MAXINE MORREY has wanted to

can remember and wrote her first

when she was ten. Coming in first, she won a handful of book tokens – perfect for a bookworm!

She has written articles on a variety of subjects, as well as a Brighton Ghost Walks book for a Local History publisher. However, novels are what she loves writing the most. After self-publishing her first novel when a contract fell through, thanks to the recession, she continued to look for opportunities.

In August 2015, she won Harper Collins/Carina UK's 'Write Christmas' competition with her romantic comedy, *Winter's Fairytale*.

Maxine lives on the south coast of England, and when not wrangling with words loves to read, sew, and listen to podcasts. As she also enjoys tea and cake, she can also be found either walking or doing something vaguely physical at the gym. You can keep up with Maxine's news on Twitter, Facebook, Instagram or Pinterest, or at www.scribblermaxi.co.uk

Second Chance at the Ranch

MAXINE MORREY

ONE PLACE. MANY STORIES

This novel is entirely a work of fiction. The names, characters and incidents portrayed in it are the work of the author's imagination. Any resemblance to actual persons, living or dead, events or localities is entirely coincidental.

HQ
An imprint of HarperCollins*Publishers* Ltd
1 London Bridge Street
London SE1 9GF

This edition 2018

First published in Great Britain by
HQ, an imprint of HarperCollins*Publishers* Ltd 2018

Maxine Morrey asserts the moral right to be identified as the author of this work.
A catalogue record for this book is available from the British Library.

ISBN: PB: 978-0-00-832296-0

MIX
Paper from responsible sources
FSC® C007454

This book is produced from independently certified FSC™ paper to ensure responsible forest management.

For more information visit: www.harpercollins.co.uk/green

Typeset by Palimpsest Book Production Ltd, Falkirk, Stirlingshire
Printed and bound by CPI Group (UK) Ltd, Croydon, CR0 4YY

To all those who still love to read a
Happy Ever After …

Chapter 1

'Yes! Just like that! More! More!' Hero Scott turned her head this way and that, lifted her arms up, then down, the movements almost automatic now as the photographer prompted her unnecessarily. Her long dark hair swayed like a glossy curtain as she tilted her chin down further, maintaining the serious look the photographer had demanded for the shoot.

The studio was lit, almost over-lit, in accordance with the style wanted for the designer's advertising campaign. Loud music by the hottest current DJ blasted from speakers. Hero closed her eyes briefly from the glare, trying to halt the progression of a headache that had been rumbling in her skull for the last half an hour. Her throat was dry and she turned to one of the assistants hovering around the set and made a quick mime of drinking. The assistant grabbed a bottle of water, undid it and stuck a straw in the top. Just as she stepped towards Hero, the photographer roared.

'What are you doing?'

The assistant froze, colour immediately flooding her face as she stood, half on, half off the background roll.

'I … erm …'

'You've ruined the perfect shot! Ruined it! Where do we find these people, for God's sake?' he asked, turning on one of the others hovering around the shoot.

'I'm sorry. It won't happen again,' came the reply from a short but perfectly dressed woman, as a vicious glance was sent towards the assistant whose eyes were now brimming with tears.

'I cannot work with such—'

'It's my fault, Armand.' Hero's educated tones rose above the noise, interrupting the photographer's rant mid-flow.

Everyone turned to look at the supermodel. She casually tucked one hand behind her, the pose confident yet aloof. Behind her back, her other hand balled into a tight fist.

'I was thirsty and asked her to get me a drink. I'm sorry if it upset your process but I thought you were taking a break for a moment. So, the fault is completely mine, not hers.' Hero gave the briefest of smiles as she turned back to the young woman and took the bottle from her, placed the straw between glossy, deep-plum-coloured lips and took a brief sip. It wasn't enough, but Hero knew better than to test this particular photographer. He was well known for his diva-type tantrums and had the ability to end a budding career with just one vicious text. Hero had known him for over fifteen years now, both of their careers blooming at a similar time. Unfortunately, as Armand's career had blossomed so had his ego – something which hadn't been all that small to begin with.

No one spoke. No one moved. All were waiting for the explosion they knew was to come.

Instead, Armand let out a dramatic sigh and made a Gallic 'pfff' sort of noise. Hero met his eyes, the short nails on the hidden hand biting in to the soft skin of her palm.

'Fine. Let her keep her job. This time!' He held up his finger, highlighting the magnanimity of his decision. Hero nodded, and beside her the young assistant let out a strangled sob of relief.

'OK. Now! Can we get on?'

Hero dropped back into action as the shutter continued on

and on, the music still pounding, her throat still dry and the headache now full blown. Armand had returned to the shoot with even more drama than it had already been infused with. Hero had been there since 5 a.m., having make-up applied, touched up, and completely changed as fashion editors assigned assistants to curate outfits for the shoot. Hero stood patiently, being handed various clothes to try. Belts put on, belts taken off, her body moved this way and that as if she were no more than a shop mannequin. Which, in some ways, she supposed she was.

The incessant shutter finally ceased as Armand scrolled through a few of the last frames, his thin face becoming even more pinched as he frowned at the back of the camera. Hero took the opportunity to stretch her body, trying to ease the tension in her back and neck as she did so. Glancing across the studio, she smiled as she saw her best friend, Anya, a blonde, willowy Swede, talking to the assistant from earlier. Anya gave her a hug and bent to say something private to her. Whatever it was, Hero was glad of the smile it brought to the young woman. There were days she hated this world. But she knew she couldn't leave. Not yet.

Anya glanced up and over at Hero, her beautiful smile and funny double thumbs up making her friend grin and giggle.

'What are you doing?' Armand's attention, and ire, was now directed at Hero. She'd protected someone else, but Armand had to be seen to win. She knew the game.

'What is this?' he yelled, pulling a sarcastic version of the supermodel's wide smile. 'I do not want this! I want serious. Sultry! Mysterious! I do not want Coco the Clown! If I want to photograph clowns, I will go to the circus! Yet today I am wondering if the circus has not been brought to me!'

The photographer blustered on through his tirade. Hero knew Anya was trying to catch her eye again, but this time she refused to meet it. Instead, she blanked her expression, applying the metaphorical mask of disinterest she wore in these, and many other, situations now. They wouldn't get to her, she told herself. At least they wouldn't see, even if they had.

'Hey!' Anya hurried over to her friend once the photo shoot finally ended, and gave her a hug. 'You OK?'

Hero nodded. 'Yes, fine, thanks. You know what he's like.'

Anya rolled her eyes in agreement.

'Is that assistant all right?' Hero asked as Anya waited for her to change back into her own clothes.

'She's fine. I know her boss pretty well and had a gentle word.'

Hero flicked a glance up as she sat and tied the lace on her designer boots. 'Gentle?'

Anya shrugged, then grinned. 'The poor thing. Armand can be so awful sometimes. He thinks far too much of himself.'

Hero stood and pulled her hair into a low ponytail before pulling a baseball cap on. They had dinner reservations at a restaurant's opening night and, now that the photo shoot had run on far longer than it was supposed to, she didn't have time to go home and change. The make-up was much heavier than she would normally wear for something like this, but it would have to do now. The cap lent an air of casualness to her look and she knew, like so much in this world, if she acted like she was confident about it, no one would know the truth.

***

'How's your head?' Anya asked as they stepped out from the Tube carriage and into the mass of life that was a London Underground station at rush hour.

'It's going off, thanks.' Hero smiled.

The women exited the station within a swarm of others before managing to disentangle themselves from the crowd to walk the short distance to the restaurant. Anya tugged on her friend's sleeve to slow her.

'What's the matter?'

Anya looked at her. 'You.'

Hero frowned.

'You still have a pounding headache, don't you?'

Anya was one of only three people who could read Hero. Everyone else was kept away from knowing what she really thought, or felt.

'No.'

Anya raised one fair and perfectly shaped brow.

'OK, fine.' Hero laughed. 'Yes, I still have it, but it is less now, I promise. Probably half of it is just dehydration.'

'Let's just go back home then,' Anya said, her voice soft and kind.

To Hero, that sounded like the perfect suggestion, but she knew Anya had been looking forward to this restaurant thing for ages now. Cooking and baking was sort of her thing. Not an ideal hobby when you were trying to keep your weight to a number decreed by the modelling agency. Hero had started running for longer since she and Anya had bought this flat together, and her friend demanded she be her guinea pig for each recipe she trialled in the gleaming steel and granite kitchen of their Kensington home.

'No, honestly.' Hero reached out for Anya's hand and gave it a brief squeeze. 'It really is going off now. I just need some water and some food and I'm sure that will take care of the rest of it. Come on.' She moved and linked Anya's arm through her own before tugging her along.

'OK. But if it gets worse again, just let me know and we can leave.'

Hero nodded in agreement. 'Promise.'

***

When Hero had begun modelling full-time, the world she had entered scared her and wore her down. She would sit at the castings, knowing that everyone there was analysing her, judging her, comparing her. She hated it. Finally, on a summer afternoon, she got up in the middle of one such go-see and walked out.

Hero sat on the wall of the ornate fountain in the gardens of the location and let out a huge sigh. It felt like a weight had been lifted off her shoulders. Another replaced it almost immediately. If she wasn't going to model, she had to find a job. The summer breeze blew the fountain into a mist and the fine spray was cool as it landed on her face. She closed her eyes to enjoy its soothing touch.

'Hello.'

Hero's eyes flew open and she found herself looking up into the face of a beautiful blonde. She was of a similar age to Hero, and looked vaguely familiar.

'Hello.'

'Are you coming back in?'

Hero looked warily at the door, then back at the blonde, then back at the door again.

She shook her head. 'I don't think so.'

The blonde took a seat next to Hero and held out her hand.

'I'm Anya.'

'Hero. It's nice to meet you.' Hero's etiquette switch engaged automatically.

'What a lovely name.'

'Thanks. My parents really liked Shakespeare.' She smiled awkwardly.

'It's very romantic.' The blonde smiled warmly again. There was an accent there, something Scandinavian, and she was the epitome of the stereotype with long, shiny, natural platinum hair, pale blue eyes and porcelain skin. Hero now remembered that she had seen her at other go-sees. That was why she looked familiar. Anya had a fantastic figure, a little curvier than Hero's. She wore no make-up, as per the preference for castings, allowing the clients to see bone structure and skin tone. Her long legs were clad in tight jeans and a white T-shirt clung to her upper curves. Anya dug in the pocket of her jeans and pulled out a fresh pack of chewing gum. She unwrapped the outer packaging then offered the pack to Hero.

'Thanks,' Hero said and began to pull a stick out of the casing. Halfway through, she stopped. 'You bite your nails!' she blurted, before looking up at Anya, suddenly realising her comment had sounded like a criticism, which it hadn't been. 'I'm sorry, I didn't mean—'

Anya laughed. 'It's OK! I do! Terrible habit. They have to keep sticking on false ones if there's any chance my hands are going to show in a shot. Or I have to place them where they won't see them. It's a bad habit but I can't stop. I just tell myself there are worse habits to have!' She laughed but both of them knew that the statement was true. Drug habits were rife within their world so, as a vice, nail biting was pretty damn tame.

Hero quickly stuck out her hands in front of her, showing her own bitten nails – a connection of imperfection with her new friend in a world of false flawlessness. She laughed properly, easily, for what seemed like the first time in ages.

Anya persuaded Hero to return to the studio, which had resulted in bookings for both of them. The encounter marked the beginning of a strong bond of friendship between the two young women. They travelled to go-sees together and eventually shared a flat, both dismissing the financially available option of each girl purchasing one separately. Anya came from a close family in Sweden and missed the company. Hero had almost no family and also missed the company. Anya kept Hero's spirits from sinking and Hero returned the favour.

'Hello, gorgeous!' Rupert Thorne-Smith wrapped his arms around Hero from behind and gave her a big kiss on the cheek. The physical contact made a difference from all the air kisses she had received this evening. 'You look bored as hell,' he said, sliding into the empty seat opposite her.

Hero smiled. 'Of course I'm not.'

Rupert screwed up his nose and made a loud 'oink oink' noise, startling the group of older, clearly loaded, women sitting next to them.

'Stop it!' Hero laughed, batting her friend on the arm.

Rupert gave one more oink for good measure before lifting his champagne glass to his lips, a devilish grin on his face. 'That's what happens when you tell porkies to Uncle Rupert.'

Hero shook her head. 'Uncle Rupert' was seven years older than her and the only man she trusted.

'You on your own?' he asked.

'No, Anya's here … somewhere,' she replied, looking around the now packed restaurant. 'I think she went off to try and talk to the chef. You know what she's like.'

'I also know what the chef is like. Real penchant for blondes. You should have brought a man. It's unlikely you'll see Anya again for some time yet.'

Hero shrugged.

'So?'

'So what?' She frowned.

'I wondered if there had been any change in the Ben Gale/ Hero Scott situation.'

Hero fixed him with a look. 'No. And there won't be.'

Rupert's face became more serious – the joker dispensed with for the moment. 'You two seemed really happy. Is it not worth trying again?'

'No. We were. Mostly. But between my career and his, it just wasn't working out.'

'But couldn't you—'

'No, Rupert. We couldn't. Besides, he's with someone else now, and so am I.'

'If you're referring to that sugar daddy, Jonathan Von Dries, then you already know my opinion of him, and your "relationship".'

'Don't be ridiculous. I don't need a sugar daddy!'

'And yet you have one.'

Hero blew out a sigh. 'I don't. And anyway, you're hardly one to talk. I'm not sure there's a lot of meeting of the minds in your current "relationship".' She made air quotes just as he had done, purposefully letting her gaze drift over to the peroxide blonde perched on the edge of a chair. His date was now on her fourth champagne and getting louder by the minute. Rupert followed his friend's eye line before looking back at her, unrepentant.

'That's completely different.'

'Of course it is. And how is that?'

'Because neither of us are wishing there was more to it than there is.'

'So, exactly the same then.'

Rupert looked at her and Hero did her best to hold his gaze. She couldn't.

'You deserve more than that, Hero.'

Her throat felt tight, and she looked away, out of the window at the passing foot traffic. Crowds of people hurried in all directions. A horn beeped and the wailing siren of an ambulance became louder as the blue lights flashed, competing with the huge neon signs for dominance. Sometimes she just wanted to get away. She didn't know where exactly but somewhere that was the direct opposite of all the noise, lights, crowds – all the constant demands on her senses. Sometimes she just wanted to sit and hear nothing but silence.

Rupert's hand caught hers across the table. 'You know it's just because I care about you.'

Hero nodded, her gaze still fixed on a point outside the window. 'I know.' And she did. Unlike most of the people she spent time with, she knew where she was with Rupert. He didn't take shit from anyone, including her, and she loved him for it.

Rupert Thorne-Smith's relationship with the model Hero Scott had always been cause for gossip. He was wealthy, good-looking, and successful with a reputation that was best described as gentleman playboy. Rupert adored Hero, but she was closer to being a younger sister to him than anything that the papers could dream up.

They had met at a party early on in Hero's career when he had found her sitting outside in the garden, away from the house and the noise and the beautiful people. She was extremely shy but something about her had made Rupert persevere – a new experience for Rupert and women – and it wasn't just her beauty. There was no doubt that the girl was stunning, but there was something else. She had looked lonely, and when he began to talk to her and ask her opinion on subjects, Rupert had never seen a person look so surprised at the interest. That night, a deep, enduring friendship was formed. Rupert took Hero to see a close friend of his, a financial whizz kid, who owned one of the top investment firms in London, and together they went over the best path for Hero to choose when it came to taking care of her earnings, which were rapidly becoming substantial. Thanks to Rupert, and Thorne-Smith Holdings, Hero's financial future was secure. She was already a very wealthy woman.

Rupert knew how the darker side of the glamorous career sometimes got to his friend. This was the side people didn't want the public to see. And to a certain extent, that wish was mutual. People didn't want to hear about the humiliation models sometimes felt, the lack of support from those who should have their backs. They didn't want to know about the drugs, the eating disorders, the ever-present knowledge that you could be the brightest star today and completely ignored tomorrow when a new star ascended. All that most people wanted to see were the highs. The glamour and glitz. The beautiful people living their beautiful lives, wearing the beautiful clothes. On days Rupert saw Hero or Anya looking exhausted, he urged them both to think about leaving modelling. Thankfully, Anya had already been thinking the same thing and was now making plans to return to Sweden and train as a chef. Having been lucky enough to sample some of her recipes, Rupert had absolutely no doubt of her success in her second career. It was Hero that held his concern.

He knew she was aware that, through savvy investments and careful control, she never had to work again. But whenever Rupert broached the subject, she would just smile and tell him not to worry. He knew that somewhere there was a reason she pushed on through, but neither he nor Anya had ever been able to find out what it was.

Hero stretched her long legs out in the hushed atmosphere of the first-class cabin. She'd come to enjoy long-haul flights, delighting in the fact that she was unobtainable for those hours. Her phone stayed switched off and in her bag – something Anya, who had completely embraced the whole Insta-life thing, teased her about relentlessly. It wasn't like Hero was stuck in the Dark Ages, although according to some of those within her circle, the fact that her phone wasn't glued to her hand and kept under her pillow meant she might as well have been. Hero smiled at their comments, but privately thought that neither of those actions seemed the healthiest and carried on doing her own thing.

And now, she had no one to answer to or anywhere else she needed to be except right here. Snuggling down under the duvet, she felt the stress leaving her body as she opened the new novel she'd bought at the airport and began reading.

When her sister, Juliet, had rung her a few weeks ago to say she had become engaged to a man she'd met on her holiday in Australia, Hero wasn't terribly surprised. Juliet had always been the most impulsive of the two sisters, and as Juliet had recounted the story of how she and her new fiancé, Pete, had met, Hero could hear the difference in her voice. Juliet was almost giddy with happiness as she told her about the sheep station that he owned and ran with the help of his younger brother, Nick, and the warmth of his mum and dad when they'd met her. A warm, welcoming family unit was something both Juliet and Hero knew very little about.

'He's a what?'

'A sheep farmer. His family own a sheep station outside Adelaide. They farm sheep. Merino sheep. Organically too,' she added, knowing how much of an animal lover her little sister was.

'Jules, I know models have a dumb reputation, but I think even I can work out what sheep farmers farm.' Hero's voice was teasing.

'I just thought you might appreciate knowing where your favourite sweater might have begun its life.'

'I'm pretty sure I knew it started off on a sheep, Jules, but thanks.'

Hero smiled under her lashes at her older sister. Despite the temptations having been scouted by a model agency when she was fifteen, Hero had continued her education, achieving good grades and fitting in modelling assignments around her academics until she was in a position to model full-time. Her looks, added to the fact that she was easy to work with, if a little distant, meant she hadn't stopped working since.

'Are you ready to be a bridesmaid for your big sister?'

'Ready and waiting.'

They had decided to marry in Australia as Pete had a large family and Juliet had almost none, only Hero. Her sister had been back in the UK finalising details on the sale of her flat, and was about to return back to Australia, and Pete. The wedding was in a month's time. Apparently, Pete's mum had been a godsend when it came to the arrangements, and Juliet was loving spending time with her and Jack, Pete's father. They in turn had loved her immediately.

'Are you really sure you'll be able to make it?' Juliet asked again. Juliet was desperate for Hero to be with her on such a special day, but she also knew that her sister's job took her all over the world. As they said their goodbyes at Heathrow, she couldn't help checking one more time.

Hero waggled her phone. 'I have the date here and I'll book the time off with the agency first thing tomorrow. No problem. If someone wants me that bad during those weeks, they'll just have to wait. And if they don't want to wait, then that's their problem.'

Juliet looked concerned.

Hero laughed. 'Oh, stop worrying. I love you. You're more important than any shoot. I wouldn't miss this for anything! And I can't wait to meet Pete either. He sounds wonderful.'

'He is.'

'Jules?'

'Yes?'

'I'm going to miss you.'

Juliet pulled her little sister into her arms. 'I'm going to miss you too,' she said, holding Hero close, not wanting to let go.

'Call me when you get home.' Hero paused for a moment and looked at her sister. 'I love you.'

'Don't! I'll cry!'

'I know. You always do, you big blubberpuss.' Hero giggled and gave her sister a huge squeeze.

'I know. I'm a wimp! And I don't care.'

Hero grinned, her own eyes dry. 'I'll be there in a month.'

Hero nodded at the dedicated first-class security area in front of them. 'You'd better go. Don't want to keep him waiting.'

Juliet reached up to hug her baby sister again. At five foot eleven, Hero was three inches taller than her elder sibling and today she wore boots with heels that took her to over six feet. Juliet's feet were snug in trainers. Hero had upgraded her sister, despite Juliet's protests, but she still had a long flight ahead, and then another hop to Adelaide. Comfort was a priority.

'I hope you're not wearing those on the day?' Hero nodded

down at her sister's footwear. Juliet followed her gaze, then laughed.

'No. Definitely not! With the groom and best man at six foot three and six foot four, I'm definitely wearing heels!'

'Good. Then if I wear flats, I won't tower over you.'

'You can be quite sweet when you want to, can't you?'

Hero pulled a face. 'Don't tell anyone!' she whispered, and then winked. 'Go on. Get on the plane, and I'll see you in a month.'

Four weeks later, Pete was back at the airport, waiting with his fiancée to meet her sister. Excited to see her, Juliet was incapable of standing still, constantly checking the screens and looking around.

Pete was intrigued. Juliet had told him all about Hero, her jet-set lifestyle, and her personality. From what he knew, it seemed that the sisters were a little like him and Nick, different in their make-up but close and reliant on each other. Even more so as a result of their parents' relative disinterest in them.

Hero stepped through the doors to Arrivals, a wheeled Louis Vuitton suitcase trailing behind her. Pete saw the difference immediately. He'd seen photos obviously, but it wasn't quite the same thing. The sisters might be similar in heart, but they didn't share such similarity in their looks as Nick and Pete did.

Pete watched as his sister-in-law-to-be glided through the crowds to meet them. Hero's brunette, waist-length hair fell in a shimmering sheet of rich brown as she crossed the space, her walk conveying absolute confidence. Her shoulders were strong and straight, with no hint of the roundness some tall people gain as they attempt to blend into the crowd. Hero certainly didn't blend. Couldn't blend. She was stunning. Completely, undeniably stunning.

Whereas Juliet's beauty was soft and crept over you, Hero's hit you straight away, right between the eyes. Pete watched the people around her and nudged Juliet as one poor guy, whose eyes were glued to Hero, got a whack from his girlfriend. Juliet pulled a sympathetic face.

'Oh dear! She can have that effect.'

Pete shrugged. 'She's very beautiful,' he said truthfully, 'but she's not you.' Juliet reached up and kissed him.

'You just remember that.'

'I hope that's Pete.' Hero appeared in front of them, a wide smile playing on perfectly painted lips. Juliet hugged her and introduced her fiancé.

'Pleased to meet you, Hero.' He leant down a placed a kiss on her cheek. It struck Hero that few men she met had to bend to do that. It felt rather nice.

Pete took control of the luggage and led the way back to the car. They loaded themselves into the off-roader and started on the long drive back to the station. Juliet filled Hero in on the wedding arrangements and their plans for after the wedding.

Chapter 2

'So that's it really. The hotel has been great about the reception considering it's such short notice.'

'That's because they don't get many weddings. Can't believe their luck at all the cash we're handing over.' Pete's eyes were on the road, and a small smile was on his lips. Juliet turned towards him.

'Maybe they're just excited. Weddings do that to some people, you know.'

'Right-oh.'

'Cynic.'

'Never.'

Juliet rested a hand on her fiancé's thigh and placed a kiss on his cheek.

Hero listened to the exchange with interest. She didn't really date as much as the media liked to make out but the men she did go out with pretty much did their best to always be in agreement with her, or let her do her own thing. That was an unconditional part of the deal. Hero Scott had known the pain of rejection before. A pain that still sliced at her heart even now, when she was in demand from all angles, commanded thousands of pounds for a shoot and could pretty much have whatever she wanted. But the pain was still there. No amount of money, investment, or any of the other trappings could soften it. Whenever she thought about it, it burned as deep as ever.

Of course, not everyone agreed with her views on dating. Rupert, for instance, usually just sat and rolled his eyes, then, with a mischievous twinkle, would tell the man in question to 'stop bloody fawning'. To their face. Hero was never surprised when she didn't see them again.

But Juliet and Pete clearly had a different relationship. From the moment they'd met, she'd been able to see that he was just as smitten with her sister as Juliet was with him. Hero was happy to see it, the knowledge allaying the remaining worry she had about her sister's whirlwind romance.

Vivid terracotta dust kicked up from the unsealed road as the vehicle drove on through the landscape. Hero watched it fill the air and swirl around the car. They'd left the city far behind them some time ago and now drove on through the countryside. Looking past the dust, she saw that this part of the country was much greener than she had expected. She'd travelled to Australia a couple of times before for work, but both of those trips had been centred in Sydney, and she was enjoying getting to see more of the country, thanks to her sister.

Pete would point out something of interest every now and then. Hero smiled and nodded, absorbing the information. Juliet had told her that she loved how laid back he was, and how his calmness seemed to seep in to her, just by being in his company. Hero could see that. Certainly, her sister looked happier and more relaxed than she had seen her in a long time. If this man and this country were the reason for that, she was immensely grateful to both of them.

Turning back from the window, she cast a glance at the front seats again and thought again about the teasing banter between Juliet and Hero's future brother-in-law. There was such love in their eyes; it had been obvious the minute she saw them together.

It struck her that her sister's marriage would be what Rupert was always saying a relationship should be. Despite the fact his own were most definitely not. But she knew, when the time came, even Rupert would settle down. It was what people did, wasn't it? And it was already happening. Anya now had her five-year plan pinned to a wall in the kitchen. All the details of the training she wanted to do, and when she would do it, before finally leaving London to return home and open up her own restaurant. Juliet would be starting a new life out here. And once Rupert found the right woman, he too would have his own life. Only she would be left. Alone. A frown creased her face as she balled her fists, pushing the thoughts out of her head.

Still, it was often the differences between the two sisters that made them close.

Hero wasn't looking for that sort of commitment anyway. Among all the men she'd met in her time as a model, she'd never yet met a man who could hold her attention the way Pete held Juliet's. And deep down, she knew that there was also a fear that she would never be able to hold a man's attention in the same way that Juliet clearly did Pete's.

Hero stole another glance. For all their wealth and status, the men Hero had dated held little interest for her. But she knew that it was a two-way street. She was a pretty trinket to be worn; they didn't know her. Not really. She wouldn't let them. She knew that real relationships meant trust, and broken trust was painful. Her past taught her that. So, she kept her feelings locked away behind a public persona that everyone thought they knew.

Juliet, on the other hand, was an open book. She even had what people called an 'open' face, although neither of them had ever quite worked out the true definition of that one. And whilst both girls had been blessed with looks, Juliet's beauty was gentle, approachable, whereas Hero's was more obvious. Occasionally it had the effect of causing people, men and women, to feel intimidated. Juliet rarely wore make-up whilst Hero never opened the door without it. Cosmetics had been banned at their school and so when Hero began her career, it was a novelty. And now it was habit. Protection. All part of the armour.

Although beautiful, Hero had been a shy child, awkward in company and content to cling to her older sister who was, by nature, at ease in any situation. When Hero's modelling career began to take off, she felt physically sick before every show at the thought of the huge numbers of people all staring up at her. But once she had been painted and preened, she was behind a mask, a character in a play. Then she could deal with the photographers, the bookers, the editors, the designers – and the world – because they weren't seeing the real Hero, just a public persona. And she'd always had Juliet to come back to. Until now.

Juliet glanced back to see her sister gazing out of the window. She was so beautiful, but Juliet wished she had left the make-up off today. To her, Hero's natural beauty was softer and even more stunning. Her sister turned and caught her.

'What?'

'What?'

'You're staring.'

Juliet smiled. 'I would have thought you'd be used to that by now.'

Hero shrugged and looked back out of the window. Pete caught the action in the rear-view mirror. He hadn't yet decided whether he was going to like his new sister-in-law or not. As a true supermodel, she led a completely different lifestyle to them, a lifestyle Pete couldn't even begin to comprehend. She did indeed have that appearance of serenity that Juliet had mentioned when she'd first told him about her sister's career, but there was something else, a coolness that was so different to Juliet's warmth. Pete pondered as to whether it was even an intentional projection. Hero had been a hot property from day one. After years of being told she was fabulous, with only Juliet to occasionally bring her back to earth, perhaps it wasn't surprising she believed a little of her own press, if that was the reason. Not that it really mattered. With Juliet living out here, and Hero jet-setting all over the world, the chances of them seeing her a lot were low, although Juliet had told him on numerous occasions how close the sisters were, and it was obvious she felt it was her job to protect and worry about her sibling. Pete could understand that. His brother could more than take care of himself, but it didn't alter the fact that Pete would always look out for him.

Still, he wanted to like her, for Juliet's sake. He cast a glance at his fiancée. She felt his gaze and turned, the same smile on her lips as the day he'd met her. The day he knew she was the one.

Juliet placed her warm, small hand back on his leg and his large tanned one curled gently around it. As the miles passed, he cast his mind back to that day. He'd entered the house with wedding bells already ringing out clear in his head, but his younger brother hadn't been convinced.

***

'I'm telling you, mate. She's the one,' Pete said as he washed his hands under the kitchen tap.

Nick opened his mouth to contradict him and remind him, 'hadn't he said that about so-and-so' when it struck him that, actually, Pete had never said that. Not once.

The brothers had both inherited their mother's good looks and their father's height. They were well built from working on the station and well educated from attending a top school in the city. The whole package made them very popular with women in the district and, between the two of them, they'd dated a good percentage. Those interested in more of a bad boy persona tended to home in on Nick whilst Pete had a more strong, silent type of reputation going on. Neither was accurate, but if it worked, they weren't complaining.

Juliet had arrived on a blistering summer's day with an Outback Discovery tour that sometimes took in the Websters' Merino sheep station. Jacob, their leading station hand, had the gift of the gab, and was therefore assigned to answer questions on the tour. He was doing his normal good work when Pete returned from mending fences out on the west paddock and caught sight of a blonde trailing at the back of the group. She wore loose cotton trousers with trainers, and her top half was swamped under an over-sized shirt. A ponytail bounced from the back of a peaked cap. Definitely not what Pete would call his usual type but something about her caught his attention.

Throwing the fencing he'd been about to unload back in the ute, Pete walked up behind the group. The blonde had fallen behind a little more now and was staring out at the vista as up in front Jacob waxed lyrical about wool fineness and weight.

'Hope we're not boring you.'

The woman jumped at the sound of Pete's voice. She turned and tilted her head back in order to meet his eyes.

'Weren't you ever told that it's rude to sneak up on people?' The admonishment came in a well-spoken English accent, accompanied by a wide smile, and teasing laughter in the gentle green eyes.

'Sorry,' Pete replied, grinning and not looking sorry at all.

The blonde smiled again and turned back to the view she had been admiring before he had interrupted. Fields stretched away to the horizon. From here, it looked and felt like they were all alone on the planet.

'I can't get over the size of it all.'

'Yeah, all the girls say that.'

The blonde looked up again and met his eyes, laughter showing in her own, 'Yes,' she said slowly, 'but I'm surprised at how big everything is.' She kept her emphasis on the word 'big' and raised one eyebrow. With that she turned and walked off to catch up with the rest of the group, leaving Pete standing on his own, a big grin plastered on his face. And already more than a little in love.

A short time later, Pete watched the group depart, his eyes focused on the mystery blonde. He didn't even know her name but, no worries, he would. The driver helped the women into the back of the tour company's four-wheel drive. Another tourist of similar age to the blonde waited to get in. She made a point of declining the driver's assistance and hopped into her seat. Pete shook his head. He was all for equality but there were people that took it to extremes and just ended up looking plain rude. He watched as the blonde took the proffered hand with a smile of thanks and disappeared into the cool, air-conditioned interior of the tour vehicle.

'We're going into town tonight,' Pete announced as he finished washing his hands at the sink.

Nick shook his head as he chewed a mouthful of beef stew. Pete dished himself out a portion and sat down opposite his younger brother. Nick was still chewing.

'What do you mean, no?' Pete asked as he forked up some of the stew.

'I'm knackered, mate!' Nick complained. 'Jacob was meant to be helping with the new shed until those flippin' tourists showed up. Joe and I ended up doing it on our own.' He took a swig from his beer and swallowed forcefully before peering suspiciously down at his stew. 'Do you know how long Mum's had this in the freezer?'

Pete looked up from his plate as he chewed. He shook his head and kept on chewing. He gave his plate a questionable look. Nick leant back and grabbed another beer from the fridge. He flipped the top off and pushed the bottle towards his brother. Pete swallowed with the help of the cool drink, glancing down at his own plate.

'Too long.'

Gathering the crockery, Nick scraped their contents into the bin, then placed the china in the dishwasher. He made a mental note to remember to turn it on before their parents returned from their weekend viewing prospective retirement properties in the city.

'Anyway, that's why we're going to the pub,' Pete announced.

'What?'

'The tourists. Or rather, one in particular.'

Nick rolled his eyes. 'Oh right. The girl you're going to marry.'

'Yep.'

Nick let out a sigh as his stomach rumbled and complained. 'Yeah, all right. Let's just hope they've got something other than beef stew.' He left the kitchen and headed up the stairs towards the bathroom for a shower. 'You're driving.' He called back.

The Outback tour group was in the pub when the two men entered a while later. Nick watched as his brother's eyes scanned the crowd for the blonde. Pete saw her. She was sitting at a small table by the window, writing. Her baggy clothes from earlier had been replaced by a long pink sundress with tiny flowers on it, and a pale lemon cardigan. The ponytail had been freed allowing soft blonde curls to bounce on her shoulders.

'There,' Pete stated, as he flicked Nick on the arm to get his attention before making his way over to her table.

'Hello again.'

The blonde looked up. She seemed surprised, but not unhappy, to see him.

'Hello.'

They looked at each other for a minute, neither quite sure what to say next. Nick looked between them, then made a small roll of his eyes.

'Hi.' He stuck out his hand. 'I'm Nick.'

'Pleased to meet you, Nick. I'm Juliet.'

Nick sneaked a look at Pete from the corner of his eye. He didn't appear to be about to speak anytime soon. His brother bailed him out.

'Pete tells me you were on the tour today. I hope you enjoyed it.'

Juliet slid her eyes back to the elder brother. 'Yes, I did.' She paused. 'Very much so.'

Pete's grin got wider. Nick smiled. He had never seen him like this. He really did have it bad. Again, there was a pause.

'I was just writing to my sister and telling her about the trip to your station.'

Pete bobbed his head happily.

Nick rolled his eyes again and couldn't help smiling. 'Well, I'm going to get us a couple of beers. Would you like a drink?'

'A beer would be lovely. Thank you.'

As Nick turned to cross to the bar, he nudged Pete and spoke in a loud whisper.

'Mate, stop just bloody grinning and say something intelligent or she's going to think you're the village idiot.'

It was busy at the bar, but Nick was happy to wait. His brother finally seemed to have got some oxygen back into his brain and was deep in conversation with the lovely Juliet. Nick had to agree there was something about the woman that made you want to know her. She was certainly beautiful, but not in a slap-you-in-the-face, obvious, movie star kind of way. It was gentle and warm but no less appealing for its softness.

Nick took the drinks over to Juliet's table.

'Here we go.' He sat for a few moments before seeing a neighbour he urgently needed to talk to and left them alone.

'Your brother is very tactful,' Juliet observed.

'Yeah, he's all right.'

Having not only learned her name, as he'd promised himself he would, Pete was also successful in persuading Juliet to change her itinerary and stay in town for a few extra days. He was up to his ears in debt to Nick for all the jobs his brother covered him for on the station whilst he showed his new love around. Juliet had been working in Adelaide for six months after leaving a job she hated in London and had taken some time off to see a little more of the expanse outside the city.

'I just decided to leave,' she told Pete when he asked how she had ended up temping in Adelaide. 'I was in London, working at a job I didn't like and I'd had enough. It was cold and it was raining so I went onto the internet, thought of somewhere sunny, and booked a flight out here.'

They were sitting on a blanket underneath a clear night sky. Juliet shifted a little and gazed up at the stars now showing themselves. 'Of course, it gave my sister a complete panic attack. She's so much more organised than me, and likes to plan everything as much as possible. We're so different in some ways but very similar in others. Does that make sense?'

'Sure. Sounds a bit like me and Nick.' Pete nodded. 'So, what does your sister do?'

'She's a model. It all seems to be going very well, although it's rather a weird choice for her really, as she's quite shy. It certainly wasn't a career she'd ever thought about taking up but she's doing great! She has this "something"... I don't have it, I don't know, a sort of serenity almost. They love that. Oh, that and the fact that she's achingly beautiful!' Juliet laughed. There was no jealousy in Juliet's tone, only pride.

'Do you see her much?'

'Yes. Quite a lot. Well, until I came out here that is, but she managed to visit me a couple of months ago after she did a shoot in Bali.'

'Nice work if you can get it.'

Juliet laughed. 'Yes! We text and call and email all the time, but I do miss her dreadfully. I worry about her too. She's nowhere near as tough as she likes people to think she is.'

'What about your parents? Do they worry as much as you do?' Pete asked, watching Juliet, and falling further and further in love with every word she spoke.

A shadow flitted across her expression before she answered. 'They passed away. Quite a while ago now.'

Pete pulled himself up. 'God, I'm sorry, Juliet. I didn't—'

'It's all right.' Juliet touched his arm and then let her hand rest there. Pete covered it gently with his own. 'We weren't close. It was a few years ago now. My parents did everything together, went everywhere together. My mother was diagnosed with cancer and passed away nine weeks later. It was all a bit sudden. Six months later we buried Dad. He just sort of faded away.'

Pete put his arm around Juliet as they sat watching the stars glisten in the clear sky. She snuggled into his warmth. 'My father was a diplomat, and they travelled a lot. I was a novelty, and Hero was … I don't know. They took so little interest in her, I couldn't help but wonder why they had her at all sometimes.

'It was heartbreaking to watch her try to please them … but she never seemed to be able to. It made me so mad. I'd look at her sometimes and there was such confusion written on her face. I know it certainly affected her confidence.'

'But being a model must make her pretty confident?'

Juliet raised an eyebrow. 'Looks can be deceiving. But yes, she's better these days. She has a couple of very good friends. And she has me.'

'So, there's just the two of you?'

'Yes.'

'What did you say her name was?'

'Hero.'

Pete paused. 'Your parents really liked Shakespeare, didn't they?'

Juliet laughed. 'Yes.'

'So she made it through school with that name?'

'We went to quite a posh school. Unusual names were par for the course.'

Pete nodded.

Juliet continued, 'Actually, it's been useful with her chosen career.'

'Easy to remember.'

'Hard to forget a Hero!' Juliet laughed.

'So why Australia, apart from the fact it was somewhere sunny? Or was that our sole attraction?'

'My father was Australian. Hero and I both have dual citizenship. We were born here but left young to be educated in England whilst my parents had various postings all over the world. I've not been back so I thought it was about time I spent some time out here myself.'

Pete sat up. Juliet followed and touched his arm.

'Pete? Are you all right?'

'Would you consider spending some more time out here?'

'I don't really know. I'd planned on staying about a year and then seeing—'

'I mean out here.' Pete waved an arm to take in the Websters' land. 'I know it's not everyone's cup of tea, being a bit remote like this but …'

Juliet shifted position on the rug. 'What exactly are you saying?'

'Juliet, will you marry me?' He paused, and then made to push away. 'What was I thinking? I should have done all this properly. You're not just some—'

'Yes!'

'What?'

'Yes!' Juliet laughed, catching his hand, and holding it up to her face. 'I will marry you.'

Pete felt his legs give way and flopped back onto the rug from the kneeling position he'd been in. He landed on his backside, and Juliet grinned, moving across the rug and plopping herself down on his lap.

'You seem surprised.'

'I am a bit.'

'At me saying yes, or the fact that you asked me?'

'Both. I think.'

Her face clouded a little. 'Do you want to take it back?'

'No!' he said, reaching for her, and pulling her close. 'God, no!'

'Then what's the problem?'

'I just – you deserve a better proposal than in the middle of a paddock on a lumpy old rug.'

Juliet smiled and raised her eyebrows. 'Actually, I think it's pretty much perfect.'

Pete recognised the smile and pulled her closer still.

'Is that so?'

'Very much so.'

Pete dipped his head, brushing the warm, soft lips of his fiancée as her fingers began working quickly at the buttons on his shirt.

***

'Here we are,' Pete announced as they pulled into the long driveway. A sign told them that they had reached 'Hill Station'.

Hero peered through the dusty windows of the vehicle and looked around. 'Where's the hill?'

'Sorry?'

'The sign said "Hill Station", but there's no … hill.' She tailed off, suddenly feeling stupid for voicing the question.

Pete smiled at her in the mirror. 'You'd be amazed at how many people don't even notice that.'

'Really?' Hero asked.

Pete's eyes flicked back up to the mirror and in that second, he saw everything he needed to. Under that apparently confident exterior was the girl his fiancée adored. For a split second, he saw through the mask, heard the hint of real pleasure in her voice at his compliment. Pete glanced back again but the childlike glint of delight had gone.

'The name's kind of a joke. My parents are Jack and Gillian. When they took over the station, it didn't have a great reputation so they wanted to change the name, do away with the stigma. One night in the pub, some bright spark said something about Jack and Jill going up the hill, and it kind of stuck.'

Hero was peering out through the dusty glass of the window as the evening sun lowered itself behind the horizon, making way for dusk to wind its way over the land.

'Jack and Gill went up the hill,' she said softly, smiling.

Juliet cast a glance at her sister and then at Pete. He met her eyes and smiled, with an almost imperceptible nod. She smiled back and released the breath she didn't even know she'd been holding. The two people she adored most in this world were right here and she hadn't realised how anxious she had been for their meeting to go well until that moment. But her fiancé's gesture told her all she needed to know.

Nick Webster watched the visitor exit the 4x4, her movements fluid. She stood for a moment and looked about her as his brother moved to the rear of the vehicle to deal with the luggage. Nick's grooming of the mare's coat slowed as he studied their guest. She was certainly taller than her sister and undeniably beautiful. Pete had mentioned something about her being some hotshot in the modelling world. Nick had let the comment roll off. Fame didn't impress Nick. People impressed him – what they did, not who they were. The brush came to a stop and Nick felt a nudge on his shoulder from the mare.

'Yeah, yeah. All right,' he soothed, taking up the motion again, his eyes never leaving the new arrival.

Juliet was showing Hero the land, pointing in various directions. Nick watched the weak remnants of the evening sun catch subtle highlights in the sleek, swinging sheet of hair. They were looking towards the west now, gazing at the low fire of the setting sun. Long, elegant fingers reached up and dropped sunglasses down in front of her eyes, freeing the hair they had secured. As he watched, she reached into the bag swinging off her lower arm and pulled out a mobile phone. Nick's mouth twitched in a smile.

'Good luck with getting a signal on that,' he said under his breath.

Chapter 3

The two women walked towards the house. Juliet's words carried gently on the same breeze that ruffled Nick's shirt and hair and he smiled at the excitement in her voice. From the corner of his eye, he saw his parents emerge from the coolness of the house and step out on the verandah to meet their new guest. His mother hurried towards the two, followed at a more leisurely pace by his father. Pete had now re-joined them after retrieving the luggage from the car. Nick watched as Juliet's sister pushed her sunglasses back up onto her head and held out her hand. His mother took it, and then swept her into a huge hug. The visitor had her back to Nick, so her reaction to his mother's normal, effusive display of emotion couldn't be seen by him but he saw Juliet subtly take her sister's hand and squeeze it.

Jack was now introduced. He was a man not given to overt shows of emotion, but he shook the young woman's hand and smiled as she said something. Nick blinked in surprise, watching as his father placed his other hand on top of their linked ones for a moment and, smiling, spoke some more to the new arrival. For Jack, that action was the equivalent of a massive hug.

'Guess she has a way of making people think she's something pretty special, eh girl?'

The mare bumped Nick's shoulder and rubbed her nose up and down, causing him to stagger a little.

'Oi. I'm not your scratching post,' he laughed, moving away.

'Well, that's all of us, except Joe and Nick. Joe's still out with his dad at the moment but Nick should be around …' Gill's words drifted off as she scanned the surroundings for her youngest son.

'There he is.' Gill spotted him. 'Nick!' She hollered across the yard.

Nick poked his head around the mare's neck and saw his mum waving him in energetically. He raised a hand in acknowledgement and gave the mare a final check before leading her back towards the stable block.

Gill was just pouring out the tea as he entered the kitchen. The others were all seated at the worn pine table that made up the heart of the kitchen. Nick walked straight to the sink and began washing his hands.

'Tea, love?'

'Please.'

Gill topped off the final mug as she announced Nick's arrival. 'And this is Nick, our youngest.'

Nick turned around to find himself looking into vibrant green cat-like eyes. They were the same as Juliet's but different. Under the blonde bobbing curls, Juliet's sparkled with mischief, whilst her sister's, framed by the sheet of dark glossy hair, had an intensity that made him catch his breath.

'Nick, this is Hero, Juliet's sister.'

'Pleased to meet you.' Her voice was soft, and the accent crisp.

Nick shook her hand and smiled. 'G'day.'

Hero held his gaze for a moment. There was a flicker of a smile before she dropped her eyes. Nick cast a private glance at Pete whose brief nod in return told him everything was good.

Nick wished he could be as sure as his brother. Something about Hero Scott already bothered him, although she'd only been there five minutes. The last thing his brother, or any of them, needed right now was some diva model swanning around and expecting to be waited on hand and foot. Typical that the first thing she did was check her phone for service, he thought, wondering just how many selfies she had taken in the car.

Nick stole another glance. This woman was certainly different from her sister, with none of the ease and openness that drew people to Juliet. He already thought of Juliet as a sister. But Hero? That act of cool aloofness she had going on already had him rubbed up the wrong way. He'd seen that moment of hesitation before she took his proffered hand as his mum introduced them. He guessed it was pretty unlikely she'd had many dealings with men who worked the land to make their income. More likely she surrounded herself with alphabet celebrities and wealthy hedge-funders, with the occasional titled aristocrat or two, just to mix it up a bit.

After seeing that everyone had a drink and assuring them all that dinner wouldn't be too long, Gill soon began talking weddings again with the girls. Nick took a seat next to his dad, and kept his gaze purposely diverted from the supermodel.

***

Dawn was breaking as Hero sat in one of the rocking chairs on the large wraparound porch of the house. She'd slept well, surprisingly for her. Not being a great sleeper, she had expected to toss and turn as she usually did, but after a soothing shower and in the homely comfort of the Websters' guestroom, she could barely remember her head touching the pillow last night. But thanks to jetlag, her body was totally out of sync so after half an hour of lying awake early this morning, thoughts racing, she'd got up, done her teeth and make-up and then pulled on an easy-to-wear maxi dress she'd been given by one of the designers – which one exactly escaped her memory – before walking quietly down the stairs and heading outside. The air was still cool at this time, and it felt fresh and clean. Hero tried to remember the last time she had smelled air like this, and failed. Streaks of orange, purple, and blue mixed in the sky as the sun tentatively poked its head above the horizon. She sat and watched, for once not thinking about the next item on her schedule. Here, she had no schedule. She repeated that thought and smiled. The patter of a dog's toenails caused her to look up and her smile became wider as the collie, Biscuit, scooted up to her and laid his head in her lap.

'Good morning to you too!' she said, her voice even softer than it usually was in deference to the still sleeping household. The collie wriggled, his tail beating faster and faster at the attention.

'Biscuit, stop bothering the guests.'

'Oh, he's really n…' Hero looked up as she spoke, her hand still stroking the collie's head as he gazed up at her with adoring, bright blue eyes. She faltered as she realised the request had come from Nick Webster. Something about this man unsettled her and had done since the moment they'd met. The smile he'd given her as they were introduced yesterday was the last she'd seen from him, at least the last in her direction anyway. Then, as now, he had a detachment about him.

Hero cleared her throat. 'He's not bothering me at all.' She tried to smile but suddenly struggled with something she could usually do on cue for camera, feeling self-conscious and awkward. Nick said nothing.

'I…' Nervously, she cleared her throat again. 'I always think it would be nice to have a pet. But I know it wouldn't be fair to an animal with the amount of travelling I do.'

'He's not a pet. He's a working dog.'

'Oh. Oh yes, well, of course. I didn't mean …' Hero trailed off, suddenly unsure what she meant.

The dog turned and sat down, his body pushed as close to

Hero as he could get it, relishing the attention. From the corner of her eye, she saw Nick give a shake of his head.

'I guess he heard you were a celebrity too. As you can imagine, we don't tend to get a lot of those around here.'

'I'm not a celebrity,' Hero replied.

Nick tilted his head and raised an eyebrow. 'Sure you're not. I'm making coffee. Do you want one? Biscuit, come here.'

The dog padded over quickly to his master.

'I don't want to put you out.'

Nick shrugged. 'I'm making coffee anyway. One more is no big deal.' He turned and walked off down the porch, disappearing into the kitchen.

Hero took a deep breath, letting it out slowly as she'd been taught in her Pilates class. It was supposed to help you relax, but right now it wasn't really helping anything. Nick Webster's presence seemed far stronger than any relaxation techniques she'd learned. And she had no idea why. Yes, he was tall, and good-looking and that dark shadow of stubble on his jaw this morning did nothing to diminish that fact. In truth, it only enhanced it. But so what? It wasn't like Hero didn't mix with good-looking people very often. Her world was practically made up of beautiful people, and none of them had ever caused the tight, fluttery feeling in her stomach before. And certainly, none of them had made her stumble over her words like a teenager before. She took another breath and began to feel her pulse rate slow. His comment about celebrity floated in her head, as did the slight disdain she detected in his voice as he'd said it.

Pushing herself up off the chair, she turned and followed the way he'd gone. As she got to the door, she hesitated. Inside she saw Nick crouched down, grinning as he ruffled the dog's fur up and down and Biscuit thumped his tail in delight.

Not a pet, huh?

Hero gently rattled the door handle a little more than she needed to, alerting Nick to her presence. He stood quickly, picking up the dog's empty breakfast bowl as he did, transferring it to the dishwasher.

'Coffee's there.' He pointed to one of the two sunny yellow mugs now sat on the worktop. 'I didn't know if you took sugar or not, but it's there on the side if you do.'

'No. Thank you.'

'Guessed not, but thought I'd ask anyway.'

'Do I look like a no-sugar coffee drinker then?' she asked a moment later, feeling the need to fill the silence.

Nick picked up the other mug and took a sip of the steaming dark liquid before answering.

'I imagine you don't consume any calories you don't have to.' His eyes met hers.

'Well, I … there is a certain amount of being aware of that,' she replied.

He raised his eyebrows briefly in reply as he looked away.

'What does that mean?' Hero asked, already knowing she was going to regret asking.

'I didn't say anything,' Nick replied, puzzled.

'Well, no. Not out loud but it's very clear you're thinking something.'

'I don't know what it's like in your world, but out here, men are allowed to have their own thoughts.'

'That's the same anywhere.'

He did the expression again.

'Clearly it can't be a very strong opinion if you don't want to share it. I get the impression you're not the type to keep your views to yourself.' Hero's voice was low but there was no doubting the annoyance behind it. What was it with this man? Why was she allowing him to get under her skin like no one else she'd ever met?

He gave a brief smile, but Hero doubted its sincerity. 'Well, then I guess that shows just how much you know me.' He drained the last of his coffee and transferred that, too, to the dishwasher.

His apparent domestication felt at odds with his character – as far as Hero had been able to actually make that out. 'Come on, Biscuit. Time to work.'

Hero's hands were still wrapped around the mug. She watched Nick take a well-worn cowboy-style hat from a coat rack holding several of them and squash it on to his head. As he got to the door he stopped and turned, watching her for a moment. A flash of something crossed his face but as Hero was still struggling to make out his character, she had no clue as to what it might be.

He nodded at her and there was the faintest hint of a smile … maybe?

'Enjoy your coffee.'

She nodded back. 'Thank you.'

With that he and the dog were out the door and she was left alone. Normally this wouldn't bother her, but today it was different. It was as though Nick Webster had taken some of the air out of the room when he left. Hero shook her head, forcing the thought to fall away. Reaching into her pocket, she pulled out her phone. The message she'd typed quickly to Anya to let her know she had arrived still sat in her outbox. She'd ask Juliet later if she could connect her phone to the Wi-Fi just so that her friend wouldn't worry. After that, she was more than happy not to get messages. Anya was already half in love with the chef she'd met at the restaurant opening and wasn't coming up for air all that much right now. Rupert was doing some deep-sea diving off the coast of somewhere she'd never heard of and, from what he'd told her, was even further from civilisation than this place. With the only other person she ever really wanted to hear from being Juliet, being unavailable actually sounded quite wonderful. No one else needed to know that she had Wi-Fi and if anyone stressed at her when she returned that they hadn't been able to get hold of her, she had the perfect excuse.

Hero rinsed her own mug and followed Nick's example of putting it in the dishwasher, then wandered slowly back out to take up her position on the porch once more. It was a shame the dog had gone with Nick. Just in those couple of minutes of stroking him, she'd felt her body relax. That was until Nick Webster had appeared.

The sound of hooves caught her attention and she looked to the right to see that very man astride a horse the colour of warm caramel. Jules had mentioned the stables yesterday when they'd got there. She could have asked Nick to show her where they were, she supposed, but somehow she got the feeling that he considered her presence here disruptive enough. From Juliet's description of him, Hero had thought she would be meeting a man of the same ilk as her soon-to-be brother-in-law. But where Pete was warm, Nick Webster was wary. From what he'd said this morning, it sounded like he had already made up his mind about her own character. The thought frustrated her more than it should. She was, after all, used to people all over the world judging her. Why should it be any different here? She scuffed the warm wood of the porch with her shoe. The answer was that it shouldn't be any different. But it was.

***

The days passed and Hero spent most of the time with her sister, knowing that she would see her far less than she was used to once she left the station for her flight back to London. It had taken just a short Tube ride in the city to visit her sister back in London. Now, any visit would have to be far more planned and calculated. Planning things wasn't an issue – Hero always had her schedule well organised. Having everything neatly arranged helped her feel in control. Besides, spontaneity wasn't really her thing. She left that to Juliet, who did it so much better. And so much more dramatically, the upcoming wedding being a prime example. Hero had worried initially but having been here for almost a fortnight now, her fears had been well and truly allayed.

Pete Webster was a good man, and he was head over heels for her sister. Although she would miss her terribly, she was glad that it was because of someone like Pete.

'You OK?' Juliet asked as she stood at the stove, preparing the evening meal. Gill and Jack had gone into the city to sign some documents in connection with the apartment they had just bought there, and the two brothers were still out working.

'Mm-hmm,' Hero replied, concentrating on peeling the vegetables in front of her.

'You don't have to do that, you know.'

'I know.'

Juliet pulled out the chair opposite her sister and sat down. 'You are happy for me, aren't you?'

Hero quickly looked up, distress showing on her face. 'Of course I am!' Juliet heard the hurt in her voice. 'Why would you ever think that I wasn't?'

'It's not that. It's just … you know. You can be quite reserved and sometimes it's not always easy to know what you're thinking, even for me who probably knows you better than anyone. I couldn't be happy here, knowing that I'd made you unhappy. We would have to work something out so that …' Juliet stopped as Hero put down the peeler and laid her elegant, wedding-ready manicured hands over her sister's.

'Jules. I am happy for you, I promise. I'm thrilled, honestly. You've found a wonderful man who clearly worships the ground you walk on, and I couldn't lose you to anyone less than him.'

Juliet blinked tears and Hero smiled. 'You're not losing me,' Juliet said, accepting the piece of kitchen towel her sister handed her and wiping her eyes.

'I know. But you know what I mean.'

'I do. But you'll always be welcome here, you know that. Gill and Jack are going to be moving to their apartment in the city as soon as we're back from honeymoon, now that they've officially retired, and there will always be a room for you here. I love Pete to the moon and back, but I can't help wishing I could somehow still be close to you.'

'We have apps and email and Skype, Jules. You'll probably get sick of me calling.'

Juliet pulled a hand out and laid it over the top of her sister's. 'Hardly. But I know the time difference will make things a bit more tricky.'

Hero gave a mirthless laugh. 'Since when did my schedule ever stick to the 9 to 5 anyway. And you know what a bad sleeper I am. It'll be nice to have someone to talk to next time I'm padding around at home at three in the morning.'

Juliet smiled but there was concern in her eyes. 'How have you been sleeping here?'

Hero raised her perfect brows. 'Surprisingly well, actually. Must be the air.'

'Or maybe you're more relaxed here, without so many people desperate for your attention.'

'Desperate is a bit of an overstatement,' she replied, glancing away.

'I'm not sure it is.'

Hero poked at the vegetables. 'How many more of these do you want?' And with that, the subject was changed. Juliet frowned at the escape her sister had made but the last thing she wanted to do was start a fight with her. It already broke her heart to know she wouldn't be physically close to her anymore, and she didn't want her worries to come across as criticism. Her sister had an incredible work ethic, but sometimes Juliet thought it too much. She was always travelling, whether that was across the city or across the world. She didn't eat anywhere near as much as she should, and when she did, it was often at strange times, or on the run. Hero wasn't stupid. Jules knew her sister acknowledged the fact that her diet wasn't the best it could be, but it wasn't something that was easy to change. It was one of the reasons she'd brought up the subject of cutting back on the modelling jobs a few days ago. Tactfully, she'd wrapped it in the wish for Hero to be available to visit more often. Her sister had nodded and said she would definitely plan to get over when she could, but dismissed the idea of working less.

'I will in time,' was all she ever said when the subject came up.

'But when will that be?' Juliet had pushed her this time.

In return, Hero had smiled that big, beautiful smile of hers before hugging her sister, kissing her temple as she pulled back. 'Stop worrying.' The glossy hair swung as she shook her head, the smile still in place.

'Well, that's never going to happen,' Juliet huffed.

Hero merely rolled her eyes and smiled.

***

The sun was fading as Hero made her way over to the stables, an apple in each hand. She approached the open door and smiled as Chester twitched his ears and clip-clopped over to her, his head already dipping down to find the food he smelled.

'Wait a minute,' Hero laughed.

'He's not great at manners.' A deep voice came from behind her. 'Sorry about that. We don't tend to get many fancy guests out this way.'

Hero didn't reply, but Nick could tell by the way her body tensed that she'd heard him. She held up the apple and the horse snaffled it with his lips, transferred it to his mouth, and proceeded to chomp his way noisily through it. Hero stroked his nose gently as he pushed his head against her, searching for the other treat he knew was still out there. Behind the curtain of her hair, Nick could just about see the smile on her face. It didn't seem to be something she did very readily, although, to be fair, she seemed to do it far more in the company of others than with him. He shifted his weight as that thought jabbed at him. The land was quiet now, with only the odd 'baa' of a sheep or two carried on the soft evening breeze. Chester broke the silence once more with his crunching as Hero gave him the other apple.

'I'd say I wasn't a fancy guest, but I think you'd probably disagree. To be honest,' she said, pulling a white handkerchief from her pocket and wiping her hands, 'I think whatever I said you'd find a way to disagree with me.' Hero glanced up, meeting his eyes.

A half smile hovered around his mouth. 'You're pretty fancy for around these parts,' he replied, ignoring the rest of her comment.

Hero turned back to the horse who was now nuzzling her neck. She tilted her head to the side and leant against him as she stroked his nose. 'I'm no different to Juliet and you seem to have adjusted to her being out here without any snide remarks. She seems to think you're absolutely wonderful, although for the life of me, I can't see why.'

The deep, throaty laugh took her by surprise. Looking up, she saw what appeared to be genuine amusement on Nick's face.

'I guess I deserved that.'

'Deserved what?'

Nick shook his head at the confusion on her face. 'Being put in my place.'

'Oh …' She wanted to come up with a witty retort, but right now the only thought in her brain was how sexy Nick Webster's laugh was. Along with the rest of him. Hero shook her head, telling herself she must have been out in the sun without a hat for too long. She wasn't attracted to Nick Webster! In fact, she couldn't think of anyone more inappropriate to have a crush on!

He tilted his head at her. 'Looks like you're having a real conversation with yourself inside your head. Care to share?'

God, no!

'I wasn't thinking anything particularly,' she said, doing her best to sound casual.

'Mm-hmm, OK.'

Hero risked a glance, and in that moment she could see that Nick clearly didn't believe a word of it. Well, tough luck to him, because there was no way she was going to tell him what she'd actually been thinking. She was pretty sure he and that ego of his would dine out on that little nugget of information every time she visited for the next several years. Instead she went back to the soothing, repetitive smoothing of the horse's nose.

'Isn't this one of those Instagram moments?' Nick asked, one dark brow slightly raised as he indicated her and the horse with his chin.

'A what?'

'An Instagram moment. Isn't that what they call it? You take a selfie with the horse and then post it with something inane like "Hashtag blessed".'

'Oh. Maybe. I don't really know. It's not something I do.'

Nick let out a puff of air through his nose that signalled either amusement or disbelief or, seeing as it was him, quite possibly both.

'Instagram or selfies?'

Hero dropped her hand and stood back from the stable door. 'Both, I guess.'

'You're kidding, right?'

She shook her head, her face serious. 'No. Why would I be?'

'I don't know. Maybe because everyone seems to be doing that these days?'

'I'm not. Are you?'

'No, of course not.'

'You seem to know an awful lot about it,' Hero prodded.

'I don't,' Nick stated, his voice firmer this time. 'I just had a fi… girlfriend who was heavily into all that stuff. It's hard not to learn by osmosis when you never get to eat a meal until it's been photographed and filtered and uploaded.'

Hero's interest was piqued at Nick stumbling in his wording.

For a moment she thought he was going to say fiancée, but she'd heard nothing from Juliet about him being engaged, which, knowing her sister, she most certainly would have. Maybe it was just all the talk of weddings and fiancées in general filtering through his head after a long day out working. 'It's pretty hard to work out which are the genuine emotions and which are faked just to make a good picture these days.'

She watched him as he took off his hat and ran a hand through his dark hair. For a moment the confident, tough guy carapace seemed to crack.

'I think you're right.' This time it was Nick's turn to look surprised.

'Wait. Did we just agree on something?' That hint of a smile became less of a shadow and more real.

'I suppose it had to happen sometime.'

'I suppose. You can write that in your blog.'

Hero rolled her eyes at him. 'OK. So, I don't have a blog. I do have an Instagram account, but mostly to keep in contact with my best friend who absolutely loves it and practically documents her whole day on it. And lastly, I am not a fan of taking selfies.'

They'd started to walk slowly back towards the house but as she spoke the last sentence, Nick halted.

'Now that I do struggle to believe.'

'Why?'

Nick smiled at her. 'You're seriously asking me that?'

'I am,' she replied, irritation creasing her brow.

'You've seen yourself, right? How would someone who looks like you not love selfies?'

Beneath the make-up, which she apparently never took a break from, Nick thought he could detect the faintest blush.

'There are plenty enough photos of me out there already. I hardly need to add to the pile.'

'That doesn't seem to stop some people.'

'Some people isn't everyone.'

'That is true.'

They'd resumed their walk, but Hero could tell Nick still didn't believe her. She let out a sigh and stopped.

'What's up?' he asked.

'Clearly you don't believe me, so here! Look for yourself.'

'I don't need to do that.'

'I want you to.'

'Why?'

'Because …' Hero had no idea why, but for some reason, she wanted Nick to know she wasn't as vain and shallow as he seemed to think she was. The idea of being bothered by this was utterly ridiculous. Those two words were applied by half the planet to anyone in the modelling world. And yes, sometimes it was true. There was vanity there just as there was anywhere else. But it upset her to think that she had been tarred with that same brush by Nick Webster. When he didn't take the phone, she quickly opened the photos tab and held it up to him.

'See?' she asked, scrolling through the photos. 'Hardly any selfies.'

He glanced at it and nodded. 'OK.' He let out a breath, something gnawing at him about the air of desperate sincerity Hero had. She clearly felt the need to prove to him that she wasn't what he thought she was. Why would one of the world's top-earning models who had people fawning at her morning, noon, and night care what a sheep farmer in rural Australia thought? Hero Scott was definitely an enigma and, beautiful as she was, Nick knew that wasn't his puzzle to work out. There was way too much potential hurt that way.

He squinted at the phone and angled it slightly, his own hand closing around hers for a moment. 'You know you have flight mode enabled on this thing?' He'd heard her asking Juliet about Wi-Fi when she'd arrived and remembered that the first thing she'd done as she stepped out of the car was type into her phone.

Hero nodded. 'Yes. I know.'

'But I thought you wanted to be on the Wi-Fi? I mean, when you're in the house.'

'I did, but only to send a message to my friend, Anya. She'd asked me to let her know that I'd got here safe.' She turned to him with a brief, shy smile. 'She worries about me.' Hero smiled and shook her head, as if the notion of anyone worrying about her was ridiculous. But just at that moment, Nick realised that he could easily spend a whole lifetime worrying about this woman. And that was exactly why he needed to keep as much distance between them as possible. He'd been pulled into that trap once before, and certainly had no plans to let that happen ever again, and definitely not with this woman. She had danger written all over her.

OK, so maybe she didn't take as many selfies as he'd supposed. And yes, sometimes, when she thought no one was looking, her beautiful face took on an expression that spoke of such insecurity and loneliness, and it pulled at his heart. None of that changed the fact that she was a world away from real life as most people knew it. Even when he'd bumped in to her at dawn, she already had full make-up on. Who did that in the back of beyond, when they were just hanging around a sheep station all day? There was still far too much coolness about her for his liking. She held herself at a distance – at least from him. And he hadn't forgotten the hesitation in the action of shaking his hand when she'd arrived, even though he'd just washed them. He guessed she wasn't really experienced in dealing with people she likely thought of as staff, up there in her ivory tower. Besides, in a couple of days she'd be back in London, with people ready to preen and pamper her at a moment's notice, and men swarming around her, desperate to be the next one in her bed. His stomach twisted at the last thought. He ignored it, telling himself it meant nothing. Of course he found her attractive. Any bloke who had a real-life supermodel come to stay with them was going to be knocked sideways a little bit. Par for the course. It was just because she was a novelty. The next time she came, it'd be different. And once the wedding was done with tomorrow, she'd be on her way, and things could finally get back to normal.

Chapter 4

Later that evening, Nick glanced down the end of the verandah to where the Websters' visitor sat on a wicker sofa, opposite Joe, playing Scrabble. His parents were in town catching up with friends, and Pete and Juliet were inside finishing off packing for their honeymoon. Nick turned his attention back to the setting sun, watching it sink slowly amidst a riot of warm colours behind a clump of distant trees. The sound of laughter pulled his gaze back; he was almost surprised to discover that it emanated from Hero Scott.

Nick knew the opinion he'd formed of her wasn't entirely flattering, and nowhere in the description did it include an enticing, carefree laugh. She'd certainly never done that in his company anyway. Was there a chance that he was wrong? What else had he missed? The rest of his family seemed to have taken to her and she to them, though not as unreservedly as she had taken to their Joe.

Joe Carter was the son of Jacob, the Websters' leading station hand. Jacob and his wife had been resident at Hill Station ever since it had acquired the name. Nick knew that the Carters had been instrumental in helping the station become the success it was today. Jacob and Maria had soon become more than employees, even more than friends. They were as much part of the Webster family as true blood, and so when Maria had finally fallen pregnant, the Websters had been as overjoyed as they were themselves.

Gill had known Maria for years. She'd always been a fragile girl, catching whatever virus passed her way, but rarely complaining. Gill and Jack knew that Jacob, although delighted about the baby, had concerns for his wife. An infection years previously had weakened her immune system, and although the doctors hadn't entirely ruled out having children, they had voiced their fears for Maria's own health should she ever fall pregnant. But the petite and fragile frame belied the strength of her will. Years of trying had persuaded her that children were not to be part of her life. Instead she had doted on the Webster boys, and that didn't change when, to her surprise, she finally became pregnant with her own child.

The young boys had been among the first visitors to see baby Joe and their acceptance and interest in him completed Maria's happiness. She knew in her heart that she would not be there to watch her boy grow into a man. The labour had been long and arduous, and every hour had taken more and more out of her. Maria had gripped Jacob's hand with more force than anyone would have credited her with. And then when the baby finally arrived, he was silent, choking on the placenta cord that had become wound tight several times around his neck. The doctors worked swiftly until, suddenly, Maria heard the most blessed sound; the sound of her baby's first cry.

Maria had taken a chance and although her body had lost, she knew as she looked down into the peaceful, happy face of her son that, given the chance, she would make the same choices. Three weeks after Joe's birth, Maria passed away.

Now, Nick watched Joe's animated face as he listened intently to something Hero was saying, smiling at his surrogate younger brother's concentration. Nick cast his mind back as he sipped his cold beer straight from the bottle, his feet balancing on the rail and his chair tipped back. It had taken a while for anyone to notice anything was different about Joe, but as he began to struggle more and more with his schooling, even Jacob could not ignore the fact that his son seemed to have more trouble with learning than the other children. Tests were run and eventually the doctors said that it was more than likely caused by the lack of oxygen at the time of his birth. If the delivery staff hadn't worked so quickly, Joe could have been a lot worse. As it was, he was several years behind his contemporaries. The local school was small, understanding, and made allowances, eventually teaching him with pupils who were closer to his mental age, rather than his physical one. There were, naturally, difficult times; Joe was a big lad for his age and being put with younger children only made the difference more exaggerated. But he had one good thing going for him – his nature.

Joe was the angel Maria had promised her husband he would be. His smiling face brought cheer to a room and every time Jacob looked at his son, he saw his beloved wife, and for that he was eternally grateful. He knew that he'd never be able to repay the kindness he had received from the Websters who had adopted both him and his son. The two boys looked upon Joe as their own brother. They'd not only stuck up for him at school, but also taught him how to look after himself, should the need ever arise. Joe had also claimed another unlikely set of allies, thanks largely to his gentle nature: girls. The girls in Joe's class had been fiercer than even the Webster boys when someone tried to pick on Joe. And that was saying something.

Joe glanced up and saw Nick looking his way. He waved with a huge smile and beckoned to him. Nick pondered, then dropped his legs from the rail, at the same time dropping the chair back onto all four of its legs. He ambled down to where the others were sitting.

'Hope you're letting our visitor win, Joe.'

'This is great! Hero's teaching me some new words and stuff. Why don't you play, too, Nick?'

'Nah, you're all right, mate.' He glanced at the space next to Hero, then lowered himself into it. 'So, what new words have you learned? I hope they're the kind you can say in polite company.'

Joe chuckled. 'Of course they are.' From the corner of his eye, Nick noticed Hero focusing on turning the letter tiles over in the lid of the box. 'And Hero says she's going to bring me some books next time!'

Nick turned his attention to the bowed head of their guest. 'So, you're coming back then?'

'It will probably be a little while, Joe. I might have to send them,' she answered without looking at Nick.

At her reply, Joe's face fell briefly before he covered it up with a smile, an expression that fooled neither of his companions. Nick instinctively knew Hero's reply had been influenced by his own presence. The look on Joe's face twisted at his insides.

'OK,' Joe agreed.

Hero leant over and touched the young man's face gently. 'But I'll see what I can do. I'm sure I can steal a few days away, and I promise to bring the books then. How's that?'

Joe's brave smile turned to one of genuine pleasure and he beamed it around as he took the lid of the box that Hero had now filled with upturned word tiles and shook it around to mix them up.

'Sure you don't want to play?' Joe asked again.

Nick smiled and shook his head, then stood and walked off in the direction of the stables. As he walked, he mused over the exchange – how Hero hadn't looked at him once throughout the conversation, how eager she had been to settle Joe, and the gentle touch she had laid on Joe's cheek. What surprised Nick most of all was that he'd found himself wondering how that touch would feel on his own skin.

As Joe shuffled the letters, Hero lifted her eyes and watched the retreating figure of Nick Webster as he strolled away. As he'd sat close beside her on the little wicker sofa, the clean smell of soap had drifted on the air and she could still smell it now. She didn't know if it lingered for real or just in her mind. Nick Webster unnerved her. She couldn't read him. He was edgy. Dangerous. An unknown quantity. Hero didn't like unknown quantities. She liked exactness. She was glad he hadn't taken up sweet Joe's offer to play Scrabble with them. She was glad that he had gone, even more so knowing that part of her had wanted him to stay.

***

'So, this time tomorrow, you'll be Juliet Webster.'

Pete's mother was almost bouncing up and down with excitement as they sat at the dinner table. Although she worshipped her two boys, Gill had always wanted a little girl. Unfortunately, complications had set in after Nick's birth and the requisite surgery meant that further children were no longer an option. In Juliet, Gill was finally getting the daughter she had always wanted.

Juliet leaned over and took Gill's hand. 'Then there'll be two of us!'

'Oh hell!' Jack groaned with a tease.

Hero watched, smiling at Jack's comment as Gill's tumbled around in her mind. Mrs Webster. No longer a Scott. No longer in England. No longer just hers. Hero looked at Juliet and felt her heart swelling as the happiness emanated from every fibre of her sister's being. Although having her move halfway around the world wasn't what Hero would have chosen for her, Pete was definitely the sort of man she would have. Pete was handsome, kind, witty, and would clearly walk through fire for his fiancée. If Hero had to lose her sister, she was glad it was to someone like him – and at least she'd had the sense to fall for him and not his rather younger brother.

Hero slid her eyes across to Nick. The brothers certainly had some similarities. Nick was also tall, had the same dark hair cut in the same short way, a warm smile and liquid brown eyes topping a strong, muscular body. It was a combination that Hero was sure must have swept many a girl off her feet and into his bed. His bed? The last thought popped uninvited into her mind, and Hero blinked, stiffening in her chair as she mentally forced the unsettling thought back out.

The slight movement across from him caused Nick to glance at their guest. He'd done his best to try and like her – although his brother had disagreed on that point. Nick had shrugged the criticism off. He didn't appreciate that snooty attitude she had, and whenever he thought maybe he'd misjudged her, he'd turn back only to find that same look of indifference on her face. Pete had defended her, saying there was more to her than that, and that Nick had to give her some leeway, citing her kindness and attention to Joe as an example. Nick had to concede on that point, but he was still wary. What was her motivation in the time she spent with Joe? Was she going to go back and tell all her friends about the charity case she'd taken on? Was it all some forward planning for yet more attention? Nick's jaw tensed at the thought that anyone would try and use Joe in that way. But as much as he'd thought about this, there was something in her face, in her touch that night he'd joined them as they played board games, that made him hesitate. If she was putting all that on, then she ought to go land a movie deal, because it had looked pretty damn genuine to him.

Still, putting that aside, they lived in completely different worlds. Nick's involved other people and, as far as he was concerned, Hero's only involved herself, perhaps Juliet, and now Joe. When it came to those two, she certainly gave the appearance that nothing was too much trouble. Anyway, the sooner she went, the better he'd feel. As a rule, Nick knew he was pretty easy on people, so having to work at something like this was a new experience, not to mention distracting. He was looking forward to getting station life back to its normal routine.

Hero moved again as she mentally tried to push the unexpected and entirely unwanted thought of Nick Webster naked in a bed out of her mind. Her gaze lifted as she did, and she found that very man watching her. She stopped mid-shift. Even with her make-up and the soft lighting of the dining room, Nick could see it. She was blushing. A smile slid onto his lips. This might be fun. He sat back in his chair, tipping it until it balanced on the two back legs.

'I reckon with me being best man and you being chief bridesmaid, we probably ought to have at least one dance together tomorrow.'

Hero smiled back sweetly, wondering if it was bad that she was secretly hoping his chair would tip over, just to wipe the smug look off his face.

'Oh, I'm sure you'll have plenty of women clamouring for your attention already, Nick.'

'Probably,' he agreed languidly, his broad shoulders lifting in a shrug, 'but I'm sure I can make space for you.'

Hero's eyes widened in disbelief at his arrogance. Under the table, he got a hard kick from his older brother. Pete knew Nick was only winding her up, but it was obvious to everyone this wasn't a game Hero Scott had ever played.

Make space! She could have slapped him.

'Well, I'm sure that's very kind of you but I wouldn't want to cramp your style.' She purposefully kept the tone light. Only two more days and she'd be gone, back to civilisation and her own world. She ignored the fact that, for some reason, she didn't feel as happy about that as she probably should have. But on the plus side, it did mean she only had two more days to put up with Nick Webster and his judging looks and suppositions about her and her life. For Juliet, Hero was prepared to be civil and play along with his silly little game.

Nick shrugged and smiled as he bounced the chair back onto the floor, garnering a reprove from his mother about the furniture as he did so. He apologised politely to her with a smile, then glanced back to their guest. She was listening to his brother rattle on about her sister. Nick smiled to himself. No matter how well she covered it, he'd got a reaction. Maybe there was hope for Hero Scott after all.

***

Hero was enjoying the wedding celebrations far more than she had expected to. What she was most thankful for was the fact that hardly anyone seemed to know, or care, who she was, outside of being the bride's younger sister. The relief in that alone was almost like a physical burden had been lifted. The only attention she'd felt unsure about was from one of the waitresses. A blonde, busty woman of a similar age to her, she guessed, whom she recognised as a barmaid from the local pub. Hero had noticed a few looks come her way from that direction when she'd been into town with Juliet. Her stomach tensed at the thought of this woman posting something on social media about her being here. Hero had always been so careful to protect Juliet's identity. The world could judge her, but her sister was entirely out of bounds. The world's obsession with social media had definitely made protecting her more difficult but, so far, Hero had managed it. The last thing she wanted now was someone giving out information about her, and the location of the Websters' place.

She'd mentioned her concerns to Juliet, who had apparently then mentioned them to her new family, as the subject had soon come up one night over dinner. Hero had given Juliet a bit of a look, feeling awkward and worrying that the Websters might think she was spoiled and full of herself, assuming people would automatically want to talk about her. She could understand an outsider thinking that. But she operated within that world, and she knew how it worked.

Thankfully, the Websters had been very understanding, telling her not to worry about it, and that they would do their best to make sure everyone's privacy was protected. That was apart from Nick. Throughout the whole conversation, he'd kept his eyes down, concentrating on his food, staying out of the conversation. It was clear that he was as keen for her to leave as she was.

Pete's parents had been very kind at introducing her to people at the wedding venue and then again this evening, but it was their son's wedding and they had plenty of their own mingling to do. The Websters were well known and well liked in the area, and Juliet was already becoming a favourite in her own right.

Glancing around the room earlier, Hero had noticed a few jealous looks being thrown her sister's way. It was understandable. Pete was handsome, solvent and a decent man – an ideal combination, and one that wasn't always that easy to find in a busy city, let alone in a remote location like this, she imagined. Even if she saw them, Juliet wouldn't take it to heart. She understood that all they saw was that an outsider had come along and snapped up one of the few eligible men in the area. In time, they'd get used to it, and her. Hero had pulled a face at her answer when they'd talked about it yesterday, wondering at the ability her sister had to always see the best in people. Hero's nature and life path had combined to make her see things differently. It was one subject that they had agreed to disagree on, several times:

'The trouble with you, Jules, is that you think everyone is like you.'

'And the trouble with you is that you don't.'

The reception was heaving, and Hero took the opportunity to step outside, breathing in the warm air of the evening as she looked up, gazing at the huge sky, stars now appearing, sparkling like diamonds on the deep blue canvas of twilight. It was years since she'd last looked up at the stars and really been able to see them as she did now. The light pollution in London, and all the other major cities she'd worked in around the world had meant she'd almost forgotten they were up there. But there they were. Hero breathed in deeply, as if by doing so she would be able to take away some of the peace and beauty with her when she left. As if by photographing this moment in the camera of her mind, she'd hold on to the feeling of calm she felt settling around her as she gazed up at them.

She jumped as a door burst open behind her, the sounds of the party within tumbling out in the night.

'All right, love.' One of the many people Gill had introduced her to earlier tapped her on the shoulder as they passed, before taking one of the chairs under an awning nearby. Next she heard the click of a lighter, and then the rhythmic movement of an ash glowing, then cooling as it moved up and down in the smoker's hand. She was thankful he'd not stopped to chat, as unsociable as she knew that sounded. Hero had never been good at small talk, a quirk that worked fine in her usual surroundings. Most people, she found, were more than happy to talk about themselves ad infinitum. Their compliments about her being such a good listener, which Hero always waved off with a smile and a head-shake, felt unwarranted. She knew the truth was that she should be thanking them. The less she had to talk about herself, the better. Magazines and social media, not to mention Anya, had told her that apparently she was looked upon as mysterious. Hero knew that others were less kind, thinking her behaviour spoke more of snobbishness and that she considered herself far too high and mighty to ever engage with those outside her immediate circle. If only they knew, Hero thought. What she'd give to have the easy-going, sociable nature of her sister, instead of the awkward, shy confines of her own.

The door behind her banged again, and several more people, in various states of intoxication stumbled out and headed towards the smoking area. Hero knew she should go back in. She didn't care about strangers thinking she was snooty, but she didn't want her own behaviour to reflect badly on her sister in her new life out here. Taking one last look at the starlit sky, she drew a deep breath and headed back inside.

Nick had intended to ask Hero to dance. Initially it had been a joke but after the wedding breakfast was over, Pete had told him he had to make good on the tease.

'She'll never go for it,' Nick replied, dismissing his brother's request.

'Just ask her, will you, mate?'

'Yeah, yeah. Right-oh.' If it had been anyone else, he'd have probably done it a lot sooner. But three minutes worth of awkward dancing with this particular woman didn't exactly fill him with glee. That was assuming she even accepted. She certainly hadn't been keen when he'd brought the subject up at the dinner table. OK, so maybe he hadn't phrased it in the best way he could have. Even behind that cool exterior she projected out to the world, he'd noticed the surprise in her eyes at his jest. Understandable, he supposed, when you were one of the world's most beautiful women and people were desperate to be in your company, even just be noticed by you, let alone anything else.

After receiving yet another loaded glance from his older brother, Nick nodded and resigned himself to going off to find Pete's newly acquired sister-in-law. It took him a little while to find her among the many guests, although he had to admit that he hadn't put too much effort into the actual act of looking, finding himself easily, and willingly, distracted. One of those distractions being in the shape of the barmaid, Susannah Dagmar. And what a shape! She'd always had a bit of thing for Pete, so Nick felt a bit sorry for her having to wait tables at his brother's wedding when she probably felt that, by rights, it should have been her wearing the white dress, not some interloper. He finally tore himself away when his mother sent him a dagger-laden glance, before making a nodding gesture. Nick sighed. Gill had never liked Susannah.

Following the direction of his mother's nod, Nick caught sight of Hero. She was sitting alone towards the back of the room looking absolutely stunning. Whether he liked her or not, Nick couldn't deny that she was beautiful. But he understood the possibility that that same beauty might keep people at a distance. Men might be intimidated and women might be jealous, wary, or both. Then again, it could just be that she was a stuck-up pain in the arse. Nick excused himself from Susannah and made his way towards Hero. Her hands were folded on her lap as she sat, back straight against the wall, looking for all intents and purposes in utter control. Out of her sightline, he hesitated as he noticed her thumb rubbing back and forth at a hangnail. Her gaze was fixed at no clear point, as though she wanted to evade making eye contact with any other guest. The gaze alone he might have put down to her reluctance to mingle in lowlier company than she was used to. But he hesitated in his judgement as he watched her hands. His time in the city had given him more than enough opportunity to observe the habits of the stressed, and he was pretty sure that was exactly what he was watching now. Damn woman. Why couldn't she just be one thing or another?

'You ready for that dance now?' Nick asked. 'I looked for you earlier, but I couldn't see you.'

Hero looked up, surprise in her eyes. The look confirmed what he'd begun to think. *Yeah, you were hoping no one would notice you sat back here all alone, weren't you?*

'I went outside for a little while,' she said, gathering herself a little as she took the hand he offered and stood. Her relief at seeing a familiar face seemed to cause that mask of confidence and indifference to slip. Nick tilted his head.

'You all right?' Even with the heat of all these bodies, her smooth, porcelain skin looked a little paler than usual.

Hero caught the concern in his voice and felt something rush through her. Looking up into the intense chocolate-brown eyes now studying her, she gave a small, embarrassed smile.

'I'm not really very good with crowds. They make me nervous.'

Nick didn't reply. He was just looking down at her.

She smiled shyly and lifted their joined hands. 'Are we going to dance or just stand here holding hands all night? Right now, I'm happy either way.'

Nick glanced down at their hands, before turning towards the dancefloor. Their path was crowded as he led the way, holding tightly to her hand, clearing the way for her with his broad shoulders. His eyes were on the way ahead, but his mind was still reeling from the smile Hero had given him.

For the past couple of weeks, they'd done nothing but rub each other up the wrong way, with a large proportion of their conversations edged with sarcasm and spikes. In company, they had silently but mutually agreed to concentrate on being polite for the sake of their respective siblings. Nick struggled with the constant control she kept about herself. There was none of the spontaneity of her sister, none of the laughter and fun Juliet seemed to naturally inspire. He'd even begun to doubt that the woman even had real emotions – something about her seemed so false, so brittle. Pete and his parents had taken to her like she was a wounded bird, but all Nick saw was self-importance and privilege.

But the smile she had just given him had blown all his beliefs about her to bits. For the first time since he'd known her, he saw what the others had been privy to all along.

They reached the dancefloor and squeezed into a space as Nick raised their joined hands and wrapped his other arm around her narrow waist. The crowd of people on the floor meant that Hero was pressed close to him. He could smell her perfume, feel her fragile build beneath his hands as well as her now uneven breaths. Looking down into her face, he saw that striking green gaze dart around as it desperately tried, and failed, to find something familiar to focus on. She felt his own gaze on her and looked up, his eyes holding hers as his arm tightened a little closer around her.

'Just breathe,' he said, softly. He kept his eyes on her until her erratic breaths steadied. Feeling his arms strong and steady around her, Hero closed her eyes and felt the world slide away. With just one movement, and with the last person she ever expected, Hero no longer felt alone.

Too near the speakers for any real conversation to take place, Hero was glad. She was tired of keeping her mask in place with Nick, but something about him had unnerved her from the beginning. He hadn't tried to bow down to her every whim like most men she knew. He made her laugh, although she did her best to hide it. The many conversations she had sat in on proved that he was an intelligent, well-informed man. She'd desperately wanted to take part in them but, despite Pete and Juliet giving her plenty of openings, she kept her participation limited, afraid to make herself look stupid in front of this man who already caused such a torrent of emotions within her. But it seemed that the less she said, the more it irritated Nick. And as much as she had tried to deny it, his reaction upset her. She'd spent the last fortnight convincing herself that he was arrogant and of no consequence. But the truth was that he excited her. She'd never felt like this about anyone. And that fact alone both thrilled and frightened her.

As Hero and Nick moved to the music, she felt the strong hand on her back. Many of the men she knew were muscular, but they were false muscles, born from spending hours in the gym, admiring themselves in huge floor-to-ceiling mirrors as they pumped iron. Nick's body was strong from hard work and hard play. She felt the slight roughness of his skin against her hand as it held her own. It felt good. Something about those men with their soft, smooth, overly manicured hands had always made her feel slightly queasy. She turned her head slightly against his chest to look at the hand holding hers. The nails were short and had been scrubbed clean. Hero smiled to herself at the effort this must have taken, knowing Nick had spent most of yesterday under the bonnet of the old ute they used to drive out into the fields.

'They are clean.' Nick leant in close to her ear when he'd worked out what Hero was studying, a smile in his voice.

She looked up, embarrassment showing on her face at being caught. But then she felt it, deep within herself, like a revelation she wasn't even aware she was waiting for. There it was, shining clear in her mind as bright as any neon sign. There was no need to be embarrassed anymore. Not here. Not with Nick. She didn't need to be afraid anymore. She didn't need to be anything but herself. As this realisation dawned within her, she turned and smiled at him again, for once not holding back. For once not smiling on someone else's cue.

Looking up at him, Hero smiled, wide and beautiful. The power of it made Nick catch his breath. This. This was what she was hiding from the world. The question was why? The smile hit Nick square in the face and didn't stop until it got to his toes, detouring several times on the way down. He pulled her closer, the surroundings too noisy for him to hear. Bending his head towards her, she repeated herself close to his ear, so close that he could feel her warm breath on his skin as she spoke.

'You have nice hands.'

The simple, almost childlike compliment only added to the feelings racing around his body. His head spun with it all. How the hell did she survive in that cold, shallow world she lived in? Nick saw now what she did her best to hide from the world at large – the shy, insecure young woman who fooled people into thinking that she was in control, completely sure of herself, and everyone around her. But now he knew differently. This girl wasn't in control at all. She was barely treading water, just trying not to drown.

Nick squeezed her hand a little in a gesture of reply and saw the corners of a smile play upon her mouth. He looked up for a moment and caught the eye of his elder brother who was standing with his new bride, talking to some relatives who had flown in from Sydney for the wedding. He nodded at them and grinned. Nick gave him a brief smile in return. As his gaze left his family, it landed on Susannah. Susannah was also watching them, but she wasn't smiling. Her eyes were on Hero, and there was something far colder in her expression.

Nick turned back to his partner and steered them away from the main crush, as well as Susannah's glare.

'Don't take this the wrong way.' He smiled as he pulled away a little in order to look into those hypnotic eyes. 'Do you want to go outside and get a bit of air?'

He felt her body relax a little in his arms as he said it. That was more than enough answer for him. In a reverse of their earlier journey, Nick once again led the way through the thrumming dancefloor and out into the cool, quiet night.

Chapter 5

Once outside, they found a bench a little away from the doors, and the smoking area, and sat down. Nick still held Hero's hand and, surprising herself, she didn't pull away. Didn't want to pull away.

'Not something you've ever fancied then, all this?' Hero nodded in the direction of the reception room they had just left. 'By the amount of six-foot-under looks I've been receiving, I get the impression that you're not short of offers.'

Nick shrugged his eyebrows. 'Nope. Not really sure it's for me.'

Hero turned a little, kicking off her shoes as she did so, and tucked her legs up in front of her. Resting her chin on her knees, she pulled a face at his reply. 'The good-looking man with a fear of commitment – isn't that rather a cliché?'

Nick caught the twinkle in those mesmerising, cat-like eyes of hers. He tilted his head at her.

'Was that a compliment? The "good-looking" part I mean?'

Hero just smiled.

'And who said I had a fear of commitment? Or is that a little projection on your part?'

Hero ignored the second question, focusing on the first. 'Don't you?'

'No.'

She echoed his head tilt. 'So how come you're not happily ensconced somewhere with a clan of little Nicholases running around?'

'Perhaps I'm just enough of a good bloke not to want to show up my big brother by getting there first.'

'Well, that's very considerate of you, if it's the case.'

'I thought so.'

'But I'm not buying that as the reason for a moment.'

'No?' He laughed.

'Definitely no.'

'OK. So maybe I just haven't found the right girl yet.'

Hero considered that. 'From what I've heard, you've conducted plenty of research in that department.'

Again, Nick saw the eyes twinkle. She was enjoying this. As much as he was? It was hard to tell.

'Research can be a very valuable tool.'

'This is true.'

'Want to help me with said research?' He flashed a grin, enjoying this rare, unguarded version of Hero.

She laughed. 'No, but thank you for offering me the chance to take part in such a prestigious and vital project.'

'No worries.'

Silence fell between them for a few moments, but it was companionable. From the open windows, they heard the DJ transition one song seamlessly into another. She turned to the sound, then looked back at Nick, a question in her eyes. She didn't really want to go back in. Not just yet. She wasn't even comfortable at parties where she did know lots of people. When you barely knew anyone and were also receiving openly questionable looks from certain females, the discomfort tended to grow. Nick understood.

'Got somewhere else to be?'

A pause. His companion shook her head. The movement was

almost imperceptible, but its ripples caused the shining locks to sway gently, catching the light of the outdoor lamp. Nick smiled softly at her, and Hero returned it. She shifted on the bench. The back slats were uncomfortable on her back. Keeping hold of her hand, Nick ran his other arm around her waist and shifted her body until she rested on him, rather than the bench. Much better.

'Truth is, I thought I had found the right one,' he said after a few moments.

Hero waited.

'Turned out I was wrong.'

When he said nothing more, she spoke. 'What happened? If you don't mind me asking?'

He didn't mind her asking. Strange really, because until this moment, he would have thought that Hero Scott would be the last person on earth he'd open up to.

As close as they were together, Hero felt the deep breath he took and then exhaled slowly as his mind worked.

'I don't know. To be honest, I thought everything was fine. I thought we were happy. We'd talked about getting married and she seemed stoked. I bought the ring, did the whole down-on-one-knee thing, she accepted, said she couldn't be happier. Then, next thing I know, I'm walking in on her in bed with her boss. Stupidly, I'd never questioned all that overtime she was doing.'

'Oh, Nick! I'm so sorry.' She gave his hand a gentle squeeze. 'I would never have said anything if …' She trailed off and looked awkward. Nick laid his cheek against her head. She felt the smile as he returned the reassuring squeeze.

'Don't be daft. It's fine. I didn't know if Juliet had told you, but I guess not.'

'No! No, she hadn't!' She pulled herself up and twisted so that she could see him. He was surprised to see she looked genuinely upset. 'Nick, I know you think I'm rather cold, but I'd never make light of something like that … of you being hurt.'

One hand gently cupped her face, the expression in his eyes soft and warm under the low light.

'I know you wouldn't. And just for the record, I don't think you're cold.'

She smiled at him almost shyly. Their initial distrust and differences had been put aside – at least for the moment. It seemed so obvious to her now. What she first thought was conceit and arrogance wasn't that at all. It was part of a defence mechanism, a shield. Creating an armour against the world was hardly something she could criticise him about when she spent so much time, perhaps too much, behind her own. She could see, feel, that it was a relief for both of them to have a break from it, even for a just a few moments, revealing themselves to each other, if no one else.

'So,' Hero began, 'you do actually have a fear of commitment, just not your own.'

He thought about that for a moment, then gave her a lopsided smile. 'I guess so.'

She nodded, understanding, empathising, before breaking eye contact with him. Nick drew another deep breath before pulling her back closer. Without thinking, Hero let her body follow, feeling the warmth of him through the fine material of her gown. His slow, steady breaths soothed her. She knew she was on dangerous ground. But right at this moment, she didn't care. Right now, it felt as though this was exactly where she should be. Resting her hands on the warm, muscular arm that encircled her waist, she didn't need – didn't want – that mask she usually wore. And as she felt his lips softly brush her hair, Hero closed her eyes and let the moment envelop her.

'You tired?' Nick's deep tones drifted close to her ear.

'A little,' she replied. The truth was she could so easily stay here with this man, feeling his strength and his comfort, and not move for the next several days. It had been a long, although beautiful, day. Emotions had run high and Juliet had burst into tears on more than one occasion, especially with Hero. Hero's eyes, as always, remained dry but Juliet knew it wasn't because she didn't care. Crying just wasn't something she did. Not for a long time. She'd smiled as the ceremony came to its climax and everyone cheered, welcoming Juliet into her new family and her new life. Again, Hero had smiled. Smiling was the only way to stop the panic rising in her. Suddenly she felt alone. Out here in this land where their father had been born but that had meant nothing to either of his daughters. Now, to one it meant everything, and Hero felt cast adrift.

'What's up?'

'Nothing.' She closed her eyes again, pushing away the panic that had begun to creep towards her again. Her hands tightened almost imperceptibly on Nick's arm.

'So why don't I believe you?'

She shrugged against him.

Feeling the soft kiss on her hair, her breaths gradually slowed. What was it with this man who could make her mad one moment and chase away her demons in the next.

'You know your sister is worried about you.' His words were a statement, not a question.

'I know. She doesn't need to be though. I'm fine.'

'She thinks you work too hard.'

'I like keeping busy.'

'There's keeping busy, and there's back-to-back assignments.'

Hero drew in a breath and let it out slowly, concentrating on the glittering stars and the warmth of Nick's body behind her.

'A girl has to pay the rent,' she said, trying to lighten the mood, not to mention deflect the enquiry.

'I don't mean to be nosy, but I'm pretty sure you've probably got that covered.'

'Maybe. But I like to be sure.'

'Why do I get the feeling there's more to this?' Nick asked, getting his answer as he felt Hero's body tense within his arms.

'Of course there isn't. I just like to be sure I'm financially prepared and independent. I know that's still quite a radical view to take in some parts, but that's what happens when you invite outsiders into your world.'

Nick smiled. 'Not me. I'm all for that.'

'Good to hear.'

'So, what do you do to relax?'

'I …' What did she do to relax? She spent time with Anya shopping, and visiting restaurants. She liked to read but the only times she ever seemed to be able to sit down with a book was on a long-haul flight like the one that had brought her here, although even then she never seemed to get far as fatigue overtook her and sleep won over reading.

'What do *you* do to relax?' Hero turned the question on him.

She felt the deep rumble of laughter as he squeezed her a little more. 'Oh no, you don't. I asked first.'

She sighed dramatically.

'And don't try and pull that diva stuff on me. I know you better than that now.'

She could hear the smile in his voice as he teased her.

'I suppose I go out with friends to relax.'

'And do you?'

'Do I what?'

'Relax. It's just that you've seemed as tight as a wound spring all day here.'

'No, I haven't.'

Nick tipped her up and twisted positions so that her legs now lay over his and she was looking up into his face in surprise.

'What are you doing?'

'If you're going to fib to me, you have to look me in the eye when you do it.'

Hero drew herself up. 'I'm not fibbing.' Was she?

In the low light from the function room's porch, she met his eyes and he knew that she was.

'I don't know anyone here. It's different.' Her voice was soft, and Nick pulled her a little closer, not just so that he could hear her but because there was something so hurt, so fractured in that tone that made him want to wrap his arms around her and protect her from whatever it was that had created that pain.

'You know me.'

A flicker of a smile danced on her face. 'I think that probably goes for most of the women in this district from what I've witnessed today.'

He grinned at her, even white teeth showing against the dark shadow on his jawline.

'Point taken. OK, so you know all our family, and most people here are pretty easy going and I find it hard to see that someone would turn down the opportunity of talking to a stunner like you.'

She dropped her gaze, knowing that, in a way, he was right. What she'd got used to at home, though, was wondering whether they were talking to her because they were interested, or whether it was because they wanted to be seen to be talking to her, or because they thought she might be useful in furthering their own cause. She knew how cynical her slant on it all was. Unfortunately, it seemed to prove itself over and over. Although, maybe here it was different.

'I didn't really know what to say to anyone.'

'You probably don't need to say much at all. Just ask about them and you'll be golden. Most people love an opportunity to talk about themselves.'

Hero let out a breath of laughter. 'That is true.'

The silence settled between them but there was nothing awkward about it. It felt natural. Companionable.

'I've never seen Juliet as happy as she is here.'

'I'd never seen my brother get such a dopey look on his face before she walked onto the property.'

'I hope they'll be happy.'

'I have no doubt about it. Although, it does mean I'm going to have to get my arse in gear and get my own house built now.'

'They're kicking you out?' Hero pulled back from his chest and stared at him, her mouth an 'o' of surprise.

'Nah, not at all. But the house should be theirs. All theirs. Of course, it's going to take a while to do anyway, but if I get started, I'll feel better.'

'Where will you be moving to? Won't it be difficult if you're still planning to help run the station?'

He wrapped his arms a little tighter around her, warmth flooding through him at her gentle, unguarded concern. Hero rested her head back against the solid wall of his chest.

'I'll still be on the property. When the place was built, I think there was some delusion of grandeur going on, and they had a gatehouse put in, near the start of the driveway.'

Keeping her head on his chest, Hero raised her eyes to Nick. 'You're not talking about that ruin on the left-hand side as you come in, are you?'

'That's the one.'

'You're rebuilding that?' The astonishment that the feat was even possible was clear in her voice.

'Mostly, plus I'll be extending it a bit.'

'That seems like a lot of work. Are you doing it on your own?'

'I've done the plans and had them approved, but not the rest. I've just been getting enough money together to make it happen.'

'Did you enjoy planning it? Juliet said you were an architect. I was kind of surprised when she went on to say you'd moved back here from the city to go in with your brother on the station.'

'Yeah, it was a change of direction, that's for sure, but sometimes things happen to make sure you end up where you're supposed to be, don't they? Sometimes all the bright lights, big city thing can wear you down.'

'It can. That's true.'

'After the whole engagement debacle, I realised I didn't want to be there anymore. I'd brought up the subject a couple of times with my ex, but it never really came to anything. We came out a few times to visit and I could tell that she was desperate to get back to the city about ten minutes in.'

'People change though. I never thought I'd see Juliet out here, on a place like this. We've only ever lived in big cities, and yet now it's hard to imagine her anywhere else. She looks completely at home.'

'I think the key is that you have to try. You have to have an open mind when it comes to change. It's always scary but sometimes you just need to give it a chance.'

'She's very lucky, and I know she knows that.' Hero smiled up at him briefly before resting her head back against him.

'Ah, I think we're the lucky ones. Finding someone as great as Jules to take Pete off our hands.'

Hero giggled, and he held her a fraction tighter, trying to remember when he'd heard her laugh like that in his company. He couldn't.

'I'm so glad your dad agreed to walk her down the aisle. She was nervous about asking him, I know.'

'Dad was thrilled. From the first time they met Juliet, they already loved her like a daughter.'

'You have a lovely family.'

'Thank you. I know I'm lucky.'

'You are.'

'It seems a shame that she had to ask Dad though. That your own dad wasn't here to do that with his daughter.'

As Hero's body stiffened, he realised there was a raw nerve there. 'He wouldn't have deserved that honour, even if he had been alive.'

Nick felt the change in her breathing. So relaxed a moment before, and now short and staccato. The tension he'd felt drift away from her was back and he kicked himself for breaking the spell. Unsure what to do, he remained still, his arms around her loosely, leaving her free to move away from him, should she want to. Slowly he moved one thumb rhythmically back and forth over the bare arm beneath his hand.

Inside Hero's head, memories spilled out. Memories that she had carefully stored away and done her best to hide. Her chest felt tight with hurt and anger that those memories still had the power within them to make her feel like she was nothing. Nothing but a burden.

'I'm sorry if I said the wrong thing, Hero.' Nick's tone was low, almost a whisper, and even without looking at his face she knew it would be full of concern.

'You didn't.'

'I know I'm a bloke, and therefore, at times will be able to put my foot in it whilst still being completely oblivious to that fact. But I'm pretty sure now isn't one of those times.'

Hero's thoughts raced, as Nick's soft, deep voice wound itself around her as tangibly as his arms. Why wouldn't those memories ever leave her? She knew they didn't mean anything now – she'd proved they didn't! She was the supermodel, Hero Scott. People paid thousands for her to endorse their product, or be photographed in their designs. People wanted her. They'd been wrong! What her mother had told her wasn't true. She knew that now. So why? Why did she still feel as if she had to prove it every day of her life?

'Talk to me.'

Hero shook her head. She couldn't. She'd not even told Juliet the full truth that day when she'd been punished and humiliated at school for crying. And Nick Webster of all people? If she hadn't told the few people on this earth she trusted, she was hardly going to air her dirty laundry to him, was she?

'I was a mistake,' she whispered, unsure of how, or why, those words were spilling out now.

'A mistake?' Nick replied. 'In what way?'

'Being born. Conceived at all.'

Nick hesitated, waiting to see if Hero was going to continue. When she remained silent, he encouraged her again.

'Lots of babies who weren't planned come into this world. They're still loved. Once they're here, it doesn't really matter if they were part of a bigger plan or not.'

'It mattered to my parents. Very much indeed.'

This time Nick remained silent, sensing that Hero needed the space and that she would fill it in her own time. He kept up the rhythmic touch of his thumb on her skin and waited.

'I was seven the first time my mother told me outright. There had been plenty of hints before, but I hadn't really understood what my parents had meant and Jules had always covered for them. No. That's the wrong phrase. She wasn't covering for them. She was protecting me. Being four years older, Jules had taken on that protective role that my parents had no interest in. But then, one day I was at home on my own. I don't really think a child is supposed to be left alone at that age, but that was the last thing on my parents' collective mind.

'Anyway, I heard my mother come in and I thought I would make her a cup of tea. I'd watched the housekeeper do it enough times, so I knew exactly how she liked it, and in which cup. I thought if I could do that for her, she would be pleased with me. For once. So, I got everything ready, but as I reached up to get the cup from the cabinet, it slipped out of my hand, smashing into tiny pieces on the limestone floor. I just stood looking at it, my seven-year-old brain desperately working to think of a way I might be able to fix it.'

Nick kept up the soothing movement on Hero's skin, but his jaw tensed as she spoke, feeling the confusion and pain her younger self had experienced. And he had a feeling it was about to get a lot worse.

'Of course there was no way to fix it. It was far beyond that. Not to mention that my parents never had anything that wasn't perfect. That was until I arrived, of course. My mother walked into the kitchen and looked at the floor which was now covered with the shattered bone china. I still had the saucer in my hand and she suddenly realised the mess on the floor had once been her favourite teacup. I think my father had bought it for her somewhere. I don't remember now.'

Hero took a deep breath, and a faint shudder passed through her body. Nick tightened his hold, pressing his lips to her hair, wanting her to know that she didn't need to be afraid anymore. His throat constricted as he heard the pain of that seven-year-old little girl come from the body of the grown woman now in his arms.

'I don't think I'd ever seen such coldness in someone's eyes before. Or since.' The statement was bald. Matter of fact.

'I mean, before that my mother barely looked at me anyway. Juliet was always the one she addressed. My father wasn't ever much interested in either of us. Anyway. My mother held out her hand towards me.' Hero gave a small, mirthless laugh. 'Stupidly, I thought she was putting her hand out for me to take hold of it. I reached for it and she snatched it back as though I'd burned her and then made things clearer for me. "Give me that, you stupid child." And she'd pointed to the saucer I was still holding. I was crying by then. I still didn't understand. Not then. But she made sure I would this time. I handed the saucer over as she'd asked. She looked at me for a second and then she lifted it high and brought it smashing down onto the tiles. I remember looking at all the mess, and just feeling … lost.'

Nick's jaw was so tense, he could feel it radiating back into his skull, but he couldn't stop it. He wanted to take away this woman's pain. He wanted someone to have stepped in and taken away that young child's pain. Resting his chin gently on the top of her head, he let her continue in her own time, his support silent but strong.

'I tried to tell her I didn't mean to do it. That it was an accident. She just glared at me and told me that I should know all about accidents as I'd been one. Obviously, I had no idea what she meant. Immediately realising that, she was kind enough to spell it out for me. They had only ever wanted one child, which was Juliet. Although, looking back now, Jules and I have come to the conclusion that having her had been more about keeping up with the Joneses, than from any true desire to actually have children. Apparently finding herself pregnant with me was one of the worst moments of her life, a feeling which was only compounded by being told that she was already too far along to "have things fixed". I can only think that the expression on my face told her all of this was just horribly confusing to me which seemed to only make her even more cross. Apparently, it hadn't even occurred to her that such things were not normally within the realm of understanding for a shy, seven-year-old girl. Luckily for me, she broke things down at that point and ensured that I understood I was just a terrible, terrible accident and she had begged for the doctor to help her get rid of me. How they had never, ever wanted another child and all I meant was that there was another mouth to feed, another schooling to pay for. Money that would have been far better spent on themselves rather than supporting a completely unwanted child. But no. Apparently I had to come along and ruin all their plans.'

Nick said nothing. What was there to say? He couldn't even comprehend the cruelty behind the words and actions of this mother. This monster.

'She didn't say another word to me after that. Just turned on her heel and stalked out of the kitchen. I can still hear the noise the tiny shards of china made as she crushed them underfoot. I was still sweeping them up a little while later when Juliet got in from school. I had a china splinter stuck in my hand from where I'd run it over the floor, trying to make sure I picked up every single bit, and she pulled it out for me. There were so many pieces and I was terrified that if I missed even one, my mother would come back and say something else horrible. I don't know … I suppose it was a coping mechanism or something.' She let out a sigh. 'I expect a psychologist would have plenty to say about it.' She glanced up at Nick and a fleeting, sad smile washed over her face. He closed his arms and held Hero close thinking that yes, they probably would. The first of which would be how the hell had she dealt with all that as well as she had?

When Nick had found out that his new sister-in-law had a high-profile supermodel sibling, he wasn't exactly thrilled. Thoughts of some diva sailing in with her own entourage, and creating a drama out of every possible crisis, not to mention the possible invasion of privacy out on their station, hadn't filled him with generous thoughts. Initially, he felt that his summations hadn't been that far off the mark. OK, so she travelled alone and had only had one freak-out involving a large spider that had decided to take a rest in her en-suite bath. By the time he and Pete had run up the stairs on hearing screaming, Hero and her sister were clutching each other's hands and had squeezed themselves in to the furthest part of the room where they were still able to keep tabs on the creature until it was safely evacuated.

Her personality though had been more of an enigma. During the past couple of weeks, Nick had given up trying to figure her out. There was so much going on beneath that calm, beautiful surface. So much that it seemed she was determined no one would see. Until now. He didn't know if it was the fact she felt like an outsider, alone within this crowd, or if it was the champagne which had caused her to drop her guard. Either way, he'd just got an insight into Hero Scott that explained a hell of a lot.

'What did Juliet say when you told her what happened?'

She shook her head. 'I didn't tell her.'

Nick sat straighter and moved so that he could see Hero's face. 'What do you mean you didn't tell her?'

She shrugged. 'She was eleven years old. What was she going to do?'

'But you were only seven! That's a hell of a conversation for a child to have had! Did you tell anyone?'

Again, she shook her head. 'No. Never. I don't … I don't know why I just told you.' Suddenly she pushed herself further away, looking into Nick's gaze, intensity shining in her eyes. 'And you can't tell Juliet! Or anyone! You have to promise!' She was breathing rapidly, her voice changing in pitch as the reality of having told her secret now dawned on her.

Nick watched her expression change as it did. Suddenly she was that seven-year-old girl again, terrified of saying the wrong thing. Doing the wrong thing. He took her face between his palms and held her gaze, waiting as her breathing slowed.

'I won't say anything. I promise. But you should tell Jules. At some point.'

'Why?'

'Because she'd want to know.'

'There's no reason to now though.' Her voice was soft, and her words almost a question. As though she wanted permission to lock this terrible, hurtful memory back in the dusty box where it had lingered for all this time. Her eyes searched his, dry but with a haunting expression that made his blood boil at the cruelty she had endured, and his heart burst at the knowledge that all he really wanted to do now was show her what real love was. A love that helped you grow and become the person you're supposed to be. The kind that let your heart soar and only ever grew more and more each day. As he pulled her close again, his mind filled with one thought. Would she stay?

Chapter 6

Nick got his answer to that the following morning. As he padded bleary-eyed down the stairs, he saw a Louis Vuitton suitcase standing by the door and followed the sound of lowered voices into the kitchen. His brother and Juliet sat at the table looking as tired as he was. Opposite them, with her back to the door, sat Hero. As the other two greeted him, she made no movement. He crossed the kitchen, heading for the coffee pot, screwing his eyes up as he went.

'Is it always this bright in here?' he grumbled, wrestling with the hangover from yesterday's champagne before pouring himself a large mug of the rich, black steaming liquid. 'Anyone else want one?'

At this prompt, his brother held out his mug with one hand whilst his other still massaged his forehead. Nick took the mug and turned back to the table, placing it back down in front of Pete before carrying his own to the table and sitting heavily down on the chair. Throughout all of this, Hero had neither spoken a word, nor looked up at him. Even now, she kept her glance away from his, concentrating instead on the mobile phone in front of her.

'Good morning,' he said, briefly leaning a little closer so that there was no doubt as to whom he spoke.

He saw her swallow before tripping out a casual, 'Morning.' Well, as casual as it got with that plummy voice. The glance she gave to accompany it was so brief as to be almost non-existent. Nick felt his muscles tighten. Last night they'd shared secrets, but this morning Hero was back behind that damn mask of indifference. The shy, vulnerable woman he'd discovered yesterday, the real her, was gone. Just as he was finally getting to know her. He rolled his neck, trying to loosen the knotted muscles.

'What's with the case out there?' He nodded towards the hall. 'I thought you were staying on a bit after the wedding, until these two jet off to Bali?'

Hero picked up the phone and began typing something. 'Yes, initially. Change of plan.'

'Right.' Nick took a sip of the coffee. 'Pretty last minute, isn't it?'

'A bit.' She was still avoiding looking at him.

'What is it then? Emergency photo shoot?'

Across the table, Pete gave him a warning glance, shaking his head briefly to try and steer his brother away.

'Something like that,' Hero replied after a couple of beats.

'Right. So, how you getting to the airport?'

'I'm taking Hero to town and she's going to catch the bus from there,' Pete answered.

'Is that why you're necking coffee like it's going out of fashion? Excuse the pun.' He glanced at Hero. 'I'd have thought you'd be spending the day after your wedding just lounging about with your new wife until you leave for Bali tomorrow? Wasn't that why we sorted out coverage for the station in the first place?' No one could miss the controlled tension in Nick's voice.

Hero shifted in her seat.

'Yep,' Pete agreed, 'but Hero's plans changed. These things happen.'

'And when they do, we all have to jump into line? Is that how it's going to be here now?' Nick shoved his chair back from the table.

Hero had kept her head down throughout the exchange, but as the chair scraped sharply, she jumped and met Nick's eyes. For that moment, he saw her. He saw the woman who'd opened up to him last night. The woman he wanted to know more about. The woman he wanted. And then she was gone. Back behind that blank expression where she thought no one could hurt her. Did she know that by doing that she was hurting others? Did she even care?

'Of course not,' Hero spoke, those cool tones completely under control with none of the fire that currently raged within his own body. 'I had no intention of putting anyone out, and I have said that I would rather get a car sent but Pete kindly offered to take me.'

Nick searched the beautiful eyes for the smallest sign that last night's soul baring had sparked something in her as it had within him, but there was nothing. Hero stood more carefully than he had, tucking the chair back under the kitchen table.

'I still can't believe you don't have a hangover,' Juliet grouched at her sister. 'You can't have had much.'

'Oh, I had plenty. Probably a couple of glasses too many, actually.' She bent and kissed her sister's head. As she stood, her eyes met Nick's and he understood the message. *It was the champagne talking, not me.* None of it meant anything.

She looked back at Pete and Juliet. 'I really can sort out transport, you know. Nick's right. You two should be here together.'

'Don't be daft. It's no problem.' Pete squeezed his new sister-in-law about the shoulders. Juliet smiled. 'Of course, we'd rather you stayed a little longer, but I know you already turned down work to be out here the last couple of weeks anyway.'

'Nick's just throwing his toys out because he feels crap,' Pete added.

Hero gave a brief smile at Pete and nodded. Nick turned his back and stared out of the kitchen window, drinking his coffee as Pete and Juliet went upstairs to get ready. His thoughts raced back to the previous night when Hero was soft, and open. She'd showed him her heart and he'd felt so privileged, knowing how hard it must have been for her. He thought that they'd taken that step together. As the night cooled, they'd gone back into the party together, but in the crush and laughter of the proceedings, her hand had slipped from his. When the party eventually wound down, he found her again, but she'd looked completely exhausted. They'd all climbed into one of the taxis they'd arranged and headed back to the station, hugging each other goodnight. It had been a wonderful, joyous day, and Nick had thought – hoped – that it might be the start of something else wonderful. But Hero's behaviour this morning couldn't have sent a clearer message. She'd said nothing yesterday about needing to cut her visit short, and he didn't believe for one minute there was any reason except that she regretted letting him get so close.

Nick turned, leaning on the edge of the worktop and watched Hero for a moment. She slid the phone into the side pocket of a small handbag.

'Got your passport?'

Hero nodded. 'Yes. Thank you.'

He shrugged. 'I just don't want my brother wasting any more time and petrol if you have to come back.'

A flash of something passed across Hero's face as she straightened her stance.

Nick pinched the bridge of his nose with this thumb and forefinger. 'Sorry. I shouldn't have said that.'

Hero shrugged. 'It's all right. It's a valid point.'

He met her eyes, trying to find the woman from last night. Hero broke the connection, looking away before he had the chance to search any longer. Nick let out a breath, long and slow.

'Have you said goodbye to Joe? He'll be pretty upset if you leave without seeing him.'

'I wouldn't do that,' she replied. 'I saw him a little earlier.'

'Was he all right?'

Her forehead creased. 'He was … a bit sad, I think.'

'I'll go and find him in a while. Check he's OK.'

'Thank you.'

Nick threw her a glance. 'I'm not doing it for you.'

Hero swallowed and nodded. 'No … I realise that. I just meant …' Her fingers worried the strap of her bag.

'Joe and his family have taken to you. For some reason.' Nick's voice had an edge to it this morning. The words that had been so soft to her last night were now sharp and cut her deep inside. She wouldn't tell him that though. She never told anyone. He was angry with her and Hero understood that. What had happened last night was unexpected. At the time it had felt so, so right but as she'd lain in her bed this morning, watching the pink smudges in the sky burn away to the deepest blue, Hero knew. Knew what she had to do. Once she had put the distance back between them, everything would go back to normal. It was for the best. For her, but also for Nick. He deserved more than she could ever give him. More than she would ever allow herself to give him. Last night, it had all happened so easily, so naturally. Sharing in the joy so evident in her sister's face, and that of her new family, she'd forgotten herself. Forgotten to pull up the drawbridge that protected her. She'd wanted to be part of that joy, and for a while she was. She'd got caught up in the wonder of the day and the feeling of security, and desire, as Nick had held her. As they'd sat in the deepening twilight, their voices low, his body strong and warm. It would have been so easy to follow her heart, knowing where it would lead her. Tiredness had stopped her last night. Reality had stopped her this morning. This family, this life, was Juliet's now. She had no claim on it. The sooner she got back to her own life, the better. There she knew where she was, what was expected of her, and what she expected of others.

'Yes. I … hope he's OK.'

Nick watched Hero as she brushed her hand across the front of her dress, the action unnecessary. She looked, as always, perfect.

Long, tanned legs ended in high wedge sandals. A dress that would look demure on others did nothing to lessen the attraction and Nick's body threatened to betray him. He steeled himself, concentrating on her as she was now. Hard, cold, and self-centred. She wasn't the soft, broken bird starved of affection now. Nick shook his head. How did he fall for that? She didn't need love. She craved attention. Why else would she carry on taking job after job when it was clear she already had more money than she could spend? Because she loved it. Hero Scott might have not had all the attention or love a child should, but she had the adoration of the world now. Nick ran a hand through his hair. How could he have been so stupid? Beautiful women were nothing but trouble.

'He'll be all right. Plenty of things come and go in life. It's the ones that stay that matter.' Nick finished the last of his coffee and put the cup in the top rack of the dishwasher. 'You should be careful with Joe. He gives his affection freely. I don't want him getting upset if you're only going to show up for flying visits and then disappear a day later.'

'I wouldn't hurt him for the world.'

Nick heard it. That slight wobble in her voice. She meant it. He'd already known that, but his point stood. Joe had quickly adopted Hero as a sister, and Nick had to admit that his surrogate brother, with his naturally sunny disposition, seemed even happier when she was here. He still struggled with his reading, but Hero was already helping with that, happily sitting near him on the porch after the day's work was done, reading together. Not to mention the pile she'd come back with for him following a trip into town with Jules one day. She'd looked happy. Relaxed. Open. The opposite of how she looked now.

'I know you wouldn't.'

From upstairs they heard a shower turn on followed by laughter. A small smile passed between them.

'I think I'm going to wait out on the porch.'

As she stepped towards the hallway, Nick moved. She met his gaze and her breath caught. He was looking at her so intensely it felt like he could see straight into her soul, see her true thoughts.

'Hero?'

'I have to go.' She started walking away. Nick reached out, catching her by the wrist. His head told him to stay away but his damn heart refused to listen.

'What—'

'Tell me why you're leaving. The real reason.'

'I just …' Her eyes searched his face and she could see her own confusion reflected in him. She couldn't finish the sentence; she wasn't even sure what she had been planning to say.

'There's no job, is there?'

Hero met his gaze and looking into those intense brown eyes, she couldn't lie. The faintest shake of her head gave him her answer.

'Is this about yesterday?' Nick reached out and took her other arm, his hands now gentle. 'If it is, then you don't need to worry. I'm not going to say anything, and I don't expect anything from you. I just want you to be yourself, relax, have some fun. You always seem so tense all the time, not to mention tired. Maybe taking a break would be a good thing?' He stepped closer. 'It's like you're afraid of everyone.' Lifting his hand, he gently cupped her face, just as he'd done last night, his touch gentle and warm. 'Nobody's going to hurt you here. I promise. I won't let them.'

Hero closed her eyes against his touch. It would be so easy to stay here, to have Nick touch her like he was touching her now. To rest against his strong, solid body as she had done last night. To be with somebody who cared. Hero opened her eyes, Nick could tell she was wavering. His heart picked up. And then he saw it. That woman was gone, the armour back in place.

'I have to go.' Hero stepped back, her voice more definite now. She took another step away from Nick, trying to put physical space between them before she got sucked back in again. Before she let herself fall again. 'I'd appreciate it if you didn't tell Juliet that there isn't a job. It would only upset her.' She gave a quick nod and pushed past him, walking out onto the porch, grateful for the breeze that cooled her face and body.

'So, what am I supposed to tell her?' The door bounced on its hinges as Nick burst through it a moment later. His face was set, his eyes dark with frustration and anger.

Hero forced herself to look at him, fighting with herself to maintain her calm expression, as inside her heart pounded so hard, she was sure he must see it.

Tell her that you got too close. Tell her that I have to protect myself. That I have to keep you at arm's length for a reason because what I really want is for you to touch me like you did just now. Tell her that I just can't take that risk. My parents didn't want me. I can't take the risk that anyone – especially you – might feel that way too once the novelty wears off.

When Hero didn't answer his question, Nick filled in the blanks himself.

'You want me to lie.' He drew himself up to his full height, frustration tensing every muscle in his body.

Hero tilted her head back to meet his eyes. 'You don't have to put it quite like that, Nick. It's for her own benefit.'

Nick rolled his eyes. 'Is that right? From where I'm standing it seems like it's for your benefit. Like everything else in your life.'

Nick knew he was being unfair. But he was angry and hurting. And feeling guilty. If he hadn't encouraged her to open up to him last night, she might not be leaving now. They might all have had more time to show her there was no one to endanger her heart out here. That she was, and always would be, safe.

'I'm sorry that you have that opinion of me.'

And she really was. Hero made to turn and walk further down the porch.

Nick blocked her way. His voice was louder now, and he was thankful the running water from the shower obscured the noise of their arguing from Pete and Juliet.

'No, you're not. You don't care what I think.'

'That's not fair. You know that isn't true!' Hero returned.

'No, I don't,' Nick snapped back as the sound of footsteps hurrying towards them got louder. 'But it doesn't matter now anyway. Last night I thought that whole ice maiden thing you do was just an act, and that underneath all that there was a decent person, someone worth getting to know.' He paused, and Hero slid her eyes up to meet his. In place of the usual warmth and laughter they held was a cold steel. Beneath the unshaved stubble, a muscle flickered in his jaw. 'It's pretty obvious now that I was wrong.'

He finished just as Joe sped onto the porch, nearly colliding with both of them. 'Why are you yelling at her?' He rounded on Nick. 'Don't yell at her!' Joe's innocent eyes were wide as he looked from one to the other.

Nick's shoulders sagged. He gave one last glance at Hero, shaking his head. 'I'm finished yelling at her.'

He brushed past Joe and walked off out into the yard. Shortly afterwards, they heard a motorbike engine start, rev twice, and quickly become distant.

Joe reached out and held Hero's hand, the childlike gesture ripping away the armour.

'What were you fighting about?'

Hero shook her head and sat down on the wicker sofa. 'Nothing. Just something silly.' She hated lying to Joe. She hated lying to herself, but right now, it was all she could do. Last night she had come closer than she had ever been to opening up to someone. She'd let Nick see the real her, the damaged soul that resided within the pretty decoration. Why, or how, it had happened, how she'd found herself in Nick Webster's arms and telling him the secret she had never spoken of to anyone, she could hardly say. All she knew was that it had. And the part that frightened her the most was that she knew she wanted it to happen again. Over and over. But it wouldn't. It couldn't.

Hero had vowed she would never give anyone the power to hurt her ever again. There had been no choice with her parents, but she made her own rules now and she'd done just fine – at least until last night, but she would collect herself again. All she needed to do was get away from here. Back into her own world. The world she understood. The world that had never touched her heart as much as this one.

'I wish you weren't leaving.' Joe's big blue eyes were sad as he looked at her. 'I like it when you're here.'

Hero turned in her seat, reaching around to hug him.

'I like it when I'm here too,' she whispered.

Joe wrapped his arms around her tightly, almost as if he thought that by doing that he could keep her there forever.

***

Nick parked the bike and made his way into the kitchen.

'Lunch is nearly ready. Wash your hands, please.'

Nick obeyed Juliet's instructions, glancing down at the place settings laid out on the kitchen table. His stomach flipped. There was one extra. She hadn't left after all.

'Four?'

'Yes. Joe's eating with us tonight.' Juliet pulled a casserole dish from the oven and placed it on a pan stand. 'He was down about Hero leaving earlier, and Jacob's in town anyway.'

'Right.' It was all Nick could manage as disappointment and guilt took turns at him. Raking a hand through his hair, he turned back to the door. 'I'll go and see where he is.' Walking out of the kitchen, he crossed the porch and leant on the porch, watching as Joe ambled across the yard, his gaze cast downwards. Beyond him the fields stretched out beneath the vast sky, its blue streaked with the faintest brushstrokes of white as wispy clouds broke up the expanse.

'All right, mate?'

Joe nodded.

'I need to ask you a favour.'

Joe looked up at him, sadness evident in his expression. 'OK.'

'Don't mention to Juliet that Hero and I were arguing this morning. OK? It was nothing and Jules is already sad that she's gone. She'll only get more upset if she knows we argued too.'

Joe nodded again. 'I won't. Hero asked me the same thing just before she left anyway, and I already promised her that I wouldn't.'

'OK.'

'Nick?'

'Yep?'

'Did she leave because you argued?'

Nick slipped his arm around Joe's shoulder. 'No, mate.' The fact was he was pretty sure it was quite the opposite. 'She was leaving anyway.'

They had just sat down to eat when they heard a car pull up. Moments later Pete entered the kitchen.

'Everything all right?' his wife asked as she got up, kissed his cheek and then set about dishing him out a plateful of food.

'Yep. She only had half an hour to wait for the bus by the time we got there.'

'Did she say when she was coming back?' Joe asked, his expression hopeful.

'No, mate. Sorry.'

Joe looked crestfallen. He returned his attention to the plate in front of him and half-heartedly took another mouthful.

Nick's conscience gave him a sharp jab in the ribs. *See what you've done*, it taunted. *This is all your fault.*

Nick knew it was probably right too. He knew what Joe was going through. He loved Hero being there too, despite the act she put on. It had slipped a couple of times, caught up as everyone was in the excitement of the wedding. He noticed it happened the most when she thought she was alone, laughing as she played with the dog or resting her head gently against the neck of a horse as her hand stroked his nose in a rhythmic, calming movement.

All just brief glimpses of the real woman beneath the armour and the make-up. But last night, everything had changed. Last night he'd really seen her. The smile she'd given him when he'd first approached her had almost swept him away. It had proved to him what he had suspected all along. That there was so much more to this woman than just the pretty exterior, however much she tried to hide it.

Of course, he was attracted to her looks. Christ, he was a male and had a pulse. What else did you need when a woman who looked like that walked into your life? But their continual spikiness with each other had kept anything else, any deeper connection, firmly out of sight. Then last night, at a wedding in the middle of nowhere, Hero Scott had dropped her shield, the carapace fractured, and the true Hero showed herself to him, and him alone. And he was lost.

Seeing her so changed back, so well protected once more, had fired Nick's frustration and screamed at him. It was that which had driven him to say the words he had today. And despite the cool eyes she kept on him throughout their exchange, he had seen her fists clench, seen the long, elegant nails she'd apparently grown specifically for her sister's wedding jam into the softness of her palms. Hero had heard him. But it hadn't done any good. After everything, she had still left.

***

'So? How was it? I've had the condensed version, now I want the Director's Cut,' Anya announced, as Hero sank down next to her on the battered old leather sofa in their favourite coffee shop around the corner from their flat.

'Good. Nice.' Hero took a sip of the strong, bitter coffee and tried not to stare longingly as a large slice of chocolate cake was delivered to the next table.

'Hero?'

'Hmm?' Hero pulled her attention back. 'Sorry. I missed that.'

'Probably because you were lusting over that woman's cake. Do you want some?'

Yes!

'No. No, of course not.' She smiled but Anya didn't return it.

'What's wrong?'

'Nothing.'

'Hey. This is me you're talking to. You've been weird ever since you got back. I thought it was just jetlag, but you usually get over that pretty quick.'

Hero hadn't mentioned anything about Nick Webster, well, no more than she needed to. If she left him out entirely and then Anya found out her new brother-in-law had a gorgeous younger brother, she'd get the full interrogation.

'I'm all right, really.'

Anya tilted her head as Hero picked at the spinach and egg salad in front of her.

'You look like you're wishing that was chocolate cake too.'

Hero let out a sigh. 'Honestly? I do.'

Anya's pale brows raised in surprise. 'I didn't think you even liked cake. I don't think I've ever seen you eat it.'

Hero stabbed a piece of boiled egg before replacing her fork on the plate and pushing the salad away. 'I do like it. I just never eat it.'

'So have a piece. One piece won't hurt.' Anya made to stand up, her eyes on the display of mouth-watering cakes on the counter.

Hero put a hand on her arm. 'No. I can't. But thanks anyway.'

'Why not?'

'Marlena said I've put on weight.'

Anya was about to laugh until she realised her friend was entirely serious. 'Then she is wrong. You look beautiful, just as you always do. Marlena needs new glasses.'

Hero gave the ghost of a smile. 'Actually, she's right. I weighed myself a couple of days ago and I have gained a few pounds. I was so caught up in my sister's wedding, I sort of forgot myself.'

'Well, I don't see it. And it can only have done you good.'

Hero pulled a face. Her booker could spot an extra pound at a hundred paces, and had no qualms about letting the model in question know, as well as anyone else within hearing distance. With eyes like a hawk and a voice like a foghorn, it was hard to keep anything on the downlow. Even someone at the top of their game like Hero couldn't afford knowledge like that, or even a rumour, to spread too far. Hero had assured her agency she would lose the few extra pounds quickly and had immediately doubled the length of her morning runs and added an extra half-hour to her gym routine. According to her scales, she was already almost back to the weight she'd maintained for the past several years. But Marlena's sharp words, as she'd scrutinised Hero the first day she'd gone into her office following the model's recent trip to Australia, still resonated in her mind.

'You know as well as I do, there are a hundred girls, thousands even, to take your place if you're looking to retire.' She'd shrugged her sharp, bony shoulders at Hero. 'It's all the same to me. I'm not the one who'll be out of work.'

Hero had gone home and stared at the woman looking back at her from the huge ornate mirror that rested against one wall in the large, high-ceilinged Georgian bedroom. Stripping off her dress, she stood there in all but the briefest of briefs and wondered how much longer she could do this. People fought to have her walk down their runway. Men wanted her on their arm, girls aspired to be her. And yet all of it was a façade. For them to be who they thought she was, she only ate certain foods, avoided those she craved, and all to look like this. Hero knew she wasn't a good role model for young women, and that worried her. She'd seen the disapproving stares, the nasty, offensive tweets about her body and although she didn't agree with the way it was delivered, she did understand the basic message. As a top model, she perpetuated the illusion of glamour, the idea that being thin brought riches and reward. But that wasn't all it brought. There was a side that people didn't see. The dark side that brought unhappiness, disillusionment, eating disorders, drug abuse, and abandonment. It was a world that fêted you when it wanted and left you in the wilderness once it was finished.

Hero turned and yanked a silk throw from her enormous bed and flung it at the mirror, its ornate edges catching the fine fabric and ensuring it stayed in place, hiding her reflection. She stood there for a moment, her mind whirling, before moving slowly across to the bed. Climbing onto it, she sat, her knees folded under her as memories of the past few weeks raced through her mind before it inevitably returned to her booker's uncompromised, harsh words. The worst part of it was that Hero knew it was true. With Juliet now settling into her new life on the other side of the world, her own world became smaller, more important. Needed. She couldn't afford to lose her place in this world, because without it she wouldn't belong anywhere.

Anya reached out and took her friend's hand within her own. 'Ignore Marlena. She's always had a mean streak. You are still the most beautiful person I know. Both on the outside and in your heart.'

Hero sighed and laid her head on her friend's shoulder. 'I don't know what I'd do without you.'

'Well, until I return home and open my multi-award-winning restaurant, you are stuck with me, so that is not an issue you have to worry about.'

Hero smiled, her friend's enthusiasm and humour warming her bruised, frightened heart.

'So,' Anya said again. 'Tell me all about the wedding, and don't leave anything out.'

Chapter 7

The useful thing about being one of the highest paid and most in-demand models in the world meant that Hero was able to still see her sister while avoiding Nick Webster.

Using work as an excuse, Hero was able to fly Juliet out and meet her at several different destinations and when, a year later, her sister's first wedding anniversary rolled around, she sent the couple a gift of paper in the form of two tickets to Paris and accommodation at the most luxurious hotel in the city. Having a shoot in the city a day later, Hero took the opportunity to meet up with them both for dinner.

'You really shouldn't have done all this,' Pete said as he hugged his sister-in-law in the lobby of the hotel. 'It's too much.'

'Not at all. Besides, it's really a gift to myself as it means I get to see you both this time.' She smiled, and Pete dropped a brotherly kiss on the top of her head.

'You know you're always welcome at the station.'

Hero smiled and nodded. 'I know. Thank you,' she said, knowing that she had no intention of returning there unless it was entirely unavoidable. She did miss Joe dreadfully though. Skype just wasn't the same. Thankfully, Pete had been happy to juggle Joe's schedule so that he could accompany Juliet on a couple of trips to meet up with Hero. But the longer she could stay away from Nick Webster, the better. Besides, from what she heard, Nick had certainly been keeping himself busy outside of work on the station entertaining half the women in the area. As time had passed, Hero had realised that she had probably had a rather lucky escape. Clearly all those soft words and gentle caresses were nothing more than a come on, aimed to add yet another notch on his bed post. He'd probably had a good laugh at the thought he'd nearly bedded the one woman who hadn't been immediately taken with him. She'd posed a challenge – and he'd nearly succeeded. Even the thought of it made her mad with herself. Of all the people to let under her defences, a cocky Australian lothario whom she may have to actually see again at some point hadn't been the best decision. Still, she'd managed it for over a year and had plans to extend that for as long as possible.

Plans, however, had a habit of changing either through design, or circumstance and this time was no exception.

'Twins?' Hero repeated, placing her champagne glass back down on the table, next to her sister's untouched one.

Juliet nodded, the broadest, most contented smile on her face. Hero shifted her gaze to Pete and saw the same joy reflected there. Her own smile broke as she leant around the booth and hugged them both together.

'I'm so happy for you. Truly. I can't think of anyone who would make better parents than you two. That's two very lucky little babies you have in there.' She laughed, as she gently wiped her sister's tears of joy away with her thumbs.

'We thought we might wait a little longer, but I guess the universe didn't agree.'

Pete kissed his wife. 'I think it might have had more to do with the two bottles of wine we got through that night more than the universe.'

Juliet gave him a patient but loving look. 'Yes, but that's a far less romantic story.'

Pete agreed and held his glass against Hero's for her toast.

'I know it's very early but knowing how busy you are, we wanted to ask you now if you would agree to be their godmother.'

Hero felt the lump in her throat as she looked between the two. 'Me?'

Pete nodded. 'Of course. There's no one else we'd rather have.'

'I … I don't know anything about babies!' Her heart swelled with joy as she laughed.

Pete wrapped his arm around his wife, the look of adoration on his face just as strong, if not stronger than it had been on their wedding day. 'Join the club. We can all learn together.'

***

Hero continued to meet her sister in various places across the globe for the next few months, telling her that once the babies arrived, it was naturally going to be more difficult, so she wanted to take advantage of the situation and pamper her for as long as possible. There was no need to tell Juliet that she was still uncomfortable about the fact that whenever she thought of Nick Webster, her stomach tightened, her treacherous mind refusing to forget the way he had felt against her as they danced. Knowing that he was happily sleeping his way around the district made her feel even more ridiculous, showing that what she had thought of as special, he apparently hadn't thought of at all. And yes, she'd panicked and bolted the very next morning, unable to even look him in the eye, but his words had lingered in her head. It wasn't the first time she'd been called a diva, and was unlikely to be the last. It came with the territory.

There were others in the same profession who most certainly subscribed to that kind of behaviour – even relished it – but Hero wasn't made that way. She didn't have the belief that she was better than others because of her looks, or her bank balance, or her fame. The quickest way for a man to lose her interest was to be rude or obnoxious to the waiting staff in a restaurant. In fact, Hero had always kept that as a benchmark. Rupert's good manners towards the servers was one of the first things she noticed about him when she'd originally met him at that party. Honestly, it would have been so much easier if they could have just worked romantically. But apparently the universe had decided that would have been far too easy and had instead thrown Nick Webster in her path.

Which was why her insides were now turning somersaults as the car she had arranged from the airport sped her ever closer to Hill Station.

Closing her eyes, she told herself not to be so ridiculous. It had been a few hours nearly two years ago and from what she heard from her sister, he certainly hadn't given a second thought to her since she left. Hero cast her mind back to the morning she'd last been at the station. Was it any wonder she'd avoided coming back here? Nick had been so quick to pin the diva label on her that morning, he hadn't even given her a chance to explain. Hero brushed a tiny piece of fluff off the silk of her maxi dress as her mind continued to whirl. But deep down she knew the truth. He had given her the chance. He'd asked her to tell him the real reason she was leaving … but she hadn't. She couldn't. The question that continued to gnaw at her though was was that because she was afraid of another rejection? Or something quite the opposite?

'Not far now, love,' the driver called back, catching Hero's eye in the mirror.

'Thank you,' she replied, already recognising the landmarks that Pete had pointed out on her first visit to the place. It had been months since she'd seen Juliet and she hadn't seen the babies at all. Work had been crazy, she'd taken a few business trips with Rupert which he'd insisted would be utterly boring unless he had company. Naturally, the papers had soon latched on to them, talking about their on-again, off-again relationship, which showed how little they knew, or cared, about the truth. There had never been a relationship to be on in the first place. At the airport, Rupert had picked up a copy of one of the many trashy gossip magazines that seemed to take up more and more space in the racks. A slightly blurry picture of them both coming out of Tiffany's in New York had sent them into overdrive. 'Hero finally to marry her own hero?' said one.

Rupert was especially fond of that one. 'I rather like that. Perhaps next time we should sort out some horse riding. I'll arrange a white charger for me and perhaps a lightweight suit of armour? You know what they say. Go big or go home.'

Hero had taken the magazine from his hands and swatted him on the arm with it before placing it back on the shelf.

'Then I think go home would be the best option in this particular case.'

Rupert had rolled his eyes. 'You're no fun.'

'Oh. In that case, I can sit and paint my toenails this evening and read some more of my book whilst you go to that – what did you call it – tedious but necessary function.' She tossed him a smile over her shoulder as she headed away to the departure lounge.

'You wouldn't do that to me.'

'I might.'

He'd caught her hand then and wrapped his arms dramatically round her. 'Do not leave me, my beauty! I repent most arduously. Your wish will be my command always and forever.'

Hero, by this time, was giggling so much at his ridiculous expression and his rather terrible but still recognisable Laurence Olivier impression, that she forgot the world for a moment. The click of a shutter pulled them both back, grins on their faces. Several camera phones were pointed in their direction. Releasing her, Rupert had taken her hand and led them at a brisk pace to the private lounge.

'You know that's going be all over those awful magazines tomorrow, don't you?'

Rupert had looked at her as they entered the quiet privacy of the room, his face serious now. 'Do you mind? I forget sometimes.'

Hero shook her head and smiled, then placed a gentle kiss on his cheek. 'Not at all. You make me remember to laugh at it all. That's definitely a good thing.'

'Here we are!' the cheerful driver said, rousing her from her thoughts as he turned the car into the long driveway of Hill Station.

Hero ran a hand over her hair and took a couple of calming deep breaths. It was ridiculous to be so nervous and, in her heart, she knew she was glad to be out here again. Away from the noise and toxin-filled air of the cities she spent most of her life in. She knew that tonight, when she looked out she'd be able to see the stars, hear the soft bleating of a sheep and nothing else. The thought alone sent a ripple of calm through her body as the car pulled up to the house.

She opened the door and stepped out, the heat of the afternoon shocking her after the cold rain she'd left behind in London and the continual air conditioning of the airports, planes, and cars. Hero closed her eyes for a moment, letting it warm her bare shoulders.

'Where do you want these?' the driver asked, as he lifted out two cases. 'Staying a while then?'

'No, not really.'

'Aah.' He smiled, as he pushed the boot lid closed. 'My wife's like that. Everything but the kitchen sink, she takes. Sometimes it feels like that might be in there too!' His tanned face deepened its crow's feet as he chuckled.

Hero gave him a smile and a large tip. The truth was that she did pack light. She'd learned to over the years of modelling and thousands of miles she'd now travelled. He wasn't to know that the larger case was filled with gifts for Juliet, Pete, and their growing family. She paused in thought as she considered that.

Why hadn't she said 'her family'? Pete was her brother-in-law and she was auntie to two gorgeous little babies. By the end of her trip, she'd be their godmother. So why did she still feel like an outsider?

'You're here!' Juliet's cry made Hero jump as the driver pulled away slowly, being careful not to cover his recently disembarked passenger in red dust.

Her sister ran down the steps of the porch and into Hero's open arms. 'Oh, Hero. I can't believe you're here at last! It seems so long.'

A wash of guilt passed over her. It had been too long. She should have made an effort to come sooner, instead of telling herself that seeing her sister on Skype was almost the same thing. Telling herself that they were both busy. She hadn't fully appreciated that until now. She held her sister back and gently wiped away the tears.

'I'm sorry. Please don't cry!'

Juliet smiled through them. 'No, no! It's fine. They're happy tears. I promise!'

Hero nodded, knowing she had her own reasons for keeping away. But in doing so, she had hurt Juliet. Not that that was something her sister would ever think or say, but Hero knew the truth.

Bending down, she picked up her cases, rebuffing her sister's offer of help.

'Come on, let me carry one.'

'No, I'm fine. You've been carrying two small humans around until fairly recently. I think you've done quite enough.'

'Don't be silly. Come on. Just let me take one.'

'How about I take both and call it even?' Pete's deep voice came from behind them as he strode across the yard, his Akubra hat shading his face but not concealing the grin on his face. He put his arms out and Hero stepped into them, his hug wrapping around her tightly.

'Good to have you back,' he said softly before releasing her.

She looked up into his face as she stood back. Did he know? Did he blame her?

'I should have come sooner.'

Pete shook his head. 'You're here now. That's what matters.'

Juliet nodded enthusiastically, linking her arm through her sister's and leading them all into the cool interior of the house.

The rest of the afternoon was spent being introduced to, and cuddling, Hero's new niece and nephew. According to their parents, the babies were already developing their own personalities with the little girl, Bridie, excitable and wriggly, while her brother, Marcus, had a more placid nature, often calming his sister down as they lay side by side on their play mat chatting to each other in a language only they understood.

The babies now put down and sleeping peacefully in their cots – a situation that may, or may not remain, her brother-in-law joked – the three adults sat around the table. Dinner had been eaten and all three now sat with a large mug of tea, chatting over a multitude of topics as the conversation swung from light to serious and back to light as they began talking about the arrangements for the children's christening.

'Mum and Dad are coming in from the city the night before and then heading out again the morning after.'

'They're off on a cruise,' Juliet filled in.

'How are they finding living in the city? Do they still enjoy it?' Hero asked, realising just how much she was looking forward to seeing Jack and Gill again.

'I think it took a bit of getting used to at first, didn't it?' Juliet said, looking at her husband.

'Yeah. It's obviously a bit different from out here. There's a lot more people and noise for a start.'

Hero nodded.

Pete smiled. 'You're the last person I need to tell that to though, I'm sure.'

'It certainly is a change.'

'They seem to be into it now though,' Juliet took up again. 'They've made quite a few friends and joined some clubs and they're always off to visit a museum or on a trip somewhere. I think, at first, they worried a bit that they'd done the wrong thing but it's all worked out.'

'Just having the flat there means there's much less for them to worry about too, and they can just concentrate on enjoying their retirement.'

'They must be thrilled about the babies though?'

Pete laughed. 'You could say that.' The broad smile on his face showed Hero his parents weren't the only ones thrilled at these new additions. She lifted her mug, catching a glance of Pete as he took her sister's hand, kissing it gently.

'It will be lovely to see them again.'

'The feeling's mutual. Mum's been nagging to get you back out here pretty much ever since you left last time.'

Hero smiled, but it felt awkward. 'I know. I'm sorry. I really did leave it too long.'

Pete patted her hand. 'Don't be daft. Everyone's busy and time just flies. You look round and another six months have gone!'

The smile became a little more natural, as Pete continued. 'Mum just adores you two. All she needs now is for you to move out here and she'd be happy as a clam I think.'

'I would too,' Juliet said, her tone telling them that she was only half joking.

Hero pushed her hair back and smiled, not looking her sister in the face. That situation most certainly wasn't going to happen. She loved it out here but there was no way she could see herself living somewhere like this. After years of living in London, with everything just a phone call or message away, coming here was an absolute contrast. And what about all the people she knew?

Why hadn't she said friends?

Hero pushed it all out of her mind and concentrated on what her sister was saying.

'So, what was all that fuss on the front of a magazine I saw a couple of weeks ago?'

Hero grinned. 'You're probably going to have to be more specific.'

'You and Rupert.'

'Again. More specific.'

'Really?'

'Oh yes. The media seem to be incapable of accepting that a man and a woman can be just friends. According to them, there are always benefits.' Hero rolled her eyes and then broke into a huge smile as Biscuit came hurrying through the door and scooted around the table to where she sat, his tail whizzing round in circles as she bent and fussed with him, laughing as he tried to climb closer for his cuddles.

'You were coming out of Tiffany's though. Is there something we should know? Has he really bought you an engagement ring?'

Hero sat up from where she'd been bent over in her chair, playing with the dog, turning back towards her sister.

'Of course ...' Her words faded as she saw Nick stood in the doorway, his eyes locked on hers.

She swallowed, her mouth suddenly dry. 'Hello.'

He nodded, the faintest of smiles flashing at her.

'How did it go?' Pete asked.

'Yeah. Fine,' Nick replied as he turned his back to the table and began washing his hands.

'Nick's been helping out one of the other stations. One of their hands had a fall off a horse and he's been out of action for a while. They've got someone coming in but had the vet coming over today and Nick offered to help them out.' Her sister filled Hero in as she stood and dished up a bowl of the delicious casserole she'd kept warm on the stove from earlier.

'Here you go.'

'Thanks, Jules.' Nick picked up the cutlery and began tucking in as Juliet cut a piece of homemade bread and put it down on a side plate next to him. 'So, sounds like I missed something. Should I be offering congratulations?' His gaze flicked to Hero very briefly before going back to his food.

'Congratulations?'

Her brow creased and Nick smiled to himself. Good to see not all city women were going for botox. That was something. Women were hard enough to figure out sometimes without chemicals taking away any tell-tale clues!

'On your engagement?' He forced himself to keep his tone light.

'I'm not engaged.'

'So what were you doing in Tiffany's with Rupert?' Juliet sat back down next to Nick. He hoped she hadn't seen him lessen his grip on the fork as Hero had replied in the negative to their questioning. Why should it matter to him whether she was engaged to that richer than God guy? They certainly seemed incredibly close, according to the magazines he'd seen on the newsstand. Just in passing of course.

'It was his parents' silver wedding anniversary. He wanted a second opinion on their gift.'

'Ohhh.' Juliet nodded. 'That makes sense. Did they like it?'

Hero smiled. 'They did. Very much so.'

'You always did have good taste.'

'Must be a family trait.' Pete grinned, straightening his shirt, and sporting a smug expression.

'Everyone has off days, mate,' Nick said, looking up and giving Jules a quick wink.

'Yeah, yeah,' his brother replied, stealing the last bit of bread off his brother's plate, laughter in both their eyes.

***

'You scrub up all right, don't you?' Juliet grinned as she held a baby in one arm and gave her brother-in-law a quick hug with the other. 'Thanks for doing this.'

He let out a breath in laughter. 'Don't be daft. I'm honoured to be asked. Although the fact that you're willing to trust me in a legal document to look after your children does make me question whether all those lost hours of sleep have affected your thinking.'

'That's what I told her,' Pete said, coming up to them, his daughter gurgling happily in his arms as she surveyed her surroundings.

'Oh shush. You know you said their godfather had to be Nick, and that no one else would do, you big softie,' Juliet teased him.

'Well, only because we'd got Hero on board already. At least we know one of their godparents has some sense.'

Nick cast a glance at Hero and rolled his eyes. She smiled and wondered again why they would trust her with something so precious and monumental as their children's lives when she had no idea what she planned to do with her own. Thankfully, she had little time to begin musing over this once more as Gill came hurrying up the steps, her arms spread wide to hug Hero.

'Oh, my darling! You're here!' She wrapped her up as Pete had done, and Hero's chest tightened at the thought that this was how her sons had grown up. Feeling wanted and loved. She envied them.

'Charming.' Hero saw Nick nudge his brother, an expression of mock affrontery on his face. 'I haven't seen them for ages either.'

Pete gave a shrug. 'Yeah. But truth is, they like her more than you. Tough, I know, but just the way it is.'

'Oh, don't be so mean.' Gill laughed, pulling Nick into her hug, but not yet releasing Hero. His hip bumped against hers as his arm moved behind her back to accommodate them all. His mum stepped back and took a hand of each of them. 'I love you both, and don't you ever forget that.'

Hero dropped her gaze, suddenly unsure of what she should do.

'We know,' Nick said, softly, leaning in to give his mum a kiss on the cheek, taking Hero's free hand within his own. 'Don't we?' He turned to Hero, his eyes giving her the prompt.

'Yes.' Her voice was soft as she replied.

Gill let her gaze linger for a moment before giving both their hands a squeeze. 'Good. And like I say, don't you forget it.'

Hero shook her head. Whatever happened, she knew she would never forget this moment.

'So! What have you been up to? Juliet said something about you being in New York with a man friend? Is there something we should know?'

'Mum.' Nick's tone had a friendly warning.

'Oh pfft.' She batted him away. 'Hero doesn't mind, do you, love?'

Hero smiled, shaking her head. For once, she didn't mind at all.

'There. See?' His mum nodded at him. 'Don't you have something to do anyway? This is girls' talk.'

Nick rolled his eyes and went off in search of male back-up as Gill linked Hero's arm within her own and repeated her question about Hero's love life.

***

Hero's smile blossomed as the pudgy little hand wrapped its fingers around one of her own and stared up at her with curious, deep brown eyes. She'd never really had the occasion to be in contact with children or babies and the first time Juliet had held one of the twins out for her to hold, she'd panicked, sure she would do something wrong. But Juliet and Pete had reassured her and helped nudge her in the right direction and now she could hardly wait each day to hold and cuddle one of these two perfect little people.

As baby Marcus closed his eyes, his fingers still clamped tightly on to hers, she swept her gaze to the man beside her. Nick was currently trying to corral one very wiggly little Bridie. She smiled as he adjusted his hold and began gently rocking her. Bridie's bright green eyes, so like her mother's, focused on him as her hands reached out for his finger which she then began trying to chew on with her mostly gummy jaws. Juliet had said that the babies had both just started teething, and Hero saw Nick flinch and adjust his hand a little as the vicar continued with the baptism.

Marcus having been done, Nick stepped forward with the now snoozing Bridie. As the water dribbled onto the little girl's forehead, her face immediately crumpled and a piercing scream filled the church. Her uncle deftly moved the now unhappily awake child and held her against him, bouncing her gently as he made soothing sounds whilst the vicar carried on rather bravely, lifting his voice occasionally to be heard above Bridie's cries. As the service drew to a close, her eyes slowly fluttered closed again, and beside her, Hero felt Nick let out a slow breath of relief.

Chapter 8

'Think you got the easier deal there.' He motioned towards Marcus, still happily sleeping.

'You seem to have the knack of calming her though,' Hero replied, smiling.

'Yeah. Case of practice makes perfect.' He turned away as someone called his name, stopping as Juliet relieved him of the child, rubbing his arm with her free hand and laughing. Hero couldn't hear the conversation over the noise of the general chatter now going on, but his words echoed in her head. She looked down at the baby in her arms. Nick had already had months getting to know these new additions to the Webster family, months of what he'd called practice. She should have been there for Juliet. She should have come over and helped – in whatever way she could. But the thought of seeing Nick again had stopped her. Yes, she had been busy with work and travelling but she should have put her sister first. Juliet had told her she was fine, but it couldn't have been easy for her with one new baby, let alone two, even if she had had a little more practice than her sister. When Hero was, most inconveniently according to their mother, born, it was Juliet who had given her cuddles and played with her. Juliet, who had helped the nanny they'd brought in. None of the nannies ever lasted all that long. As soon as their mother saw anything like affection towards this new charge, they were out. Hero looked down into the peaceful face of Marcus who was now waking, his eyes searching out this new environment. She smiled down at him and spoke softly, drawing a smile from his happy little face.

'He reminds me so much of you.' Juliet smiled, as she rocked Bridie gently. 'Apart from the eye colour. That's all Pete's side. But his curiosity. His calmness. You were just like that.'

Hero turned and saw the tears shining in her sister's eyes.

'Jules, please don't cry. What's wrong?'

Juliet smiled through her tears. 'Nothing. I mean, I just wish ...'

Hero frowned. 'You wish what?'

'This ...' Her sister moved, her hand under the baby spreading to indicate the family and friends that now surrounded them, laughing, talking, and fussing over the children. 'This is how it should have been. This is the love that you should have been given.'

'Oh, Jules.' Hero leant her head against her sister's. 'I had you, and that is more than enough for me.'

'I don't know why they treated you the way they did.'

Hero shrugged, turning her face away. 'It doesn't matter now.'

Across the room, Nick watched Hero drop her gaze from her sister, an expression of pain on her face as she did so. She'd moved so that Juliet wouldn't see. But he saw. He knew the secret she still kept from her sister. How cruel her mother had been to a child who had never asked to be born. Nick could only empathise with her, and knew he and Pete had been so lucky to be born into this family. A family that extended their love to anyone who needed and deserved it. His eyes fell on Joe, who saw and waved, his surrogate brother's happy smile releasing his own.

As he turned his head, his glance caught Hero's. The pain no one was supposed to see left her face. Within a moment, her expression became unreadable. A flesh and blood mannequin.

Nick felt the fire in his soul burn with frustration at this woman. He thought he'd be over it by now, but when he caught the glimpses of what she kept hidden, it seared into him once more. Nick turned away, angry with himself for letting her get to him. If that was how she wanted to live her life, then so be it. He didn't want to get involved. He'd tried that once before, and for a few wonderful hours he'd seen the softness within. She had surprised him that night, allowing him into her thoughts as she had, sharing secrets she'd kept for so long. It was though the world had shifted around him. Stupidly, he'd thought it actually meant something, but Hero had disavowed him of that belief completely the next morning as she'd sat at the kitchen table, eyes on her phone, luggage packed and ready to go with barely a look in his direction. He shouldn't be surprised. It wasn't the first time he'd been played by a woman, but he wasn't a fool. He had no plans to repeat the same mistake with this particular one again.

Pete hadn't said anything after Hero left, but he wasn't stupid and he knew his brother. Which was probably why he asked the one question he did.

'Did you sleep with her?'

Nick had shaken his head, doing his best to not let his thoughts go down that particular 'what if' trail. The last thing he'd needed at that particular moment was an overactive imagination. Hero Scott had made it clear that her use of him was over. He'd entertained her at the reception but now she was heading back to the real world. Or at least the world that was real to her – however fake it seemed to others.

***

As the babies grew, Hero returned to the station for more visits. Her guilt at staying away so long prior to their birth still nagged at her and she was determined to make up for it. Although her sister and brother-in-law seemed happy to see her more, Nick

Webster certainly didn't seem to share their feelings. He'd been polite at the twins' christening, almost friendly, but they had never reconnected like they had at the wedding. Hero knew it was her fault. She knew she'd hurt him that day when she'd left with barely a backwards glance. She'd seen it in his face, but opening up to him had been an accident. An accident brought on by joy and fear, love and champagne. She'd felt so out of place at the wedding, despite everyone being so kind and welcoming. Well, apart from that one waitress who'd been throwing dirty looks her way the whole evening. Nick had come to her at the right moment and suddenly she'd felt … safe. Like she was home. Hero knew that was ridiculous. This life wasn't for her. And Nick Webster definitely wasn't for her. Most of the time they just rubbed each other the wrong way. So why was it him she'd opened up to? Why did he know the secret scar that she had never told anyone, not even her own sister?

Juliet worried about him. As she did about everyone, but Nick had taken a special place in her heart. He was as much a brother to Juliet as she was a sister.

'I do worry about him,' Juliet said as they cleared the last bits of wrapping paper from the floor and put it into a pile.

'He's a big boy, Jules. He can look after himself, I'm sure.'

'Hmm. I know it was a while ago now, but finding his fiancée cheating on him cut him deeper than he likes to admit. I don't think he's as tough as he likes to make out.'

'For goodness' sake, don't let him hear you say that. I'll probably get blamed for being a bad influence on you.'

Juliet shook her head. 'What is it with you two?'

Hero fished out another piece of rogue wrapping paper from under the sofa and squashed it down into the bag.

'What?' she asked, not looking up.

'You two. You're just … I don't know. You seemed like you were getting on well at the wedding but ever since then … you're just so spiky with each other.'

'We're just different, Jules. You can't expect everyone to be as lovely as you.'

Juliet put her hand on her hip. 'Stop trying to sweet talk me.'

Hero laughed. 'I'm not. I promise. It's true though.'

Juliet smiled. Her sister had a soft, pretty laugh but it was a sound she heard all too rarely. She knew her sister found it difficult to relax with people. She was better here, even more so when Nick was out of the room. Juliet had noticed them dancing at the wedding and asked her about him, teasing, but Hero had just shaken her head and told her she was imagining things. Eventually Juliet let it drop. There was no point in pushing it for the few times a year that she got over to visit. Juliet knew from experience that the more she pushed, the more Hero would clam up.

'How on earth did they get paper right back here?' Juliet laughed, throwing two balls of wadded up wrapping paper out before backing out from behind the Christmas tree.

'I think they were just excited.' Hero smiled, adding them to the rubbish bag she held in one hand.

'That's hardly surprising.' She gave her younger sister a look.

'What?'

'You know perfectly well what I mean. You spoiled us all rotten. Again.'

Hero shrugged. 'It's Christmas.'

'Yes. This time. But you do this every time. You know you don't need to. We love you just being here. The kids have been getting excited for weeks.'

Hero looked up, her face radiant at the mention of the children. They didn't have expectations of her and they didn't judge. Her friendship with young Joe was the same. She could be herself completely with them.

'I'm their godmother. I'm allowed to spoil them.'

'So, what's your excuse for the rest of us?'

Hero sat back on her knees. 'It makes me happy. Besides, what else would I spend it on?' Hero took the hand her sister offered her and stood. 'Please, Jules. You're all I have. Just let me do this.'

Nick and Pete approaching the living room caught the last of the conversation. Exchanging a glance, Pete shook his head at Nick. Nick held his brother's gaze for a moment before entering the room after him.

'Two little monsters sound asleep as requested.'

'I'll take this out.' Hero picked up the rubbish bag and headed out to the shed closest to the house, where several plastic crates lined one of the shelves, neatly labelled in block letters. She began unloading the wrapping into the appropriate box.

'Want some help?'

Hero jumped. 'God, you frightened the life out of me. But no, thanks. I'm nearly done anyway.'

The silence of the night was broken only by the rustle of the paper as Hero squashed the last of it into the box.

'Thanks for the riding coat. You shouldn't have though.'

'I could hardly leave you out.' It was a statement of fact more than anything.

Nick stepped closer, leaning on the shelf. He ran a hand across his face, a shadow of dark stubble framing his jaw. 'Why do you do that?'

'Do what?' she asked, applying a level of concentration to her task far deeper than was required, keeping her eyes lowered.

'That!' He waved a hand. 'Act like that. Like you don't care about anything. Or anyone. We all know it's not true.'

Hero folded the bin liner unnecessarily, waiting for him to leave. But he didn't. He raised his eyebrows expectantly.

Hero sighed. 'What?'

'I'm waiting for an answer.'

'An answer?'

'Yes.'

'And what exactly was the question again?'

Nick gritted his teeth, doing his best to control his temper.

Hero could see the flicker in his jaw but kept her expression blank. She had to. It was the only defence she had.

'The question was why you feel you have to put on this act? I can maybe understand that you have to do it in your career, but you don't need to do it out here. Surely you know that!'

Hero's heart was racing but she knew she couldn't show him. She waited a beat before meeting his eyes coolly. 'There is no act, Nick. This is me. I'm sorry if you don't like it but I can't really help that. This is who I am.'

He looked down into the startling green eyes, studying the face with its perfect make-up, as always, before replying softly. 'No, it's not. This isn't you at all.'

Hero stepped back. Her eyes flashed for a moment before she covered herself. Nick wasn't sure whether it was insecurity or anger. Probably both.

'I really do advise you to stick to the day job, Nick. It would seem your psychology degree is a long way off yet.' Grabbing the empty rubbish bag, she pushed past him and strode back into the house. Nick watched her go. However much she denied it, there was no escaping the fact he'd hit a nerve.

***

'Are you sure you can't stay a bit longer?' Disappointment sounded in Juliet's voice. 'The children would love it so much if you could. They'll be so disappointed when Jack and Gill bring them back from the city tomorrow.' She tilted her head. 'We'd all love you to stay longer.'

Not quite all of you …

Hero bit down on her bottom lip. 'I know. I'm sorry. I hoped I'd be able to. But a shoot I'm doing has got moved up, and I can't back out of it. I'm really sorry, Jules. I'll make it up to you.'

'There's nothing to make up for. It's just nice having you around.'

Hero smiled briefly as she finished packing her case. She really had hoped to stay out here longer this time. There was so much space, physically and metaphorically. Just you and the sky, with several thousand sheep thrown in for company. Every time she returned to her own world after being here, it seemed to suffocate her a little more. But she couldn't. Not now. Nick's words the other night had unsettled her. The truth unsettled her.

He was right about it. About everything. But she couldn't help it. There was no way he could understand. She didn't expect him to. But, as much as he railed against it, she needed that shield. It was her only protection from the world. It kept people out, kept them away from her real feelings. Kept them from damaging them. It was a matter of survival. She'd learned from an early age, courtesy of her mother, that being open with people just made it easier for them to hurt you, and her career had only reinforced that. She'd never had a thick skin, so she'd had to work out a different defence strategy. But was Nick right? Had she done it too well?

Back when Juliet was in England, it had been easier to let her in, lowering the defences to one of the few people she trusted. But as the miles between them had grown, Hero had retreated into herself more and more. Rupert didn't stand for it and she loved him for that. Anya just rolled her eyes and made her laugh, but as Anya's own romantic relationship had become more serious, along with her plans for returning home, Hero had seen her less and less and it had all just become a habit, an automatic setting that Hero fell into almost each and every day. It was, she knew, becoming more permanent. Just as Nick had said. And something about him knowing that frightened her.

'So it's not something that can be moved?' Juliet kept her tone conversational, but she knew there was something off with her sister. Hero had had that emotionless expression on her face almost constantly since late on Christmas Day, not to mention the fact that she'd barely looked at Juliet the whole time she'd been packing. There was something more to Hero's inability to extend her stay than she'd said, and Juliet got the feeling that it had nothing to do with her job.

'Not really. I told them a while ago that I was flexible on dates, but I just sort of forgot about it.'

'Right.' Juliet nodded, knowing for sure now that her sister was covering something. Hero was the most organised person she knew. She planned everything. Had to, almost, it seemed. Juliet suspected it gave her sister the feeling that she was in control of at least some small part of her life whilst the rest of it was run by agents and bookers and commented on almost constantly by the press. The sort of flexibility she'd mentioned wasn't something she gave. Ever. It had caused some to label her as self-important and a diva – Hero knew that and accepted it, balancing that against the confidence of knowing her schedule exactly. It was, she'd told Juliet before, non-negotiable. Her sister's strength in this belief had surprised Juliet but Hero had shrugged it off, claiming it as one of the benefits of being successful. Her reply hadn't been egotistical. It was just fact. Which was exactly why Juliet didn't believe Hero's explanation as to why she was leaving the station first thing in the morning.

'This is me you're talking to,' she tried again, her voice soft.

Her sister gave the briefest of nods as she folded the last items into her case. 'I know.'

'For God's sake, Hero. What's going on with you? Why do you insist on running away all the time?'

Hero looked up, shocked at the pain in her sister's voice.

'Jules ...' She leant across the bed, covering Juliet's hand with her own. 'Honestly, I'm not running away. Everything's fine.' Hero smiled but it didn't feel right. Juliet was the one person she never, ever wanted to lie to, but she didn't know what else to do. Turning back to the case, she checked it was secure before lifting it down off the bed and carrying it over to the door.

Juliet leant back against the headboard, her mind trawling back through the past few days, turning them over in her mind, looking for any clue that could explain her sister's suddenly amended plans. She sat up as something jarred in her memory.

Hero saw the change in her sister's expression as she pushed herself off the bed and half ran out of the room, storming down the stairs two at a time.

'Jules?' Leaning over the bannister, Hero saw Juliet's blonde curls disappearing into the kitchen. Running down the stairs, she heard the sound of the kitchen door being pulled open, then banging on its hinges heavily. Hero ran after her, desperate to stop her sister, sensing where, or rather who, she was headed for.

'What did you say to her?' Juliet spat at her brother-in-law, her words loaded with fury. Nick and Pete both straightened up from where they had been studying a sickly tractor.

'Jules?' Pete said, his forehead creasing in surprise.

Beside him, Nick's expression seemed almost expectant. As though he'd been waiting for this. His brother's frown deepened.

'What did you say to my sister?' Juliet yelled. 'Tell me! She'd been planning to stay on longer this time and now she's not, and it's because of you. I know it is! So just what the hell did you say to her?'

Nick opened his mouth to say something, but Juliet was there before him.

'You just couldn't be nice, could you? Couldn't just try for a bit longer?' Her voice broke and the tears that threatened burst through. Pete threw down the wrench he'd been holding, wrapping his arms protectively around his wife.

'Come on, love.' His voice was soft, the tone soothing.

Nick swallowed hard. His insides twisted with guilt, knowing that he was responsible for his sister-in-law's tears. He loved Juliet and he'd die to protect her, but he couldn't protect her from this. No one could.

'I don't understand,' Juliet sobbed. 'You're a good man, Nick.

You always do your best to get on with everyone. Why can't you just accept my sister for who she is?'

Nick dropped his gaze to the ground. Letting out a breath slowly, he looked back up and met Juliet's pleading look.

'Because she doesn't accept it herself.'

Pete's eyes narrowed. This wasn't what he was expecting. He'd expected Nick to deny it, shrug it off. His wife could get a little over-protective about Hero sometimes. It was understandable. Underneath all the show, she worried that her sister was lonely, and, despite plenty of reassurance to the contrary, Juliet still felt guilty that she may have added to that loneliness by moving way out here.

A cry of pain left Juliet as she lunged for Nick. 'You—'

'Stop it!' Hero cried, running into the barn, and straight into the path of Juliet as she broke away from Pete. Nick didn't move. The two sisters collided, Hero stumbling backwards into him as she blocked Juliet's attack. Catching Hero, he steadied her as she regained her balance, then let his hands drop again to his sides.

'What are you doing?' Hero's eyes were wide in shock as she stared at her sister.

'He's sending you away!'

'No! He's not!'

'Yes, he is.' Juliet turned her tear-stained eyes on her little sister, her breath hitching in her chest, the tears flowing freely now. 'I don't want you to go! I'm afraid I'm going to lose you, Hero. You slip away a little more each time. I used to be able to see behind that bloody mask you wear but now it's there nearly all the time. Even with me.' Drawing a breath, she looked cautiously at Nick. Hero followed her sister's gaze. She took a step, placing herself in front of him, breaking Juliet's line of vision.

'Nick didn't do anything, Juliet, so don't start on him.'

Behind her, Nick blinked. Hero Scott was definitely a woman of surprises. She was the last person he'd thought would ever jump to his defence. Especially when he knew he didn't deserve it.

'I just thought he—'

'He didn't. Whatever you think. He didn't. We might never be the best of friends, but Nick would never intentionally upset me because he knows in doing that, he would be hurting you, and both of us know he wouldn't do that for the world.'

Juliet looked from her sister to Nick, then back to Hero again. 'So why are you leaving?'

'I told you.'

Juliet's eyes searched her sister's face but there was nothing to read there. Her gaze slid up to meet Nick's.

'I just wish you could be friends.'

'We are. In our own way.' Hero moved a little, tilting her head catch Nick's eye. He understood the silent plea.

Nick nodded, the briefest of smiles showing agreement. What she'd said was true – for the most part. An uncomfortable knot still sat in his stomach, knowing he was responsible for all, or even a part of this. Juliet had been so excited her sister was coming, especially as she'd half got her to agree to extend the visit. He hadn't planned on calling Hero out. If the truth were told, he didn't want Hero to leave either. Ever since the night of the wedding, when he had finally slipped under her defences, his insides still did a little flip whenever he remembered the smile she had given him, how she had felt in his arms, her head resting on his chest, the pleasure he had felt at her childlike compliment on his hands. Not once had he ever been able to get back under those defences – but he hadn't forgotten a moment of it. Whatever happened, that memory was lodged in his heart, his soul, forever.

Juliet switched her gaze between them before letting it rest on Hero.

'You'll come back soon though?'

'Yes. I promise.'

Juliet nodded in acceptance, a loose tear running down her face as she did so. Hero stepped forward, hugging her sister tightly, hating that she was responsible for a part of her sadness, if not all of it. Juliet released her, then looked up at Nick, her eyes searching his face for forgiveness. He shook his head and pulled her close.

'I'm sorry,' she whispered. Nick's hug tightened a little and Juliet knew she was forgiven.

Stepping back, she reached for her husband's hand. Pete gave his brother an exasperated look then led his wife out of the shed, leaving their respective siblings alone together. When Nick was sure that the others were out of earshot, he turned to Hero who was now leaning on the open doorway of the shed, watching the retreating figures enter the cool interior of the house.

'Is she right?'

Hero didn't turn. 'Of course not.'

'Really?'

'Yes. Look, I know you don't like me—'

'I do like you.'

Hero turned, astonishment clear on her face.

How could she ever think that he didn't? Nick pushed through. This door had been opened and it was now or never. There was only so long they could carry this charade on. At least there was for him.

'Juliet's right though. I still stand by what I said the other night, and what she said today. I like you, but the woman I like disappears more and more behind this other persona and I'm really not keen on her. She makes me nervous.'

Hero sat down heavily on a hay bale, and at his words she looked up.

'You seem surprised.'

She shifted across on the bale to make room for him. It was a snug fit for the two of them. His hip rested against hers but she didn't move.

'I've just always had the impression very few things, if anything, would make you nervous.'

'I'm not sure whether that makes me sound tough or just arrogant.'

'Probably a little of both.' Hero shrugged, but for once, he saw the honesty in her expression.

They sat for a few more moments in silence.

'Are you still leaving?'

'I have to.'

'Why? You said before your ticket was open-ended. Why not stay a few more days?'

'I just can't.'

Hero saw the muscles in Nick's jaw tighten. He turned, his leg bumping against hers in the sudden movement. A shiver of pleasure rippled through her at his touch. How ironic it was that this man could stimulate her body, her mind, so easily and unknowingly and yet he had no wish to. The men she'd dated, she'd slept with, those who had prided themselves on their skills – not one of them had ever come close to the effect that Nick Webster had just by looking at her.

'Look me in the eye and tell me you can't stay.'

Hero's game face met Nick's gaze. She saw the tick in his jaw, the steel in his eyes. He saw the lie.

Hero looked away. She was tired. Tired of trying to prove to him that she was something she wasn't. But she'd spent such a long time building it up, adjusting, perfecting, it was hard to remember now a time she'd been without it. Her mother had put her on the first step of this path and her career had helped push her along it. Nick, Juliet, even Rupert – none of them could understand how exposed she felt in her professional life. In this celebrity-obsessed age, the lines had become blurred between what was personal and what was professional. Blurred and removed. The media, the public, everyone felt like they owned her. She was high profile. People who had never met her, who knew nothing about her, looked on from afar and passed judgement. It had begun to destroy her. Now it was just a matter of survival.

Nick stood, Hero immediately feeling the loss of his warmth against her.

‘You need to be careful about whose lives you’re playing with.’

Hero stood and frowned at him. ‘What’s that supposed to mean?’

‘Exactly what it sounds like,’ Nick replied. ‘You come here and give your sister hope that she’ll have more time with you and then you change your mind. Every time you do it, you crush her that little bit more.’

‘That’s not fair! You know I’d stay if I could.’

Nick shook his head. ‘No. I don’t. And they don’t either.’ He jabbed a thumb back towards the house. ‘And it’s not just Juliet. It’s Joe too, and now the kids. Juliet might understand, but the others? All they see is you leaving when they’ve built up their hopes of seeing you for longer! I don’t know how it works in your world, but here that’s a pretty shitty thing to do.’

‘I would never hurt them. Even you must know that!’ Hero’s voice was strained but her eyes were dry. She saw Nick study her for a moment as if searching for something. Whatever it was, it was clear he didn’t find it.

‘No, Hero. I don’t. And if you want to know the truth, they don’t either.’ His voice was soft now. The anger had left now, replaced by … what? She met his eyes. There was nothing there. Nothing she could read and for the first time, Hero realised something. Those few people she loved in this world? This was what they saw in her. A blank canvas. No hint of the emotions that swelled within her. To them she was detached. Disinterested.

‘Please don’t say that,’ she whispered, pain flooding her heart.

Nick didn’t even look at her now. ‘I’m not one of your hangers on, Hero. I’m not going to tiptoe around you, and tell you how fantastic you are when the truth is you’re hurting people – children – who mean the world to me.’ He turned now, the soft brown of his eyes now dark with determination and defence. ‘We’re real, Hero. We’re not toys you can pick up and put down whenever the fancy takes you! What’s your sister supposed to say to the twins when they come back and you're not here? Joe is going to be heartbroken. Again.' He snatched his hat from his head and ran a hand through his dark hair. 'You come here thinking that if you bring expensive presents, it absolves you from your crappy behaviour!'

'I don't think that! I—'

Nick cut her off, the dark eyes flashing with anger once more. 'You need to decide. You're either in or you're out. There are no half measures. You've spent the last five years playing with emotions out here and it needs to stop! You need to decide on something for once and stick with it, not run away every time something spooks you!'

She threw her hands up. 'Why does everyone keep telling me I'm running away?'

Nick gave a mirthless laugh and shook his head. 'I know you're not stupid, Hero. Have you stopped to think that maybe if everyone is telling you the same thing, it might mean that it's true?'

'No. Because it's not!'

'Right,' Nick replied through gritted teeth as he struggled to rein in his temper.

'You don't get it. Just because everyone is saying the same thing doesn't mean that it's true. If that were the case, I've been pregnant, engaged and on drugs at least three times!'

Nick narrowed his eyes at her. 'Are you seriously comparing your family to the media?'

'No. I …'

He stepped back, his expression icy. 'You know what? Never mind. That actually explains a hell of a lot. Good to know where we stand in your eyes.'

'Nick! I didn't mean …' She caught his arm, but he shook off her hand as quickly as he would a scorpion. Hero flinched.

'Don't,' he snapped. 'Just … don't.' He didn't look at her, instead he lifted his wrist, glancing quickly at his watch. 'You should get on. We wouldn't want you to miss your bus and force you to stay one more godforsaken day out here.'

'You know that's not how I feel about it here! That's not fair!'

Nick threw up his hands. 'For fuck's sake, Hero! Life isn't fair! And if you want to know the truth, not one of us know how you feel about being here. Nobody has a bloody clue about what you feel about anything! Or even if you feel anything at all. And you know what? We're all pretty tired of trying to work it out. Your world might put up with this shit, but out here in the real one, we don't have time to tiptoe around you, trying to work out what it is you want from us. We have real lives, and real things demanding our attention. The last thing we need is you pulling this act every time you come out!' He let out a sigh as he rammed his hat on, before looking back at her. 'The best thing you can do for all of us now is just go back to London. Go back where you're supposed to be.'

Chapter 9

Pete and Nick walked up to the car, the dust settling gently in the still of the early evening. In the end, Juliet had decided to take Hero all the way to the airport, enabling them to have a little extra time together. As she was heading to the city anyway, she picked the children from their grandparents on the way back, saving them the drive.

'Heya rugrats!' Pete laughed as the children ran into his legs. 'Everything all right?' he asked as he bent and kissed his wife.

She nodded. 'Yes. I think so.'

Pete tilted his head in question.

Juliet shrugged. 'She seemed … I don't know. A little quieter than usual, I guess.'

'Probably just thinking about work.'

She smiled. 'Yes. I expect so. Are you two done?'

Nick, who was now giving Marcus a piggy back, nodded. His mind was turning over what his sister-in-law had just said about Hero. He felt a twist in his stomach. He hadn't meant for it to end the way it had, but she just made him so mad! As they got to the porch, Nick bent his knees and Marcus slid off.

'Dinner should be ready any time. I just need to get these two to wash their hands and faces and then I'll dish it up.'

'I can do that,' Nick replied, herding the children through the kitchen.

Juliet tossed a smile over her shoulder. 'Thank you.'

Nick nodded, feeling undeserving of her smile. Hero obviously hadn't told her sister about their argument, and clearly she hadn't guessed. But he knew his words had got through. She might not have shown it on her face, but he'd seen her knuckles whitening as she'd kept her fists at her side. Had he said too much? Or had he not said enough?

After supervising his godchildren into being mostly clean for dinner, Nick took a seat at the table, gratefully accepting the cold beer his brother poured him. Staring down into the golden liquid, the words he'd thrown at Hero this morning rang around his head. He shouldn't have let her go like that, not with those damning words in her ears. He should have gone after her. Told her why she made him crazy, and why he wanted her to stay. Told her, finally, that he'd fallen in love with her that night, the night of the wedding, and no matter what he did, who he dated, or how cool they acted with each other, that feeling refused to go away. And, despite everything being against it, each time she visited, it only got stronger. It was frustration that had driven him to act the way he had, say the things he'd said. Frustration because he knew what was beneath that layer of protection and it drove him crazy when she shut him – and everyone else – out.

Nick picked up the glass and swirled its contents. The conversation replayed over and over in his mind like a broken record. If there had ever been a possibility of something blossoming with Hero Scott, he was pretty sure he'd now blown it to smithereens.

'What's wrong, Uncle Nick?' Bridie's high sing-song voice broke into his thoughts. 'You look sad.' His niece glanced at her mother.

Juliet nodded and Bridie climbed down from the table. The little girl walked over and stood next to Nick, looking up expectantly. Her uncle smiled and pushed his chair back so that Bridie could climb up onto his lap. Getting herself comfortable, she then studied his face, her own serious. Nick looked down into the striking green cat-like eyes, replicas of her mother's. And her aunt's.

'Are you sad because Auntie Hero left?'

'She had to go back to work, sweetheart.'

Bridie let out an impatient sigh. 'I know, but is that why you're sad?'

Nick studied the open, honest little face. It was amazing how astute kids could be without even trying. It was all black and white to them; no greys, no slight shading. Just one or the other.

He threw a glance at the clock. 'It's pretty late. Isn't it about time you two munchkins had a bath?' Bridie screwed her head around to look at the clock, delicate little arms still clinging around his neck. She turned her head back and tilted it at him.

'Will you read us a story after?'

'Of course.'

'OK.' Bridie slid off his lap and ran around the table to her mother as Nick got up and headed to the back door.

'Let me know when you're ready for your story,' he called. There was a click as the door closed behind him.

Juliet rose from the table. She took Bridie's hand and ushered her and her brother out towards the stairs and the children's bathroom. As she left, she shared a glance with her husband. Neither of them had missed the fact that Nick had studiously avoided answering his niece's question.

Later that night, Pete and Nick sat out together on the verandah. Juliet had turned in early, tired after the long drive, and a little tearful as she always was for a couple of days after her sister left. The brothers sat in companionable silence, drinking their cold beers as warmth radiated from the land. Above them, stars began to push through the fabric of the twilight to glint and sparkle. Nick stared up at them, thinking of a previous time he'd sat and gazed at them.

'So, did you tell her?' Pete asked, his tone casual, conversational.

'Tell whom what?'

'Hero. Did you finally get around to telling her that you like her?'

Nick threw a look at his brother before turning back to the stars. 'Don't know what you're talking about, mate.'

'If you pull the other one, it'll play "Oranges and Lemons".'

Nick closed his eyes.

'I've nowhere else to be, so I can wait all night,' Pete added.

His brother turned to look at him. Pete gave him a palms up gesture. Sometimes it annoyed the hell out of Nick that he could be read like a book by those in his family.

'Right-oh,' he said on a long exhalation. 'Potted version. She knows I like her. God knows why any of us bother to though with that bloody mask of control she wears most of the time.' He swigged at his bottle.

'That what you fell out over?'

'She tell Juliet that?'

'Nope. She hasn't told anyone anything, from what I can see,' Pete said, quietly. 'But you just did.'

Nick met his brother's eyes. They were calm, with a hint of a smile in them. Nick held the gaze for a moment, shook his head slowly and returned his attention to the midnight blue sky. He was caught and he knew it.

'Does Juliet know?'

'We've both just put two and two together.' Pete shrugged, taking another swig of his beer. 'Something happened at the wedding, but you told me you didn't sleep with her—'

'I didn't,' Nick broke in.

'I believe you. But something happened. Hero took off the next day and you were like a bear with a sore head for weeks. You're a pretty easy-going bloke these days but she really seems to know how to push your buttons. Logical thinking means either you can't stand her, or you really like her. I might not say much, but I've got eyes and I know my little brother.'

Nick let out a long sigh. Strangely, it was almost a relief that Pete knew. 'Every time I've thought about it, something happens. It's like … she's afraid.'

'Maybe she is.'

Nick thought about that. Thought about the secret she'd told him that night. Maybe Pete was right. Could it be that she did care about him but she was afraid that, if she made a step towards him, held out her hand to him as she had done to her mother all those years ago, he'd crush her in the same way? How could he make her believe that he'd never do that, not to her. Never to her.

'I'm not sure she wants to hear it. She's not exactly a fan of people getting too close.'

'Couldn't get much closer than she is with Joe and the kids.'

'That's different. She …' How could Nick explain something to his brother that he didn't understand himself. 'Joe, and the kids, they're innocent. She knows they'll never hurt her, so she lets them in.'

'What about you?'

Nick dropped his eyes from the heavens, fixing his gaze somewhere out in the darkness of the land stretching away in front of him. 'That night? Your wedding. You were giving me gip about dancing with her, so I asked her. Honestly, I expected her to send me packing but she didn't. She gave me this look … I can't explain it … it was like …' He paused, remembering the moment, trying to find the right words. 'It was like she was drowning in quicksand and I was throwing her a lifeline. For a few hours she was this completely different person to the one she'd been up to then. All we see is this stunning, confident, kind of snooty woman but that night I got to see someone even more special, more beautiful.' He took a last swig of his beer then let it rest on his thigh, worrying the label with his fingernails.

'I guess she regretted opening up to me because she left the next day and she's never let me anywhere near that close again.

I wish to God she would. I know she lives in a different world, not to mention the other side of it, but …' He didn't need to finish the sentence. Pete understood.

'I've been trying to take it easy, play along, but that bloody mask doesn't crack. All this time and I'm still no nearer to her. I tried to just forget, chalk it up to experience and move on, but I can't. I just end up comparing everyone to her and no one comes up to scratch.' He raked a hand through his hair before tipping his head back, exhaling a long, low breath. 'I said stuff I probably shouldn't have, but I was just so bloody frustrated. I just wanted a reaction!'

'Well, it looks like you got your wish.'

Nick pulled a face. 'Thanks for your support.'

Pete shrugged.

'Does Juliet still think Hero went back early for a work thing?'

'For the moment.' Low light filtered through from the dining room and Pete used it to study his beer bottle. 'Hero did a pretty good job of convincing her whilst she was busy defending you.'

'She only defended me because she didn't want Juliet and I to fall out. Hero may be selfish but she's not stupid. She knows we all have to live and work here together.'

'She's not selfish, Nick, and you know it.'

Nick turned at the serious tone his brother's voice had taken on.

'We were lucky. We had a loving, stable childhood. Those two girls were put in boarding schools whenever possible and farmed out to distant relatives when it wasn't. That's going to leave anyone with a scar. People deal with things differently. Juliet's managed things a little better than Hero, maybe because she was older, but the truth is, sometimes we need to make allowances.'

Nick moved his attention back to the swathes of dark land in front of him. Juliet had managed things better than her sister, that was true, but only he and Hero knew the true reason for that. And as much as she drove him up the wall, she'd confided in him and he would take that secret to the grave.

'Look, I'm not saying Hero's perfect.' Pete shrugged. 'Who is? And yes, she can be hard to figure out at times, but I think she's worth the effort. And you do too, or you wouldn't be getting so worked up about it.'

Nick tipped his head back and stretched his neck, rolling his head first to one side, then the other.

'Just give her a break, mate. OK? Next time she comes, start again. She's never had anyone but Juliet and then I stole her all the way out here. It's a strange kind of world she lives in, being judged on nothing but purely how she looks. It's no wonder she's built up some defences.'

Nick winced as he cast his mind back to the parting words he had fired at Hero earlier.

Pete turned, catching his brother's expression. 'Oh, no. I know that look. What did you do?'

Nick gave him the highlights of the argument he'd had with Hero earlier that day.

Pete rolled his eyes. 'Oh bloody hell, mate. I thought you'd calmed down as you got older.'

'I know, I know.' Nick held up his hands, palms out. 'She just makes me so … argh!'

'Yeah, I know. And that's exactly why it bothers you so much.' Pete stood, his arms reaching for the sky as he stretched. 'Don't worry, mate.' He clapped his brother's shoulder as he headed for the door. 'She'll be all right. Don't worry. Juliet got her to promise to visit again soon. Just start again then.'

***

'We totally should have done this ages ago,' Anya said, tossing her bag into the boot of Hero's classic MG Midget.

'We should.' Hero agreed, hurriedly shutting the boot and

scooting around to the driver's side, trying to get out of the teeming rain as quick as possible. Every time she came back to London after staying with her sister out on the station, it seemed colder and greyer. She'd walked out of Heathrow Airport a few days before New Year's into torrential rain, and it had barely stopped since.

'I'm sorry I've not spent as much time with you as I should have lately. I am a bad friend.'

'Oh, don't be silly,' Hero replied, plugging in her seatbelt. 'We've both been busy, and you have a very good excuse in that you're planning a wedding, as well as getting things in place to open your restaurant, not to mention house hunting back in Sweden.'

Hero checked her mirrors and pulled out into the busy London traffic. Rain hammered on the roof and windscreen as its little wipers swished on double speed.

'You do promise to come and visit when I go back?'

Hero flashed her a brief glance of acknowledgement before returning her eyes and concentration on the road in front of them. 'Just try and stop me. Anyway, we're going to be together more for a while with this new contract. You might be sick of me once we've got all these shoots done.' Hero grinned.

'Ha! Never. I think it's going to be fun doing this together.'

'Me too.'

The contract with Sacha Cosmetics was a huge deal with both women signed up for the next three years. Sacha had broken away from the mould with this new planned campaign, opting for two looks instead of the traditional association of one face for the brand. Anya, with her blonde, fair Nordic looks was to be their spring/summer/daytime face whilst Hero's dark hair and jewel-green eyes made her perfect to carry the mantle of the autumn/winter/evening look. Top names had been vying for the contract, but a twist of fate had intervened. One of Sacha's executives, stepping out of a meeting to take a telephone call, let her gaze drift as she listened to the caller drone. Further down the hall, she noticed two women enter an adjoining office together. The shining dark hair of one had contrasted with her colleague's fair looks and a lightbulb pinged bright in the exec's brain.

The security of the deal gave Anya the freedom she'd been aiming for to concentrate on other areas of her life which were now taking precedence. Modelling had funded her true dream and this joint contract alongside Hero would keep finances topped up as she began a new stage of life. For Hero, not only did it give her the same guarantee of security as Anya, but even more than that, it meant the joy of working alongside her friend.

Anya looked around, her bright smile a contrast to the miserable winter weather outside. 'I love this little car. It's so cosy!'

'Isn't that just another word for small?'

'No! It's super cute. I'm so glad you bought it.'

'If you remember, I kind of had to. You wouldn't stop going on about it until I did.'

Anya shrugged. 'I can't drive so you getting it was the next best thing. Obviously.'

Hero laughed. 'Obviously.'

'Besides, you know it was a sound investment. Classic car prices have been going through the roof the last few years. Those financial guys at that party were telling us that, when they were banging on about investment opportunities.'

'Were they?'

'Yes! Weren't you listening?'

'Sort of.'

From her peripheral vision, Hero saw Anya turn a little in her seat. 'You've been very quiet since you got back from your sister's. Are you sure nothing happened?'

'No, nothing.'

'You miss them.' There was no question, just an understanding of fact.

'I do,' Hero replied, her concentration still on the road ahead. They'd left the city now, headed in the direction of the exclusive spa where they'd booked a week of rest and relaxation. First on the list for Hero was a really good, deep tissue massage. She'd had tension knots in her neck and shoulder ever since she'd left Australia. Perhaps taking this time away from everyone, save her best friend, was just what she needed.

'Would you ever go out there?'

'Huh?'

'To live, I mean,' Anya elaborated.

Hero paused for a moment before answering, her thoughts engaged in just how well that would go down with one particular resident. The words 'lead' and 'balloon' came to mind.

'No. I don't think so.'

'Why not? You said it was a large property. Surely there would be space?'

'Yes … it's not that.'

'What is it then?' Anya's enquiry was soft and considered.

Hero rolled to a stop at a set of traffic lights, letting her head fall back against the rest.

'There is something, isn't there?' Anya persisted.

Hero let out a small sigh. 'Yes. But it's … complicated.' She put the car in gear as the lights began to change. 'Can we talk when we get to the hotel?'

Anya covered her friend's hand briefly as it rested on the gearstick. 'Of course.' Turning her attention to the window, she squinted, trying to see past the rain into the darkness. 'Where are we anyway?'

'Not far now. Maybe ten, fifteen minutes.'

'Ooh goody! First bottle of champagne is on me!'

Hero laughed. 'Aren't we supposed to be all healthy, just drinking wheatgrass smoothies and eating vegetables all week?'

Anya screwed up her perfect nose and gave a derisive snort. 'I hope not! That sounds terrible, but you go ahead if you want to.'

'No thanks, your version sounds much better! I'm going to need a drink to unwind from this journey for a start.'

A mobile phone gave out a ping and the two women drove on, the silence companionable as Anya replied to the message. By the smile on her face, Hero guessed it was probably her fiancé. Anya was naturally light-hearted and ready to smile, but the smile she reserved for her husband-to-be was different. There was so much love behind it that it spilled out and you couldn't help but notice.

Hero concentrated on the road ahead. She hadn't told Anya, or anybody, about Nick – about how she'd opened up to him at the wedding and how incredible, how right, it had felt. Not a word about how comfortable she'd been in his arms and how just a look, a smile, made her body react in a way she'd never known. She felt the familiar stab as his last words to her echoed again around her mind. They had wounded her deeply, for the simple reason that they'd come from him of all people. She knew that meant something. And deep down, she knew they hurt because they were true. He was right about the protection she'd built around herself, but she'd been in this place such a long time, she wasn't sure how to get out of it, and keep her heart intact.

Those harsh words had pushed her towards the clarity she should have found years ago. She knew now that she should have spoken to someone, confided, long before tonight. But she knew Anya would understand. She wouldn't be offended that Hero had kept these things to herself. They'd both been dealing with the whole crazy fame thing for years but Anya, somehow, had still managed to begin a new career, and fall in love. Maybe that meant there was hope for Hero too? Maybe one day she would find someone else who looked at her the way Nick had done that evening as they'd sat under the star-studded twilight. She'd never forgotten that look. She never would. But she'd pushed him away. Kept him away. Forever running away – just like he'd said. And she'd kept on running. But where had it got her? She couldn't run from that memory of his eyes, dark and caring, or the last time she'd seen him when his look had sent a splinter of ice deep into her heart.

That ice would never melt, she knew that. But his words about confusing Joe and the children, as well as her sister, were burned into her brain. Hurting them was the last thing she had ever wanted to do but now that Nick had held a mirror up to her behaviour, she realised that was exactly what she'd done. Replaying her sister's words that day, the crack in her voice, the tears pouring down her face, Hero felt an almost physical pain knowing that she was responsible. But it was going to change. Starting tonight.

Now that she'd made the decision to tell Anya everything, she felt lighter, instinctively knowing it was the right decision. She would need her friend's help to get out of this path she had furrowed. It was long and deep, and she would need Anya's guidance to navigate an escape, but her faith in her friend was strong. They'd been there for each other throughout their careers and would continue to be, whichever way their lives moved. It was a promise they'd made years ago and one they renewed annually, usually with a bottle of champagne or two. Hero had kept things from Anya, just as she had kept things from everyone. That was going to change. This spa break was the first step in a new direction. It was scary, but Anya would be there, and Hero knew she wouldn't let her fall.

Her friend stretched, as much as someone her height could in the small car. 'I do see what you meant about it perhaps being not so great for longer journeys. Perhaps you need another car for these?'

Hero raised her brows. 'It's hard enough finding space to park one vehicle anywhere remotely near the apartment in London, let alone two.'

'Yes. I suppose that would be true. I know. Next time we do this, we'll call a limo. Have someone else take us there. Not only will we have a little more room, but we will also be able to start on the champagne earlier!'

'Now that,' Hero replied, 'sounds like a very good idea.'

'It's a deal then.'

'Absolutely. Not long now though, the turning for the hotel is just another mile or so.'

'Yay!' Anya cheered. 'Hot tub here we come!'

They never saw what hit them. Lights blinded. Anya screamed. Tyres squealed. Metal collided, twisted and groaned. The car spun again and again, Anya's cry piercing through once more. They hit something. Hard. The spinning stopped immediately. Abruptly. And so did Anya's scream.

Hero sat in the dark, eerie hush and felt something wet running down her face. Pouring in through the shattered glass, the rain was making her legs and face wet. She tried blinking the liquid from her eyes but still it kept coming. Her head pounding, she called Anya's name, trying to twist around in the buckled seat. There was no reply. Hero cried out again, fear cracking her voice. Nothing. She strained to try and see her passenger. Her best friend. It was impossible. Her own body was pinned close to the dashboard, her legs immoveable among the mangled wreck of metal that had once been a pristine little sports car. Struggling, she finally managed to free one hand and reached out, feeling beside her in the cold, dark silence until she found Anya's hand and held it tight.

'It's all right, Anya. I can hear somebody coming. We'll be out soon.'

Anya didn't answer. Pain and fear built within Hero's own body and she felt herself sinking down into the horror, afraid that she might drown in it if she allowed her eyes to close as they so desperately wanted to. Forcing them to stay open and holding tightly to Anya's hand, she couldn't understand why the voices were taking so long to come nearer. She knew she was losing the fight and her chest heaved as thoughts of those few people she loved filled her mind. Hero closed her eyes, letting the darkness envelop her, the voices drifting away until there was nothing.

Chapter 10

The paramedics hurried through the doors of the Accident and Emergency Department, running alongside the trolley they had just brought in.

'What have we got?' Dr Jacobs asked, looking down at the silent figure they wheeled in. A drip was already in place, and a collar had been fitted around her neck. The features were almost totally obscured by blood.

'RTA. Head on with a lorry and another car. Looks like the truck had a blow-out and crossed the reservation straight into their path. We'd have had to get the air ambulance out if the hospital hadn't been so close.'

Jacobs nodded. 'Take her straight up.'

The medic continued his hand-over. 'She was unconscious when we got there. Took a while for the fire crews to cut her out. Injuries to the head and face, possible internal bleeding, broken left humerus, possible damage to the ulna.' The medic paused for breath as they manoeuvred the patient into the lift that would take them up three floors to the trauma suite, x-ray, and operating rooms.

'She also has an open fracture of her right tibia, fibula and femur.' He glanced back across at the doctor. 'Whole leg's a bit of a mess really.'

'Have we got a name?'

'She's wearing a bracelet with the name "Hero" engraved on it. I'm guessing it's that.'

The doctor paused at the unusual name. 'As in "Much Ado About Nothing"?'

The paramedic shrugged. 'If you say so.'

The lift pinged, announcing its arrival. The doors opened and a medical trauma team, already prepped for surgery, met them. The paramedics relinquished their duty as the team swarmed around the trolley, disappearing into the emergency suite. A triage nurse waved the paramedic crew over to her desk.

'Do you have any more details?' she asked.

'Only these. One of the firemen picked them up as they were cutting her free.'

He handed over two portfolio cases. The nurse unzipped the first leather folder. The medics leaned in to see what it contained. Inside were photographs and tear sheets from magazines featuring a tall, long-legged brunette with a sultry smile and hypnotic green eyes. The nurse flipped through the pages silently before unzipping the second portfolio case. It contained similar pages, but this time a Nordic-looking blonde gazed out at them, complete with perfect cheekbones and stunning figure.

'They're models?' The medic stated, trying to reconcile the photographs in front of him with the broken body they had just rushed into surgery.

The nurse frowned as she registered his words. 'They? They were both in the car?'

The medic nodded.

'Where's the other one?' she asked, already fearing the answer.

A second nurse joined them, dishing out mugs of instant coffee to her colleagues. As she did so, she caught a glance at the portfolio open on the desk. 'Oh wow. Hero Scott. She's stunning. God, I wish I looked like that!'

All three turned their heads at her comment. 'What?' she asked, frowning.

'Do you recognise this one too?' The older nurse asked, holding up a page of the blonde's collection.

'Of course. That's Anya Svenson. She and Hero just signed a huge cosmetics deal together.' She glanced again at the portfolios and frowned. 'How did you get these?'

***

On the other side of the world a telephone's shrill call broke the silence of the night. Pete shoved a hand out from under the duvet to silence it. Missing the handset, he caught the lamp instead, knocking it to the floor.

'Bugger.'

The noise continued.

'Are you going to answer that?' Juliet's muffled voice grumbled from the pillow.

'I'm trying!' he whispered loudly, despite the fact he was fairly sure the kids would be awake by now anyway.

'Put the light on, for God's sake.'

'I can't. It's on the floor.' Pete snatched again blindly in the dark and made another unsuccessful grasp for the receiver. As he waved his hand for another swipe, the noise stopped. A second later a knock on the door was swiftly followed by Nick entering his brother's bedroom without waiting for an answer. Beneath his tan, Nick's expression was as pale as the moonlight that illuminated him.

'There's a Dr Penland from London on the phone. It's Hero. She's been in an accident.'

Half an hour later Juliet sat at the kitchen table in shock. As Pete suspected, the children had indeed woken, and after a while, two sets of little feet padded downstairs.

'What's going on?' they asked, rubbing their eyes sleepily.

Nick glanced at Juliet. She opened her mouth, but shock had robbed her of words. Instead she just tightened the white knuckle grip she had on her husband's hand. Pete exchanged a look with his brother. Nick nodded and left the room, chivvying the children up the stairs in front of him.

'Why is Mummy crying?' Bridie asked as her uncle tucked her back in to bed.

'She's fine, sweetheart. Nothing to worry about,' Nick replied, in what he hoped was a reassuring tone before going on to tuck Marcus in too. He could only wish and hope it was the truth. Juliet hadn't been making a lot of sense, but they'd seen the look on her face as she'd listened to the doctor. Whatever he'd been saying, it wasn't good.

Nick closed the door to the children's bedroom and waited outside for a few beats, listening for any movement but the kids were both asleep almost before he'd left the room. Slowly he descended the stairs, making his way to where Jules now sat, white-faced and red-eyed at the kitchen table.

'Is Hero OK?'

Juliet opened her mouth to speak but the words refused to come.

'Come on, love, it'll help,' Pete said, encouraging her to take a little more of the brandy he'd poured.

With a shaking hand, Juliet took the glass and forced some of the warming liquid down. Nick waited as Pete sat, his hand still in his wife's vice-like grip.

'We're not sure, mate.'

Nick stared at his brother, then glanced across at Juliet. She took another sip of the brandy, as the blood in his own veins turned icy. Pete, although down to earth, was also the family optimist. The fact that he hadn't answered a simple 'yes' spoke volumes.

'It's pretty bad,' he continued, his voice low. 'They've operated but the next forty-eight hours are crucial.'

Nick took the brandy his brother held out, leaning on the table for support as he did so. Finishing the shot, he moved and placed a kiss on the top of his sister-in-law's head.

'I have to go,' Juliet announced, stirring Pete and Nick from their own silent thoughts. 'I have to be there. I have to be with her.'

'If that's what you want.' Pete squeezed his wife's hand.

'But the children—'

'We'll sort it. Mum and Dad will come out and help for as long as they need to.'

Juliet ran a hand over her temple. 'I can't just sit here, waiting for the phone to ring. Waiting for them to tell me she's …' She didn't voice the final word, as though afraid that by saying, she might make it true. Pete moved his chair closer to his wife's and gently pulled her out of it onto his lap and into the protective shelter of his embrace. Juliet buried her head in his shoulder, sobbing once more with such feeling it ripped at Pete's very core. Rocking her gently, he made soothing noises as his own mind whirled.

How could this be happening?

He stroked his wife's hair as he gently rocked her. Juliet and Hero, through their parents' disinterest, had forged a bond that tied them to each other irrevocably. If Hero didn't pull through this, Pete worried what that could do to his wife. Resting his chin gently on Juliet's head, he let out a long breath as he thought about the young woman lying broken in a hospital bed. She might act aloof, but Pete knew there was a lot more below that surface than she made out. He'd seen the look on her face when she thought no one could see. There was a lot more loneliness and fragility to his sister-in-law than she'd ever confess to, and that worried him. Hero was in a bad way. Would she have the strength, the willpower, the wish to fight for her life? Within his arms he felt Juliet shuddering as the tears flowed again. Holding her a little tighter, he raised his gaze and saw his brother sat at the table, his expression dazed and numb. Silently, he willed Hero to fight like he knew she could. She had to. Her life literally depended on it – and although she may not know it, so did others.

***

Nick sat staring at the screen, his face lit by the eerie blue-white light of the computer, the only illumination in the dark panelled study.

'Anything?' Pete asked.

Nick jumped. He'd been so absorbed in his own thoughts he hadn't heard his brother enter the room. Pete walked up and stood at Nick's shoulder.

'Um. Yeah. Some. Where's Jules?' Nick asked.

'Lying down in the living room, clutching the phone like her life depends on it. Or Hero's.'

Nick's stomach churned and roiled. Pete ruffled his brother's hair, a gesture he hadn't made for years. The tenderness of the moment set free a tear that rolled slowly down Nick's face. He was staring at the screen, but his mind was elsewhere. Pete squeezed his little brother's shoulder. He guessed the one thing running through Nick's mind was that the last words he'd spoken to Hero had been hurtful and cold.

She'd been due to fly over next week for a month's break, before she began shooting on a new contract and Pete knew his brother had been rehearsing how to apologise almost since the moment she'd left. But instead she was lying in a hospital intensive care unit, on the other side of the world, closer to death than to life. What scared Nick the most was that he might never get the opportunity to tell her how sorry he was and how much she really meant to him.

'So, what did you find?' Pete said, pulling a chair across to sit next to his brother.

'This one's probably the best.' Nick pointed to some flight

details on the screen. 'Qantas, via Melbourne. Leaving tomorrow morning. There's still a few seats left. Do you want me to book one?'

'Yep. Jules will be better off with her sister, whatever. I'll ring Mum in a couple of hours and get them to come and stay to look after the kids. I've no idea how long she'll be gone, but Mum'll understand.'

Nick nodded numbly. He clicked with the mouse and began filling in the details on the booking page of the website. 'I need your credit card.'

***

Juliet handed over the fare and exited the black cab. She was shocked at the amount of reporters camped out around the hospital. She knew her sister was high profile but until this moment, she hadn't understood quite how high. Suddenly, the cool persona that Hero presented made a lot more sense. And, with the accident happening within hours of the press conference for a mould-breaking cosmetics deal, the media had pounced.

Juliet entered the hospital without incident. Hero had always been careful to avoid any involvement of Juliet in her professional life. She knew the tabloids loved to look for any angle on a celebrity and it didn't matter who they used or destroyed in the process. Hero was vehement that she would not subject her sister or her family to that sort of exposure and she'd made good on that promise. Glancing at the gathering outside, Juliet realised that couldn't have been easy. Guilt gnawed at her as she made these discoveries. She'd thought Hero had just been protecting herself, and of course she had been. But she'd been protecting those she loved as well. Until that moment, Juliet hadn't understood just how much. She stopped at the elegant reception desk and asked directions to Hero Scott's room.

The receptionist's face was expressionless. 'I'm sure you

understand that a lot of people have been requesting to see Miss Scott. Could I ask your name and your relationship to Miss Scott please?'

Juliet blinked and stared for a moment. It was only then that she became aware of two large men dressed in dark suits and wearing radio earpieces waiting by the door. Security. Yet another reminder of why Hero had withdrawn behind a mask of indifference if this was how she had to live her life. Or end it.

'My name is Juliet Webster. I'm Hero Scott's sister. The hospital rang me.'

The receptionist nodded as if to say, 'Is that the best you can do?'

'I see.' The woman shuffled some papers and seemed to be making no move to accept the story.

A bundle of pure exhaustion and shock and fear, Juliet cracked. 'We had a call from Dr Penland to tell me there had been an accident and that my sister might die. I've just stepped off a bloody long flight and I'd rather be with her than standing here talking to you so if you can stop just bloody faffing around, I want to see her. Now!' Juliet drew breath and knew she probably looked a state after all the travelling, not to mention now stood here yelling like a fishwife. Quite the opposite of Hero's signature serenity and elegance. She didn't care. All she wanted was to be with her baby sister.

'Just a moment please, Mrs Webster.'

Juliet stepped back from the desk, taking the passport she had slammed down as identification with her. She closed her eyes and took a couple of deep breaths. God, how she wished Pete were here with her. But they had decided that it would be better if he stayed at the station with the kids, and Nick. Her in-laws should be there by now and they really didn't want to upset the children any more than they already were. Their father staying with them gave it all some sense of normality, however engineered that may be.

'Mrs Webster? I'm Dr Penland.' A man who looked to be in his early forties with a kind face held out his hand. Juliet shook it, accepting his request to accompany him. As Juliet entered her sister's room, she was glad the doctor was with her. Despite all the images and fears her own mind had conjured in the hours since they'd had that dreadful call, Juliet was still completely unprepared for the sight that met her. She'd never seen so many tubes and machines. A framework was over the lower half of the bed, keeping the linen off Hero's legs. Beeps and whooshes from the machinery were the only noises. And there, in among all the electronics and mechanics lay her little sister, broken and bruised. Juliet's knees buckled. The doctor steadied her, then pulled a chair across, easing her into it as he motioned to a nurse for a glass of water.

'Thank you.' Juliet's voice was barely audible.

She hadn't taken her eyes off the figure in the bed. Pulling the chair closer, she gently took one of Hero's hands in her own, careful to avoid the canula secured in the back of it. Her skin was soft and cool. She smiled through the tears that were now streaming silently down her face. Hero's hands were always cold. 'Cold hands, warm heart,' she'd always said, and no matter what the appearance, Juliet knew that was absolutely true.

'Is she going to be all right?' Juliet managed eventually.

The doctor shifted his focus from the patient to her sister. This was never easy.

'She's held her own so far. That's a good sign, but she's not out of the woods yet. We did a brain scan when she was brought in because of the head trauma but it came back clear. She was very lucky in that respect.'

'But the bandages?'

'Your sister suffered head and facial lacerations during the impact. The deeper ones have had to be stitched but we've used hair ties for the more superficial ones on her head wherever possible to minimise scarring. Most of the facial ones will fade in time too. The most serious one, as you can see, is the one across her forehead.'

Juliet looked at the line of neat stitches that stretched from the centre of Hero's forehead across and down to her cheekbone.

'The laceration there was far deeper than the others, but I called in a plastic surgeon colleague of mine who has the highest reputation to assist me on this. As far as we can see, it doesn't seem to have damaged any muscles or nerves. It will fade over time, but its severity does means that it will be more visible than some of the others.'

Juliet stared at her sister's face. What wasn't covered in stitches or gauze was purple with bruising. She knew what the doctor was saying, as kindly as he could, knowing that she would in turn have to deliver the message to her sister. Hero's career, one based purely on looks, was over. That glittering, shallow world wouldn't wait for her injuries to heal, or accept that that perfect face, lean and lithe body was now damaged, probably irreparably. All that was gone.

'What else?' Juliet forced herself to ask, drying her eyes on a handkerchief with one hand as the other held tightly to Hero.

'She suffered internal bleeding, but we luckily managed to control that quite quickly. She has a broken left arm. The other main injury is to her leg. I'm afraid it was broken in several places. We've put pins in to help it mend but it'll be a while before she can walk on it again. She's going to need a lot of physiotherapy. It's quite possible that she'll always need to walk with a stick, but it's impossible to say for sure at this point. Different people heal differently. She was fit and healthy before the accident, I understand?' Juliet nodded. 'The muscle tone on the other leg is good. It's really a case of wait and see.'

Juliet thought of Hero's graceful, serene walk, the way they had chased around with the children after Christmas lunch just a couple of months ago, the unrestrained joy in her sister's face and the laughter that accompanied it. Dr Penland laid a gentle hand on her shoulder as her tears ran freely again. She barely noticed him withdraw from the room, quietly closing the door behind him.

It was three more days before Hero's vital signs stabilised and three more after that before she opened her eyes and looked blankly at her sister. Her brain, fuzzy with medication, tried to make sense of where she was and why Juliet was there holding her hand, looking pale and drawn.

'What happened?' she whispered eventually. Her voice was dry and weak.

'There was an accident, sweetheart. A lorry blew out a tyre and crossed the central reservation onto your side of the road. It hit your car into another one.'

There was no flicker of recognition on Hero's face. Dr Penland entered the room, catching the conversation. Juliet looked at him, confusion and worry in her eyes. He answered her unasked question as he made some checks on his patient.

'It's quite normal for some amnesia following a trauma. Sometimes it comes back, sometimes it doesn't.'

Hero blinked with tired, drugged eyes. 'Trauma?'

Juliet stroked the dark hair. 'It's all right, darling. Everything's all right,' she soothed as Hero drifted back to sleep. But Juliet knew that was a lie. Everything wasn't all right. Apart from Hero's own injuries which she was clearly still unaware of, and the likely sudden end of her modelling career, Juliet had to find a way to tell her sister that Anya, Hero's best friend and ally, hadn't survived the accident. Jules knew that would be the hardest thing she had ever had to say to anyone – and she worried that receiving that news could send Hero straight back on to the critical list.

It took a few more days for Hero to awaken enough for any real conversation to take place, but once she was lucid enough, Juliet broke the news about Anya. Hero's good friend, Rupert, had been in and out all of the time, checking on her, keeping a lid on the media's hounding. He was as devastated about Anya as they both knew Hero would be, but had agreed that the news was probably best coming from Juliet.

Hero listened to the words her sister spoke, feeling dazed and confused. It couldn't be true. The many medications she was on must have affected her understanding. It was impossible that Anya was gone. But the look on her sister's face told her it was true. She lay there, staring at the ceiling, waiting for the tears to come, wishing for them in the hope that they would take away some of the pain that squeezed her heart until she felt it might burst. But her eyes remained dry.

***

Juliet had been in England for three weeks when the man knocked on the door to the private room. Hero was sitting in bed, propped up on pillows and staring at a daytime television show rather than the ceiling for a change, trying to decide which was more entertaining.

The visitor made to enter before stopping short. Juliet saw his eyes take in the damage to Hero's face and body and the shock at seeing it showed clearly on his own face. Quickly, he made an effort to cover it, giving them both what was clearly a practised smile. Juliet was unsure whether to return it.

Hero spoke first. 'Hello Jonathan.'

Juliet took the opportunity to excuse herself. 'I'll just—'

'No!' He held out a hand, palm towards her, then glanced briefly at Hero, his eyes unable to linger there. 'I didn't realise you had company. I'll come back later.'

But Hero had seen it. That look in his eyes. He'd seen the metal framework piercing her leg, the plaster cast on her arm, the stitches on her face and the short fuzzy patches on her head where yet more stitches hid. But he hadn't seen Hero. It was all so obvious to her now.

'No, you won't,' Hero stated softly, her tone flat.

Guilt flushed the man's face. She held his gaze a moment longer then looked back towards the television, a sign for him to leave. Making no objection, he stepped back and, in her peripheral vision, Hero saw the door close. His feet had never even crossed the threshold.

Juliet retook her seat, frowning at her sister. 'Who was that?'

'Boyfriend, I suppose you would call him,' Hero answered, her voice empty of emotion. 'Or rather ex-boyfriend as it would appear.'

'You didn't give him much of a chance, darling.' Juliet was, as usual, ready to see everyone's point of view, but her mind was also still trying to align the word 'boyfriend' with the man she'd just seem. Expensively dressed, elegant and well spoken, the visitor had to be at least twenty-five years older than her sister. Hero had never mentioned him. Juliet hadn't even known Hero was seeing anyone.

'He wasn't looking for a chance, Jules.' Hero flicked off the TV with the remote and turned back to her sister. There was a strange expression on her face. 'I was a trophy, that's all. He's twenty-seven years older than me but he's successful, dresses nicely, keeps himself fit and was nice to me. It was a suitable arrangement for both of us.' Hero turned her attention to the sheet over her, smoothing it unnecessarily with her one able hand, unable to bear the expression on her sister's face.

'The accident altered the arrangement. I wouldn't have expected him to stay.' Hero gave a shrug automatically, wincing as pain shot through her.

Juliet's green eyes were wide in amazement, and concern. 'It sounds more like a business arrangement than a relationship, Hero.'

'I suppose it was in a way,' she replied, refusing to meet her sister's eyes.

Juliet felt the sadness within her, and guilt that she shared such love with Pete when her sister was so very lonely. At that moment, more than anything, she wanted her husband's strong arms around her.

'Did you sleep with him?'

Hero rolled her eyes then stopped mid-roll when it hurt. Everything bloody hurt.

'Sometimes.' Finally, she met her sister's gaze. 'Don't look at me like that.'

'Like what?'

'Disapproving.'

'I'm not!'

'Yes, you are. You're as bad as Rupert. I don't expect you to understand, Jules. It doesn't matter now anyway. I won't be seeing him again.'

Juliet stared. It all seemed so cold, so matter-of-fact. She knew her sister and, however she acted, this wasn't her. Not really. Juliet knew that behind what the public saw, she didn't truly have the cool, detached personality required for such an arrangement.

'Did you love him?'

'No,' Hero replied softly. 'But he was nice. I liked him and we had fun.'

'Don't you want more than that?'

'What else is there?'

'Love.'

Hero shifted in the bed. Her rear was sore from sitting in the same position. She took hold of her sister's hand and touched the simple gold band on her finger.

'Not everyone gets what you and Pete have, Jules. It's beautiful. You can see the love in your eyes, and in his. He'll look at you in the pub when it's heaving with people and it's like you two are the only ones in the room. It's precious.' She smiled but there was so much sadness in that smile, Juliet's heart nearly broke. 'Not everyone gets that lucky, or is that privileged.'

Juliet laid her other hand over Hero's. Her sister was right; what she and Pete had was wonderful. Hero had used the right word. They were incredibly privileged to share what they did, and they knew it. She missed him so much.

'That doesn't mean you should give up.'

'You don't miss what you've never had.'

'I don't believe that and neither do you.' Juliet's voice was firmer now. Suddenly she was furious at Hero for wasting her life like that, letting a man use her like some bimbo.

But her sister's comment had given her away. The mask was slipping. Perhaps it was already gone, shattered at the moment of impact like so much else. Juliet realised the truth. Hero wanted love just like everybody else but the fear of being rejected had won. She was too afraid of losing love to ever let herself find it.

In the days and weeks following the accident, Hero didn't have the energy or the ability to provide herself with the mental armour she had created before. Juliet stayed with her, taking her for walks around the hospital after they had begged the doctors to let her exchange her bed for a wheelchair, just a few moments of freedom and fresh air. Juliet was her shield now.

Hero envied her sister's ability to interact with others so easily and make friends. Hero had been surrounded by people in her career, but she knew the truth. They weren't friends. Most were acquaintances, nothing more. They had sent flowers but not visited. The bouquets were, of course, delivered by hand. All those beautiful people, doing their best to avert their face from the press whilst still ensuring that the cameras got their best side.

Jonathan had come, that was true. She still wasn't sure why. Maybe she had been hard on him as Juliet had said, but she'd seen the look on his face when he had seen the changes in hers. She didn't want to give him the chance to tell her that she had been a mistake for him too. Juliet had been accurate in her observation – what they'd had wasn't really a relationship, not in the way Juliet had, or in the way Hero really wanted.

There were constant requests for visitors throughout the time

Juliet stayed with her sister, and Rupert had been a godsend when it came to deciding who received permission, which was very few, and who was turned away. He knew who came because they cared and who had come to make themselves the centre of attention, or to collect fodder for gossip columns.

Juliet had met Rupert a few times before when she'd lived in London and been inordinately glad to see him when he'd burst in through the door to Hero's hospital room a few hours after Juliet had arrived. He had been buried in meetings in New York when his secretary had finally managed to reach him with the news of the accident. He'd left there and then, taking the first flight he could get back to London.

Hero had been quiet at the hospital since Jonathan's visit. She'd actually been a little surprised at seeing him at all. Rupert had never approved of the situation. He felt, as Juliet did, that Hero was no more than decoration which annoyed him, knowing that she was so much more than just a pretty face. However unhappy Rupert had been to put Jonathan on the approved list of visitors, he'd felt that Hero may want to see him which overruled his own gut. However, once he heard how the meeting ensued, and Jonathan's barely concealed repugnance, Rupert went through the roof and Hero, startled at his strength of feeling, made him promise not to punch him when he voiced a desire to. His anger only increased when he saw Jonathan two days later at a function, now with a true bimbo on his arm. It was only his love and respect for Hero that made him walk away. Of course, he hadn't promised not to get the louse blacklisted from every good restaurant and influential party for the foreseeable future, so that would have to do. For the moment at least.

Chapter 11

When Juliet came back from the garden area, where she'd been Skyping Pete and the children, Hero was lying in the bed, staring at all the flower bouquets now filling her room.

'Everything OK?' Hero asked as she came in.

'Yes. Biscuit stole a sausage sandwich Nick had made for his lunch yesterday, which the children found hilarious.'

The smirk on Hero's face indicated that her sister agreed.

'Jules, would you mind passing me the cards from the bouquets, please?'

Juliet scooped up the pile and handed them over. Hero took them, reading them silently. She smiled briefly a couple of times then stopped.

'Nick sent flowers?' she asked, looking up from the small card with a mixture of surprise and pleasure.

'Mm-hmm. He rang to ask me what your favourites were.'

Hero stared for a moment then nodded faintly, her throat too constricted to reply in words. Juliet put Nick's flowers on the table where Hero could see them properly. She touched the blooms and couldn't help but think of the man who had sent them as she returned her attention to the card in her hand.

Dear Hero, I'm pretty rubbish at saying the right thing as you know, and I'm sorry we parted like we did. I should never have said that stuff. I really am sorry. Hope you like the flowers and we're all looking forward to your next visit. I'm not going to say I know what you're going through – I don't. I can't even begin to know that. But I do know you're an incredible woman and that you can get through it. We're all here for you, and always will be. Love Nick (and Biscuit). xxx

Juliet watched as her sister read. Nick and Hero always managed to rub each other up the wrong way during her visits but she got the feeling that both still looked forward to the confrontations. Hero was accustomed to people, especially men, succumbing to her every whim, whether she asked them to or not. Nick didn't succumb to anyone's whim. He wasn't built that way, and Hero wasn't used to that. It meant she had to make an effort, and Nick could tell when she was genuinely interested in something and, at those times, his attention was boundless. If he sensed the opposite, he wouldn't waste either of their time.

But for the most part, Hero was interested. She loved watching Nick and Joe training the new horses, joining the ride out to check fences, and laughing at the dogs as they bounded across the backs of the sheep. And Nick loved showing Hero different aspects of the station, loved that she was interested unlike some of the women he'd spent time with. They didn't care about how the property was a success so long as it was.

They all noticed that Hero's mask of indifference occasionally slipped when she and Nick talked about the station, but it was never discarded for long once the conversation changed to other subjects. Juliet had seen the frustration in her brother-in-law's eyes at the continual shutting out, and she understood it. Nick wasn't the only one Hero shut out. Despite accusing Nick of scaring Hero off at Christmas, she didn't blame him, although she had been unable to stop Nick blaming himself, even more so since the accident. Juliet had been worried when Hero happened to let slip that Anya had been planning to move back to Sweden. Knowing that Hero would once again be living alone, knowing how unhappy she had been before, had concerned Juliet no end.

Two neat piles of cards now sat on the adjustable table next to Hero's bed. One comprised those from her sister, Pete and the children, the one from Nick and another from Juliet's in-laws as well as a funny, not to mention rude, one from Rupert involving a comment about hospital gowns. She leaned over and dropped the rest in the bin.

'Jules,' she said, looking up, 'would you be able to do something for me?'

Half an hour later, two black cabs sat outside the hospital, each packed with bouquets. Juliet instructed one to take its contents to the hospice Hero had often passed when she'd taken her early morning walks. Juliet had had to explain the area she meant, as Hero hadn't been able to remember the name. The driver nodded.

'I know the one,' he replied, glancing at his fare. 'These will certainly bring a few smiles.'

Juliet thanked and paid him then turned to the other driver, asking him to deliver his flowers to the Royal Hospital at Chelsea. Hopefully the flowers would bring smiles to the faces of the scarlet-coated pensioners too.

While Juliet took care of the donations, Hero sat alone in her room, bereft of flowers now, except for the few bouquets she had chosen to keep, knowing that those had been sent from the heart. She picked up Nick's card again, looking down at the words, written by a stranger in a London florist, and ran her finger over the text before folding her hand around it. It was still there when Juliet returned from downstairs as Hero drifted back into the drug induced sleep that helped dull her pain.

It was another week before Hero finally managed to convince

her sister she was fine. She would still be in the hospital a while yet, but she was healing, even if it was frustratingly slow, and Rupert was visiting every day even though she'd told him not to. Pete and the children needed Juliet far more than she did now.

'Don't you ever cry?' Juliet asked when she pulled back from her third attempt at a goodbye embrace.

'Sign of weakness, Scott!' Hero half smiled as she impersonated their old headmistress.

Back at school after her mother's shocking disclosure, this cold, sharp-featured woman had found Hero sitting alone and crying. There was no attempt at understanding or comfort. Instead, she had unceremoniously dragged the child back to her office and given six swipes of the cane across her palms. The charge had been self-indulgence. Hero had never cried since. But Juliet wasn't smiling at her sister's mickey take.

'Why were you crying that day? You've never told me.'

Hero rested back against the pillows her sister had now plumped three times in the last five minutes. Jules was right. She'd never told anyone – except Nick Webster.

'Does it really matter now?'

'It does to me.'

Ordinarily, Hero would have evaded the question, or batted it away with a change of subject but, now, for some reason she didn't want to. Or perhaps it was just that she no longer had the energy to.

'Did you know I was a mistake?' she asked as Juliet perched on the very side of the bed, careful not to knock her sister's injuries accidentally.

'A mistake?'

'Yes.'

'No. I mean, our parents weren't exactly the warm and fuzzy kind, but I don't think they ever considered you a mistake.'

Hero smiled and the sadness it contained broke her sister's heart.

'Do you remember that day you came home and I was clearing up broken china?'

'Yes. With your hands! And you had a big shard of it stuck in your palm.'

'I did. But my big sister took care of it.'

Juliet placed her palm gently against Hero's undamaged cheek, who moved, accepting the touch as she closed her eyes.

'What about it?'

Hero took a deep breath and relayed the circumstances that had led to the splinter, and to the cane. As she finished, Juliet's tears were flowing once more.

'Why did you never tell me?'

'There was nothing you could do, and I knew it would upset you, just as it has now.'

Juliet shook her head. 'Please. Never do that again. Never try to protect me. I want to know, even if I can't help. Please!'

Hero nodded her agreement, passing her sister another tissue from the box sat on her table.

'I can't believe you've been carrying that alone all these years.'

'Not quite all of them.'

Juliet paused in wiping her eyes. 'You told someone else?'

Hero gave a brief, but awkward smile. 'The last person I thought I would really.'

Her sister frowned.

'Nick.'

'Our Nick?'

Hero nodded. 'I know. It surprised me just as much.'

'When?'

'The evening of your wedding. I was feeling a bit overwhelmed, and after a dance we went outside for a bit, just to get some air. I don't really know how or why, but I ended up telling him this secret I'd managed to keep hidden for so long. I'm assuming, by your reaction, he's never said anything.'

'No,' Juliet replied. 'But then I wouldn't expect him to. As far as Nick is concerned, and as crazy as you seem to make each other, there's no way he'd break a confidence like that.' She stroked her sister's dark hair. 'I'm glad you told someone. I only wish it had been sooner.'

'There was nothing you could have done.'

'No. But still …'

'I know. And I'm sorry.'

'Oh, my darling, there's nothing you need to be sorry about. I can't believe that woman' – in her fury, Juliet couldn't even bring herself to refer to her as Mother – 'could be so utterly, utterly callous. She didn't deserve such a beautiful daughter like you.'

Hero held tight in her sister's embrace. 'She didn't deserve either of us.'

'You know, it is OK for you to show your emotions to cry. No one will judge you now.'

'I know. I think … I don't know. I guess I just got out of the habit.'

'It might help.'

Hero returned her sister's sad smile. 'I keep telling myself that. But they still won't come. I only wish they would.'

Juliet held her tight, the gesture saying more than any words could, before finally leaving. Rupert had arranged a private car to take her there and upgraded her ticket, as requested by Hero, to first class. After everything she had done for her, throughout her life, not just since the accident, Hero felt she had a lot of making up to do. She knew she'd never be able to repay her entirely, but she would do what she could, whenever she could.

Hero gave a small wave, watching her sister disappear through the door back to her own life, her own family. Back to Pete and the children – and Nick. His image in her mind brought Juliet's earlier comment about relationships, and more specifically love, flooding back to her.

That doesn't mean you shouldn't try.

The words echoed around in her head as Hero closed her eyes and remembered the effect that Nick had on her every time he touched her, however innocent that touch, every time he even just looked at her. How she had wanted to try – almost had – all those years ago. But, lying in her bed that night, still able to feel the touch of his hand, the solid feel of his body as she'd lain against him, both looking up at the stars, the doubts had crept in. She'd been a mistake to someone before. What if Nick, in the clear light of the morning, no longer shared that same want? Seeing rejection in his eyes as she had seen in her mother's had driven her back, made her run every time he got too close. But now, as she lay in the quiet room, alone once more, another thought broke free. Was it just a fear of rejection that had scared her, or was it something else altogether? Had it really been the possibility that Nick actually did feel the same as she did that frightened her?

Hero pushed down with her arms, positioning herself straighter. Even that small effort was exhausting. Pausing for a moment to gather her breath and strength for the next step, she looked down at her leg, still a mass of dressing and pins, the other undamaged but wasting, the muscle tone already gone. Reaching across to the side table, her hand closed around the item and she brought it back, laid it in front of her momentarily. It had been sitting there for a week now, taunting her with what it would reveal. Juliet had tried to encourage her to do it before she left, but Hero knew this was a step she needed to take alone. Carefully, she turned the mirror and brought it slowly up to her face.

Hero stared at the reflection. She felt strange, almost detached from the image she saw there, as if it wasn't her. But it was. The realisation seeped in. This. This was what she now looked like. Would look like. This was why Jonathan had fled. And why they'd kept the mirrors away from her initially.

She wanted to put the mirror down, but she couldn't. It was as though someone else held it there, forcing her to see her true self. For once. Small cuts were dotted around her face, healing now with dark red crusts. Glass cuts, she suspected. Vaguely she remembered Dr Penland explaining things to her, but she hadn't been ready to see anything then. She ran a hand over a patch on her head. The precisely cut, always shining hair now hung limply past her shoulders, and in places all that was left was a fuzzy dark patch, the skin underneath stitched. Slowly Hero focused back on her face. Her eyes were sunken, rimmed with dark shadows and fading bruises and her skin, once creamy, now looked pale and drawn. And then there was the scar. A long, angry line stretched across her forehead down her temple where it was joined by another from her cheekbone. She touched it gently. The skin around it was still swollen, even now, although there were no actual stitches visible. The plastic surgeon who'd assisted with her surgery had removed the outer stitches a few days after the accident when Hero had still been barely conscious. Juliet had told her that he'd explained that he'd stitched deeply first, and those would dissolve in time. Removing the external ones early meant that she should have a neater result in time, without the cross lines that were common in many scars.

Hero replaced the mirror. The worst was over now. At least now she knew. The life she'd known until now was over. Juliet hadn't said it in so many words, probably because she hadn't known how, but the career she'd built for the last fifteen years was over. In one split second, her life had changed irrevocably and her best friend's had ended. If only they had left five minutes earlier. Or five minutes later. What if ... Hero closed her eyes. There was no point in going down that road. There was no what if. There was only now.

She thought back to what Juliet had said shortly before she left, about having Hero out to stay with them for a while, once she was well enough to travel. There was plenty of room and they'd love to have her, especially the children. Pete had commissioned a swimming pool for Juliet's birthday last year, and her sister had emphasised how beneficial swimming would be in rehabilitation for Hero's leg, an opinion backed up by her doctor.

Hero turned and looked at the mirror, now lying face down on the side table once more. She made her decision. As much as she wanted, and likely needed, to be with Juliet, she wouldn't go. Not now she knew. She was only just holding on as it was. The thought of seeing the same look on Nick's face that she had witnessed on Jonathan's would break her entirely.

***

The summer months passed but Hero barely noticed them. The doctors had given her a worst-case scenario in regards to her leg but she was determined to prove them wrong; she would walk without a cane.

The physiotherapist assigned to her was pleasantly surprised by Hero, vowing to always think twice now about believing what she read. Instead of the prima donna she had been expecting, she found a rather shy, likeable woman with a determination that belied her fragile looks. That same determination sometimes pushed Hero to try too hard and the physio had to convince her patient on a regular basis that she literally had to walk before she could run. Her weary body demanded rest. Disregarding that would only undo all the good work they had already accomplished.

Hero watched the raindrops race each other down the windowpanes. Focusing past them, she gazed down at the Kensington street. Pavements shone with the downpour and people raced past, their faces shielded by umbrellas of varying hues. Rupert was in California on business and Hero was now half regretting rejecting his offer to accompany him. At least the weather would have been an improvement. But she still didn't feel up to seeing people. Not yet. She had no idea what to say to people who didn't know her and asked what she did for a living. Or to the people who knew her background and who, in turn, still had no idea what to say. Her career had defined her. Now that it was gone, there was no definition, no structure to her life. Every day she found herself staying in bed longer and longer. What was the point of getting up? She had nowhere to be, nothing she had to do. She couldn't remember exactly when she had stopped bothering to get dressed, but as with a lot of things now, all she could think was, *what's the point*?

She'd rowed with Rupert a few weeks ago about that particular subject, his frustration with her evident as he'd told her flat out that she might feel better if she at least took a little pride in her appearance. Hero called it a row, although in truth she hadn't made much contribution to the actual conversation excepting a non-committal shoulder shrug. She hated seeing him upset, especially knowing how incredible he'd been after the accident, taking care of not only her, but also making sure Juliet ate and slept as much as she should. But just getting dressed wasn't going to make any of this go away. People kept telling her things would become easier with time, but it wasn't getting easier. It was painful and raw.

Hero wrapped her hands around the mug of steaming hot chocolate and took a sip, its heat warming her from the inside. Turning away from the window, she caught sight of the photographs on a side table. There were several of Juliet, Pete, and the kids; one of her and Nick that Juliet had snuck when he was showing her a Brumby they were about to break in. Hero's eyes rested on the next photo. It showed her and Anya standing on a bridge on the Seine, the wind whipping their hair, their perfect faces laughing and happy.

Hero smiled as she remembered the trip. It had been a last-minute decision, one of Anya's specialities. She had burst in one afternoon after a terrible go-see and announced that they were going to Paris for Hero's birthday. Hero had given up fighting her on these spur of the moment announcements – it was easier just to go along with it. She remembered how they had each thrown a few clothes in a bag, called a cab to take them to the station and bought two tickets on the Eurostar, first class, of course.

Closing her eyes, she could still see her friend. Laughing, teasing, gossiping. Anya was supposed to have been getting married this year and instead she'd been buried at the same church. She missed her so much, her smile, her laugh, her company. In the seven months since the accident, Hero had barely seen anyone. It had shown up, painfully, the fact that many of the people she had met through her career were not friends. They were acquaintances, nothing more, and sometimes not even that.

Partly, it had been her fault. She knew that. Knew that she should have made more of an effort with people, like Anya had with her, but it had never come easy to her. And then there were the ones who wanted to be seen with her because of what she was, not who she really was. How to tell the genuine from the fake? Not that it mattered anymore. Hero was no longer a part of that world, their world. Anya had been the only one she had trusted to be true in that one. And she was gone.

It had taken ages for Hero to accept Anya's death. To really believe that her friend was gone. Forever. Even now she still expected Anya to come bursting through the door with some scandalous piece of gossip or the latest bargain. The flat was so lonely without her. She was lonely without her.

Hero forced herself up, taking the now empty mug out to the kitchen. As she did, something caught her eye and her footsteps slowed. Putting down the mug, she moved her hand to the boxes of pills stacked in neat piles on the dresser. Her fingers ran lightly over the top of each one. Some were for the pain, some to help her sleep when flashes of bright lights and screams haunted her dreams. The others? She couldn't even remember now. Didn't even bother to try most days. As she'd said to Rupert – what was the point? Hero sat slowly in the overstuffed armchair that stood next to the dresser, staring at the innocuous looking boxes. It would be so simple, so easy. No more pain, no more guilt at being the one to survive, no more loneliness. A single tear escaped from Hero's eye and ran slowly down her cheek. She waited for more. It might help, Juliet had said. But no more came. She reached out, nothing in focus but the small boxes that rested there. Picking one up, she opened it. It was almost full. Doing the same with the second, she found it to be the same. One by one she pushed the capsules from their foil, placing them in neat piles back on the dresser.

As she began work on the final strip, the telephone rang. Its shrill electronic call pulled her from her trance. Reaching out, she picked up the receiver, mostly just to stop the noise tearing through her skull.

'Auntie Hero? It's me. Marcus.' Her nephew's chirpy voice with its broad Antipodean accent was clear on the line. 'Hello?' he said again.

Hero couldn't speak. Her eyes were fixed on the collection of drugs inches away from her.

'Mum!' Somewhere in the distance, she heard Marcus call for his mother, and then mumbled voices before Juliet's voice came on the line.

'Hero? Hero, darling, are you there? Please answer me!'

Hero's voice was small and scared when she finally spoke, and she saw nothing but the pills in front of her.

'Jules?'

'Hero, sweetheart. What's wrong? What's going on?'

'I don't want to do this anymore. I can't.' The pain tore through her as she spoke, her throat constricting.

'What sweetheart? Do what? Please talk to me!' Juliet felt the ice filling her veins, chilling her to the core despite the warm spring day. As Nick and Pete walked into the kitchen, they stopped short, watching as the colour drained from Juliet's face.

‘Who’s on the phone?’ Pete asked his son who was now busy driving a small car around the kitchen table.

‘Auntie Hero.’ He jumped his car off the end of the table and headed off into the playroom. Exchanging a look, Pete and Nick sat down silently at the table, listening as Juliet gave instructions to her sister.

‘It’ll be all right, sweetheart. I promise. Just get the next flight out and call me with the flight number. I’ll be waiting for you.’ She paused for a moment, as she looked a question at her husband. He reached out and squeezed her hand. ‘We’re all here, darling. It’s going to be OK. I promise you. You’re not alone. We’re all here, waiting for you. OK?’

She spoke a little longer then reluctantly replaced the receiver. Looking up, she met the silent enquiry of their eyes.

‘Hero is coming to stay for a little while. I know I should have checked with you both, but it was—’

‘What’s going on, Jules?’ Nick interrupted.

Juliet stared at him. Then at her husband. ‘I don’t know … I think …’ She swallowed hard and tears filled her eyes. ‘I can’t lose her! Not now!’ Her voice broke in a sob and Pete stood quickly, wrapping his arms around his wife. He had no idea what was going on but whatever it was, he would be there for his wife, and her sister. They all would.

***

Juliet didn’t relax until she saw Hero walk through the Arrivals doors. But as she took in the change that had occurred in her sister, the relief was short lived. Hero’s limp was pronounced but she refused to rely on any form of crutch. The confident walk that belied her shyness before had gone, her dark head was bowed. The green eyes lifted nervously, breaking their link with the floor only to search for Juliet among the crowd. Relief flooded both faces. If Hero could have run to her she would have. Instead she locked eyes with her, holding on with them as she weaved her way through the other travellers. Juliet knew now for certain that she had been right to dictate her sister onto the next flight out. The intensity of pain in her little sister's eyes devastated her. She didn't dare break the eye contact. It was Hero's lifeline until she could get through.

Hero almost fell into her sister's open arms as she guided them aside, away from the stares of others. Hero looked different but there would still be people who might recognise her, and the media were still on the hunt. That was yet another bonus for being out here. In London she still had to hide. It didn't matter out on the station. No one there would judge her. There, all she would receive was love.

It was quiet in the house when the two women finally arrived back from the airport. Juliet explained that, as it was a school break, she'd arranged for the kids to spend some time at their grandparents' place in the city, along with Joe whom the kids rarely wanted to go anywhere without. It would give Hero a chance to settle in a bit before they came back and started bombarding her with demands for attention. She stole a glance at her sister as they sat, Hero lowering herself to the sofa a little awkwardly.

'Have you slept at all?' Juliet asked, her hand covering her sister's.

Hero looked startled at the question. 'A little.'

'I thought the doctor gave you some pills to help?'

Hero nodded. 'He did.'

And then Juliet knew. The broken look on Hero's face told her everything her words didn't.

'Oh my God! That's it, isn't it?' Her voice was almost a whisper. 'That's what you meant on the phone. I thought I was overreacting but … you didn't …?'

'No.' Standing, Hero limped across to the window, finding it easier to talk as she looked out across the fields dotted with sheep.

'I had them all piled up. Neat little piles. And then Marcus rang.' She turned back to face her sister. 'I'm so, so sorry, Jules. I never meant ...' Her voice tapered away.

'Would you have done it?' Juliet forced herself to ask the question.

'I don't know,' Hero answered softly, honestly. Hero shook her head as she looked at her sister. She knew it wasn't the answer Juliet had wanted to hear. 'I'm so sorry,' she said again. Her voice was low and unsteady. 'It's just that I felt so, I don't know, just ... adrift. The flat was so quiet and lonely without Anya.' Hero stopped and gave a sad laugh. 'She was always so bloody noisy, even when she was trying to be quiet. And messy. She was the messiest person I have ever known. It used to drive me up the wall but now the place is so clean and tidy and it's awful. I'd do anything to bring her back and find clothes in every room and mugs on every surface. I miss her so much, Jules!'

Juliet watched her sister. There were no words to say that would comfort her.

'I haven't even cried. Can you believe that?' Hero asked, anger in her voice. 'What sort of person does that make me? My best friend died beside me and I can't even cry for her!'

'That doesn't mean you don't care.'

'Doesn't it? I don't know anymore. I've spent most of my life building a barrier to protect myself from being hurt, or abandoned or whatever and where has it left me? Why couldn't I deal with Mum and Dad like you did? You didn't shut yourself off from everyone, or push them away. You kept your belief in people and found all this.' She waved a hand, encompassing Juliet's world.

'I wasn't carrying around that spiteful knowledge Mother imparted on you. You've done a hell of a lot better than most people would in the same circumstance. We're not all made the same, Hero. People deal with things the best way they can.'

'I know.' Hero's anger died as quickly as it had risen. Turning back to the window, she spoke again. 'I just wish I'd been made more like you.'

Juliet stood, crossing the room to hug her sister. 'You are who you are, Hero. And you are good and decent and kind and loving. I know that. Pete knows that, and so do Nick and Joe and the kids. Anya knew that too. It's why she chose you to be her friend.'

Hero asked, her face filled with pain and confusion, 'Then why can't I cry for her?'

'You're grieving, sweetheart. Just because you haven't physically cried doesn't mean that you're not, or that you don't care. The tears will come. When it's time.'

Juliet took a seat on one end of the big, squishy sofa, pulling Hero down gently next to her. She looked exhausted.

'Here,' Juliet said, and her sister followed her direction, too tired to do anything. Laying her head in her older sister's lap, Hero closed her eyes. Juliet rested one hand on her sister's jutting hip bone while the other stroked the smooth, dark hair. The combination of exhaustion, relief, and Juliet's rhythmic motion hastened Hero into the much-needed embrace of sleep. Juliet sat back and thought again of her sister alone and staring at the drugs that would make it all go away forever. She looked down at the sleeping face and her blood ran cold. As if feeling her gaze, Hero opened her eyes blearily.

'Go back to sleep, sweetheart,' Juliet whispered.

Hero obeyed. Within moments, her breathing was steady and slow again. A tiny fragment of the emotions raging within her had been released, and Juliet was glad of that. She knew it was going to be a slow process, but Juliet promised herself she would be there for her every step of the way.

Hearing footsteps some time later, she leant towards the open door a little, putting a finger to her lips as her husband and Nick entered the living room. Pete crossed the floor and kissed his wife before looking down at Hero with a question in his eyes.

'She's going to be fine,' Juliet said, determination in her hushed words. 'It's just going to take a bit of time.' Hero barely stirred. 'I don't think she's slept much recently. I don't really want to wake her. Could you take her upstairs for me so that she can rest until dinner's ready?'

'Right-oh.' Pete lifted Hero effortlessly from the sofa. She slept on. Nick hadn't moved since they had entered. He watched Pete carry her out and started as Juliet touched his arm.

'Penny for them?'

'Huh? Yeah, right. What?'

'You finished for today?'

'Yep. You want me to do anything? Peel some spuds or something?'

'That would be great. I'll be back down in a minute.' Smiling at him, she patted his arm in gratitude, before crossing to the door to check on Hero.

'Jules?'

She turned.

'You really think she's going to be OK?'

Tilting her head a little, she smiled. The look in her brother-in-law's eyes confirmed what she and Pete had suspected for a long time. Nick's feelings for Hero ran a lot deeper than he had even begun to hint at.

'She'll be fine, but it's going to take time and she's going to need help.' Juliet let out a sigh. 'She lost her best friend, her career, and got dumped by her boyfriend, in one fell swoop. Added to that, I think her leg is more painful than she lets on. Because of the injuries, and the fact that her career is over, she thinks her looks and appeal are gone too. Those two things have been synonymous with one another for so long, it's hard for her to believe that it's not true. It's a hell of a lot for her to deal with, but she's here now, with her family, and I think that's a good start.'

Nick didn't reply, but Juliet hadn't missed the shadow that had passed over his face when she'd mentioned the existence of a boyfriend.

'I'll go and get …' He didn't finish the sentence, jabbing his thumb towards the kitchen instead.

'That's great. Thanks.' Touching him gently on the forearm, Juliet then turned and headed out of the room and up the stairs.

Chapter 12

Nick's stomach was doing somersaults as he waited for the two women to come down the stairs for dinner. He busied himself with pouring drinks for everyone until he heard an uneven step on the stairs and Hero limped self-consciously into the kitchen, Juliet at her side. The difference in her demeanour was the first of many changes Nick took in. For the first time since he'd met her five years ago, she was free of make-up. But there was one thing that remained exactly the same, if not stronger. She was beautiful. All Nick saw was Hero. The relief at seeing her back at Hill Station combined with the rush of desire this woman always fired within him stunned him for a moment and all he could do was smile at her.

'Hi,' he managed eventually. 'Had a nice sleep?' Nick groaned inwardly at his lame conversation, but Hero didn't seem to mind.

She gave him a small smile and nodded. 'Yes. Thank you.' She paused. 'How are you?'

'Good, thanks. Starving.'

Pete pulled out a chair for Hero and she slid into it. The dinner was relaxed and although she was quiet, Hero contributed now and then. Nick topped up her wine glass and returned the smile she gave him in thanks. Juliet asked her sister's opinion on a matter and Hero turned her attention across the table. Taking the opportunity to quietly study their guest without, hopefully, looking too creepy, Nick considered the changes fate had wrought on Hero since she had last sat at this table. The dark hair was a little shorter and she now had a fringe and long layers that fell slightly across one eye. Hero peeked from behind it, as did the large deep scar the new hairstyle did its best to disguise. It was strange to see her with no make-up. Nick felt almost like he was seeing her for the first time. The conversation swung back towards him, and Hero turned, meeting his eyes. Her beauty still took his breath away, just like it had done the first time he had seen her, however much he had tried to deny it. Except now there was something different about it, something that had nothing to do with make-up. It was softer now, more approachable, more real. That mask of protection she'd worn before that had been the subject of such contention between them was gone, shattered in the same instant that had taken her best friend and changed her life forever.

***

Hero was quiet during the first few days at Hill Station. She walked around the property, exercising her leg, although she was yet to accept the offer of using the pool, remaining self-conscious of the angry scars that would be on show. Gradually though, she began relaxing into the land, and this new passage of life. She didn't know how long she'd be staying, and she didn't think about it. One of the many lessons she had now learned was just to enjoy today. Tomorrow would come soon enough. Or not.

Juliet stood at the kitchen window, watching as Hero made her way over to feed the chooks.

'Who are you spying on?' Pete teased, coming to stand behind his wife before following his wife's line of vision.

'I'm not spying,' she said, batting his arm, as he wrapped them around her waist. 'I hope I've done the right thing bringing her out here, Pete. It's a completely different way of life from what she knows.'

'That fact could be the best thing about it.' Pete squeezed his wife's waist, leaning round to drop a kiss on her furrowed brow. 'Stop worrying. She'll be all right. I'll see you later.'

'Making the most of the peace and quiet before Joe and the kids get back?' Nick called out when he saw Hero standing on the bottom rung of the fence watching two half-broken Brumbies dance about, the now empty bucket from the chicken feed dangling from her wrist – a definite change to the five figure designer handbags that had often swung there before the accident.

Hero turned her head at his approach and gave a warm smile in response to his question. 'I can't wait to see them all.'

Reaching her, Nick turned, resting his back against the same railings. 'The feeling is mutual, believe me.' He laughed and her smile increased. He turned again, focusing his attention on the horses. Looking at Hero like that was causing all sorts of effects that Hero wasn't anywhere near ready to deal with yet. She had enough to cope with, without him adding to the situation. They stood in silence for a few moments, watching the horses.

'Pete said you've just started breaking them in.'

Nick eyed the animals, squinting briefly as he concentrated. 'Yep. Still a fair way to go yet though.'

'I'd never really seen any like this, you know, in real life, before I came here. At the stables where I used to ride, they were all just there. Ready and waiting.'

Nick nodded, never taking his eyes from the Brumbies. Glancing at him, Hero caught his expression.

'I know what you're thinking.'

Nick shrugged. 'I wasn't thinking anything.'

From under the shade of the battered Akubra hat she'd found on the coat rack, Hero rolled her eyes.

'Nick, you have never treated me with kid gloves. Please don't start now.'

Smiling now, Nick faced her. 'Right-oh. So what was I thinking?'

Hero turned back to the animals. 'You're thinking that everything's always been pretty much ready and waiting for me in my life.'

Nick smiled and shook his head, but his lack of response made her think that perhaps the thought had crossed his mind, even briefly.

Hero stepped down off the fence. 'I guess I'm paying for it now,' she said, taking a step back towards the kitchen.

Nick's expression darkened as he straightened away from the fence sharply and stepped across Hero's path, his face inches away from hers as he looked down.

'You're not paying for anything. What happened wasn't some sort of retribution, Hero. Don't even begin thinking that. It was an accident. A horrible accident – wrong place, wrong time. But that's it. End of story. Understood?'

Hero nodded, green eyes wide, stunned at the emotion in Nick's voice.

'Right. Good,' he continued, clearing his throat, his tone calmer now. 'You were right before. I've never treated you with kid gloves. I don't believe in it. And you've never indulged in self-pity before.'

'I didn't have to before.'

'But you could have done. Your parents' attitude to you could have made you bitter, but it didn't. I think it just made you afraid. But that's all in the past now, Hero. You're in a place where people love you.' She was looking at him so intensely with those incredible green eyes … Nick gripped the set of keys in his hand tighter, rushing on. 'We'll make a deal. If I don't treat you with kid gloves, you don't indulge in navel gazing. Deal?'

His terminology brought a smile to her face, and she held out a hand. 'Deal.'

'Good.' He shook the offered hand. 'Now, do you want to come out and check the fences with me?'

Hero's smile faded, replaced by a look of awkwardness as she cast her eyes down, then back across to the house. Everywhere but at him.

'I … won't be able to ride again for a while yet. If ever. But thanks for the offer.' Her tone was civil, but he knew that hint of defensiveness from old. Stepping around him, she made to walk off.

Nick grinned, glad to see that the fire was still burning in there somewhere. Reaching out, he grabbed her shirtsleeve.

'Still got that stroppy streak then I see?'

Hero blinked as he stopped her, catching her breath. Nick's confident, lazy smile should really have infuriated her, but it was having quite the opposite effect. She tried to think of a suitably pithy comeback, but all her mind could focus on was Nick's strong hand which had now wrapped loosely around her wrist. Deciding the best thing was to keep silent, Hero raised her eyes in question instead.

'I wasn't going on horseback. I'm taking the bike.' He nodded at the off-roader parked next to the barn. 'It's a bit bumpy. Think you're up to it?'

'Yes,' Hero replied without hesitation, just as Nick knew she would if she thought he was challenging her. It was instinctive. Hero had had to prove herself one way or another her entire life. That wasn't something you could just switch off. It would take time, but Nick hoped that, out here, she'd learn that she didn't have to prove herself anymore. That it was OK to want to from time to time, but that there was a big difference between wanting to, and feeling like you had to every single day of your life.

Walking over to the bike, Nick swung one long leg over the saddle, then started the engine.

'You know, you don't need to change the way you do things just to make me feel included.' Hero hesitated beside the machine, her voice raised to be heard over the motor.

Nick looked round at her and rolled his eyes. 'Just get on the bike,' he said, holding out a hand for Hero to steady herself as she climbed on. As she did so, memories from taking limo-bikes around the various Fashion Week cities flashed in her mind. Nick kept the bike steady as she landed a little heavily on the seat behind him, waiting as she adjusted her position in order to find the most comfortable position for her damaged leg.

'Ready?'

'Yes!'

'For God's sake hold on. I don't want to face your sister if you fall off.'

'I won't.' Hero wrapped her arms around Nick's waist. 'Just go!' she called, urging him on. Nick grinned, hearing the smile in her voice.

Hero knew Nick was taking it easy, but the sensation was still wonderful. Her hat now hung down against her back and the breeze whipped the hair from her face, exposing the scar she did her best to hide at all other times. They rode along the fence lines, checking for damage and, when they stopped, Hero noted down the places that would need to be revisited in the ute with new fencing and tools.

'Thanks,' Hero said, handing Nick back the water bottle he'd brought as they leant back under the shade of a tree for five minutes. 'By the way, you didn't answer my question earlier. I thought you normally check the fences on horseback. Did you take the bike today for my benefit?'

Nick sighed. 'Some and some. But the bike needed a run and so did you.'

'Oh I did, did I?'

Nick had been resting back on his elbows, but at Hero's question, he rolled on his hip to face her.

'You're enjoying it, aren't you?'

Hero looked back at him, seeing that expression of certainty on his face. He smiled. She was doing her best to maintain a cool expression, but he could see the humour in her eyes.

'It must be such a strain being right all the time.'

Nick stretched onto his back as he answered. 'Yeah, it can be, but you learn to deal with it.'

'Wow,' she answered flatly.

Nick laughed, even white teeth showing against his tanned face. He stretched again. Hero watched him, unable to look away. No one had ever caused the kind of feelings that Nick fired in her and no matter what she did, she couldn't stop them. It had happened the first time they had met, only increasing with every visit. It didn't matter if they were arguing or laughing – Nick Webster was still the only man she had ever wanted with so much desire. Tearing her gaze away, Hero got up and went over to lean on a fence post, staring out at the paddocks stretching before her. She and Nick had flirted before the accident but they both knew it was just entertainment, a battle of wills. He'd found her attractive, she knew that, and the feeling had certainly been mutual. Of course, there was no need for him to know that she'd never felt like this about anyone before, so overwhelmed with her feelings and desire. He seemed to believe that she was an experienced woman of the world, and so she'd let him think that. But then she'd lowered her guard with him at the wedding. He'd come to her when she'd felt lost, and alone, and the way he had made her feel – protected, safe – had felt so right, like a perfect fit. But it also terrified her. That feeling that someone else could be responsible for her feelings, her heart. As much as she wanted him, she knew it was too much of a risk and promised herself that she would never let him that close again.

After that, the only time she'd ever really relaxed with Nick was when they discussed aspects of the station, the jobs to be done, and the reasons why. Hero allowed her real character to show on these occasions, excusing herself with the reasoning that talking about the life here couldn't be personal. It was these moments Nick had cherished. Her occasional moments of haughtiness irritated him, but she was a good verbal sparring partner and once the children had arrived, she'd begun visiting every few months and the discussions about the station had also started to become more frequent, both of them finding ways to spend time together without facing up to why.

But none of that mattered now. Nick Webster was one of the most eligible bachelors in the district. Handsome, intelligent, with a slight bad boy taint from his younger days when he had got into more than his fair share of scrapes. Many of the single women had their eye on him, as well as a few married ones. Mothers pretended to disapprove but he was courteous and respectful of women, and as his temper had calmed with maturity, they had soon come around. The fathers were less of a problem. Nick was honest, could defend himself if needs be, and owned half of one of the largest, and most successful properties in the area. Any daughter could do worse. Nick certainly had his choice of women and Hero wasn't stupid. Plenty of them were vying for his attention. Before the accident, she might have been able to compete with them, at least on a looks basis, but not now. The irony of the situation wasn't lost on her. Since the accident she no longer wore the mask that had so irked Nick in the past but now that she could finally be herself, it was clear that friendship was the only relationship Nick was interested in.

'We'd better get back,' Nick said, getting up and busying himself with strapping the water bottle back on the bike.

His head was down, and Hero took the opportunity to thank him for the flowers he had sent to the hospital. It was easier to do if she didn't have to look into those melting brown eyes.

'I know it's rather late, but I don't think I thanked you for the flowers you sent. After the accident. They were beautiful.'

Nick swung a leg over the bike. 'No worries,' he replied, sitting up and meeting her eyes.

Damn. Hero smiled briefly and then looked down, studying the ground for dips as she walked the short distance back to the bike.

'I thought Juliet said you sent all the flowers away?' His voice was soft, enquiring.

'I did. Mostly.'

'Right,' he said when nothing else came to mind.

She was at the bike and level with him, now that he was sitting.

'I've had a lot of time to assess the way I've treated people. I tried to be all cool and in control, but I think it came across as … uncaring, and I'm sorry for that.' She raised her eyebrows and smiled awkwardly. 'I don't know why I'm telling you all this now. Anyway, the flowers were lovely and much appreciated. I'm not sure they were deserved because I've been fairly beastly to you, in the nicest possible way of course, ever since we met.'

'Oh, I don't know. I think the beastliness was pretty even. And besides, you have your moments.'

His expression was serious, but his voice was soft as he held out a hand to assist Hero onto the bike. She reached for him, her eyes missing the rut that her foot twisted into. Grabbing for her, Nick leant further, at the same time ensuring the bike didn't fall on top of them. Hero tumbled away from him, brushing his fingertips as she fell. Wincing, Nick swore and was already off the bike as she landed heavily on her bad leg.

'Are you all right?' He bent down, trying to put an arm around Hero to help her up but she waved him off, pushing herself up from the ground with her palms.

'I'm fine.'

But Nick had seen the pain in her face as she landed. He rubbed his forehead in irritation.

'You know, it's all right to ask for help sometimes. It doesn't make you a bad person.'

'Stop fussing. I tripped. It's no big deal.'

Nick squinted at her, then turned away, lifting the bike back up off its side. Climbing back on, he reached out, holding Hero's arm tightly as she got on. Feeling her body slide against his own and her arms wrap around him, he started the engine.

Juliet was just coming out of the house as they rode up. She smiled and waved, her expression changing as she realised who the bike pillion was. Changing direction, she headed straight for them.

'What the hell are you doing?' she yelled at her sister as Nick steadied Hero's dismount.

'Checking fence lines,' Hero replied calmly. 'Thanks for the ride, Nick.' She turned away and began walking towards the house. Giving her brother-in-law a glare, Juliet then tilted her head, brow furrowed as she watched her sister. Nick followed her sight line. They both saw it – she was limping more heavily than usual.

'You fell off, didn't you?'

'No,' Hero replied, turning. Her face was impassive.

Juliet turned to Nick. He, on the other hand, had guilt written all over him as he pointedly studied the bike.

'I knew it! What were you thinking taking her out on that?'

'Oh, for God's sake, Juliet!' Hero took the few steps back to them. 'He didn't kidnap me! He asked if I wanted to go and I said yes. And I'm glad I did. For the first time in months I actually felt like I was alive!'

They were both staring at her. Juliet spoke first, softer now. 'But you did fall off?'

'No. In order to have fallen off, I would have had to have been on the bike in the first place. I stepped in a rut and lost my balance. I could have done that anywhere.'

Juliet looked back at Nick. His expression had cleared. Her sister was apparently telling the truth.

'Now, if it's all right with you I'm going to go and soak my bruised bum in a nice hot bath.' Hero didn't wait for a reply before turning back and heading in towards the house.

'And you can wipe that grin off your face!' Juliet said, eyebrows raised at Nick, whose mind was pleasantly engaged in thoughts of Hero soaking anything in a nice hot bath.

'Heard you went out on the bike earlier?' Pete grinned at his brother as they sat on the verandah for lunch.

'Don't you start.'

Juliet came out from the house, placing two cold beers in front of the men, before taking a vacant chair.

'Many fences down?'

'Couple need repairing out on the south paddock. Nothing too bad.'

Pete nodded, making a mental note as he took a bite of his sandwich. Nick picked up his own, before putting it down again, his mind elsewhere.

'Is she OK?' he asked, now looking direct at Juliet as the moment replayed on a loop in his mind. 'I tried to grab her as she fell but I was on the bike, and she was just out of reach. I couldn't get to her.'

Juliet smiled softly at him and patted his arm. 'She'll be fine. She'll be down soon.'

'She didn't cry,' he said, switching focus between his two companions. 'She really went down hard on that leg and barely made a sound.'

Juliet craned her neck and looked back through the window, checking for her sister. 'At school, we had a very strict headmistress. She caught Hero crying once, shortly after my mother had been particularly cruel and she was understandably rather upset. Anyway, this awful woman laid into Hero about crying being a sign of weakness and all that crap, gave her the cane. I think she was trying to make her cry again. But she never did. Even to this day, as far as I know.'

'But she must have done after the accident. Losing her best friend like that?'

'You would have thought so, wouldn't you? But she couldn't. She wanted to, I know, and she feels like she's a terrible person for not doing it but … it's like she's forgotten how.'

***

The children were bouncing to get out of the car before Jack had even pulled it to a stop outside the house. They raced up to Juliet, powering into her as they wrapped their arms tightly around her, accepting her kisses before seeing their father and uncle pull up in the ute.

'Dad!'

Marcus was hugged, kissed, swung around and dangled upside down, giggling all the while. Bridie was content to be picked up by her uncle, cuddle his neck and survey the world serenely from this new perspective.

'Where's Auntie Hero?'

'I think she's out feeding the chooks.'

Nick plopped Bridie back down and she and Marcus broke into a run. Their aunt appeared a couple of minutes later with a child firmly attached to each hand. She wore a pastel-blue ankle-length sundress with a white linen shirt open over the top to protect her from the sun. Her hair was loose with a wide ribbon of the same blue acting as a headband, and today, as had become the norm since she had arrived, her face was free of make-up. Pete watched his brother from the corner of his eye, smiling as he, in turn, watched her approach.

'There's someone else who'll be eager to see you.' Pete smiled as she came up to them. He tilted his head back towards his parents' car. Jack and Gill were staying over for a few days, and Joe was now busy helping them unload their bags.

'The kids had strict instructions not to tell him you were here. He thinks you're arriving next week. You didn't tell him, did you?' Pete asked the children in a serious voice. They both shook their heads vigorously, proud that they had been included in the keeping of this important secret. Hero stroked Bridie's hair as Marcus moved on to his uncle and began trying to tackle his left leg. Nick swept him up in one easy motion and tucked him under his arm.

'Shall we?' he asked Hero, indicating the way with his free arm as if they were preparing to enter a formal dinner.

She nodded, blinking slowly in acceptance, her smile widening as his own showed. They began walking towards his parents' car, Bridie still clinging to Hero's hand as Nick's captive wriggled and giggled under his arm. Pete walked alongside his brother.

'Dad! Help!' Marcus was now hiccupping in laughter.

Pete looked around. 'Did you hear something?'

'Dad!' Marcus squirmed, his giggles infectious.

Nick stopped, turning one way, and then the other. 'I'm sure I heard something.' Marcus giggled even more, setting off both his sister and his aunt. Winking at Hero, Nick then carried on walking. A little flushed, Hero was glad she could use the weather as an explanation although she knew the true reason for the sudden rush of blood was due to something far closer to home than the sun.

Juliet and the new arrivals turned as the commotion got closer. Laughing, Joe then did a double take as he realised just who was holding Bridie's hand.

'Hero!' He hurried up to her, flinging his arms around her, nearly knocking her off her feet in the process. Nick's free hand was at her back, steadying her, warm and strong through the thin fabric of her dress.

'Steady on, mate!' Nick laughed.

'Sorry!' Joe replied, pulling away before frowning at his surrogate brothers. 'You said she wasn't coming until next week.'

'Well, you know how it is,' Pete explained. 'Mum and Dad were really looking forward to seeing you and if we'd told you a beautiful woman was coming, we'd never have got rid of you.'

Joe blushed scarlet and Hero batted her brother-in-law on the arm. 'Don't be so mean.'

Pete pulled a 'Who? Me?' face, silently pointing at himself before looking innocently at Nick. His brother just shrugged as he released his nephew.

Hero raised an eyebrow, but there was a smile on her lips. 'Come on, you lot. I want to hear all about your trip,' she said, herding the new arrivals towards the house.

The two brothers watched the group walk back, stopping at the porch for Hero to receive a hug from their mother, watching as she spoke to her and stroked the glossy dark hair. Juliet called out that dinner would be ready in half an hour then disappeared into the cool interior of the house with the others. The brothers set off at a stroll for the house to greet their parents and wash, ready in time for dinner. Pete glanced sideways at Nick.

'What?' Nick asked.

'Have you told her yet?'

Nick glanced across, opening his mouth as he prepared to fend off Pete's enquiry with a vague denial of understanding, but Pete met his eyes with a look that told him not to bother. Nick closed his mouth and focused back on their destination.

'Nope,' he finally replied. 'She's not ready.'

Chapter 13

'So, have you kept in touch with anyone since you came out here? I mean, I know you didn't feel up to it at first but now you're getting back on your feet, no pun intended?'

Hero smiled at the unintentional choice of words. 'No, not really.' They were sitting on the porch steps as the last efforts of daylight weakly lit the land in front of them, turning everything a soft gold.

'There's no one you miss?'

'Not now, no.'

Nick knew she was alluding to Anya. He squinted at the dying rays of the sun as it cast long shadows on the nearest paddock. Hero nudged him with her body.

'What?'

'What?'

'I can see the cogs whirring. What is it?'

Nick shrugged. 'I wasn't thinking anything in particular.'

'Fibber. You had your "thinking face" on.'

Nick threw his head back and laughed. 'I have a "thinking face"?'

Hero couldn't help but be caught up in the joy of Nick's laughter. 'Yes, you do! Your brow wrinkles and your eyes go all squinty.'

'Oh, that sounds really attractive!' replied Nick, his relaxed laughter building.

'Some might think it is.'

Nick raised an eyebrow and gave her a smile. 'Is that so?'

Hero shrugged and looked away, but Nick saw the smile. 'I only said "some" and "might".'

'And what do you think?'

'I think that you haven't answered my question, and I asked first.'

Nick let out a resigned sigh. 'Fair enough. I was just surprised there's no one you miss from back home now that you don't travel back and forth.'

'I do miss Rupert, obviously.'

Nick thought about that. Catching his expression, Hero nudged him.

'Not like that. We're just good friends. He was amazing after the accident, handling the press and everything else. He kept them away from me, and more importantly, from Juliet. I don't know what we would've done without him, I'll never be able to thank him enough for that.' She glanced at Nick. The expression was back.

'You're doing the face again. What now?'

Nick half smiled, amused and intrigued that she could read him like that. 'Promise not to get stroppy?'

'No.'

Laughing, Nick accepted the answer. He knew she'd never agree and he loved her honesty. But it had been worth an ask anyway.

'OK. Well, it's just … I mean, look at you! I can think of one method of showing gratitude that most blokes would be falling over themselves to suggest!'

Hero pulled a face at him. 'Yes, look at me. Maybe you were right at one time, but not now. I'm not that person anymore.'

Nick raised a questioning eyebrow.

Realising how her words had sounded, she suddenly raised

her own brows. 'I mean, not that I ever was "that" kind of person,' she said, hurriedly. 'I've never slept with anyone for, or to repay, any favour. Ever,' she added after a moment. A faint blush showed on her cheeks.

Nick grinned. 'I never thought you had.'

'So why did you look at me like that?'

'Like what?'

'With the whole raised eyebrow thing.'

Shrugging, Nick set his expression to innocent. 'Sorry, don't know what you're talking about?'

Hero narrowed her eyes. 'Yeah, right,' she replied, punctuating the statement by poking her tongue out at him, mostly for lack of anything better to say.

Nick laughed again, which only resulted in receiving a dirty look – but he saw the humour in her eyes. How far they'd come! He'd certainly received enough filthy looks off her in the past that he was easily able to tell which were real and which were in fun. And to be fair, he'd dished out enough of his own. He just wished it hadn't taken such a catastrophic event for him to find the real Hero once more – and for her to find herself.

'You're still beautiful, Hero. You shouldn't say stuff like that.'

This time the look was softer as she glanced over before turning her gaze on the horizon.

'Thank you. But we both know I'm not the trophy some people once thought I was, and whilst you see beneath the damage, a lot of men, especially in that world, wouldn't.'

'Then I think that says far more about them than you.'

He saw the smile.

'Yes, I think you're right.'

'I don't get it though.'

'What?' she asked, turning back to him once more.

'You're an intelligent woman. Why'd you even bother with men like that?'

Hero took a deep breath of the cooling night air, letting it out slowly. 'Honestly? I think it was just easier. I gave them what they expected.' She tapped her knee against his. 'Get your mind out of the gutter, Webster, not like that.'

'And there was no one you really cared for? Or cared for you. You know, who treated you like a person, rather than an accessory?'

'Yes, there was one.'

'Am I allowed to ask who?' Nick knew he was torturing himself. The thought of anyone touching this woman in the way he wanted to, kissing her, taking her to bed, shot arrows of jealousy deep into his heart. But he needed to know. Should anything ever come of their friendship, he didn't want any secrets. Of course, that also depended on whether he ever got up the courage to try and make something come out of their friendship in the first place.

Hero turned, leaning back against the rail. 'Why are you so interested?'

'I'm interested in you.'

'Why?'

'Because we're friends.'

She smiled. 'Yes, we are.'

Returning the smile, Nick curled his fingers around the bannister, hoping that would help control the desperate urge he had right now to pull her close against him and show her just how friendly she made him feel.

'If it makes you feel any better, it was one of your countrymen.'

'An Aussie? Well, that's something.'

'Yes. Ben Gale.'

'The racing driver?'

'Yes.'

'Right.' Nick knew all too well that Hero had dated the Formula 1 driver for quite some time. He was a fan of the sport, and of Gale. Although, admittedly, his support of the man had petulantly dropped a little the first time he saw a shot of him with his arm around Hero during some TV coverage. Both Gale and Hero were private people and hadn't flaunted the relationship as some of the more glitzy couples in the paddock did. But, of course, the media loved it.

Gale was a tall, good-looking, down-to-earth Aussie, and Hero was the perfect partner for the world he operated in. Much to her surprise, Ben turned out to be quite removed in both manner and personality from many of the other Formula 1 drivers she'd met. Ben wasn't into all the show and glamour of the racing world. He hadn't moved to Monaco as many did, and he wasn't big on attending all the starry events that surrounded the sport – but there was no way he could avoid all of them. Team sponsors made certain demands upon the drivers in return for the eye watering amounts of money they spent for the exposure. That was the deal. And Ben was certainly up for a good time and a great party as much as the next person. He just didn't feel the need to 'be seen' as some others did.

'It was nice, and unexpected, to find someone else who also lived in a crazy world but was still on my wavelength,' Hero explained to Nick.

'So, what happened?'

'Nothing really. It just got difficult to spend enough time together, especially during the racing season. He was never in one country for very long and I was all over the place with work too. I went to as many races as I could, but obviously he had a lot on his mind those weekends, so it wasn't exactly "quality time" for either of us. But we took what we could get, and I was happy to see him and to be as supportive as I could of his career.'

'And I bet the sponsors loved it. You certainly seemed to bring them more coverage.'

Hero shrugged it off. 'I don't know about that. I was concentrating on Ben and his race. I hated it though at times. I know they've made the cars safer over the years, but he was still hurtling around a track at ridiculous speeds. I was always so grateful when each race was done, and he was safe.'

'So, you cared about him. And he cared about you?'

'Yes,' she replied, simply.

'But you couldn't make it work?'

In the dim twilight that now surrounded them, Nick saw a look of sadness cross Hero's face.

'No. As much as we both wanted it to work out, sometimes things just aren't meant to be.'

'Have you seen him since you split?'

'Yes. The split was a joint decision really, so it was all amicable. We still enjoyed each other's company so staying friends was a good option when we realised that a romantic relationship was no longer really possible.'

'I take it he knows about the accident?'

Hero flashed him a look as if to say, 'It'd be pretty hard not to know'.

'Yes. He was actually one of the first to get to the hospital. I don't really remember too much. I was pretty drugged up at the time. Probably just as well. But I've seen him a few times since and we keep in touch with email and messaging and stuff.'

Nick listened, processing the information.

'And?'

'And what?'

'Do you think there's a chance that you'd get back together with him? I mean, there was obviously a connection there and now you'd only really have his career to work around – I mean, at the moment, not that I'm saying yours is—'

'It's all right, Nick,' she said, smiling at his efforts to untangle the knot he was currently tying himself up in. 'You can say it. We both know my career is over.'

'Not if you don't want it to be.'

'The one I had is. There's no getting around that. And I'm OK with it now. Really.'

'OK.' Nick let out a breath, slowly, doing his best to keep the conversation casual. 'So, you're free to spend the time with Gale that you didn't have before. Could you make it work now? I mean, would you want to?'

The night was overcast now, hiding the moon and making it difficult to see the expression on Hero's face.

'To be honest, I'd not thought about it.'

Good one, Nick. He gave himself a mental kick for possibly planting a seed which could well grow into something that would come back and bite him.

'So, if he turned up here tomorrow and said, "Let's give it a go", what would you say?'

'I hardly think that's likely.'

He spread his hands. 'Humour me.'

'Oh, I don't know, Nick. I'm not used to that world anymore, and Ben was always quite protective of me anyway and now, even more so. I think it would be difficult for both of us, trying to make that adjustment back into the spotlight again with the added pressure of people's morbid fascination with the accident. I mean, he's retired from actual driving now, but he's still involved in that world and you know what the media are like.' Nick heard her shift in the dark. 'Besides, he's never mentioned a wish to get back together.'

'Did you give him a chance to?'

'What does that mean?'

Nick shrugged. 'Just that you can be a little determined at evading people when you want to.'

'I don't evade people!'

'You don't always answer questions if you don't want to.'

'To be fair, neither do you.'

Nick had to concede she had a point.

'Anyway, I'm answering this one, aren't I?' she challenged him.

'True. I didn't say you hadn't got better at it.'

Hero laughed. 'Wow. Was that a compliment?'

'If it walks like a duck …'

'You two want a drink?' Juliet called, the screen door squeaking as she stuck her head out, squinting at her brother-in-law and sister who were sitting chatting in the dark.

'Ooh, yes please!' Hero pushed herself off the railing and headed towards the pool of light now spilling out onto the wooden deck.

Nick followed, aware that he still hadn't got a definitive reply from Hero about Gale. Yep, she had definitely improved, but she hadn't lost her knack at evasion either.

***

And the day had been going so well. Nick tensed as he heard the familiar voice behind him.

'Well, well! Nick Webster! It is my lucky day!'

But not mine, Nick thought as he turned towards Susannah's voice. He'd had one date with her sometime after Pete's wedding as part of his failed 'Forget Hero Scott' campaign. But one date had been plenty. Susannah had a hell of a figure, but something about her made Nick feel uncomfortable. The night ended early and he'd retreated home, pre-empting his brother's enquiry with two words: 'Don't ask.'

But Susannah Dagmar, having missed out on Pete, still had her sights firmly set on the youngest Webster brother, and she wasn't about to give him up without a fight. Stalking was too strong a word. Persistent might be more accurate.

'She really doesn't give up, does she?' Pete had observed a while back after yet another encounter with Susannah in town. 'Were you two actually on the same date?'

Nick had blown out a sigh. 'I hate to say it, mate, but Mum was right. I should have kept well away. I can't get rid of her. She just doesn't get the message.'

'Don't worry, mate. She will.'

Pete was wrong. Several years and countless men later, Susannah was still clinging to some imagined claim. Nick Webster was the man for her. He would realise that eventually. And there he was, looking as gorgeous and sexy as ever leaning on the back of the ute, reading something and squinting like he always did when he concentrated. His long legs were wrapped in dark blue denim and tanned, strong forearms contrasted with the white of his folded back shirt sleeves.

Nick jumped at her greeting, a curse word mumbled in surprise under his breath.

'G'day, Susannah.'

'G'day yourself.'

'Waiting for Pete?' Susannah started again when Nick went back to reading his paper.

'Nope.' He replied with a glance and a half smile. It might have helped if he could be outright rude to her but, even with Susannah, good manners prevented it.

'Oh.' She paused, shifting her weight from one high-heel clad foot to the other. 'You going to the Sullivans' ball this year?'

'Expect so.'

Susannah pulled at the already straining halter-top she was wearing. Nick caught the movement as he turned the page of his paper, concentrating on the article. God knows what had possessed him to go on even one date with Susannah. Obvious women weren't really his type. Guiltily he adjusted his position on the vehicle. Actually, he knew exactly what had possessed him. Susannah was everything Hero wasn't. It was a stupid idea, and it hadn't worked anyway. Not that he had expected it to. At least he hadn't slept with her. Sometimes you had to be thankful for small mercies.

'So, who you taking?'

Clearly, she wasn't going away. Nick gave up trying to read his paper.

'Huh?'

'To the ball? Who are you taking?'

He shrugged. 'Haven't given it much thought.' *Liar.*

'Pat McKenna's asked me.'

'Pat's a good bloke.' Pat was a good bloke. Nick just hoped he knew what he was letting himself in for.

'Yes, he is. Very good.' She lowered her voice. 'But he's not you, Nick.'

Nick straightened away from the back of the ute and moved towards the driver's door. 'We've been over this, Susannah. We went out. It didn't work. End of story.'

'You didn't give it a fair go, Nick!' Her voice was back up to its normal octave.

'Look, Susannah. I don't know what else you want me to say. I'm sorry, but I'm not interested.'

'Shall I come back in a while?'

Nick and Susannah both turned at the sound of Hero's voice. Caught up in their argument, neither had heard her approach. Susannah didn't miss the way Nick looked at the new arrival. The way he had never, would never, look at her. Rage boiled inside her. She'd seen them together that night of the wedding. Him holding her close, them talking together, laughing together. Nick hadn't even asked Susannah to dance once she'd clocked off. Not once. Well, little Miss Perfect didn't look quite so perfect now, did she? Susannah had heard all about the accident. She'd found every online article she could about it and read them all. Twice. It had helped numb the pain of Nick's rejection a little, if only temporarily.

'G'day.' Susannah pushed past Nick, putting on her friendliest voice. Nick's defences flew up. 'I'm Susannah. You're Juliet's sister, aren't you?'

Hero shook the hand she was offered. 'Yes, I am.' She returned the smile and then glanced at Nick. His face was serious and wary.

'So, you're staying at the station for a while, I hear?'

'Yes,' Hero replied, smiling as she placed her purchases in the back of the ute. Nick decided it was time to leave. He had an idea where Susannah was going with her 'casual conversation' and it wasn't anywhere good.

'Come on, we're late.' His voice was sharp.

Hero looked up at him as he stood behind the bleached blonde. He was edgy. Uncomfortable. Nothing like his normal relaxed self. She couldn't remember anything that they were late for but clearly Nick wanted to leave.

'Well, it was—'

'I was sorry to hear about your accident.' Susannah interrupted Hero, looking anything but sorry.

Nick's insides went cold.

'I read that you were really badly scarred, but you don't look too bad. I mean, considering …' Susannah paused, blatantly running her gaze up and down, lingering on the deepest scar on her face, peeking from behind her hair. Hero dug her nails into her palms to stop herself from pulling her hair further around her face as a shield. 'I guess the media always exaggerate that kind of thing.'

'They—'

'Didn't your passenger die? Your best friend, wasn't it? You must feel pretty guilty, you know, as you were driving.'

'Hero. Get in the ute.'

Hero was still. Just staring at Susannah.

Nick called again. 'Hero!'

She jolted out of her shock, looking up at Nick as he opened the door for her. Her eyes locked on to his and something inside him crumbled as he saw all the pain and confusion there.

'Come on, we're going home.' He helped her in, closing the door with a slam. Susannah stood her ground as he stormed past her and around to the driver's side.

'Doesn't say much, does she?' she called after him.

Nick was too furious to speak. Yanking open the driver's door, he was already backing the ute out as he pulled it shut. As they drove off, he glanced over at Hero, but she was staring out of the window, lost in her own thoughts and memories. Painful thoughts and memories made raw. Nick gripped the steering wheel tighter, his knuckles showing white.

'I'm really sorry about Susannah.'

'It's not your fault.' Her voice was flat. 'Besides, what she said was true. The papers do exaggerate. It helps sell copy. I dealt with it for long enough.' She looked away from the window at him and smiled. 'It's really not a problem.'

But Nick had seen the look in her eyes as Susannah politely assaulted her with words and cut her with suggestion. It most definitely was a problem.

'Look—'

'Could we not talk about this anymore? Please? Really, I'm fine.' Hero changed tack. 'What's her problem anyway? Or is she just like that with everyone?'

'Her problem isn't with you. It's with me.'

'So why did she …' The penny dropped. 'Oh! Well, next time you see her, do me a favour and put her mind at rest. Tell her I'm not a threat to her or anyone. As she so rightly pointed out, although my scars aren't "too bad"' – she punctuated the words with air quotes – 'I hardly qualify for Miss Australia.'

Nick could quite happily have choked Susannah right at that moment.

'Don't believe anything Susannah tells you.'

Hero let out a sigh. 'Oh, Nick. It's not a case of believing. It's a case of accepting. I have to live with the fact that I survived and Anya didn't. And that it shouldn't have been that way round. It was my car, and I was driving.'

Nick shook his head. 'You can't keep doing this to yourself. All the witnesses said there was absolutely nothing you could have done. It's amazing you survived at all!' His blood chilled as he said the words. In London, Juliet had tracked down the fire crew who had cut her sister from the car, wanting to thank them for everything they had done. They'd told her that, from experience, they really hadn't expected to find anyone alive in the wreckage.

'Yes, I can. Like she said, it was my car. I was driving. I should have—'

'Should have what?' Nick's anger bubbled.

'I don't know!' she yelled back. 'I just …' She paused, her voice fading until it was even softer than normal. 'I should have done something.'

'It was an accident, Hero. You have to know that. To believe that. There was nothing you could have done. You were fighting for your own life.'

Hero looked away. Nick understood that there was nothing he could say that would ease the pain for her. That survivor's guilt would most likely never leave her entirely, but he hoped that over time, it would at least become less intense. He glanced again. Her reflection showed pain, but no tears.

Chapter 14

Hero had been staring out of the window for over half an hour in silence when she turned back to Nick.

'So, is Little Miss Tactful like that to Juliet?'

'Nah. She wouldn't dare. That sister of yours is a little fire-cracker when she needs to be.'

Hero considered that and smiled. Juliet believed in the innate goodness of people, but she wasn't gullible. It obviously hadn't taken her long to get the size of Susannah Dagmar.

'So why me?'

Nick let out a sigh, and stared straight ahead.

'Susannah's jealous.'

'Jealous? Of what?'

'You.'

'Me? I don't think so! Did you actually hear that conversation?'

'Hero. I saw her watch you walk into Pete and Juliet's reception that night. She practically turned inside out with envy.'

'That was then.'

'Yes. But she knows that even after everything you've been through, you're still twice the woman she'll ever be.'

'Yeah right!' Hero snorted in disbelief. 'She practically took out my eye with that cleavage. She's most definitely more woman than I'll ever be.'

Nick laughed in spite of himself, his eyes flicking over to Hero and momentarily down to her, much smaller, chest. She caught him and yanked her shirt across.

'Do you mind?'

'Sorry.' He laughed, giving her a sheepish look. 'But I meant what I said before.' His eyes were back on the road.

'I thought you said you weren't going to be nice to me.'

'I never said that. I said I wasn't going to lie to you. There's a difference.'

'So what are you doing now?'

'Telling you the truth. You're still beautiful, Hero. Inside and out. Whether you believe it or not. Everyone can see it, including Susannah. Which is why she was such a bitch today. Maybe it makes her feel better about herself. I don't know.'

Hero studied Nick's strong jaw line for a moment. 'Well then, maybe she should try snarfing down a huge bar of chocolate instead. Works for me.'

They pulled up outside the house and soon each had a small child clinging around their necks. The confrontation of the afternoon was lost within their laughter. But Nick was worried. Hero was still burying her pain.

'See anyone in town?' Pete asked as the four adults sat on the verandah after dinner.

A bottle of red wine was on the table and two sleepy children were tucked up in bed. Nick looked across to Hero, but her eyes were faraway, staring out at the paddock to where the last rays of the day's sun warmed the earth.

'No one special,' Nick replied non-commitally, busying himself with topping up each of the four glasses. Replacing the cork, he took a sip of the wine. 'Saw Susannah Dagmar.'

'Oh God! She's not still after you for another date, is she?'

Juliet laughed, half in disbelief, half in despair.

Juliet had never been able to like the woman. She was shallow and a back stabber in her opinion. And she wasn't alone in those beliefs. At Juliet's comment, Hero met his eyes, a question in her own. OK. So, he hadn't quite told her everything.

'And what did she have to say? Ask you if you were going to the Sullivans' ball, did she?'

Susannah had trailed Pete for a few years but when he'd got engaged to Juliet, she switched her attentions to his brother. And there they seemed set to stay. Since his broken engagement, Nick dated plenty but none of it was serious. Susannah obviously figured she'd be the one to change all that. Pete felt a chill run down his spine at the thought of having the woman as a sister-in-law. Living close! Not that that would ever be an issue. Juliet would have been packed and gone before the woman had even stepped in the door. Or more likely, she would just have electrified the property's entire fence line.

Nick nodded as he sipped his wine. 'She's going with Pat McKenna until she gets a better offer.'

'She won't. Pat's a good bloke.' Pete echoed his brother's earlier sentiments.

'Too good for her.'

Pete frowned. 'You all right, mate?'

Susannah was a total pain in the backside, and it really was about time she got the message, but Nick didn't normally let it affect him this much. There was something else. Nick looked up from his glass and met the question in Pete's eyes, indecision playing on his mind.

'She said … stuff. To Hero.'

'What?' Juliet exploded.

Pete put his hand on his wife's arm. 'What do you mean?' Pete glanced at Hero, who was now glowering at Nick.

'It was nothing,' Hero answered, her tone definitive, hoping that would put an end to the conversation.

But Juliet wasn't ready to give up. 'So what did she say?'

Hero gave Nick one last shot with her eyes before she answered her sister.

'Honestly, Jules, it was nothing. She said she was sorry to hear about the accident and repeated a few of the things from the papers. That's all.' She gave her sister a smile. 'Not especially tactful but nothing I haven't heard before, and nothing I can't deal with. Really.'

Her tone told them the subject was dropped. Pushing her chair back, she rose. 'I'm going to go in, if that's OK?' Picking up her glass, Hero made her way to the study, stopping to kiss her sister on the cheek as she passed. She avoided looking at Nick completely. When Juliet was sure Hero she'd gone, Juliet pounced on him.

'So what did she actually say, the little bitch? I'm going to kill her!'

Pete let her rail. He tended to agree.

'Pretty much what Hero said. She did say she was sorry about the accident, but it was the way she said it.'

'Sorry, my arse,' Pete interjected.

'Exactly. Then she went on about how the papers reported that Hero was really badly scarred and how it didn't actually look so bad after all. Then she said about Anya dying in the accident and how she must feel guilty because she was driving. All that sort of shit. That was when I shoved Hero in the ute and drove off.'

'Shame you didn't back over the pneumatic bimbo whilst you were at it.' Juliet's normally smiling face was black with thunderous rage. Nick and Pete exchanged a glance before they burst out laughing, in spite of the situation. Juliet's assault was so ungenerous and so un-Juliet!

'It's not funny,' Juliet protested as her husband put an arm around her shoulder and pulled her close into a kiss.

'You're very sexy when you're angry, do you know that?' Juliet pretended to bat him off, but her smile shone through.

'Oh, stop it, you!' She turned back to Nick. 'How was Hero? Really?'

Nick drew in a breath. 'She glossed over it, like she always does but …' He hesitated, unwilling to burden his sister-in-law with more worries over Hero.

'I want to know,' she insisted.

He looked at her squarely. 'I saw her eyes, Jules. It was enough.'

Nick knocked on the study door.

'Come in.'

He turned the handle and stepped inside, closing the door behind him. Hero looked up from the screen of her laptop.

'Go away.'

'You just said "come in".'

'I didn't know it was you then. Now I do, I've changed my mind. Go away.'

He made a buzzing noise and put on a cheesy voice. 'Sorry. I have to take your first answer.'

Hero glared at him, then dropped her eyes back to the screen. Nick took a seat opposite the desk. Hero surfed for a few more minutes, then looked back up.

'Did you actually want something?'

'I had to tell them.'

'No,' she said slowly. 'You didn't. If they had needed to know, I would have told them myself.'

'No, you wouldn't.'

'That's precisely because they didn't need to know.'

'They want to know, Hero. They care about you. If someone upset you, they—'

'She didn't upset me.' Hero struggled to keep her voice even. She hit the Windows key on the keyboard, clicked on Shutdown and closed the lid of the laptop.

'Don't walk away on this, Hero.'

'I'm going to bed,' she replied, picking up her laptop and leaving the room without looking back.

'Right then. That went pretty well, I thought,' Nick said aloud to the empty room, before eventually following her out. Pete walked by, seeing Hero disappear from the balcony at the top of the stairs, before taking in his brother's expression.

'She forgave you then?'

'Oh yeah. No worries.'

***

Susannah's spiteful words were still ringing in Hero's ears a week later. She had driven over with Nick to the neighbouring property, owned by the Sullivan family. Every year they held a ball. It had been held as a giggle initially years ago but had since become an annual fixture on the district calendar. Hero had kindly been included in the invitation, and Juliet felt her sister really ought to pay a proper visit before the actual day. She was also worried. Hero was still avoiding people, something far easier to do out here, and Susannah Dagmar hadn't helped.

Hero had been introduced to the Sullivans at the wedding and they'd met again in town from time to time, but Juliet wanted her sister's friendship with their neighbours to be everything her own was. Hero hadn't missed the irony of the situation – she'd spent her whole career socialising at the most exclusive clubs and parties in the world, mixing with actors, racing drivers, billionaires, and other high flyers, and now here she was worrying about meeting a neighbour. How the world had turned.

'Just go with Nick. It'll be fine,' her sister reassured her, almost bundling her bodily into the ute.

And it was fine. More than fine. Sarah Sullivan was a warm, motherly figure who whisked Hero away for lemonade whilst Nick and Sarah's husband, Bill, went off to discuss station life. Sarah talked and Hero listened, gradually relaxing enough to contribute. Nick smiled when he and Bill rounded the corner of the house to find Sarah and Hero laughing as though they had known each other for years.

‘Got time for a beer, Nick?’ Bill asked.

‘’Course he has, haven’t you, love? Sit down.’

Nick sat and took the cold beer Bill handed him, pleased to see Hero happy. It was the first time she’d really relaxed since the incident in town. Juliet had been right to insist that Hero come with him.

‘G’day Nick. You skiving off again?’

They turned to see Paul, Sarah and Bill’s son striding up the verandah towards them.

‘G’day mate.’

Paul leant down and kissed his mother on the cheek, stopping as he caught sight of Hero sitting opposite. Nick saw the way he looked at her and felt the blood thump in his veins. He took another pull on the beer. Paul was one of his oldest friends. Their lands backed against one another, they had grown up together and attended the same schools. They shared the same dreams, the same sense of humour, and, apparently, the same taste in women. One in particular had tested their friendship to its limits a few years ago, and although Nick had forgiven Paul for moving in on his girlfriend, it was the kind of thing that was hard to forget entirely.

Sarah made the introductions. ‘Paul, you remember Juliet’s sister, Hero, from the wedding? She’s staying with them for a while.’

Paul swung a glance at Nick, grinning. ‘Lucky them. It’s very nice to see you again.’

Hero smiled, and said hello, shaking the hand he offered. As he sat, Paul took in the changes that time had wrought since the last time he’d seen her from a distance on a visit to her sister. He hadn’t forgotten the first time he’d seen her at Pete’s wedding when Nick had been hogging her nearly all night. Not that he could blame him. He would have done the same, given the chance. And, of course, he had heard about her accident. A scar showed on her cheekbone, but she wore her hair differently now which hid much of the damage. From what he heard the ex-model now walked with a limp, but she still remained one of the most beautiful women Paul had ever seen. It was different now, a more natural beauty, but still stunning. Paul lifted his drink, observing the interaction between her and his friend, trying to work out whether there was anything between them now. He'd made that mistake a few years ago, and nearly lost Nick as a mate. It had been a stupid thing to do and he'd never do that again. But if she was free …

'So I hear you're bringing Susannah Dagmar to the ball?'

Sarah looked horrified. 'Oh, Nick, you're not.'

Hero smiled, seeing the tease in Paul's eye.

'Over my dead body.' Nick finished the last of his beer. 'Anyway, I believe someone else has the pleasure of her company that night.'

'Oh, they'll have the pleasure all right,' Paul blurted before remembering they had company.

'Paul!' His mother admonished but Hero was laughing.

'Don't worry. I'm not exactly her greatest fan.'

Nick watched, pleased to hear Hero laughing, even if it had been instigated by another man.

'I hear you met Paul Sullivan,' Juliet mentioned, her tone just that little bit too casual.

The two women were hanging out washing on the line that ran around two large shady trees.

'Mm-hmm.'

Juliet pegged up a pair of child's jeans. 'Did he have much to say?'

'Not especially. We were all just chatting.'

Juliet nodded and picked up a T-shirt from the basket as Hero fastened a tiny pair of silk Agent Provocateur knickers to the line. She felt her sister's eyes on her.

'What?'

'What?'

'You're angling at something.'

'No, I'm not.'

'Yes, you are. Spit it out.'

'Paul's a nice chap,' she said, concentrating on pegging out the T-shirt, a studied casualness to her tone. 'That's all I was saying. I just thought it might be nice if you two were friends.'

'Friends.'

'Yes.'

'Right.' Hero smiled, shaking her head as she picked up a peg for the matching silk bra. Her sister was a terrible liar.

'Morning.' Nick touched his hat as he walked by.

Turning in surprise, Hero blushed, snatching the bra back down before shoving it behind her back. Nick's gaze took in the matching thong on the line and she didn't miss that hint of smile as he walked on.

'I can't remember the last time we did this,' Juliet laughed.

Sarah had offered to babysit for the evening whilst the Websters, together with Joe and Paul went out for a meal in town. They had booked rooms at the pub so that everyone could have a drink and not worry about the time. It was a surprise for Joe's birthday and he had been so pleased, joy written all over his beaming face. He even beat Nick at pool.

'I obviously taught you too well,' Nick conceded as he handed Joe the pint they had put up as a stake.

'Well done!' Juliet and Hero each hugged Joe and gave him a kiss on the cheek. He giggled, blushing furiously.

'Hey! If you had told me that was part of the prize, I'd have tried harder,' Nick teased.

'I'd still have beaten you,' Joe declared confidently.

Hero laughed, hugging him again. Then she reached up and gave Nick a kiss on the cheek too.

'Consolation prize.' She grinned.

Nick felt the embers burst into flame at her touch. Her cheeks were pink from the wine and Nick guessed it was probably that that had led her to kiss him, but he didn't care. Not right now anyway.

After closing, the group made their way to the second floor of the pub, and their accommodation for the night. They had economised on rooms. Juliet and Hero shared one, Joe and Pete another and Nick and Paul the third. The two old friends chatted briefly through their beer haze before sliding happily into oblivion. Both had studiously avoided the subject of Hero.

The next morning, earlier than any of them would have preferred, the group were getting ready to head home. Paul sat astride the motorbike he had driven into town, chatting with Juliet and Hero. Joe was already in the truck's back seat catching up on some more sleep whilst Pete and Nick settled the bill inside.

'You'll be riding one of these by yourself soon. I've seen you out with Joe and Nick checking the fences on the property lines.'

Hero pulled a face. 'My sister has finally calmed down enough to let me ride pillion without a fight, but I think we might be a little way off me controlling one myself.'

Paul glanced at her leg then back up. 'How is it now?'

Hero smiled. His question was honest and to the point. He hadn't skirted around like some people did. Paul reminded her of Nick in that way.

She shrugged it off. 'I make sure I exercise it and stuff. It all helps.'

Back at the reception desk, Nick put the money Paul had given him for the room in his wallet and tucked it back in his pocket.

'What are you grinning at?' Pete asked as he caught a look at his younger brother's face. His own head felt like it had a hammer drill bouncing around inside it and his brother was grinning. It just wasn't right. Nick didn't answer, but carried on grinning. Pete gave him a look, guessing what, or more accurately who, had instigated that smile.

'Yeah, yeah. Right-oh,' he said walking out, the sunlight making a further attack on his fragile state.

Nick followed. He was looking forward to the ride home. It was cosy in the truck with three in the back, especially when two of those three were him and Hero. His face fell as he stepped out into the sunshine just in time to see Hero climbing onto the back of Paul's bike, her dark glossy hair spilling out from beneath the crash helmet.

'Paul's going to take Hero home as it's a bit of a squash,' Juliet explained as the brothers approached them. She kissed two fingers then transferred the kiss to her sister's nose through the open visor. 'Drive carefully,' she said, giving Paul's arm a squeeze.

He nodded and revved the bike as Hero placed her arms around his waist. Nick watched as they drove off, dust blowing out behind them.

'You getting in, mate?' Pete nudged.

Nick stepped up into the back silently, hefting Joe's sleeping form up enough to sit down and close the door. Joe slid gradually down in his slumber until his head was resting on Nick's upper arm. Nick left him there. He looked peaceful. Wasted, but peaceful.

They passed Paul on the driveway, him coming out as they drove in. He slowed the bike next to Pete's open window.

'One sister-in-law delivered safe and sound.'

'Thanks, mate.'

Paul shook his head and, through the visor, his eyes glinted in a smile as he placed one foot back on the bike.

'My pleasure entirely. See you later.'

Hero had just made tea as the others entered the house.

'Oh! Good girl,' Pete laughed. 'We'll make a station hand out of you yet.'

She poured the tea into mugs and passed them across the table. Nick gave Joe a nudge with his elbow as his head nodded and his arms slid slowly down the table. Joe sat up with a start.

'What? I'm awake.'

Hero pushed his tea towards him, as Juliet nodded at her sister.

'We're going over to the Sullivans' to pick up the kids after this. Do you think you can manage without us for a while?'

Pete rubbed his chin in mock thought. 'And just how long is a while?' He raised an eyebrow at the two women. The ball was coming up and he knew Juliet was absolutely dying to talk about it with Sarah.

'Well, I suppose that depends if we get chatting.'

'Ha! "If", she says, "if"!' Juliet flung a tea towel across the kitchen and hit Nick instead.

'Oi! What did I do?'

Pete stood and slapped his brother on the back. 'You're related, mate. That's enough.'

***

'We'd better be getting back.' Hero checked her watch.

'OK,' Joe agreed happily, immediately making more of an impression on the soft drink in front of him.

They were sitting in the shade of a large tree in the pub's beer garden snatching a cool refresher after picking up some groceries for the station. They'd beaten the lunchtime rush and had the garden to themselves.

'You ready for a game of Scrabble after dinner tonight?'

'Definitely!'

Hero and Joe's tradition of Scrabble had been established from the first visit she paid to the station. As a consequence, his reading had also vastly improved, especially lately with the time that Hero was able to spend with him on it. Joe took another gulp then thought of something.

'Could we—' He broke off and his face darkened as a shadow fell across the picnic table.

'G'day Joe.'

Joe mumbled a reply and concentrated on finishing his drink. Hero's defences flew up as she felt Joe's leg start to jitter under the table, a nervous habit. He was normally such a peaceful soul, the nervous tick only showing when he was stressed. Whoever these men were, they clearly unnerved him. It was definitely time to go.

'Not with Nick and Pete today then?'

Don't answer, thought Hero as she finished her own drink, but Joe automatically shook his head. His leg jittered even more. Hero saw the two men exchange a glance.

'Come on, Joe.' Hero rose from the table.

'Hope you're not going on our account.' One of them stepped close to her, his face in a smile that showed no warmth, but something far more disturbing.

Hero's blood chilled. He was so close. Too close. It had been years since she'd had to deal with unwanted attention like this. She, like every woman, adapted her routines, her way of life, in an effort to keep herself as safe as she could. Back home, she never left anywhere alone in the evening, and if she did have to, always arranged a car through a trusted limo service. Occasionally, if there had been any hint of extra unwanted attention, the agency had employed a security team to keep an eye on their most precious investments. Hero focused and tried to remain calm, concentrating instead on getting Joe away from a situation that was clearly upsetting him.

Chapter 15

'Aren't you going to introduce us to your lovely friend, Joe?'

'No.' Joe still didn't meet their eyes.

'Come on, Joe. We really have to go. Excuse me.'

The man didn't move. Hero tried to retain her dignity as she struggled to get her bad leg out from under the picnic table, cursing inwardly at its inflexibility.

'Want me to give you a hand there?' The man's hand slid around her waist and down her thigh.

'Don't touch me!' Hero yelled, jabbing him hard with her elbow at the same time as Joe made a lunge for him.

'Leave her alone!'

She heard the sudden intake of air as her elbow connected with the man's throat, but Joe hadn't seen the second man's foot as he stuck it out, tripping him. He went down heavily, his shoulder hitting the table and his head hitting the bench before landing sprawled on the grass.

'Joe!' Hero called, yanking her leg free, glaring at the men as she bent down to check on him. They stood back from her now, one of them rubbing his throat.

'Oh, Joe.' She laid her hand on his face gently as several people, hearing a commotion, emerged from the inside of the pub.

'What's going on? Oh my God! You all right, mate?' Doug, the bar owner caught sight of the blood now flowing from a deep cut on Joe's forehead. 'Come on. Let's get you to the doc's.'

Doug and a regular eased Joe to his feet and gently led him inside. Hero glanced behind her. The two men were lingering back in the shadows of the tree, swigging at their bottles, the one who'd touched her openly glowering.

'You all right, love?' Doug's wife touched Hero's arm. She jumped.

'Yes. Sorry. Thank you. I'm just a bit worried about Joe.'

'He'll be all right. Don't you worry.'

They were sitting in the corridor of the town hospital. It wasn't huge but, thanks to a large donation by a grateful, and wealthy, ex-patient, it was well equipped. Hero sat in the hushed quiet, her fingers nervously twiddling the pendant on her necklace. She breathed in the hospital smell, struck that even on the other side of the world, the buildings all had that same smell.

'I hate hospitals,' she said quietly.

Doug and his wife looked across, but Hero didn't look back. It was as if she had uttered the thought unconsciously. The two exchanged a glance, as if to say, 'I'm not surprised'.

Hero was sitting at Joe's bedside when Nick and Jacob entered the room. Joe's right arm was in a sling and butterfly stitches held closed the cut on his forehead.

'Dad! Nick!' He smiled sleepily.

A purple bruise was blooming around the cut and the dose of painkillers administered earlier had begun to work their magic. Jacob leant over the bed and kissed the unbruised side of his son's forehead.

'What happened, son?'

Joe met his eyes for a moment, then looked behind him at Nick. 'Roy and Ethan Burrows.'

Nick's jaw set, his whole body tensing at the answer. 'They started on you again?'

'They asked if I was with you and Pete.'

'Yeah, because they know they'd get their arses kicked again if you were.' Nick's voice was low but loaded with anger.

'Again?' Hero looked from Joe to Nick.

'Then what?' Nick carried on, ignoring the question.

'We were leaving but Roy stood in Hero's way, so she couldn't get out from the bench properly.'

Something twisted inside Nick and his eyes darted across to Hero. Her gaze was down, concentrating on Joe's hand as she held it within her own.

'She asked him to move but he didn't ,and he put his great paws on her. She told him to get off but he just laughed so I went for him. To get him away from Hero. That's when I fell.'

'He didn't fall. The other one tripped him,' Hero pointed out. She tilted her head and caught Jacob's eye. 'I'm so sorry about all of this.'

Jacob smiled and reached over, patting the hand that held his son's.

'Don't be daft, love. It's not your fault. Those two idiots never pick on anyone their own size. They've been trying to bully Joe for years, but they only ever try it when he's on his own. Last time they didn't see Pete and Nick until it was too late. Guess that's why they checked this time.'

'Well, he got an elbow in his throat for his trouble this time.'

'Atta girl.' Jacob winked.

Hero looked back at Joe who was now quietly dozing off. He gave her a sleepy smile which she returned, before gently brushing the hair away from his eyes.

'My hero,' she whispered, smiling.

Jacob watched the woman's tender touch. They had a special bond, those two. Had done from the first day Hero had walked in. Cool and elegant, she'd taken to his son immediately and he to her. Jacob had to admit he'd been surprised. When Juliet's sister had arrived, looking exactly like something out of a fancy magazine, he was sure that Joe would have been the last person she'd befriend. But it had turned out quite the opposite. They'd go on walks, and sit for ages after dinner playing Scrabble as she helped him with words. Joe had always had a gentle, happy nature but since Hero had been here full-time, his smile seemed brighter and his education had certainly improved.

Jacob knew that he and Joe were lucky to live at Hill Station. Jack and Gill had kept him going when he thought his heart would break after Maria's death. They'd helped him bring up his child, loving Joe as if he were their own, and giving him two surrogate brothers who would defend him with their last breath. Juliet had slipped easily into Gill's role, feeding them often and checking after them like a mother hen. And now there was Hero.

Hero had a role all of her own. A sister and a friend, spending time when the others had chores to do, or were too tired after the day. Joe had always loved books and reading. He was still a slow reader, but Hero would sit with him patiently, often for hours, as he read to her. If he got stuck on a word, she'd tell him what it was, get him to repeat it checking that he understood the meaning. Once he was happy, off he would go until he got stuck, and the process then repeated.

Joe's eyes opened again and looked directly into Hero's. 'You all right?'

'I'm fine. Stop worrying and get some rest.' She fussed with the sheet but they all saw the fleeting shadow across her face.

Hero smoothed the bedlinen unnecessarily, trying to shake off the feel of the man's slow, threatening touch, the alcohol-fumed breath on her cheek as he had leaned against her. Nick watched her. She was definitely more shaken up than she would admit to. It was time to go home.

'You're going to stay tonight then?'

Jacob looked up at Nick. 'Yeah, if that's all right with you and

Pete. They want to keep Joe in for observation because of the bump on his head. I can drive back as soon as they release him. The other ute's still in the pub car park. I'll go and get it later.'

'OK. We'll see you when we see you. No rush. Just make sure he's OK. If you need anything, you know where we are.'

Joe's eyes had now been closed for a while, and Nick's voice was low in deference. He leant across, pushing the rebellious bit of hair away from the younger man's eyes again, as Hero had done. As tough as Nick liked to appear, Joe was still the equivalent of his baby brother. The fact that idiots like the Burrows took advantage of his gentle nature made him even more protective. Not to mention furious.

'Do you want me to stay?' Hero asked Jacob.

'No, love. It's all right. You go home with Nick and get some rest. We'll see you tomorrow.'

Hero nodded and got to her feet. As she moved, Joe stirred and opened his eyes.

'We were supposed to play Scrabble.'

Hero leant and kissed his forehead. 'We'll play tomorrow.'

Nick stood back and let Hero exit first. He made to follow but Joe called his name.

'Go on,' he told Hero. 'I'll catch you up.' Nick re-entered the room, stepping up to the bed. 'What is it, mate?'

'Is Hero OK?'

''Course. You just get some sleep.'

Joe blinked, forcing his eyes to stay open against the drugs. 'She was frightened, Nick. Roy wouldn't rack off, and he was …' He paused and looked at his father. 'I didn't like him treating her like that. It wasn't right.' Jacob nodded at his son, a silent acknowledgement that he had done the right thing.

'I know, mate. It's all right. She's fine now. Now don't go trying to be a hero for any of these pretty nurses in here. That's enough for one day.' Nick winked, briefly laying his hand on the young man's shoulder.

Joe smiled with sleepy eyes. He saw Hero through the glass, waiting at the corner. As his friend, his brother, caught up and spoke to her, she turned and waved, before they both disappeared from view. Joe closed his eyes completely and drifted off into peaceful sleep. Hero was safe now. She was with Nick. And Nick loved her. He could tell.

Nick held open the passenger door and Hero got in, waiting for Nick to walk around. He slid behind the wheel, started the engine, and pointed the vehicle home. He stole a quick glance at his companion, but she was staring out of the window, looking back at the hospital they had just left.

'I'm really sorry about this.'

Nick took his eyes from the road for a second. 'What?'

'All this.' She waved her hands, trying to encompass the whole afternoon's events within the gesture. 'Joe getting hurt and stuff.'

Nick squinted out at the late afternoon sun. 'It's not your fault.'

'Yes it is. I couldn't get my stupid leg out of that bloody table. If I had, we would have been off, and Joe wouldn't be in the hospital.'

'Roy and Ethan are troublemakers, Hero. They would have started something anyway. They don't show up too often, but when they do they've usually had a few. Joe's an easy target. It's probably just as well you were there, to be honest. And well done on the elbow jab. I'd like to have seen that.'

Nick tried to lighten the mood a little, but the truth was he couldn't handle the thought of something happening to Hero, or the thought of those bastards even touching her. But his words were true. If she hadn't screamed out, there was no telling what they might have done to Joe. They turned, the afternoon sun hitting them straight in the eyes. Nick flipped down his sun visor.

'You don't have to make everything OK, Nick. I know it's my fault.'

'What?'

Hero's voice was unsteady, and she took a breath to calm it. Nick looked across at her. It was clear all this had freaked her out more than she was prepared to admit. But was she just talking about today? From what he could tell, the lines were blurring. The best thing he could do was just get her home.

'Why don't we talk about this later?'

Hero flipped down her own visor viciously as the sunlight streamed head on into the car. 'I don't want—' Something hit her thigh with a thud.

Jules was always stuffing her sunglasses behind there. Hero moved her hand down to pick them off her lap and screamed, yanking the door open as she did so. Nick swerved and made a grab for her. With one hand holding onto Hero's arm and the other on the wheel he skidded to a stop in the dust. Hero had stopped moving but her eyes were wide and focused in terror. Nick followed her petrified gaze. A huge grey spider was moving slowly down her thigh. In a second, he had reached over and scooped the creature up, flinging it out of his own window. When he turned back, Hero was out of the ute, brushing frantically at her clothes. Nick swore at the seatbelt as he fought to get out. Finally, it released and he ran around the vehicle to where Hero was hysterically brushing at her clothes.

'It's gone, Hero. It's gone.' Her frantic motions continued. Nick reached out, taking hold of her shoulders. 'Hero. Look at me.' His voice became stern. 'Hero!'

She looked up then, her expression seemingly one of shock at seeing him there. But she wasn't the only one in shock. For the first time in years, the beautiful green eyes that Nick loved so much were washed with tears.

'It's OK, sweetheart. It's gone. It's long gone. Everything's fine now.'

Hero blinked at him, the movement dislodging the first tear. A second chased it down her cheek. She issued a small sound and began to shake. Nick's throat closed, and he folded her into his arms, letting her cry for everything that had happened.

Nick's back was against the ute as they sat in the shade of the vehicle. Gradually Hero's sobs became softer and finally ceased. She was curled up against him, the damaged leg held out straighter. Her head was on his chest and his arms were wrapped protectively around her. Nick could have stayed there forever.

'I guess we should go home.' Her voice was soft, and raw from crying.

'When you're ready. No rush.'

She pulled away a little and tilted her head to look at him. Her nose was red and her eyes were puffy and swollen. Nick looked down and fell in love a little bit more.

'Was it poisonous, the spider?'

Nick shook his head. 'Nope. It's called a Huntsman. Ugly bugger, and it might be a bit uncomfortable if it does bite you, but it's not poisonous.'

'Do they always hide behind sun visors?'

'Sometimes. They like the dark.'

Hero leant back against his chest. 'Well, I think it's sneaky.'

Nick smiled and dropped a kiss on the top of her head without thinking. 'I don't suppose he was too chuffed at getting tossed through the air, so we're probably about even.'

Hero giggled with a hiccup from the recent tears.

'I'm sorry I freaked.'

'No worries.'

'I don't normally do that.'

'I know.'

Hero sat in the protective warmth of Nick's arms, her head on his chest, listening to the slow, steady beat of his heart. It was such a nice place to be. Nothing mattered when his arms were around her. She had felt it that first time they had danced together, and now he had made the world go away again.

Nick realised Hero's breathing had slowed. He craned his neck to see the face pressed against his shirt. Her eyes were closed and her lips slightly parted in sleep. Nick felt his face flush as a hot surge of desire rushed through his body. Get a grip, he berated himself.

'Come on, Sleeping Beauty, let's get you home.' He pulled them both to their feet and led his charge to the passenger door. Hero walked with him sleepily, hesitating as he opened the ute. Nick grinned.

'It'll be miles away by now. Or concussed.'

Hero smiled, but her eyes showed uncertainty. Nick leant past her and checked the visors and the dashboard for any more creatures that might be lurking.

'Coast is clear.'

Hero was asleep again almost before he'd pulled back onto the road, still not stirring when they reached the station. Nick lifted her out of the ute and began carrying her towards the house. Juliet and Pete met them at the door.

'Oh my God! Is she all right? Where's Joe? What happened?'

Nick looked past his sister-in-law and raised an eyebrow at his brother. 'Which one do you want me to answer first?'

Juliet was only half listening, as she stroked the hair away from her sister's face.

'She's been crying!' Juliet was as shocked as Nick had been.

'Yep.'

Nick started towards the stairs. Within seconds Juliet was behind him again. 'Nick? What's happened? Why has she been crying? She never cries. Did—'

'It's been a long day, Jules. And no, it wasn't me, before you ask.'

'I wasn't suggesting that at all.'

Nick laid Hero down on the bed, forcing himself to resist the urge to lie beside her, before looking back at his sister-in-law. His smile was disbelieving. Juliet drew herself up in defence.

'Well, you do have a knack of getting to her.'

'I'll leave you to it.' His smile stayed, as he passed by.

Juliet called him as he began to close the door. He stuck his head back around.

'Thank you.'

'Don't thank me. Thank the spider.'

'Huntsman then, was it?' Pete asked after they had eaten and got the children bathed and packed off to bed.

'Yep. Big bugger too. Must have been behind the visor. Hero flipped it down and out tumbles our furry friend. Lands smack on her leg and starts crawling around.'

Juliet shuddered as Nick recanted the trip home.

'She freaked for a bit, then just started crying.' He took a sip from his bottle. 'I guess it was the catalyst she needed. It's been a long time coming. I just hope that it helps.'

Nick opened the children's bedroom door and peered in. Marcus was going through a stage of falling out of bed in his sleep. They were currently taking it in turns to check on him. Only his nephew's top half had migrated from the bed. Nick picked the child up and eased him back into the bed, tucking the sheet in a little firmer. He then picked up Bridie's stuffed toy kangaroo, it having obviously hopped out of bed after the little girl had fallen asleep. Nick laid Bounce next to his niece's pillow. He knew she would only get in a state if she woke up in the night and couldn't find him, then closed the door silently behind him.

As he walked past Hero's room, he hesitated. Part of him said to keep on walking and that he would see her tomorrow. But the other part of him told him that tomorrow wasn't soon enough. He just wanted to check on her. Make sure she was OK. But what if she woke when he was there? Nick closed his eyes, opened them, then headed on towards the stairs. As he started down, Juliet appeared at the bottom.

'Kids OK?'

'Yep. Marcus was half out and Bounce was all the way out but they're both safely tucked back in now.'

'Thanks.'

Nick took a step down.

'Did you check on Hero?' Juliet asked.

'No.' Nick was glad that the only illumination was the children's nightlight plugged in on the landing. He felt his cheeks flood warm.

'Would you mind? Just make sure she's all right?'

'Right-oh.'

Nick left the door ajar and stepped into the room. Hero was still lying in the same position he had laid her in hours ago. Juliet had removed her shoes, but she slept in the sundress she had been wearing earlier. Nick looked around and saw a lightweight silk quilt lying over the Lloyd Loom chair in the corner. He picked it up, laying it carefully over the sleeping form. She didn't stir. The emotional outpouring, long overdue, had completely exhausted her. Sleep was the best thing. Stepping back to leave, Nick found a creaky floorboard. Its loud protest seemed deafening in the quiet room. Nick glanced back, expecting her to wake, but she merely changed position a little, the slow, rhythmic breathing unchanged. Nick lingered a moment longer. The movement exposed the scar she did her best to hide. It was deep, running from the centre of her forehead to her cheek. The surgeon had been excellent, but Hero knew there would always be a scar remaining, an everlasting reminder of the destruction those few moments of time had wrought.

It did nothing to lessen her beauty to Nick – he rarely even noticed it. Hero was still the most stunning woman he had ever met. She had captured him from the first moment, despite their differences, or maybe because of them. Seeing her injuries only made Nick care for her more, and wonder at the pain she had suffered. Glad now that she had at last released even a part of it, Nick turned and left the room, leaving Hero to her dreams.

***

Hero sat on the step, hugging the mug of coffee Juliet had made for her before disappearing back into the house to help her son with his homework. It was a task that often fell happily to Hero but today her brain was just too sleepy. A fact she found amazing considering that she had just spent almost all of the past twenty-four hours asleep. When she did wake, she'd taken one look in the mirror and turned away. Her eyes were sore from crying and the puffiness remained. Hero took a sip of the coffee and waited for the caffeine kick to hit her bloodstream.

And then she smiled. She had puffy eyes and it didn't matter. She didn't have to put iced towels on them, or cold teabags or, the worst, haemorrhoid cream! They could stay puffy and no photographer, editor, or make-up artist would yell, fret, or even care. It felt wonderful.

Looking up, she saw Nick ambling across the yard. He wore dark jeans, well-worn yard boots and a blue checked shirt with the sleeves rolled up exposing tanned, muscular arms. Hero felt the now familiar rush pulse through her body.

'About time you showed up,' he called out as he approached, his face shaded from the afternoon sun by his favourite hat.

She grinned and poked out her tongue. Nick reached the verandah and leant against a support. His smile faded a little.

'Feeling better?'

Hero took another sip of the coffee and smiled awkwardly. 'Don't do things by halves, do I?'

'Nope.'

She put the mug down on the wooden floor and wrapped her arms around her knee. She looked up at him from under her eyelashes.

'I feel a bit ... silly.'

'Why?'

'You know ...' She waved her hand from the wrist.

Nick pushed off the post and budged her along the step, sitting down next to her. 'Do you feel better?'

His mouth held the promise of a smile, but his eyes were serious. She couldn't avoid the truth when he looked at her like that.

'Yes.'

'So what's the problem?'

Hero ran her finger to and fro in the red dust that had settled on the verandah. 'I'd just maybe rather have done it in private,' she replied, concentrating on the patterns her fingers were making.

Nick gently caught her hand as it drew its dust pictures. Hero looked up.

'If it makes you feel better, I'm glad you didn't do it in private. I'm glad that I was there.' He leant over and kissed her cheek. It was so soft, so gentle that for a moment, Hero thought she had imagined it. But her hand was still in his. She lifted her eyes, meeting his gaze.

'I have to get back to work,' he said, squeezing her hand before leaving, his pace quicker than it had been on his approach.

'You all right, mate?' Pete asked when he saw Nick with his head under the tap outside the wool shed. His brother stood, turning off the tap.

'Fine. Just hot.' He ran his hand through his hair, replaced his hat and hurried off. Pete watched, half puzzled, half amused. 'Right-oh.'

Chapter 16

Slowly, Hero began to open up. It had taken too long, but the outpouring of grief, anger, and pain experienced that afternoon in Nick's arms had been truly cathartic. It was Christmas Eve and Hero had been roped in to referee an impromptu football match that had sprung up. Jack stood with her, explaining what was allowed and what wasn't. Family, neighbours, and friends had descended on the station. Children raced around, wearing themselves and each other out, laughing and hollering almost as much as the adults. Hero blew the whistle as Pete tripped his little brother.

'Oh! Pete, really!' His mother admonished.

Nick writhed around in mock pain as Pete stood over him and shrugged his shoulders innocently at her.

'Foul, Mr Webster.' Hero grinned.

'It was an accident!'

'Oww!' Nick groaned loudly from the floor.

She walked over to where he lay and crouched down. 'Can you walk?' Her voice was gentle, its softness washing over him.

Nick opened an eye, then sat up slowly, heroically. 'I don't know. It's my knee.'

'Oh dear.' Hero pouted at him and, for a moment, Nick's protests of weakness were the truth.

He watched as she kissed two fingers, then transferred the kiss to his skinned knee, just as she had done earlier to his niece after Bridie had taken a tumble.

'Is that better?'

Nick nodded stupidly and grinned. Pete shook his head, a wide smile breaking out across his face. He put his hand out to help Hero haul Nick to his feet.

'Pathetic, mate,' he whispered in his brother's ear. Nick nodded again, happily agreeing. As he got to his feet, three other players dropped to the ground, calling the ref's attention.

Hero laughed, laughing up at Nick. 'I blame you for this.'

'OK.'

Hero glanced over to where Juliet sat with her in-laws and the Sullivans. One of the men feigning injury was Paul Sullivan.

'Let him suffer!' His mother called out, at which point Paul stopped acting for a moment and looked over.

'Mum!'

Hero in the meantime had walked over to Stefan, one of the Sullivans' stockmen. Reaching up, she placed the whistle around his neck and winked. He grinned back.

'New ref,' she called out, as the six foot five, brick-outhouse-built man made his way onto the makeshift field, amusement twinkling in his eyes, 'Did someone need something kissing better?' He boomed.

Miraculously, the three men's injuries immediately healed and play continued.

Walking back to position having scored a goal, Nick glanced over to where Hero was now sitting on a metal bar fence, talking to the other stockmen, who were pointing every now and then. Nick surmised that they were explaining the nuances of Australian Rules Football to their new companion. Her eyes followed the game, and she cheered loudly when his team got the ball. He couldn't believe the difference in her from when she'd arrived, all those months ago. She'd been scared and nervous and insecure.

But gradually, she had settled into her new life in the Outback with them, giving her body and mind the time to heal. She took an interest in what they did there, how the station ran, helping with what she could. He'd always loved his life out here, but every day now held the added bonus of seeing Hero.

That day, as she'd sobbed hysterically in Nick's arms, the final barriers had been torn down. It had marked a turning point in her and Nick's relationship, as the shared experience brought them closer. Nick's physical and emotional support at the time had proved to her that he was a man she could rely on. As a friend, at least. Hero was still unsure whether Nick would ever want to take it past that level. It wasn't like he was short of offers, and she hadn't exactly given any inkling that she would be receptive in the past. But that was the past, Hero told herself. If she was to make a success of life out here, she had to move on. Coming to terms with her grief had been a step towards that. She knew she fell far short of being a natural with the land sometimes, but she tried, and as far as the people that mattered were concerned, that was the most important thing she could do.

***

'I really don't think this is such a good idea, Jules.'

Hero was sitting in her dressing gown, prodding irritably at the sponge rollers her sister had wound into her hair several hours ago.

'No. You're right,' Juliet replied.

Hero breathed a sigh of relief. But the respite was short as her sister then continued.

'It's not a good idea. It's a great idea!'

Jules looked up from ironing Pete's dress shirt and saw the pained look on her sister's face. Standing the iron on its end, she crossed the room to Hero, resting her hands on her sister's shoulders, talking to her reflection. 'It's going to be fun. It'll do you good to get out.'

'I'm fine here. I like it here.'

'Hero. The Sullivans' ball is one of the social events of the year out here, and believe me,' she laughed, 'there aren't all that many, so you have to make the most of the ones that do come along.'

Hero frowned, turning away from the mirror. 'I've had enough social events to last a lifetime.'

'Oh, come on. It's a great laugh and it'll be nice to see the boys dressed up for once.'

Hero faced her sister. 'And that's another thing. It was unfair of you to lumber Nick into taking me.'

Juliet took a deep breath, trying not to lose patience. She knew it was just nerves on Hero's part. This would be the first major social event for Hero since the accident. It was a huge step, and Juliet did her best not to lose sight of that.

'Nobody would consider taking you as being "lumbered" as you put it. Besides, he volunteered.'

'Yeah, I bet,' Hero mumbled.

'Look. The invitation has been accepted and we have to leave in an hour, so just go and get ready, will you?'

'But—' Hero stopped mid-protest as she caught a look at her sister's face. 'Fine.' She pushed herself up from the dressing table to leave. As she did so, Pete strolled in.

'Thought you two would have been getting ready by now.'

Hero winced at her brother-in-law and risked a glance back at her sister. Juliet flashed her husband a filthy look. 'In between putting the children down for a nap, getting yours, mine, and their clothes ready, not to mention persuading my sister to actually even attend this evening, I've been rather busy!'

Hero's gaze had dropped to the floor. When Juliet had finished, Hero looked up and exchanged a look with Pete. He pulled a face that said 'Oops' and crossed to where his wife fumed. He dropped a kiss on her head, and slipped his arms around her waist, as she half-heartedly batted him off. Hero turned to leave.

'Don't you want to go now?' Pete asked.

Hero turned back. 'Actually, I never wanted to go but somebody answered on my behalf.' She raised an eyebrow.

Juliet was unapologetic. 'You could hardly refuse. They're our neighbours. It would have been rude.'

'Not thinking of standing me up, are you?'

Nick stood in the doorway, a hand resting at shoulder height on each side of the frame. He wore black dinner suit trousers and no shirt. His hair was dark and damp from the shower. Hero opened her mouth, then closed it. She tried again.

'Um.'

Nick raised his eyebrows in anticipation as he awaited his answer, his body still blocking the only exit.

'I … um,' Hero stumbled.

Juliet ended her sister's anguish. 'Of course not. She was just on her way to get ready, weren't you?'

Hero dropped out of her daze. 'Yes. Just … on my way.'

She pointed needlessly towards her own room and walked to the door. Nick shifted to the side. Just enough. His eyes lingered on the curlers nodding on Hero's head as she passed.

'I can see you.' Hero edged past him, before glancing back over her shoulder. It was easier to talk the further away she was from Nick's half naked body.

'What?'

'I'll leave them in if you're not careful.'

Nick straightened away from the doorframe. 'Is that a promise?'

Hero rolled her eyes and shook her head, but there was no mistaking the smile on her face as she reached her room.

'Go and put a shirt on. You'll scare the children,' she called as the door closed behind her.

Nick's smile widened.

'Where's Bounce? Dad! I haven't got Bounce!' Bridie wailed as she wriggled under the seatbelt.

'Isn't he in the bag?'

'No! I was going to carry him. Dad!'

'All right, Bridie. We won't go without him.'

Pete and Nick had been given the task of packing the car and the children. A job that was now pretty much done, except for the missing Bounce. Juliet appeared on the porch.

'Have you got Bridie's Bounce?' Nick asked as he approached.

'No. Should I have?'

'No. It's all right. I'll go and get him. You get in. Where's your sister?'

'Just coming, she said.'

Nick jogged into the house and towards the stairs. As he placed a foot on the bottom one, he heard a step above him and looked up to see Hero stood at the top. She held an evening bag in one hand and Bounce in the other. And she took his breath away.

'I assume Bridie probably wants this chap?' She held up the toy kangaroo.

Nick swallowed. 'I … um … yeah. I was just … coming to get it.'

'Everyone ready now?'

Nick nodded. Far less effort.

Hero descended the stairs. She wore an emerald green, full-length silk gown, with ribbon straps and a cowl neck. The bias cut skimmed her curves and caused the fabric to shimmer in the late afternoon light now streaming through the window. Nick, mesmerised, remained where he was, reaching out to take Hero's hand as she approached his position.

'You look very nice.' She smiled up at him.

Nick was still staring. 'You're beautiful.' His voice was soft.

Hero smiled, almost shy, her hand still in his.

'Nick!' Pete's voice bellowed from outside, shattering the moment.

'Coming!' Nick yelled back.

'Bring Hero as well, will you?'

'Yep.'

Silence returned. Hero risked a look at Nick and grinned. 'We'd better go.'

Nick took Bounce with one hand and Hero's hand with the other and walked out to the porch. Pete and Juliet were already in, their bodies twisted around, talking to the children. Nick stuffed the soft toy under his arm as he paused to lock the house, his other hand still holding Hero's as they began walking to the car. Nick's pace was fast, and Hero laughed as she gripped his hand tighter.

'Hang on! I've got a dodgy leg and I'm incredibly out of practice with these shoes!'

Nick glanced down at Hero's feet as she walked. Her skirt was hitched up revealing strappy, block heeled sandals in the same fabric as the dress, adding another three inches to her height.

Juliet glanced up, seeing Nick approaching the vehicle. Bounce was in one hand, and with the other he held tightly to her sister. Hero was laughing as she held up the hem of her dress, concentrating on her steps in the now unfamiliar heeled shoes. Happiness radiated from both of them.

'Wait, wait!' Juliet called, quickly pulling her phone out of her sequinned clutch as she got out of the car.

'Oh, Jules.' Hero dipped her head and made to push past Nick.

'Come on. You look so beautiful! Let me have a picture.'

Hero shook her head, still not looking at the camera. 'There's plenty of pictures out there, Jules. You don't need any more.'

'Come here.' Nick smiled, catching her waist. 'Let your sister take a photo.'

Hero glanced up at him, and he saw the insecurity in her face.

'Come on. You look bloody gorgeous. I need evidentiary proof that I got to take the most beautiful woman in the state to this party.'

Hero shook her head, laughing up at him.

'Auntie Hero! You look like a princess!' Bridie breathed, her little hands resting on the open window.

'There you go, Princess.' Nick grinned, pulling her close. 'Now, smile for your sister.'

Hero turned her head, looking out from under her fringe. The scarring had faded a lot in the past year, and in years of modelling she'd learned plenty of tricks from the talented make-up artists she'd worked with. But, suddenly faced with a camera, even one in the hand of her own sister, her insecurities kicked right back in. Nick felt her body tense. He kept his arm at her waist and bowed his head, laying it gently against hers.

'Just breathe,' he said, echoing the phrase he had calmed her with all those years ago at the wedding.

Hero looked up, meeting his eyes. She nodded, almost imperceptibly, then leant her head against the front of his shoulder, smiling at Juliet, letting her take the picture she wanted.

Reaching the car, Nick presented his niece's toy with a flourish. Bridie squealed, grabbing her companion.

'Thanks, Uncle Nick.'

Nick helped Hero in to the back seat. Marcus was peering out of the window, already pulling at his tie, and patiently ignoring his sister as she bounced Bounce on his head. Hero shuffled next to her niece who grabbed her hand.

'Budge up.' Nick jumped in, nudging Hero with his hip.

'Oh! I thought you were getting in the other side.'

Hero slid herself and Bridie up to make room for Nick.

'Marcus likes the window seat.'

Hero didn't answer, her attention on Bridie who now had hold of her aunt's wrist and was absorbed in catching the sunlight with the diamond bracelet that glittered there.

Pete heard his brother's comment, catching his eye in the rear-view mirror. Nick flashed him an innocent look as they pulled out. Both of them knew that Marcus wasn't fussed in the slightest about what seat he had.

All the local children were running around in the garden when they arrived. Pete parked the car and released Marcus and Bridie into the fray. The Sullivans pulled out all the stops for this ball, including hiring staff to show guests to their rooms, take their coats, fetch them drinks and any other little chore that might be too trying.

'Websters,' Pete said, handing their luggage over.

'Very good, sir.'

They were staying over tonight, as were several other families who, like the Websters, would all be in the same room. One family, one room. The women and children had already claimed possession of the bed. Pete and Nick would be on the floor tonight.

'Shall we go in?' Juliet put on her poshest voice, not that different to her everyday one but without the slight Australian twang she had picked up during her marriage. She slipped her arm through her husband's. Nick offered his arm to Hero, glancing at her as she curled her hand around his forearm. He saw the shake in it as she did so.

'You all right?'

She smiled but it was a little lopsided. 'I haven't done this sort of thing in a long time.'

Nick put his other hand over hers. 'Don't worry. It's only the dress that's formal. Everyone is just the same.'

She nodded but looked far from convinced.

'Don't you all look gorgeous?' Sarah Sullivan rushed over in a swish of blossom-pink taffeta, kissing and hugging them all. Bill followed at a more leisurely pace, kissing the women and shaking hands with the brothers.

'Good turnout,' Pete noted.

He knew most of the people, but there were a few new faces.

'Yes. You know, I worry every year that we'll do all this and then no one will turn up—'

'And then everyone does,' her son finished for her as he reached the group. He too exchanged handshakes, kisses and compliments, though his eyes lingered a little longer on Hero. Nick saw it, feeling a glow of pride in his chest as she still clung to his arm.

'Now, girls. One of my nieces is going off to Europe. Seems

to be the thing to do these days, I don't know. Anyway, I told her you were from London and she has a pile of questions for you. You don't mind if I borrow them for a while, do you?' Sarah turned to the Webster men. They shook their heads, knowing that it was a rhetorical question anyway. Hero let go of Nick's arm, seeing the slight nod and smile of encouragement from him as she did. Sarah whisked them away as Bill began asking Pete's opinion on a new stock line he was thinking of introducing. Nick and Paul stood in companionable silence, watching the retreating figures of the three women.

'Lucky bugger,' Paul stated.

Nick grinned.

Hero was surprised by how much she was enjoying herself. She knew a lot of the people, even if only by sight. She had been sitting with Sarah's nieces for nearly an hour now as they bombarded her and Juliet with questions on what they should see, where to stay and what they shouldn't miss on their trip to Europe. When Nick passed by and smiled, one of them proceeded to blush furiously, as the others giggled.

'He's so gorgeous,' she said dreamily.

'He's Hero's date,' her sister added, pointedly.

Hero felt for the girl as she turned a deeper shade of crimson.

'Not exactly,' Hero replied, smiling, and tactfully changed the subject.

Eventually one of them plucked up the courage to ask Hero about modelling. Hero knew it was bound to happen at some point. She answered the young girl's questions, and found that it was easier than she had expected to talk about the life she had left behind. The way she had lived a lifetime ago.

'Hello.' Hero walked over to stand next to Nick.

He turned and smiled. 'Hello yourself. Having fun?'

'I am.'

'You sound surprised.'

'That too.'

'Would you like to dance?'

'I think that would be very nice.'

Nick led Hero out onto the cherry wood dancefloor that had been laid especially for the event. Slipping one arm around her waist, he gently took her hand in his, and closed his fingers around hers. They moved slowly to the music. Although Hero's leg had improved, helped by the fact she'd finally taken up the offer of using the pool, there was certainly not going to be any jitterbugging in her future. This, though, was just fine. Actually, it was a lot more than fine.

Hero tipped her head back a little. Even with the heels, Nick still had the height advantage.

'Are you having a good time?'

'I am now.'

'Ooh! Mr Smooth!'

'That's what they call me.'

'Really? That's not the name I heard,' Hero teased, an even look on her face.

Nick squeezed her waist, and she giggled. Releasing the squeeze, he kept her close as the song changed. He brushed his cheek against her hair, breathing in the smell of her. Hero's own breath caught. It was the slightest touch, but it sent flames of desire soaring up her spine.

'Glad you came?' he whispered into her hair, smiling as the soft curls nodded against his cheek.

Chapter 17

Much to Sarah's disgust, Pat McKenna had indeed brought Susannah. In Sarah's opinion, which she made no bones about stating, the woman's heels were too high, her neckline was too low, and her dress was too short. Nick and Paul exchanged a look. Hero tactfully looked at the floor and remained silent.

'Oh hell. She's coming over.'

They all looked involuntarily to where Susannah was pushing through the crowd, a distinct wobble in her gait. It was unclear as to whether that was due to the too-high heels or the champagne. Probably both.

'Hello, Mrs Sullivan. Lovely party.' She leaned a little as she said it, the already unstable cleavage now looking dangerously close to the edge. She batted her eyes in hello to Nick and Paul, blatantly showing them what she thought they were missing.

'Thank you, dear.'

Pat strolled up behind them. 'G'day.'

Nick and Paul nodded their G'days. Susannah leant heavily on her date's arm.

'And this is Juliet's sister. Remember I told you about her.'

I bet you did, Nick thought, glancing at Hero, seeing the smile she had fixed on her face. He flicked his gaze to Paul who met it, understanding the unsaid words.

'Pleased to meet you.' Pat stuck out his hand and smiled.

Hero took it, her fake smile replaced seamlessly with a genuine one. She couldn't blame him for having poor taste in women.

Hero felt Susannah's eyes boring into her. 'What a lovely dress!' Susannah looked it up and down. 'I bet it was expensive, or was it a freebie from when you used to be able to get stuff like that?'

Hero shrugged her shoulders, the fixed smile now back in place as she did her best to ignore the dig. 'I don't really remember to be honest. It's quite old.'

Susannah smiled, just as falsely. 'Of course, I could never get away with a neckline like that. Too much cleavage.'

She glanced at Hero's far flatter chest with an icy look, a triumphant smirk on the scarlet lips. Her smugness fired something protective in Sarah.

'Yes, dear, well, you do seem to have rather a lot,' Sarah said, with a smile.

Paul snorted, deftly turning his laugh into a cough as Nick slapped him on the back.

Susannah's head snapped around to face her host, unsure as to whether she had just been insulted. Smiling stiffly, she excused herself and left. Pat nodded slightly awkwardly and strolled after her.

Hero and Juliet were the daughters Sarah had never had. When Hero arrived, Sarah had to admit that she'd had hopes for her with Paul, especially now he'd moved back from the city into the annexe of his family home. It was obvious Paul would have been more than happy to go along with that, had things gone that way. But Nick Webster was his best and oldest friend and it was clear to him, to all of them, that Nick already had pretty strong feelings for Hero. The boys had fought once before over a woman, but she knew her son had learned a lesson and, thank goodness, they'd managed to rebuild their friendship. She just had to hope now that Paul found someone equally as lovely as his friend had.

Sarah had watched the exchange between her neighbour and Susannah with interest. Susannah was a trollop, it was that simple – but she was also jealous. And jealousy was an ugly thing. Hero had been through enough. Yes, Hero was beautiful and yes, she did have Nick, or she would have if the boy ever got around to doing something about it, but she had not asked for either. And God knew she had suffered for her art. Enough was enough.

'Mum!' Paul laughed when he was sure Susannah was out of earshot.

'What?' Sarah was unrepentant. 'She started it.'

Nick and Paul exchanged a look that said 'fair enough.' Hero leant over and kissed Sarah on the cheek.

'Thank you.'

'My pleasure, love. Don't let her get to you. You look absolutely beautiful and she'd kill for your figure. That's why she's such a cow about it. That and other things,' she added vaguely, but included Nick in her glance. 'Don't let her spoil your night.'

'I won't, I promise.'

'Glad to hear it. Now, by my count, I see two gorgeous men, two even more gorgeous women and a wonderful band . . .'

Paul stepped in. 'Hero, would you like to dance?' He shot Nick a playful look, 'With someone other than him?'

Hero laughed and took Paul's hand, following as they threaded through the crowd to the dancefloor.

'Looks like you picked the short straw, love!'

'Oh, I don't know.' Nick's dark eyes flashed with merriment as he took Sarah's arm and followed the others. 'You know what they say about older women.'

Sarah laughed and blushed at the same time. 'Cheeky boy. Wait until I tell your mother!'

'You all right?' Paul asked Hero after they had been dancing for a little while.

Hero knew he was referring to the encounter with Susannah.

'I'm absolutely fine.' She read his face for a moment. He wasn't sure. She smiled to reassure him. 'Honestly, I really am. But thank you for asking.'

'No worries.' He returned the smile, once again thinking that Nick really was a lucky bugger.

The night ended with more hugs being exchanged between the Websters and Sullivans as they made their way up to the largest guestroom. There had been far too much champagne all round, with each refill being excused as 'it's only once a year'. Paul was now happily cuddling Hero.

'Oi, mate.' Pete nudged him. 'That one's ours.'

'Erm. Excuse me?' Hero poked her brother-in-law in the chest. 'I do not belong to … argh!'

Paul dipped, throwing Hero over his shoulder and running off up the corridor, the two of them giggling all the way. He dived into a bedroom then stuck his head out.

'Bring her back now, son.' His father wore a grin that matched his son's perfectly.

'Aww, Dad!'

'I know. I know. She's lovely, but you can't keep her.'

'But, Dad!'

'Come on. Give her back now.'

Hero, who had been giggling the entire time, now had the hiccups. Nick laughed at them both as Paul pretended to slouch back up the corridor towards the others, before bending to release Hero. She wobbled a bit from being upside down. Nick placed a hand gently on her waist to steady her as they crept into the guest bedroom assigned to them and did their best not to wake the sleeping children.

Hero and Juliet commandeered the en-suite bathroom to change into their nightclothes, as the men stripped down to their boxer shorts in the bedroom. Nick was waiting at the door to clean his teeth when the two emerged. Juliet reached up quickly and planted a kiss on her brother-in-law's cheek before scooting around the bed and shuffling up next to her children. Pete leant over to say goodnight to his wife, and they soon began giggling like teenagers. Nick and Hero grinned.

'Had a good time?'

Hero nodded emphatically. Her curls were gone, tamed into two pigtails, and the elegant dress had been replaced with pyjamas. The make-up was also gone, her face scrubbed clean for the night, and to Nick, she was just as stunning.

'Thank you for bringing me.'

'My pleasure.' He paused, then slowly leant towards her. Without warning, she hiccupped. She looked absolutely mortified, and Nick couldn't help laughing. Maybe it was for the best. This probably wasn't the best time or place to do this … whatever it was … anyway.

'Goodnight.' Nick bent his head, placing the kiss on her cheek instead.

''Night.'

Nick returned from the bathroom minutes later to find everyone asleep. He nudged Pete awake and prodded him towards the bathroom. Hero was lying on her back in the bed, with Bridie snuggled up into the crook of her arm, one arm flung across her aunt's stomach. Juliet was on her side, facing away from them. Marcus had decided he wanted to be with the men and was sprawled out on the floor. Nick settled down alongside. Pete would take the space opposite.

When Nick woke a few hours later, Pete wasn't there. Blearily, Nick looked towards the bathroom. He could see light filtering out from under the door. He rubbed his eyes, rolled over, and then crept towards the bathroom door. It wasn't locked. Pete was, as Nick suspected, snoring on the floor.

'Oi! Wake up, you mongrel,' he whispered.

Pete grunted in response, batting Nick off. Nick persevered. Juliet would not be happy to wake up and find her husband asleep in the toilet.

'Get to bed.'

He hauled Pete up and supported him to roughly where the spare mattresses had been laid out for them, then let go. Pete dropped onto it and started softly snoring again. Nick looked over at the bed as his eyes adjusted to the dark. Hero was in much the same position, but Bridie had wriggled over and now lay with her head on her aunt's stomach and her feet on her mother's. All three looked comfortable so Nick went back to bed.

'Apparently, I tried to steal you last night. I'm sorry about that.'

Hero waved away Paul's apology. Large black Chanel sunglasses shaded her eyes, but her head still felt as if it were being sliced in two.

'Not a problem. Shame you don't remember it though. It was pretty funny.'

'Actually, I do. But I thought if I was in trouble with you – or anyone – about it this morning, denial was the safest option.'

Hero slid her glasses down her nose and looked over the top at him. 'Coward.'

He grinned back.

'Right. You ready?' Pete nodded towards his sister-in-law.

'Yep.'

Hero thanked the Sullivans again and Paul gave her a hand up so she sat beside Nick, whose head was already laying back against the headrest, eyes closed. Paul shut the door and waved them off. On the first turn Nick's head lolled onto Hero's shoulder. Leaning her own against it, she dozed off.

***

'Now, you're sure this is all right?' Juliet asked her sister and brother-in-law for roughly the twelfth time.

'Yes!' They answered in unison.

Hero bent and hugged her. 'You know I love you, but please, Jules, just get in the damn car!'

As an anniversary surprise, Pete had arranged a weekend in the city, just the two of them. Nick and Hero had been more than happy to look after the children and they had finally got Juliet in the car.

'Bye!' The children waved them off further up the drive then went back to their game.

'Dinner is in an hour you two,' Hero called up to them. They waved in response.

'What's for dinner?' Nick asked.

Hero shrugged. 'Something that takes less than an hour to cook.'

Hero had turned out to be a pretty good cook considering she had never had to bother for much of her life. Juliet had shown her the basics when she'd come to live with them and Hero had gone on from there. It was as much of a surprise to her as to anyone to find that she actually enjoyed it. She would spend hours poring over recipe books, and loved to experiment on the family with new dishes.

'Are they asleep?' she asked when Nick returned from upstairs later that evening.

'Pretty much. Would you like a glass of wine?'

Hero looked up from closing the dishwasher door. There was a lopsided smile on her face.

'What?'

'Actually, I'd rather have a beer.'

Could this woman get any better? Nick grinned to himself and pulled another beer from the fridge.

They made their way out to the verandah, as was the norm after dinner, and sat for a while in companionable silence. The night was warm and humid, and dark clouds danced overhead.

'Storm coming.'

'Do you think it'll hit before the morning?'

Nick shrugged and took a pull from his beer. 'We're prepared if it does.'

Hero nodded. 'OK.'

Nick looked over at her.

'What?'

'Nothing.' He raised the beer to his mouth. 'It's just that Jules hates storms, and so does Bridie. I just wondered if it ran in the family.'

Hero shrugged. 'Never bothered me. And you kind of learn to get pretty good at shutting out any sort of din on shoots and backstage at shows if you want to keep any sort of sanity.'

'Fair enough. But if you change your mind … you know. I mean, you can always sleep in my bed if you're frightened.'

She looked back at him slowly. He was trying to keep a straight face, but it was clearly a struggle.

They had come so close at the Sullivans' ball, but not quite close enough. Two days after that, three of their stockmen had gone down with a virus that was sweeping its way through the district. Nick and Pete had been run off their feet trying to cover. They'd dragged themselves into the house at night to eat, barely tasting the food, they were so tired. The men were back now and things had more or less returned to normal, but catching up had left very little time for any personal life.

'Sorry, but I'm not frightened.' She laughed, 'Besides, I'm not sure that would be such a good idea.'

'Really? I think it's a bloody marvellous idea!'

Hero laughed. Nick's feet were up on the balustrade and his chair was tilting back. His whole being was relaxed; a man happy in his own domain.

'You really are a smooth talker, aren't you?'

Nick laughed against the top of his bottle before taking another swig. Looking across at his companion, he reached over and pulled the chair she was sitting in nearer. When he spoke, his voice was soft and low.

'I get the feeling you've heard enough smooth talk to last a lifetime.'

'You don't know the half of it.'

Nick smiled in the dark. 'So tell me.'

And she did. The light faded, the last sliver of moonlight disappearing behind thickening cloud as they sat. The temperature dropped and Nick fetched a couple of blankets. Hero told him of her childhood, her discovery by a model scout and the mad life she had led as a top model in high demand. In turn, he told her of his early life on the station, how much he missed it when he went to boarding school, and his plans for the future. She also asked him about the women he had dated, teasing him that it might be easier for him to tell her who he hadn't been out with.

The conversation then turned back to her and she told Nick about the men she had seen once or twice, and how difficult it was to tell whether they wanted to know her or the person they thought she was. And then she told him about Jonathan.

'It wasn't a conventional relationship, but I imagine it is more common than people think. We were attracted to each other, interested in what the other had to say, and under no illusions.'

'But you didn't love him.'

'Not in the way you're talking about. But I did care about him.'

'Did he care about you?'

Hero tried to see Nick's expression, but it had been too dark hours ago. 'You don't approve.'

'I'm just trying to understand.'

Hero took a slow breath. 'I thought he did care. Don't get me wrong. I knew he didn't love me. As I said before, it was a relationship of convenience, it sufficed both our needs. But to answer your question, yes, he did care. At least I thought he did. But then I saw his face that day he came to the hospital. Eventually.'

'People handle shock in different ways,' Nick said, trying to sound understanding when that was the last thing he felt like doing for this bloke.

'Maybe. But he never came back.'

'Juliet said you pretty much told him not to.'

'Maybe,' she said again. 'But if I'd said the same to you ...' Hero left the obvious unsaid.

Nick understood. Of course he would have returned, whatever she'd said. He hated to ask the next question, but he needed to know. 'Do you wish he had?'

'What?'

'Come back.'

Hero thought about it. Every moment was agony for Nick. He needed to know that she was sure, that she wanted to be with him because it was him, not because he was the next best available.

'Perhaps I did at the time. Once Juliet came back here I was so lonely. I concentrated on getting better, but you can't do that twenty-four hours a day. When I went back to the flat, it was even worse. It was so silent without Anya. It didn't matter if the TV was on or the radio. It didn't matter how much noise there was, it was still silent. I don't suppose that makes much sense.'

Nick felt for her hand in the darkness and held it. 'No, but I think I know what you mean.'

'I don't think I actually missed Jonathan. I think I just missed someone. Someone I could trust and talk to.' Her voice softened. It sounded like she was crying. 'Someone to hold my hand.'

Nick brought his other hand up and touched her cheek. Finding it wet, he leant towards her, tenderly kissing away her tears.

'I'll always hold your hand,' he whispered.

His lips moved to hers. Hero leant into him. She had waited so long for this, and her body cried out for more. The chair scraped as Nick moved closer, his hands travelling over her body, exploring in the dark. He pulled back to catch his breath.

'You wouldn't believe how long I've wanted to do that.'

'Then why did you wait?'

'I didn't think you were ready.'

'I probably wasn't.' Hero paused, and when she spoke again Nick could hear the smile in her voice. 'But I am now.'

Nick groaned involuntarily as he pulled her onto his lap, tasting her with his mouth and hands, smiling against her skin as her hands ran under his shirt, fingertips teasing his spine, sending shivers of heat throughout his body. His hands moved to Hero's blouse, his lips trailing kisses in the wake of his hands as he deftly undid the buttons. As he got to the fourth, the phone rang. Hero pulled away.

'Leave it.' Nick's voice was husky and thick.

Hero sat back on his lap. 'I can't.' She pushed herself off him. 'It's late.'

Nick looked up at her in the darkness, understanding. She had to make sure. Juliet had received that call once and Hero couldn't ignore the phone's ring. Nick caught her hand and stood up.

'I'll get it.'

Juliet sounded more than a little drunk when Nick answered the phone.

'I just wanted to check everyone was OK. There's a storm coming. It was on the news!'

'Yes, Jules. I know. We're all fine. The kids are asleep.' Nick raised his eyes at Hero and grinned.

'You know what Bridie's like in storms.'

'I do. We're both here. She'll be fine.' He squeezed Hero's hand.

'OK, I love you. Tell Hero I love her too.'

Hero leant against Nick into the phone. 'I love you too.'

There was the sound of shuffling and Pete's voice chuckled down the line. 'Excuse my wife. She's a bit pissed.'

'I am not!' came a distant retort.

Pete snorted in disbelief. 'You all right, mate?'

'Yep.'

'Kids all right?'

'Yep.'

'Hero all right?'

'Yep.'

'Right-oh. I'm going to take my drunk wife to bed then.'

'More than I need to know, mate.'

Pete laughed and hung up.

Nick replaced the receiver. 'Your sister is sozzled.'

'I don't think your brother is entirely sober either. He's obviously a bad influence on her.'

Nick slid his hands down to Hero's waist and pulled her close. 'It runs in the family. Now, where were we?' Hero moved against him just as light flooded the room. Almost immediately, thunder broke over the house.

Nick dropped his head onto Hero's shoulder. 'I don't believe this.'

On cue, Bridie's cries rang out from above. They made their way up the stairs and pushed open the door to the children's room. Marcus was already out from his bunk and sitting with his arm around his sister as she bawled.

Nick hunkered down in front of them. 'Hey? You trying to drown out the storm?'

Bridie nodded sadly, tears streaming. She jumped as another clap broke above them. Quickly scooping her up, Nick glanced over to Hero. Marcus's arms were around her as she stroked his hair. Nick jiggled Bridie in his arms and extricated a weak giggle.

'How about we all camp in my room tonight?'

Bridie nodded, as did Marcus. He wasn't terribly bothered about the storm, although even he had to admit it was a big one.

A few minutes later, Hero had grabbed some blankets and they were all sitting snuggled up on Nick's double bed. He was doing his best to read them a story over the rolling thunder and rain that now beat against the window. The storm gradually began to move off, the thunder claps although just as constant became fainter, and the children finally dozed. Nick looked over at Hero lying on his bed, her arms around her niece. He gave her a gentle nudge.

'See you took up my offer then?'

'Hmm?' She raised a sleepy gaze as she shifted position.

Nick's breath caught as he looked down at her beautiful face. It was a face of calm, the face he loved. He bent, softly dropping a kiss onto her hair.

'Never mind. Go to sleep.'

Chapter 18

'Come in,' Nick called, looking up from the desk as Hero's face popped around the door.

'How are you getting on?'

After a day working hard out on the station, Nick had been in the study with the accounts for the entire evening. They were due to be sent tomorrow and he just wanted to go over them one more time, not that there should be any discrepancy. He just liked to make sure everything was right.

'Fine. I'm done.'

'Oh good. I'm going up now. I'll see you in the morning.'

They had decided it best not to spend the night together whilst they were in charge of the children. Kids had a habit of appearing at the most unexpected of times, so it was safer that way. Safer, but driving them crazy. She started to close the door.

'Hero?' Nick called out and a moment later, her face appeared again. 'Have you got a minute?'

In answer, she opened the door further and stepped into the study, the light from the hallway briefly silhouetting her body under the thin-strapped white cotton nightdress she wore, as she automatically pulled her dressing gown together and belted it. She closed the door behind her.

'What's wrong?'

'Nothing. I want to show you something.'

Hero crossed to the desk where a large sheet of paper had been unrolled, the edges weighted down with a couple of paperweights.

She cast her eyes over it. 'Are these the final plans?'

'Mm-hmm.'

'And that bit there is the extension?'

'Yes.'

Hero looked over the design, lifting the paperweight to see the plan underneath, asking more questions. The drawings were for the renovation and extension to the Gatehouse. It had taken longer than he'd hoped as he'd wanted to put aside a certain amount of money himself rather than start with a huge loan, and Juliet and Pete had been happy to have him live at the main house for as long as he wanted. Juliet especially had loved it, enjoying the bustle of a family, so different to her own childhood. The previous owners had let the building fall into ruin, and his parents hadn't thought much about it, but Nick could see its potential. The work had begun in earnest some months back now and the extension was nearly finished. It was finally beginning to look like the house he'd kept in his mind for so long.

Hero perched on the edge of the desk, as Nick leant back in the chair, answering her questions. Her cheeks were still pink from her bath, and the glossy hair cascaded down her back in a shimmer of chocolate brown.

'It's going to be wonderful, Nick.'

'I hope so.'

'Do you think you will be accepting visitors?' Her tease was shy, and all the more tempting for it.

A slow smile crept onto Nick's mouth. He lifted the paperweights and the plans pinged back into their rolled-up state. Moving them aside, he placed a hand each side of Hero's hip, sliding her along the desk until she sat in front of him, her toes swinging just above the floor.

'That would depend entirely on who they were.'

Nick's hands dropped, then slid slowly back up Hero's legs, lifting the nightdress with it.

'Nick. We can't … the children.' Her voice was low, husky with the want her mind fought to overrule.

He pulled back, raking a hand through his hair. 'No. Sorry.' He stood, putting distance between them in the hope it would cool his raging desire. It didn't. Especially when Hero moved from the desk, immediately closing the distance between them again.

'Goodnight.' She reached up, kissing his cheek, before leaving the study, pausing for a moment at the door as she cast a glance back, meeting his eyes and knowing her own reflected the same hunger as his.

Nick listened to the sound of soft footsteps on the stairs before hearing her door click shut. The sooner he got the Gatehouse finished, the better. If he didn't, he was going to go crazy.

***

'Just going over to check on the renovations,' Nick called out to Pete as he wheeled the motorbike out from the shed when they'd finished for the day.

'OK. See you later.' Hero was walking out as Pete headed in. 'You off to see how the house is getting on too?'

'No, I was just going to see how that poorly lamb was doing.'

'You're more than welcome to come,' Nick offered. 'We can check on the lamb on the way back.'

'Sure you don't mind?' She smiled.

''Course not. Hop on.'

The workmen had finished for the day, and the only sounds were from the animals out in the fields, their calls drifting on the gentle breeze. The house was coming along well, and Hero loved seeing Nick's animation and excitement as he showed her around. They were now in what was to be the study, and Hero was looking out of the unglazed window, taking in the view that Nick would have when he came in here to do paperwork.

'What do you think?'

'I think it's looking amazing! It's going to be beautiful, Nick.'

Smiling, he brushed a bit of dust from the dark tresses. 'I think it's going to be beautiful too,' he whispered into her hair as his lips grazed her neck, his hand sliding around her waist, pulling her close before moving lower.

Nick's touch set off flames in Hero that she couldn't control. Didn't want to control. Not any longer. His warm, strong hands moved under her skirt and reached her hips, his skin slightly rough against hers, but the touch gentle. Hero thought it the most perfect combination. Then he moved to between her thighs and she lost the ability to think at all. Her hands reached for him as she moaned softly, her eyes closing. Suddenly, his touch ceased, and she opened her eyes, searching for the reason it had stopped, and desperate for it to begin again. Nick's eyes looked almost black with heat. But his hands remained where they were. Away from her.

'What's wrong?' she asked, her voice thick with longing, as she attempted to pull him closer to her.

'Nothing,' he replied softly, sliding his hands back up her body, unable to keep the distance his mind was telling him to. 'Oh God, Hero, absolutely nothing. But I need to know that this is what you want. That you're sure.'

Hero slid her hands around his neck and pulled him as close as she possibly could, kissing him softly. She tilted her head back, so that she was looking directly into his eyes, now dark with passion. 'I don't think I've ever been more sure of anything in my entire life.'

It was all Nick needed to hear. He bent his head and kissed

her, soft at first and then harder as she responded in a way he had never dared to hope. His hands explored her body as he laid her back gently, roaming over the smooth skin, touching the scars she had kept hidden, every touch bringing her nearer.

'Nick, please,' she whispered as his hands grazed her thighs, before moving away again, teasing, tempting. His only response was to smother her plea with another kiss as he let his fingers trail across her. Soft, tender kisses trailed down over her throat as he pulled at the lacing of her top, revealing her breasts, the nipples hard and erect with wanting. His tongue flicked at them, then teased again slowly, as Nick explored her, taking her into his mouth, sucking, tasting. Hero turned her head to the side, a soft moan escaping. Nick's weight shifted and Hero felt him against her, knowing that he wanted her as much as she wanted him. His hand slid downwards again, and she breathed his name softly as her lover's fingers once again began their teasing dance. Moving against him, Hero heard his intake of breath, increasing her desire for him even more. Her mind was losing focus – all she could feel was Nick's weight against her and his fingers driving her into ecstasy.

Nick whispered her name, his breath warm and enticing as his lips brushed her ear. She turned her head and opened her eyes, looked into his, and his hand moved away from where it had been taking her. She found his hand, trying to push it back to where she was desperate to have it in order to continue her pleasure, but Nick was stronger. His hand twisted and held hers, moving her arm up until it was above her head. Hero felt the heat soar again as Nick smiled, covering her soft mouth with his own and moved one hand downwards again, bringing Hero to the brink. She moaned against him, her pitch raising as she moved closer. She was so close! He pulled back, his hand still moving against her.

'You sure you want this?' he whispered.

'Yes! Oh … I … yes!'

His fingers and the gentle, secure weight of his hand on her wrist had made coherent thought almost impossible.

'I have to be sure,' Nick whispered closer as one finger slid inside her.

Hero's breath caught and her face buried itself into the curve of his shoulder. It was all becoming too much, the passion building as Nick teased her with both his body and his voice. He knew she wanted to cry out, to scream in ecstasy and he played on it to make the flame burn white hot.

'Let it out, Hero.'

Nick slid another finger inside and Hero forced her head against his shoulder to stop herself from calling out. It was the last barrier. Something she couldn't take back. But God! She wanted to scream with the sensation he was driving her to.

Nick felt his own desire building.

'I want to hear you.' His voice was soft, but rough with desire and his lips brushing against her ear felt so sensual. As he moved faster, Hero pulled back from his shoulder, wide eyes focused on his. She was breathing heavily now, beautiful mouth parted as small moans left her body. She felt it, and so did Nick. His speed increased and Hero struggled against the wave she felt building inside her. Finally, the final defence fell, crashing down as Hero cried out his name in ecstasy, her eyes closed as her body bucked beneath him, flowing through her in waves, Hero thought it might never stop. And she didn't care because it felt so good. Finally, the shuddering subsided and Hero opened her eyes. Nick was looking back at her and smiling.

'Hello.'

'Hi.' She thought she'd be embarrassed but it all felt so good, so right. There didn't seem to be any need. All she needed now was more of him, something Nick was happy to comply with as Hero pushed at his jeans with wantonly urgent hands.

She woke later, stiff from the hard floor and the workout they'd both had. She glanced at Nick's closed eyes and moved his wrist gently to see his watch.

'Plenty of time yet.' His voice was sleepy but she could hear the smile in it. She wiggled around until she was facing him.

'I thought you were asleep.'

'Sorry to disappoint you.'

'Oh, I'm not disappointed.' She slid her hands over the muscular arm that wrapped around her body, then moved down his back, before brushing along his upper thigh. 'I'm not disappointed at all.' Her touch had woken him in more ways than one. Nick pushed himself up onto one elbow and played with a strand of her hair.

'You're amazing.'

'Yeah, yeah. I bet you say that to all the girls.' Hero looked at him from under her lashes. 'Don't forget, I know you. Those smooth lines won't work on me.'

Nick raised an eyebrow. 'Is that right?'

'Yes.'

'So how come you're lying on a bloody hard, very uncomfortable floor with me then?'

'You know, nobody likes a smart arse.'

'You do.'

He had her there. She reached up and ran her fingers though his hair. It was sticking up at odd angles.

'Yes, you're right, I do.'

'Hero?'

'Yes.'

'I don't say that to all the girls.'

She believed him.

***

'I know this is a bit of an odd request, mate, but I need to borrow a woman.'

'Oh,' Pete replied, a smile curling onto his lips. 'Right. Help yourself.'

Paul grinned back.

'I've got some dinner dance thing tonight. I had someone lined up, but she's gone down with the flu. It's one of those things that's going to look a bit odd if you turn up on our own. Apart from which I'll be bored out of my mind. I wondered if Hero or Juliet would mind a trip into the city for a free dinner.'

Pete shrugged his shoulders. 'Probably not. They're inside. Got time for a beer?' Pete pulled the screen door, heading for the fridge and grabbing two beers as he relayed Paul's request to his wife as he did so.

'I'd love to, Paul, but Bridie's temperature's still high,' Juliet replied. 'I don't really want to leave her. Hero's free though, aren't you?'

Hero looked up from the cookbook she was studying. 'I, well, yes but, I'm not really sure ...'

'There's nothing to it. All you have to do is look pretty and stop me from going insane, and you already have part one covered.'

Hero rolled her eyes at him. She knew he was only putting on the smooth talk for a laugh. Hero wavered. She really didn't want to go to the function but neither did she want to let a friend – which was what Paul had become – down.

'I'd really appreciate it, Hero. The hotel is holding a second room in the event that I can manage to persuade someone to come with me.'

'It's just that I wanted to be here for when Nick got back from droving.'

Pete waved a hand as he finished his beer. 'He won't be back until after lunch tomorrow at the earliest.'

Hero was cornered. 'OK. But don't say I didn't warn you. Social mingling is not my forte these days.'

'Excellent. Thanks, love. I owe you one.'

***

The evening was nowhere near as bad as Hero expected it to be. Paul was a fun companion and kept her amused with a running commentary on the people attending.

'Paul, dear boy!'

Paul raised his eyebrows at Hero quickly as they were approached by a distinguished looking gentleman. 'Eccentric but astute,' he whispered before his hand was swept up and pumped furiously.

'Carlton, great to see you.'

'And you, dear boy, and you! And who is this lovely lady?'

'This is a friend of mine, Hero Scott. Unfortunately, my date has the flu so Hero kindly stepped in to prevent me being the sad bloke who had to attend on his own.'

Carlton Barnes roared with laughter and slapped Paul on his back, almost managing to wind him, despite Paul's size. After kissing Hero's hand, Carlton turned and scanned the room.

'There's someone I'd like you to meet. Nowhere near as delicious as your guest, but might be useful and jolly good fun. Where has he got to? There he is.' Carlton flapped his arms to another guest. As he approached, Hero saw who it was.

'Rupert!'

Carlton and Paul looked at her. 'You know him?' Paul asked, surprise in his voice.

'For ever!'

'Hero? Is that really you?'

'I was going to introduce you, but it appears there's no need.' Carlton laughed, tailing off as Rupert rushed up and swung his friend in the air.

'You look fabulous! Stunning! Lots of other good words!' Hero laughed and batted him on the shoulder to put her down. 'I was going to give you a call to meet up but then they moved the meeting in New Zealand to earlier tomorrow so I've got to shoot off. I'm so happy to see you but what are you doing here?' Rupert laughed.

'I came with a friend. Oh! I'm sorry. Paul Sullivan, this is Rupert that Juliet told you about.'

'Uh oh.'

'Don't worry. It was all good.' She laughed, reassuring him. 'Paul's parents' own the neighbouring property to Hill Station.'

Hero sat with Rupert and caught up on the gossip. He regularly sent her emails offering the latest scandalous event but him relaying them to her in real life was so much better.

'So, where's the infamous Mr Webster?'

'Droving.'

'Honestly? I thought they only did that in the movies.'

'No, it's actually for real. Some old friends needed to move some of their cattle. They're short of hands so Nick volunteered to help. He's back tomorrow, thank goodness.'

'And Paul is?'

'Just a friend. His date went down with the flu and he needed to borrow a trinket. Juliet volunteered me, and as it happens, I have plenty of practice at that sort of thing.'

'Something tells me that there's more between you and this Nick chap than trinkets.'

Hero smiled, taking Rupert's hand, her eyes saying everything he needed to know.

Driving back from the city the following morning, Paul glanced across at his passenger. 'Thanks for coming with me, Hero. I know you didn't really want to.'

'That's OK. It was actually quite fun, and such a wonderful surprise to see Rupert there so I'm glad I did.'

They were approaching the town and Paul turned the ute into the pub car park.

'Thirsty?'

'Gasping.'

Susannah watched from the corner of her eye as she dried glasses. Paul Sullivan and Hero Scott sat at the other end of the bar. The Websters and Sullivans had been close ever since Jack and Gill had bought that run-down old station, and the friendship had extended down to the next generation. Susannah picked up another glass and started on that. Sarah Sullivan had taken

Juliet Webster under her wing when she had moved out here, especially when Juliet's own in-laws had moved to Adelaide to retire. From her actions at the ball, it was clear that Hero Scott was also now a favourite of Sarah's. She'd made no secret of the fact that she would have been more than happy for her son to get together with Hero. But it didn't seem likely that was going to happen. Hero Scott had cast her spell over Nick Webster the moment she landed, and Paul Sullivan certainly seemed pretty happy with his serial dating, although he seemed to be seeing more of that skinny lawyer he brought in the pub sometimes. No, it was more likely that Gill Webster, rather than Sarah Sullivan, would be getting Hero Scott for a daughter-in-law.

The glass slipped from Susannah's hand as the thought burned in her brain. The sound caused her customers, including Hero and Paul, to look up. Susannah gave them a fixed smile.

'Butterfingers,' she said as another thought began to form in her mind.

***

Paul didn't even see the blow coming. Grabbing his shoulder, Nick spun him around, letting his fist fly. Paul was on the ground, with a bleeding nose, wondering what the hell was going on before he knew it. He looked back up at Nick. If it had been anyone else, anyone other than his best friend, his reaction to retaliate would have kicked in immediately but shock and confusion had temporarily overwhelmed him. But none of that meant he wasn't furious.

'What the fuck was that for?'

Paul stood up and stepped forward, just as Joe ran up and stood in front of him, his own face showing as much confusion as Paul's. He and Pete had seen Nick pull up in the old ute, slam the door and then, with no warning, punch his friend, causing both of them to sprint over and stand between the two men.

Juliet stepped out onto the porch with fresh lemonade, her smile disappearing as she put the tray down heavily on the verandah table, its contents clanging against the metal of the tray. Blood was streaming from Paul Sullivan's nose and her own brother-in-law seemed to be the culprit. She glanced back at her sister, now staring at the same scene in horror. The crash of the tray caused the men to look over. Juliet was shocked at the look in Nick's eyes. Quickly she spoke to Hero, who disappeared back inside. Marching over, Juliet was thankful that the children were still at school and not witness to the scene.

'Just what the hell is going on?'

She stood between them, looking from one to the other.

'When you find out, maybe you can tell me.' Paul wiped at his bloody nose with his shirtsleeve.

'Oh, don't act so bloody innocent!' Nick fired, 'You couldn't wait, could you? So much for that promise you made about never taking another woman from a friend! You've wanted Hero since the first time you saw her. I hear you both had a good time in the city. You know what? I hope it was worth it, mate.'

'Nick?' Hero responded before Paul could. Standing on the porch, a bowl of water in one hand and a cloth in the other, her expression was pure pain. Juliet threw her brother-in-law a filthy look and stepped across to take to the water and cloth from her sister. Hero relinquished them without looking, her eyes still fixed on Nick in disbelief. Juliet began to clean up Paul's face, swatting away his protestations with a look.

Hero stepped closer. 'What is it exactly that you think we've done?'

Pete had dropped his grip from his brother's arms and stood watching the exchange, his face unreadable. Joe stood alongside him, confusion showing clearly on his.

Nick turned to look at her, eyes cold. 'Do you really want me to answer that?'

Hero could hardly speak. The pain she felt was almost physical, like Nick had reached in and ripped at her insides.

'How could you?' she asked, her voice almost inaudible.

Nick's eyes flashed fury. 'Excuse me? How could I? What about how could you? I thought we meant something to each other and then I find out that no sooner am I gone, than you're off to some hotel in the city, screwing my best friend. I guess we really did wake up that libido of yours. One bloke's not enough—'

The slap cracked like a whip in the still afternoon. A tear ran slowly down Hero's face, her hand stinging from the strike.

'I thought we meant something to each other too.'

With that she turned and walked back into the house, closing the door quietly after her. The others watched her exit and then all eyes turned back to face Nick.

Pete shook his head and looked at his brother. 'You stupid bastard.'

Juliet picked up the bowl and the cloth. She stopped in front of Nick, her eyes red with unshed tears.

'I hope you know what you've done.'

Nick suddenly had the most awful feeling that he did.

The four men were silent as the kitchen door slammed under Juliet's violent hand. Paul took off his bloody shirt and threw it in the back of the ute, checking his T-shirt. Still clean at least, protected from the blood by the shirt. He looked across at his neighbour.

'Stopped at the pub on the way home, did you?'

Nick didn't answer.

'I'm assuming you got your so-called information from Susannah Dagmar.'

Nick looked everywhere but at him. It was enough confirmation for Paul.

'Jesus, Nick! What is wrong with you? Why would you believe anything that tart tells you? You know what she's like!'

He moved towards his friend. Pete saw Joe shift as if to stop him, and laid a hand on Joe's shoulder. He knew Paul wasn't going to punch his brother although, right now, he wasn't sure he would try and stop him even if he did. Nick had pulled some stupid stunts in his time, but this had to rank as one of the stupidest. He felt like punching him himself.

'So what did she tell you?' Paul asked.

'Does it matter now?'

'You punched me in the face, mate, so yeah, I think I have a right to know.'

Nick let out a sigh and sat down heavily on the step of the verandah. He dropped his head into his hands, his fingers locking together in his hair.

'Just something about how she was sorry to hear I'd broken up with Hero. I didn't take much notice at first, and just kind of ignored it. But she carried on, saying maybe you were more Hero's type anyway, being the smart businessman and that. How you'd know to take her to the sort of places she was used to and so on.' He dropped his hands into his lap and looked up. 'The way she said it, there was something about it, so ...' He raised his eyes. 'Stupidly, I asked her what she meant. That was when she said you two had been to the city for the night, some flash hotel. I guess I let my imagination do the rest.'

'And a fine job it did too' – Paul dropped down next to Nick – 'just as she knew it would.'

Nick turned to his friend. 'I'm sorry about your face.'

'Yeah. I'm sorry about yours too.'

Nick rolled his eyes, but the glimmer of amusement faded as he thought about what he had just done.

'I shouldn't have doubted you. Either of you.'

'No. You shouldn't.'

Nick let out a sigh. 'I think I may have just made the biggest mistake of my life.'

'I think you may be right.'

'I'd better go and try to talk to Hero.'

Paul stood and walked to the ute. Nick walked with him. As they reached it, Nick stuck out his hand. Paul looked at it for a moment then took it.

'Good luck, mate.'

Paul leant out his window as he put the ute into gear. 'You know, Pete was right though, you are a stupid bastard.'

Nick didn't reply. His own mind was telling him the same thing.

Chapter 19

They did their best to keep up a pretence of civility for the sake of the others, especially the children, but no one could miss the tension that had surrounded both of them since the incident with Paul, or the fact that Hero had once more begun to retreat back into herself. When she could, Hero did her best to avoid him and he did his best to try and apologise. It was a little over a week later when he literally bumped into her by the wool shed as she swept it out, ready for the arrival of the shearers the following day. Nick walked in and Hero went to move past but he blocked the way.

'Excuse me.' She didn't look up.

'This is stupid, Hero. We need to talk.'

She shifted her weight to the other foot, waiting, still refusing to meet his eyes. Nick gently took her arm and led her to where a few hay bales stood. Hero sat down as Nick let her sit down on one as he knelt in front, taking her hands in his.

'I said I was sorry.'

'I know.'

'I was stupid and I made a mistake, a huge one, and I can't even put into words how much I wish I hadn't. I was stupid to listen to Susannah but her words brought everything back, what happened before – my fiancée cheating on me, and the whole thing with Paul before. But I should have trusted you. I should have trusted Paul. I was just so afraid of losing you and I've ended up doing that anyway. I am so sorry, Hero. You don't know how much. I don't know what else I can say.'

'There is nothing else to say.' Her voice was flat, emotionless.

Nick slid his hands from hers to her waist. She moved away. 'Please don't.'

It was hard enough to bear the loss of him without him reminding her how good he felt. Or how good he made her feel.

Nick dropped his hands to his sides, shaking his head. 'I'm sorry. I just miss you so much.'

'I have to go.'

She pushed past him, tears burning her eyes. It was impossible. She couldn't do this. Not anymore.

'Don't you feel anything for me?' Nick's voice cracked as she hurried past him. His words made her stop, and for the first time she raised her eyes to his. 'I still love you, Hero.'

She smiled at him sadly. 'I love you too,' she replied before walking away. Nick caught up with her, catching her arm to slow her, but she spoke before he could.

'It won't work, Nick. I'm sorry.'

'How do you know if you won't give it a try?'

She stopped. 'We tried. It's over. End of story.'

Nick's temper frayed in desperation. 'So that's it then? Just like that?'

'No. Not just like that, but because relationships are built on trust! If you don't trust one another you have nothing. So we have nothing.'

His face was full of so much pain and regret. He suddenly looked so small, like a child. It would have been so easy to reach out and just hold him. But she couldn't. Hero knew that if she did, she wouldn't let go and she had meant what she said. He hadn't trusted her. And that betrayal was worse than anything.

***

Hero sat at the bar and waited for the bus. Telling Joe and the children had been awful. Trying to be brave for them and Juliet was awful. Everything was just so bloody awful! The taxi arrived after Pete and Nick had left for work. Juliet hugged her sister, closed the taxi door and watched the dust trails until she could see it no more. Then she sat on the step and began to sob.

It was there the two brothers found her a short while later, having returned for the post hole maker Pete had asked his brother to put in and that he had consequently forgotten. Pete let him off, knowing his mind wasn't quite on the job at the moment. Pete raced out of the ute when he saw her.

'Juliet? Jules? What is it, love?'

Pete's arms wrapped around his wife as he tried to coax out the reason. Nick stood apart from them, allowing them privacy. After a little while she looked up and found Nick with her eyes.

'She's gone.'

One look at his brother's ashen face told them all who she meant.

'When?'

'After you left this morning.'

'Where?'

'Back to London.'

'To do what?'

'I don't know.' Juliet's voice was soft. She held no blame for him anymore. She had seen enough since it had all happened to know how much Hero meant to him and how her leaving would devastate him, but she couldn't stop her.

'I don't think it's important. The most important thing to her was that she wasn't here anymore.'

Nick stared at his sister-in-law. His mind spun. A month ago life had been so perfect. He was on the land he loved, with the woman he loved, watching the plans for their own house finally come to fruition. And then in one stupid, jealous moment, he had wrecked everything. And now she was gone.

The dirt kicked out from the tyres as Nick sped along the track. He didn't know what time the bus was due, and could only hope that he arrived before it did. He had to stop Hero from leaving. Before she had come to Hill Station, Nick thought he had everything that he wanted. He worked hard, but he played hard too. And he'd thought that was enough. Until Hero had arrived for good and changed everything.

***

Hero sat at a table, playing with the paper straw in her drink. She had cried the entire way in the taxi. The driver had said nothing, silently handing her a box of tissues as they pulled out onto the road, his actions earning him an extra generous tip when he dropped her off in town to wait for her bus. The pub was quiet, thank goodness. Hero was in no mood to chat this morning. Doug had served her the drink and seen her suitcases.

'Going away then?'

She nodded as she took a sip of the fruit juice.

'Don't stay away too long, will you?'

Hero gave him a watery smile, shook her head, hating the lie.

The bus wasn't due for a while. She tried to read but she couldn't concentrate, the words swimming in front of her eyes. She didn't want to be here. She wanted to be back on the station that she had grown to love, with her family and the animals and most of all with Nick. *But you can't*, she told herself, *so just deal with it – this is the right thing to do. If he doesn't trust you now, how can you have a future with him?* Because he knows he made a mistake, she countered as the argument continued spinning in her mind. Because the jealous cow planted a seed in his head when he was overtired and stressed from a difficult drove. Because he knows he can. Her mind fought back and forth, building on the headache she already had from crying. She dropped her head down onto her arms.

'Can I take that?' Bright red fingernails reached out for the empty glass like talons.

Hero jumped at the voice, sat up, and found herself looking directly into the face of the woman who had started this whole emotional landslide.

'Oh. I didn't realise it was you.' Susannah's smile was fixed and triumphant.

Hero knew she looked tired, but she was far beyond caring what this woman thought about her now. Everyone knew that it was pretty hard to keep a secret in the district and, judging by the look of that smug smile she was wearing, she'd obviously heard the news about Hero and Nick.

'Congratulations.' Hero's expression was steely cold. Susannah's smile slipped a little, discomfort beginning to shadow the waitress's face. Hero didn't care. It wasn't like she would be back here for a long time, if ever. She and Juliet had already worked out places they could meet, taking holidays together. It had worked before, and she would make it work again.

'For what?' Susannah shifted from one high heel to the other.

Hero rose, gaining the height advantage despite the woman's shoes. 'You did it.'

'Did what?'

'Nick Webster. He's available again. That's what you wanted, isn't it?'

'I don't know what—'

'Don't even bother, Susannah,' Hero cut across her. 'I know what you told him and for a moment …' She held up a finger, and Susannah took a step back, her façade of nonchalance slipping away. Several other people had drifted into the pub and were now all listening intently. Not that they didn't already have the measure of Susannah's character but the Websters were a popular lot. You didn't upset them without upsetting a lot of other people.

Hero continued. 'Just for one moment he believed it. But you knew that would happen, didn't you? You knew his history and you played on it. All you had to do was plant the seed. The rest would take care of itself. So, congratulations. You won. We're finished and I'm leaving. So what do you think will happen now, Susannah? Do you think Nick will realise the error of his ways and come rushing into your arms, thanking you and begging you to marry him? Is that what you think?'

Hero advanced on the other woman again who by this time was backed up against the bar. Doug and his wife were watching from the side, and by the looks of it Hero had a feeling she might have just helped Susannah lose her job. Somewhere inside she felt a little bad that she didn't care.

'I notice he didn't ask you!' Susannah spat back at her.

For a moment, Hero stood watching the woman, a look of surprise on her face. And then she began to laugh. With all the emotions of the past ten days colliding, the laughter was an almost hysterical release.

Susannah stared at her, fury in her eyes. How dare the woman waltz into town looking like that and steal the man who was supposed to be hers, then accuse her of wrecking the relationship! OK, so that part was true, but it served her right. She didn't deserve him anyway. But now the pommie bitch was laughing at her? Actually laughing at her, in front of everyone.

'Just what the hell is so funny?'

Hero stepped back, gathering herself. 'You! You actually think that's going to happen. Well, I'm afraid I have some bad news for you. Your name is lower than mud at the Websters', and that includes Nick. We might be over, but I guarantee he wouldn't touch you if you were the last woman on the earth.'

'We'll see!' Susannah screeched as Hero reached down for her bags.

'She's right. I wouldn't.' Nick's deep, rough-edged voice made them both turn to where he was standing in the open door. As he walked towards Susannah, the contempt on his face was clear for all to see. 'Everybody here knows what you are, Susannah, so I won't spell it out but above all you're jealous.' His glance took in Hero's luggage, before focusing coldly back on the blonde. 'I hope you're happy now. But a word of advice: don't ever, ever come near me or any of my family ever again.'

Hero watched him and watched the look on Susannah's face. Watched the hopes crumble. Ordinarily she would have felt sorry for her, but right now there wasn't enough room for her own pain, let alone someone else's. She bent again to pick up her case but Nick took it before she could, gesturing for her to go ahead of them as they headed out of the building.

'Nice speech.'

'Ditto.'

They fell into silence. Hero squinted into the sun to watch the road, waiting for the bus to rumble into view. Nick took the sunglasses he had perched on the top of his head, handing them to her.

'Here.'

It was such a small gesture, but it made her pain burn even brighter.

'Probably not much call for them in London at the moment.'

'Take them anyway. Something to remember me by.' He tried to smile but it wouldn't stay on his face. Tears shone in his eyes. 'Please don't do this, Hero. You said you loved me.'

This was why she had left in the way she had. This was what she couldn't bear.

'I do.'

Nick closed the distance between them. 'So why are you leaving?'

Hero looked up the road again. The bus was coming. Nick

saw it too. She looked back at him, and when she spoke her voice was raw and broken.

'Because I love you.'

Doug had phoned Hill Station when Nick Webster came back into the pub and ordered his first double. Two hours later, barely conscious, his brother took him home.

To her credit, Juliet didn't blame her brother-in-law for Hero's departure. Of course he'd been stupid but factors had conspired to make the outing between Paul and Hero seem more than it was. If Nick had been around when Paul came to ask if he could borrow one of the girls for the evening, Susannah wouldn't have been able to deceive him. If Bridie hadn't been running a temperature that night, Juliet would have gone instead. If, if, if. Besides, there was no need for her to heap blame upon Nick. Nobody could blame him more than he blamed himself.

Nick lay in the dark, staring up at the ceiling. He rolled his head, glancing at the clock. 3 a.m. Another hour or so and he could get up. Get on with something. The nights were the worst. That's when he had the time to think; to think about her face, her voice, her laugh, her touch. His whole body ached for her.

Hero had been gone three months now. Nick had wanted to find her, go after her, but where? She hadn't told Juliet where she was staying. Knowing that her sister never had been able to bear seeing anything in pain, animal or human, she had kept in touch, but her location remained a secret. If Juliet saw Nick suffering, she would have to tell him. The sisters kept in touch by email and apps, but Hero only called when she knew Nick would be out at work.

Hero kept telling herself the pain would dull in time, but she had a horrible feeling she was lying.

***

Pete watched his younger brother through concerned eyes. Nick had been chopping and splitting logs for three hours straight, the drink Juliet had made sat untouched where she had left it. His shirt was tied roughly around his waist and the sweat ran off him in streams. It was the same with every job he undertook these days. He pushed himself to the extreme, immersed himself in the task to the point of exhaustion. It was how he got through the day. Pete didn't know how he managed the nights.

Joe followed Pete's gaze. He watched Nick for a few more moments.

'Hero's not coming back, is she?' Joe's eyes were still fixed on Nick.

Pete pulled his own gaze away.

'I don't know, mate.'

Joe had always been treated as an equal on Hill Station. Pete wasn't about to start lying to him now. Joe and the children had been told that Hero had to go away for a while, maybe a long while. It had seemed the best option at the time. Juliet had wondered aloud whether the phrasing Hero had used was a psychological thing for Hero. If she didn't say she was going away forever, then maybe it wouldn't seem so real.

'Getting on that bus must have made it pretty real.' Pete's retort had been uncharacteristically acidic.

It had been the night Hero had left. His wife was on the permanent verge of tears whilst his brother was upstairs unconscious through alcohol. Pete cursed himself as he saw the look of pain and shock on his wife's face at his outburst, quickly stepping across the kitchen, kissing the top of her head in apology as he wrapped his arms around her, holding her close. Pete was angry. Not just at Hero, but at Nick too. They'd had something wonderful. Something that not everybody got to have. Something like he was lucky enough to share with Juliet. And they had thrown it all away. In a matter of moments, they had let jealousy and pride ruin the most precious thing they had.

But Pete was a pragmatic man. He knew that there was nothing he could do on this one. No way he could ease the pain that his brother, and he was sure, Hero, still felt. He didn't know where she was or know anyone that might. All he could hope was that Juliet would eventually get through to her, make her realise what she had left. Although, as her sister had requested her not to talk about Nick the first time Juliet had mentioned him, that particular task was proving difficult. Alternatively, he had to hope that Nick would meet someone else and get over her. But even as one of life's optimists, Pete knew that the chance of the latter happening was pretty slim and certainly wouldn't be for a long time yet.

As the two men went back to their task, Pete shot a look across at Joe. His leg was jittering. That happened a lot lately. Joe shifted, shifting his weight onto the betraying leg. His eyes darted from point to point. Pete frowned.

'What's up, mate?'

The younger man's eyes found Pete's. They were filled with worry and fear, and sadness. He shifted again.

'I heard some of the blokes talking. They didn't know I was there ...' He paused, looking down, unable to hold Pete's gaze. 'They said that Nick was working himself into an early grave.'

'Ah, mate. You know better than to listen to station gossip.'

Joe moved his head in a yes and no kind of way.

'Don't worry. Nick's going to be just fine.'

Joe nodded. They took up the task in hand again. Pete knew he hadn't assuaged any of Joe's fears. The problem was that, even to his own ears, Pete's assurances rang hollow. The truth was, he was afraid that the men might actually be right.

***

'You all right, love? You look a bit pale.' Sarah Sullivan touched Nick's face as he bent to kiss her cheek.

'I'm fine, thanks.'

Behind him, Bill Sullivan shook his head. That boy was far from fine. Paul strolled out from the house.

'G'day Nick.'

'Paul. You ready?'

'Yep.'

He kissed his mother goodbye and slid into the passenger side of Nick's ute. They passed Paul's own on the way out.

'Still up for sale?' Nick asked, nodding in the direction of the vehicle.

'Why? You interested?'

'Nope.'

'Good. Bob Markham's coming tomorrow afternoon to pick her up.'

Nick glanced in the rear-view mirror. 'Is he picking up all the crap in the back too?'

Paul grimaced. 'No. I have the pleasure of that particular task tomorrow morning. God knows what I'll find in there. Assuming you don't get me too drunk tonight.' He did his best impression of coy and batted his eyelashes.

Nick glanced over, the briefest of smiles fleeting across his features. 'Silly bugger.'

They drove along in silence for a while. They'd known each other long enough not to have to fill it. Eventually Paul spoke.

'Nick?'

'Yeah?'

'You look like shit, mate.'

Doug did a double take as Nick Webster walked in with Paul Sullivan. Nick looked terrible. His face was drawn, even when he smiled which didn't seem to be very often. He was still as broad but the energy that had once surrounded him, that zest for life, had disappeared. Doug had a good idea exactly when it had gone, and which bus it had taken. In its place was a weariness, a feeling that Nick was merely going through the motions.

The landlord had known the Webster boys forever. Two peas out of a pod, he called them. They had always been good lads essentially, high spirited and fond of the women, but that was no bad thing, not in this country. Pete had taken the road to wedded bliss several years ago now. He was a one-woman man now, two if you counted little Bridie. Doug had never seen him happier, and he had thought, as many others had, that Nick might be heading down the same road with Pete's sister-in-law. Until Susannah Dagmar had stuck her oar in.

'G'day lads.'

'G'day Doug.'

Paul spoke their order and gave the place a quick scan over, seeing who was there, and who wasn't. 'No Susannah tonight then, Doug?'

The barman cast Nick a quick glance but his face remained expressionless. The mischievous light in his eyes had died months ago. There was nothing.

'No. She left. Few months ago now. Turns out we were over-staffed.'

He didn't look up, but the corner of Nick's mouth twitched. It might even have been a shadow of a smile.

The two friends shot a couple of games of pool, talked with neighbours. Nobody asked about Hero. Not that they weren't interested. It was just that it was clear for everyone to see what her leaving had done to Nick Webster. Nick knew people talked but he'd been past caring a long time ago.

They were sitting at a corner table wincing occasionally when the screech of a visiting hen party grated. They were from the next town apparently. Paul cynically reasoned that it was easier to cover up any misdemeanours that might occur when they didn't happen on your own doorstep. It was getting late and the two men were just finishing up when one of the party appeared at their table looking mortally embarrassed. From the 'L' plate strapped to her front and back, it was obvious which one of the party she was.

'Hi.'

They returned the greeting and waited. There was clearly a reason for her being there. She was pale, pretty, and looked to be in her early twenties. She threw a self-conscious look back at her friends. The men followed the look automatically to where the group of women sat. They were of varying ages, all making gestures encouraging her to get on and do whatever it was she was supposed to do.

'Um. I'm really sorry about this.' Her embarrassed glance went from Nick to Paul, and back to Nick again. They in turn exchanged a look between each other.

'Sorry for what, exactly?' Paul asked, a smile in his voice.

The girl picked a beer mat from their table and began turning it around in her hands nervously.

'I'm supposed to … well, the thing is. Um … we saw you both come in earlier and everyone said how we had come to the right place.' Her blush deepened. 'And then one of the girls said that she didn't think you would be much fun. That you looked a bit … well … miserable.' She glanced up from twiddling the cardboard and met Nick's eyes. The poor woman looked like she wanted the floor to open up and swallow her whole. She took a deep breath and pushed on. 'But I told them I didn't think you looked miserable. I just thought you looked sad.' She returned her eyes to the beer mat, rushing on before either man could stop her. 'The others started teasing me. They gave me a forfeit.' She looked up.

Nick looked at her. There was a hint of a smile.

'And what is your forfeit?'

She blushed crimson again. 'To get a kiss. From you.'

Nick looked down at the floor, shaking his head and smiling a little more.

'Hang on. What about me?' Paul interjected, 'Doesn't anybody go for the happy, smiley type anymore?' The look of mock indignation on Paul's face dissipated both Nick's and the girl's embarrassment. She started to laugh.

'Actually, my mum said she'd like quite like to take you home.'

'Your mum?' Paul looked down the length of the pub to see

an older, not unattractive, woman finger waving at him. He waved back, a little unsure.

Nick swung his concentration back to the young woman in front of them. 'When are you getting married?'

'Saturday.'

'Is he a good bloke?'

Her smile broadened, lighting her whole face. Nick didn't need an answer now, but she replied anyway.

'Yes, he is. He makes me happy.'

Nick stood. 'Then hold onto that. Sometimes a love like that only comes once in a lifetime. Have a beautiful wedding day, and a very happy life. Congratulations.' He then bent, placing a kiss on her cheek in full view of her friends who immediately started whooping and cheering.

'Thank you,' she said, once again turning scarlet. She made to step away then turned back. 'I hope that whatever it is you lost, you find again.'

The two men watched her walk away. Her words tumbled around in Nick's mind. He wanted that too. So much. But the likelihood of that happening grew less and less every day.

They were about halfway home when Paul asked, 'Have you heard anything?'

Nick knew what he was referring to.

'No.' Paul saw his friend's grip tighten on the steering wheel. 'Nothing that's meant for me anyway. She sends her sister emails, only calls when she knows I'll be out of the house. Juliet has no idea where she is.' Nick took his eyes off the road for a moment and looked across at his friend. He knew he was lucky he could still call him that. 'I don't even know where to start looking.'

'What about the old boyfriend? Rupert or whatever his name was. The guy we bumped into in Adelaide.'

'He wasn't a boyfriend. Besides, I don't know his surname. I know he owns some huge company, but I don't know the name of that either.'

'Useless bugger.'

In the glow of the dashboard, Paul saw Nick raise an eyebrow in a conciliatory gesture. They drove for a bit more.

'Do you think she's with him?'

Nick couldn't help but smile. Paul was direct, as always. It was one of his best qualities.

Paul caught the expression. 'What are you smiling at?'

'The fact that you ask exactly what you want to know.'

'Mate. You've already punched me in the face ...' He let the sentence drift off and shrugged, as if to say, 'What else can you do?'

'You're never going to let me forget that, are you?'

'Nope,' Paul confirmed. 'So. Do you?'

'What? Think she's gone back to be with him? I don't even know anymore. I know they were really good friends, and I don't think he ever accused her of sleeping with somebody else. Has to be a bonus point to him. It wouldn't surprise me if something happened between them.' He glanced at his passenger. 'Did she look interested when you met him, you know, in the city?'

Paul shook his head. 'No. Not at all. But you hadn't acted like a total idiot then.' He paused. 'Well, no more than usual.'

'Thanks for that.'

'No worries. Do you think she'll go back to modelling? She might be easier to find if she does.'

'No. I don't think so. I know she's had offers to do some stuff. The scar on her face is much fainter now and she covers it pretty well if she wants to. But even if it wasn't, I think they'd still want her – just for the kudos.'

Paul sensed something. 'But you don't think she'll do it.'

'No. I don't. I don't think that's who she is anymore.'

Chapter 20

'You know, the agency still calls asking if I know where you are. If you'll be making a comeback.'

'You don't and I won't.'

Rupert put down the hot honey and lemon drink he'd made her on the mirrored glass side table, before flopping into the armchair opposite and meeting Hero's large, green, permanently sad eyes.

'I know.'

Hero picked up the mug. 'I do appreciate your confidences, Rupert.'

'I know that too.'

She closed her eyes and sipped at the drink. She had finally relented and let him visit at the small cottage she'd rented in a remote village in Cornwall. The building was perched high on the cliffs with floor-to-ceiling windows that gave uninterrupted views of the Atlantic breakers as they crashed dramatically against dark, jagged rocks. Hero would sit, often for hours, just watching. It wasn't that she was particularly a fan of the sea. It was more to do with the wildness of it. The remoteness.

'So, how are you feeling?'

Hero had been down with the flu for three weeks now. It had

finally begun to release its grip on her, but she was exhausted. More than once it had crossed her mind that during the past couple of years, the worst thing she had suffered from was a cold. Nick had made fun of her red nose, sore from blowing, but had soon made it up to her, bringing hot soup Juliet had made and keeping her company until she fell asleep. God, she missed him so much.

'Hero?'

'Pardon?'

'I asked you how you were feeling.'

'Oh. OK. Much better. Thanks.'

'Hero?'

'Yes?'

'Don't take this the wrong way …'

'Yes?'

'You look terrible, darling.'

'Thanks, Rupert. Love you too.'

He crossed the room and sat next to her. 'You know what I mean. Why don't you come back up to Town, be with people, get back into it?'

'I'd much rather not, thanks.'

'But—'

'Rupert. I stayed in London for a month when I got back. It was awful. I felt like I was suffocating. That's why I came here.'

'OK. Then can I ask you something else?'

Hero answered with her eyes.

'Why don't you go back?'

Hero frowned. 'Did we not literally just have this conversation?'

'I'm not talking about London. I'm talking about Australia. The station.'

Hero looked up at him sharply. She blinked away the initial stun of Rupert's question, and when she spoke her voice had a raw, cold edge.

'You know exactly why.'

Rupert shrugged.

Hero's temper broke through. How could he even ask that? He knew she would go back in a minute if it were that easy.

'And what the hell is that supposed to mean?' Hero imitated the shrug back at him, somewhat stiffer and full of anger. She was on her feet now, the blanket she'd been wrapped in abandoned on the chair as she paced unevenly up and down the small room. Her leg was stiff and sore, aggravated by the cold weather and the ravages of the ache-ridden flu. Rupert still hadn't answered. He was about to when Hero started again.

'I can't believe you could even ask that! You know what he accused me of and you know that I would never, ever do that! Not to anyone. And never to him. You know how I felt about him.'

'Correction. I know how you feel about him,' Rupert finally replied, putting the emphasis firmly on the present tense.

Hero stopped pacing. He was right. She knew he was, and so did he. But it didn't matter. She looked around the room avoiding Rupert's confident, concerned gaze.

'Sit down, darling.'

All of a sudden, she was tired. So very tired. Taking his advice, she sank back onto the sofa. Rupert reached over, gently taking her hand.

'When I saw you back in Adelaide, you looked amazing. Not that you don't normally, but there was something else. Something I hadn't seen before. You looked radiant.'

Hero made a small, derisive sound.

'I know that's a rather old-fashioned word, and probably a cliché too, but there's really no other word suitable. You did. You sparkled! In all the time I've known you, I've never seen you as happy as you were that night, Hero. And now look at yourself.'

Hero lifted her head and looked taken aback.

'I'm sorry, darling, but it's true. You're thoroughly miserable, you're so low that you catch every virus passing within a five-mile radius, you—'

'Is this supposed to be helping?'

Rupert sighed and took her other hand. 'I'm just pointing out the facts.'

'Yeah, thanks for that, Rupert. I was a little unsure of them.' Hero snatched her hands away and bumped up a seat on the sofa, away from him.

'Don't be sarcastic, Hero. It's not attractive.'

'You know what, Rupert, I really don't give a shit.' Her tone was defensive as it struggled to mask all the hurt she was desperately trying to contain.

Rupert let out a sigh. Hero got back up, crossing the room to stare out at the waves. The wind was picking up and the white horses seemed to grow wilder with every wash.

'So that's it then?'

Nick's exact words. She could hear his voice, see the pain in his face, and the anger, and the love. She didn't turn but Rupert knew. This too was something new. He shook his head. He had never seen Hero either as happy, or as sad.

When she had cried herself out, Rupert looked into the beautiful green eyes, now swollen and red.

'I'm sorry if what I said hurt you, darling. I just want the best for you.'

'I know.'

Rupert paused. 'There is such a thing as forgiveness.'

'No. I can't, Rupert. We were supposed to be in love! You can't just go around accusing people of things like that.'

'Haven't you ever made mistakes, Hero? Said something you wish you hadn't?'

I'm leaving sprang to mind.

'This is different.'

Rupert looked at her for a long moment, and then threw up his hands in resignation.

'I don't know what else to say.'

Hero closed her eyes. Nick's words yet again.

'You obviously had something with this chap. Something amazing. And he clearly felt the same way considering he waited years for you.'

Hero rolled her eyes. 'He was hardly saving himself.'

Rupert waved her comment away. 'Whatever. He made a big mistake believing the word of some cheap barmaid, I admit that, but it's amazing what you think sounds reasonable when you've been awake for far too long which, from what you told me, was the case. Alongside his history, it unfortunately made for the perfect storm.'

'That's no excuse.'

'No. It's not. I'm just saying people make mistakes. Intelligent people learn from them. You were happy. I just want you to be absolutely sure that you think walking away is the right decision. You're going to have to go back out there at some point. You know that. They're your only family. If you go back and this man is with someone else, married to someone else, I just want you to be able to say, "What I did was right for me." And not through any sense of injured pride either, but because you know in your heart that it was the right thing to do.'

'Rupert?'

'Yes?'

'If he had cheated on me, would you still be telling me to forgive him?'

'Good God, no. I'd be telling you to forget the ungrateful fool!'

Hero smiled through the tears that still washed her eyes.

Rupert touched her face. 'But he didn't though, did he?'

Hero shook her head, her throat too tight to speak. Rupert's words were circling around in her head. Nick with someone else. Nick married to someone else.

'Why don't you call him?'

Hero shook her head and smiled at him sadly. 'I can't.'

'Can, but won't,' Rupert corrected.

Hero looked away.

'Fine. I've said my piece. You win. Except from where I sit, it seems like a very hollow victory indeed.'

'I agree.'

Rupert threw his hands up. 'So why not call the man then?'

'Because it's too late, Rupert!'

'How do you know?'

Hero gave a bitter laugh. 'Because I do. For God's sake, you saw his photograph. Women practically fall at his feet. I don't think his bed would have been cold for very long.'

Rupert began the long drive back to London. The rain that had threatened all day had made good on its promise and was now bouncing off the Aston's windscreen. Rupert thought about Hero, and the comment about her ex's attraction. So, there was a little streak of jealousy in her after all. Just like the ex. Just like everyone else. He knew she wouldn't call him. Not yet. But he'd got the feeling that she might find out from her sister, in an oh-so-casual way, what the chap in question was up to, and that was, at least, a start.

Hero sat staring at the email. She had written the usual – talking about the weather, what she had been doing, which wasn't much thanks to the flu, about the books she had been reading and a couple of interesting programmes she'd watched. She asked about Pete and the children. She had also asked about Nick. Just casually, slotting it in there between everything else. She knew Juliet would pick up on it straight away, however she tried to disguise it. But she had to know. Rupert's words had been taunting her. Sneaky Rupert. Clever Rupert. She smiled to herself as she read the email again and then hit the save button. Switching off the laptop, Hero popped it in its protective bag and picked up her suitcase. The taxi was just drawing up as she shut and locked the front door.

'Taxi for Barker?'

'That's me,' Hero called, answering to one of the old pseudonyms she had employed in her previous life. She smiled at the driver. He smiled back. It wasn't very often women who looked like that smiled at him and he made the most of it.

'Heathrow then?'

'Yes please.'

'Long drive.'

'Yes.'

'So, you renting this place then?'

'Yes.'

The cabbie gave up, concentrating on the road instead. The woman was polite, but she obviously wasn't interested in conversation. She looked as if she had something else on her mind.

'And get some sun,' Rupert had said as he pulled away. 'Your body's probably missing it!'

Hero smiled to herself. She had taken two pieces of Rupert's advice in one go. He might actually faint when she told him.

'Have a nice trip,' the driver said, handing over the expensive luggage. She rewarded him with a wide smile and a big tip.

'Thank you.'

She checked the desk number required on an overhead screen, then walked leisurely over to it, heading for the first-class check-in where an attractive brunette sat at the desk. Her name tag read Polly Myers.

'Good morning.'

'Hello.' Hero smiled at her as she handed over her passport.

'Thank you. I'll just check your details.'

The customer service agent opened the passport to check against the tickets booked. Like she needed the passport to tell her the woman's name. *Vogue* was her bible. How could she not know the woman standing before her, especially after that horrendous accident? She seemed to have dropped off the face of the earth after that. All the tabloids had run stories of how badly scarred she was, how she would never walk again, how her agency had dumped her the minute the story broke. Polly knew the majority of it was just filler.

Hero Scott had been critically injured, yes, and Anya Svenson had been killed in that road accident. The police had confirmed that much on the evening news, but little else had ever been released to the public. The so-called news articles that had littered the media and internet said very little and what they did wasn't substantiated. In time, *Vogue* had done a very tasteful piece on the two star models in their prestigious September issue, documenting how their careers had begun and how they had ended. They had also stated that the agency that had represented the two had not dumped Hero Scott, but would be keeping her contract open indefinitely, should she ever choose to return to modelling. Those in the know had commented that it was more as a sign of respect than a business proposition, but still. It had silenced the red top rags and become one of the biggest selling issues in its history. Polly had felt a sense of pride at that. *Vogue* had, in a very classy way, stuck its tongue out at the tabloids and said, 'So there!'

Hero watched the agent tapping at the keyboard with perfectly manicured nails. Subconsciously she balled her fists to hide the state of her own nails. Amazingly, on the station they had been in pretty good shape. One of the first things Juliet had done when Hero came out to live with them was instigate a regular girls' night. Every couple of weeks the bathroom was commandeered and they would sit and do each other's nails, deep condition their hair and slap on face masks. Bridie had soon wanted to join in and they made a big fuss of including her in the treatments. One of Hero's favourite pictures of her niece was of her wearing a full organic face mask, her hair in a towel and a huge grin. How she missed them. All of them.

'All done, Miss Scott,' said Polly, handing back the passport together with a boarding pass after checking in Hero's single suitcase. 'Have a good flight.' She then indicated the way to the first-class lounge.

Polly guessed that the ex-model probably knew the way, having flown with them in that class plenty of times before, according to her screen, but it was never polite to assume. She smiled again as Hero turned back towards the main body of the airport. There were no other customers waiting so Polly watched her walk away. There was a definite limp, but she still managed to look graceful. Wow! Hero Scott. Polly had been dying to ask her where she had been all this time, whether she would ever be going back to modelling, what she had been doing, but the young woman valued her job far too much to do that.

There were certainly benefits to having money, and travelling first class was one of them. Hero sat in the serene, exclusive departure lounge, and signed on to the complimentary Wi-Fi network on her smartphone. She re-read the email she'd written earlier, changed a typo and sent it off. Standing, she made her way over to the snacks and drinks, helping herself to some of both before heading for a comfortable armchair tucked away in the corner. Some people stared, whether it was from recognition or attraction, it didn't matter. Hero never noticed.

'Sorry to see it go?' Sarah Sullivan asked as the dust trails kicked out from behind Paul's old ute.

'Yeah. A bit. Still, I do have a shiny new toy to play with now.' He grinned and looked over to where a brand-new scarlet red 4x4 sat gleaming on the driveway.

Sarah laughed and reached up to pat her son's cheek. 'I don't know. You boys and your toys. Your father's exactly the same.'

Right on cue, her husband stepped from the house out onto the verandah. 'Not taking my name in vain again, are you?'

Sarah laughed and turned to link her arm in Bill's. 'Would I?'

'Gone then, has it?'

'Yep. Oh, and thanks for clearing it out for me, Mum. I do appreciate it.' Paul gave her a squeeze.

'Yes, yes. Don't worry, you'll make it up to me.'

Paul had had honest intentions of clearing out the accumulated junk himself, but a call had come in from his office and the telephone had been subsequently glued to his ear for the following two hours. His mother had brought him a coffee at one point and had seen that he was going to be tied up for some time yet. Bob was due to pick up the ute later that day and he wasn't going to be happy if it was still filled with all Paul's rubbish.

'I threw most of it out, but there's a little pile of things I wasn't sure about so I've left them for you to go through.'

Paul saw where she was pointing and wandered over, as his parents disappeared back inside the house. He prodded the pile. Looked like most of it could go. A card slipped off the desk and fluttered to the floor. He picked it up and made to toss it back on the pile. Then he looked again.

Sarah and Bill peered out the window as the sound of crunching gravel and spinning tyres drew their attention.

Joe read the card. 'Rupert Thorne-Smith. Thorne-Smith Holdings.'

'Tell Nick this is The Rupert. Hero's Rupert.'

'OK. He shouldn't be long.'

'Good. Give it to him as soon as you see him. I reckon this bloke might be able to give us a clue as to where Hero might be. It's got to be worth a try anyway.'

Joe nodded in agreement, a flash of hope in his eyes.

Paul clapped him on the shoulder. 'Let's hope, eh?' he said before heading back out to his car.

Joe put the card in his top pocket and waited for Nick.

Nick was unloading sacks of feed into the storage shed when he saw Joe hurrying towards him across the yard.

'All right, mate?' he said, stretching his back as he straightened.

Joe held the card out in front of him. 'Paul came over and dropped this off. He said to give it to you as soon as I saw you.'

Frowning, Nick took the card and read the name.

'It's Hero's friend. The one that helped with the hospital stuff and that she met in Adelaide.'

'Yep. I know.' Nick's voice was flat as he stuck the card into his pocket and returned to unloading the feed.

Joe watched in confusion.

'If you're not doing anything, you can give me a hand with these,' Nick said, seeing Joe still standing there. But Joe didn't move.

'Aren't you going to call him?'

'Who?'

'Rupert.'

'I don't know.'

Joe's face screwed up in confusion. 'But he might know where she is.'

Nick shrugged. 'Maybe. Maybe not.'

'Isn't it worth a try?'

'I don't know. I'll think about it. You going to give me a hand with these or what?'

'No!'

Nick turned at the severity in Joe's voice. 'What's wrong with you?'

'What?'

'Everything all right?' Pete asked, as he and Juliet got out of the ute they'd just pulled up in.

'Yes,' Nick replied.

'No!' Joe said, at the same time.

Pete arched an eyebrow. 'So which is it?'

'It's nothing.' Nick shot Joe a look, but for the first time in his life, Joe ignored him.

'It's not nothing! You've got the chance to find Hero and you're not even going to bother trying? I don't understand!'

'You know where Hero is?' Juliet asked, a mixture of surprise and hope in her voice.

'No.'

Pete scratched his head. 'Then what the hell is going on?'

Joe started before Nick could. He'd always trusted Pete and Nick, trusted them to make the best decisions. But not this time. From what he could see, Nick was about to make the second worst one of his life. 'Paul came over earlier and dropped off one of Rupert's business cards.'

'Hero's Rupert?' Juliet asked.

Nick looked away.

'Does he know where she is?' she prompted impatiently. Unknown to anyone, Juliet had rung Rupert a couple of times after Hero had first left, begging him to let her know where she was, her mind rushing back to that day Hero had phoned, sounding so small and broken. He promised he didn't know where she was – which was true. But he couldn't promise to tell her if he came to find out. Not if Hero asked him not to. As much as Juliet had sobbed over his answer, she also understood it. Rupert had shown his loyalty to her sister at the time of the accident. She would never be able to thank him for what he'd done back then. She just had to trust that, if Hero was in need ever again, he would be there for her if Juliet couldn't be. She hadn't told anyone she'd called. Hadn't wanted to raise her, or anyone else's hopes.

'I don't know. But isn't it worth trying to find out?' Joe asked.

'Well you ring him then!' Nick snapped, slamming the tailgate of the ute shut.

'Nick!' Pete warned him.

'What? You think a bloke like that is going to tell me where she is, assuming he knows at all? He's going to be loyal to her. They might even be an item now for all we know! As far as he's concerned I've hurt her. Badly. I'm the last person in the world she'd want him to tell.'

'Which is why it has to be you who calls!' Joe shouted back at him. 'I know I'm not exactly the brightest bulb on the Christmas tree but even I know that! If it's any of us, Hero is going to think that it's only us that want her back. Not you. Unless of course, you don't. In which case, you don't deserve her anyway!' Joe's chest heaved, and tears shone on his gentle face. He glared at Nick who, like the others, stood looking at Joe in surprise. Joe had never spoken to Nick, to anyone, like that before. Silence hung between them. 'I need to get back to work,' Joe said, breaking it as he spun on his heel and strode off across the yard.

'I'm going to go and see if he's all right,' Juliet said. 'I've never seen him like that before.' Her expression was as upset as Joe's had been as she hurried after him.

'None of us have,' Pete replied, looking pointedly at Nick.

'Don't!' Nick warned. 'Don't you start too!' Yanking open the driver's door, he got in, revved the engine and sped out of the yard, the wheels sliding on the loose dust as he did so.

It was dark when he pulled in to the drive of the Gatehouse. He'd spent the afternoon just driving, until eventually he found a spot under the shade of a huge tree, and having pulled the ute to a stop, he'd sat for hours, staring out at the scenery without seeing any of it, images of what had, and might have been filling his eyes instead.

Nick hated to go to bed now. Often he would wake up on the sofa, having put the action of going upstairs off a moment too long. He'd moved into the now completed Gatehouse but for all the years of planning and excitement and dreaming, the event had been an anti-climax. For years he had thought that it would be perfect. And then Hero had returned to them and the pipe-dream thoughts he'd occasionally entertained of her being a permanent part of his life became reality. Nick had shared the plans of the house with her, asking her opinions and, when he felt she was ready, asking her to move in with him. Her beautiful smile, the laughter in her voice as she'd accepted still rang in his mind clear and joyous.

The house had been completed only a few weeks after she had left him outside the pub in town. He'd stood there, watching the dust as the bus barrelled down the road away from him, hoping that she would turn around, at least give him one last look. But she didn't. Still he stood, wanting, waiting for the brake lights to flash, for the bus to stop and for Hero to step off, back out into the glare of the sun, back into his life. But it didn't. And she didn't. Lying on the sofa, he reached out, snagging his phone from the coffee table Hero had picked out. No missed calls. No messages.

Chapter 21

Nick knew that it was incredibly bad manners to ring anyone at such an ungodly hour, but he couldn't wait. He'd made the decision and now he had to put his thoughts into action.

'You'd better have a really good explanation for this.' Paul Sullivan's sleep-drenched voice croaked into his ear.

'I need a favour.'

Half an hour later the two men were in Paul's new car, heading for the city.

Paul yawned loudly, not even bothering to cover his mouth. There was no one around at this time of the morning to notice his lack of manners, except Nick, but he didn't count as he was the one responsible from pulling him away from his warm, comfortable bed in the first place. He flashed his friend a tired, disgruntled look but Nick could see the smile that lay beneath. There was no point in telling Paul how much he appreciated his help, and his friendship. It was unspoken, as always. Nick knew that he was lucky he could still call him that.

Pulling into the drop-off area, Paul knocked the gear stick into neutral. Glancing at his friend, as Nick grabbed his bag from the back seat, he could only hope this scheme worked.

'OK then. Here goes nothing.'

'Think positive, mate.' Paul leant over from the wheel and gave his friend a hug. He knew that this, that Hero, meant everything to Nick. 'Good luck.'

'Thanks, mate. For everything.' Jumping out of the truck, he gave a quick wave and then he turned and headed into the building.

'Well, what friend? Where?' Juliet asked, reading Nick's note over her husband's shoulder as he sat at the kitchen table.

Pete flipped the paper over briefly to see if he had missed anything. 'Dunno. Doesn't say.'

'Do you think he's all right?' Juliet was as concerned about Nick as everyone else. Plus she was desperate to tell him that Hero had finally asked about him. Although her sister's email had been sent several days ago, their connection had been playing up and Juliet had only just got it today – after Nick's sudden, and unexpected, departure. Juliet plopped down heavily on the chair next to her husband and sighed.

The cancellation flight Nick had been waiting for finally arrived and he was called to the desk to ask if he wished to accept it. Nick handed over his credit card taking his seat shortly afterwards on a Qantas flight, routing via Sydney to London Heathrow.

Nick gave the taxi driver the address, before settling back in the seat and trying, unsuccessfully, to get warm. The driver caught his passenger's accent and made a remark about the change of temperatures. Nick agreed grimly that it was definitely a little chillier than when he'd left home. He returned to gazing out of the window at the unfamiliar surroundings of London. As the icy wind whistled over the car, Nick shivered involuntarily. In his haste he had thrown on his lightweight jacket. If he was to find Hero at all, he'd need to buy some warmer clothes or risk freezing to death before he ever got the chance to see her.

The cabbie sat in the traffic and cast a glance back at his fare. For a big bloke, it was amazing how small the man had managed to make himself. The driver turned a dial on the dashboard and warm air gushed out with even more vigour.

Thorne-Smith Holdings. Nick read the elegant brass plate that announced the company within the building he stood before. He looked at his watch. 8.30 a.m. He didn't know if anyone would even be here yet, but he was prepared to wait.

'Do you have an appointment?' the receptionist asked.

'Not exactly.'

Nick had already noted the security guards. He would have to handle this carefully, calmly. They looked as if they would have no compunction about tossing him back out into the cold, and he hadn't even begun to thaw out yet.

'I don't have an appointment. I did leave a message, but I had to leave for the airport before he got back to me.' Nick smiled. He knew he probably looked pretty rough after all the travelling and lack of sleep, nothing like the average visitor to the premises. At least not by the looks he was drawing from the employees as they filtered into work, some suspicious, some intrigued and some just plain bored at the thought of another day stuck in front of a computer terminal. Nick felt a pull inside for the station and pushed it back. He looked back at the receptionist. She was young, pretty, very blonde. She was also looking a little unsure. Nick felt bad about compromising her – but he'd come this far and there was no way he was leaving.

'I'm really sorry to cause any inconvenience. Can't you just say I pushed my way through?' A glimmer of humour in the soft brown eyes, contrasting with the dark shadows beneath them.

The receptionist giggled, a little nervously. 'I'm not sure that would be all that believable.' Surreptitiously she indicated the two large security men.

'I'm a black belt in Karate?' Nick suggested, smiling in an attempt to hide his increasing frustration and desperation.

The woman thought for a moment. 'Let me try something, but I can't guarantee anything.'

A short while later, Nick stepped out of the lift onto thick, expensive carpet. From here, the level he had been directed to split to the left and the right. To the left was a large boardroom with glass walls. He looked back the other way and saw a woman, older than the last, with a posture that said friendly but efficient, sitting at a desk, evidently waiting for him. Nick moved silently on the soft carpet, the thud of his heart drowning out the faint classical music playing from unseen speakers.

'Good morning. Mr Webster, I presume?'

'Good morning. Yes, it is.'

'My name is Janet Haynes. I'm Mr Thorne-Smith's personal assistant. Firstly, I want you to know that it's highly irregular that you have even been allowed up here without an appointment, but Amanda is new and not quite used to the system yet. Secondly—'

Nick interrupted her. 'Please don't take it out on her. I didn't mean for her to get into any trouble.'

'Well! Chivalrous to boot. I'll have to tell her to add that to her list.' The woman was smiling.

'Excuse me?'

'Young Amanda rang up to tell me that she had just sent up a gorgeous man, tall, dark with an Australian accent, and a sexy smile. I'm assuming that's you. She obviously didn't see your gallant side.'

Nick half smiled. The woman was teasing him.

'Oh, I'm not all that gallant,' he replied, thinking of the words he had thrown at Hero months ago now.

'Is that so? It's only fair to tell you that I've been doing this job for far too long for your charms to have the same effect on me as they did on my young colleague. I enjoy my job here. I'd like to keep it.' She looked back up at the visitor. He didn't look affronted by her remark, just tired. Very, very tired.

'I completely understand that, but I do really need to see Rupert. I mean Mr Thorne-Smith. It's extremely important.'

Wasn't it always?

'Which company are you from?' The man's appearance and manner of dress was unlike anyone her boss normally held meetings with.

'I'm not here from a company. I'm here to see him on a personal matter.'

'I see. Can I ask the nature of this matter?'

Nick regarded the woman for a moment. Without telling her, he knew there was no chance of progressing any further.

'It's regarding Hero Scott.' Nick saw the shutters slam down, the friendly tone disappearing completely.

'I'm afraid we cannot help you in that matter. Now, I'm sorry but you'll have to leave. I really don't wish to have to call security.'

Nick blinked at her. Realisation dawned. She thought he was some sort of paparazzo. 'I'm not a reporter.'

'No. Of course you're not,' she replied flatly, meeting his eyes.

'I promise. I'm really not. My name is Nick Webster. My brother is married to Hero's sister, Juliet. Hero's been living out on the station with us.' Janet watched as the Australian paused to take a breath and ran his fingers through the already untidy brown hair. 'She left seven months ago and I really need to find her. Please.'

'Nick Webster, did you say?'

Nick nodded, and the PA rustled through some notes on her desk. She pulled one out.

'You left a message on the answerphone.'

'Yes. But he didn't return my call. I couldn't wait, so I came over.'

'Mr Thorne-Smith has been in New York on business. He's due back in today.'

'Oh.' He looked back at the woman. 'Does he know where Hero is?'

Her tone was a little friendlier again now, but she remained professional. 'I'm afraid I really couldn't tell you that.' She paused for a moment as a cold fear washed over her. 'Is there something wrong? Her sister?'

'No.' Nick smiled, trying to reassure her. 'Everybody's fine.' *Except me.*

'Rupert's due in shortly. I will tell him you're here, but I can't guarantee that he'll see you. If he chooses not to, there's nothing more I can do.'

'No, I understand. Thank you.'

'Why don't you sit down? Would you like a coffee, hot chocolate? You look absolutely frozen.'

'No. I'm fine. Thanks.' Nick still felt like ice, despite the warmth of the office. A hot drink would probably help but he was so nervous, so desperate for this to work, that the thought of food or drink made him feel sick. He stepped back, perching on the edge of a modern-looking sofa. It wasn't very comfortable but it was stylish and he guessed that was its purpose. The PA was busy typing something.

'Can I ask you something else?'

Janet stopped typing and smiled. 'You can ask.'

'Do you know if Hero went with him to New York? I mean are they … is she …' Nick rubbed his brow, struggling against jet lag, exhaustion, and plain desperation.

Normally Janet would never even consider answering such a personal question concerning her boss but the pain in this man's eyes was so clear, she decided to bend her rule. Just this once.

'Yes, I do know. And no, she didn't. And, as far as I'm aware, assuming I understand what it is you're asking, no. But, again, only as far as I'm aware.'

Nick nodded. 'OK. Thank you.' Now, Nick just had to hope she was right.

Nick was gazing blankly out of the window, looking down on the world below, watching the traffic, the people, the signs, but he wasn't really seeing any of it. Janet occasionally stole glances at the visitor. He looked dead on his feet, but she guessed there was no way he would leave without seeing her boss. Janet knew that Rupert knew where Hero was, although he'd not shared the information with her. Or anyone. So whether he'd surrender it to this man was anyone's guess. She didn't like his chances much. Rupert had always been fiercely protective when it came to Hero Scott.

The lift pinged softly causing both Janet and the visitor to look up. A man strode confidently into view. Nick waited. He had no idea what Rupert looked like. In his overwrought state, he hadn't even thought to Google him.

'Hello Janet. How are you?'

'Fine thank you, Rupert.' From the corner of her eye, she saw the visitor bounce to his feet, his face apprehensive. 'Did you have a good trip?'

'Yes, very good thanks,' he replied, smiling warmly as he took the messages his PA handed him, and began walking towards his office.

'Mr Thorne-Smith?'

Rupert turned and looked at the man who had spoken. He'd ignored him previously, knowing Janet had kept his own diary clear today, as he'd requested her to. Hero's taxi was dropping her back here later and they were going to order Chinese when he hoped she was finally going to tell him what decisions she'd apparently made whilst soaking up the sun in the Maldives.

'That would be me.' His expression was half smile, half frown. There was something familiar about the man, but he couldn't place him. Rupert glanced over to Janet. She opened her mouth, but Nick jumped in.

'My name is Nick Webster. I'm afraid I don't have an appointment, but I need to talk to you urgently.'

'Nick Webster?'

'Yes.'

Rupert nodded. 'Then you'd better come in.'

Rupert showed Nick into his office, indicating for him to take a seat as he poured two coffees from the pot that Janet always started for him, before handing one to Nick.

'No than—'

Rupert motioned for him to take it. 'It'll help warm you up. You look frozen to the bone.'

Nick took the bone china mug and sipped the hot liquid, feeling it burn down into his throat and chest.

'Better?'

It was. 'Yes. Thanks.'

Rupert took a sip from his own mug, booting up his laptop at the same time. He looked across at Nick.

'So, what is it that you think I can do for you, Mr Webster?'

'I need to know where Hero is. I don't know who else to ask.'

'She's been back for months. Why now?'

'I didn't know where to look before. A friend of mine found your business card the other day which is when I called.'

'Is this the friend that was with Hero when I ran into her in Adelaide?'

'Yes. Paul Sullivan.'

'The same friend you accused Hero of sleeping with and whom you subsequently punched?' Rupert raised an enquiring eyebrow as he took another sip of his coffee.

Nick's shoulders slumped. Why had he thought Rupert would tell him where Hero was? Rupert was Hero's closest friend and Nick had hurt her. What had ever possessed him to believe that he'd help him find her?

'Yes.'

'I see.'

Nick's voice was hoarse with tiredness and emotion. 'Please. I just need to talk to her.'

Rupert studied his visitor. So here was the man that had finally unlocked Hero Scott's heart – and then shattered it. There were photographs of them all together in Hero's cottage, but he looked so different today. That was why Rupert had struggled to place him. It was as though all the energy had been sucked out of him. Nick's eyes held the same expression as Hero's had done ever since she came back. Pain, hurt, but most of all, emptiness.

'Where are you staying?'

'Sorry?'

'Which hotel?'

'I, erm, I haven't really …' He drifted off. Was Rupert going to tell him where Hero was or not? 'I came straight here off the plane.'

'Well, I suppose that explains a few things.' Rupert cast an eye over Nick and smiled. He pulled a desk drawer open and reached into it, lifting out a small key ring with two keys attached which he handed to Nick.

'Here. We have a corporate apartment for clients when they visit. It's vacant at the moment. I'll ask Janet to call you a taxi to take you there. Just announce to the concierge that you are with Thorne-Smith Holdings. Janet will tell them to expect you.'

'But—'

'Just go and get some sleep. I'll call you tomorrow and we'll talk more then.'

Nick squinted for a moment, rubbing his hand across his forehead. 'Are you going to help me?'

Rupert looked back evenly. 'Mr Webster—'

'Nick.'

'Very well. Nick. Firstly, you broke her heart. Hero is the most loyal person you could ever hope to meet. Despite her previous career, she is painfully shy, it takes a long time to really know her, but I guess you already discovered that. Her trust isn't easily won. You won it and you lost it. I don't like that you hurt her. Hero is very special to me.'

Nick felt his blood turn to ice. Were they together? Had his PA been mistaken?

'But I also saw her before this all happened, at the function in Adelaide. I've never seen her so happy. And that too was because of you. For that reason alone I will tell her that you wish to see her, but I make no promises to you. If she says no, I won't side with you. My loyalty is to Hero. I hope you understand that.'

'I do.'

Nick stood and for the first time since Rupert had met him, there was something else in the other man's eyes. Hope.

'When will you ask her?'

'When she gets back.'

'Back?'

'Yes. She's on holiday. I told her to get some sun.' Rupert smiled and raised his eyebrows. 'Amazingly, she actually took my advice!'

'Oh. Right.'

The disappointment on Webster's face was almost painful. Oh dear, these two really did have it bad.

'Cheer up. She'll be back in a couple of days and then we'll see. In the meantime, why don't you go back to the apartment and get some sleep?'

True to Rupert's word, the concierge at the apartment building was expecting a Thorne-Smith guest and directed Nick to the correct floor. Nick fished out the keys, unlocked the door, and stepped into a modern, spacious luxury apartment, decorated throughout in neutral tones. Two pale, squashy sofas took pride of place in the living-room area, one of which faced the huge window that gave out onto a sweeping vista of the capital. Nick wandered around slowly. On the opposite side of the room from the sofas, a dining area with blonde wood chairs upholstered in the same cream fabric as the other furniture. He moved on to the other rooms. There were two bedrooms, furnished in the same pale, neutral colours. Nick dropped his bag in the closest one. The main bathroom was white and slate grey marble with a pile of thick fluffy towels stacked neatly on white ladder shelving.

Finally, he wandered back out and into the kitchen. It too was white with expensive looking stainless-steel appliances breaking up the expanse. He nosed about in a couple of cupboards, finding them fully stocked with non-perishables, pans and dishes. Whether any had ever been used was another story. He noticed a pile of takeaway menus on the counter and flicked through them. By the looks of things, these had been well used instead. Nick's stomach growled loudly. Rupert had said that Hero wasn't due back for a couple of days anyway. He was so tense – in fact he found it hard to remember the last time he hadn't felt tense. But he was here now, and soon he'd find out whether he had lost her forever.

Right now, he needed a hot bath and then he'd order in some food. His body clock was all over the place, but he knew he needed to try and get some sleep. If he was to get a second chance with Hero, he wanted to make sure that this time he at least had a clear head.

Returning to the bathroom, he set the taps to full flow and tipped in some of the salts that sat on an inset shelf. Straightening, he caught a glimpse of himself in the mirror. He wondered now why Rupert had agreed to see him at all. Perhaps it was a good thing he hadn't been able to see Hero straight away, looking as he did. If she did agree to see him, turning up looking like some sort of wild bushman wasn't exactly the image he wanted to project.

Nick washed off the last few bits of soap and ran a hand over his jawline. Much better. Shrugging off the clothes that he felt he'd been wearing for a week, he stepped in the bath, the water washing over his tense, taught muscles. Laying back, he closed his eyes, thinking of Hero.

Feeling at least clean if not relaxed, Nick pulled out a T-shirt, boxers and a pair of stone-coloured cargo pants Hero had bought him on a trip to the city and put them on. Sitting on the bed, he knew he really ought to go and order some food, try and get his body in sync with the new time zone. Just five minutes. He'd close his eyes for five minutes and then he'd definitely get something to eat.

Hero shifted position in the back of the cab. Her stomach was grumbling, and she frowned again at the fact that Rupert had stood her up. She knew it was unfair, not to mention ungracious to be cross at him, but she was tired and hungry, and that was never a good combination.

'I'm really sorry, sweetheart,' Rupert had said as he came out of his office to meet her, 'Something's come up and I can't put it off. Would you mind terribly if we did this tomorrow night?'

Hero was stalled. She had made her decision. She was going to go back, to see Nick, to see if she was too late to salvage the best thing that had ever happened to her. And Rupert had helped her come to that decision – a decision that had made her happier than she had been in months. She desperately wanted to take him out to dinner instead of just getting takeaway to thank him. To thank him for not giving up on her.

Rupert had never given up on her. He had cared for her and loved her. It had taken Hero a long time to believe that Rupert saw beyond her looks, that he spent time with her because he enjoyed her company. He did, however, freely admit all those years ago that when she accompanied him to a function, he knew all the other men were as jealous as hell, and that was, apparently, 'great for a chap's ego'.

She knew she owed Rupert more than she would ever be able to repay him. After the accident, Rupert had been the one to deal with the agency, the press, and the apartment. But, tired and hungry, she was still cross at being packed into a cab, and told to order something in, with Rupert saying he would call her tomorrow. Now she was decided, she desperately wanted to share that with him, and take that first step back towards the station – and Nick. That was, if she hadn't left it too late.

The cab began to slow in front of a sleek, glass fronted building.

'Here we are, Miss.'

Hero thanked the driver, handing over the fare and tip as a doorman moved to assist her with the luggage. She smiled at the concierge, letting him know that she would be staying in the Thorne-Smith Holdings apartment for a few days. *Just until she could get a flight back to Adelaide.* The concierge nodded, advising he had been told to expect her. The porter took her luggage, placing it on a brass luggage trolley and proceeded into the lift. Hero smiled. Slight overkill, she thought, looking at the little case sitting forlornly alone on the trolley, but she had learned long ago, so much was about style, and how things looked rather than substance or practicality.

People paid a fortune for these apartments and part of that was to get the right address, and service to impress. It suited Rupert's company perfectly, increasing in value enormously. She had done well. No, Rupert had done well for her – as he always had. This apartment actually belonged to Hero, another of the investments Rupert's friend managed for her. Thorne-Smith Holdings leased it from her on a permanent basis.

The lift gave a soft ping and the doors slid noiselessly open. Stepping from its mirrored interior into the corridor, the porter indicated the direction with his hand and followed. Hero checked the numbers and then slid the key into the bottom lock. It didn't turn. Hero frowned, before trying the top lock which opened silently. She stepped into her apartment, surveying it for the first time since it had been purchased.

'Where would you like your case, Miss Scott?'

'Just there's fine. Thank you.'

As she closed the door behind her, her eyes swept over the lock. She must remember to mention to Rupert that the bottom one hadn't been thrown. It was likely just an error by a busy cleaner, but she knew he'd want to know everything was being done just so.

Walking across to the huge window, she gazed down on

London, beautiful as it twinkled in the twilight. It had been a long time since she'd seen it like this. The years of parties and functions and the whole of her crazy, busy modelling career seemed a lifetime ago. She wondered, had the accident not made the decision for her, how much longer she would have gone on, burning herself out a little more every day. Her mother's words that day had imprinted themselves onto her brain. They'd resented the expense that came with this unwanted addition and she'd worked and worked, never feeling it was quite enough. She'd been determined to support herself, always. Never again would she be made to feel a burden to anyone. That thought was always in the forefront of her mind. Crouching there, loitering. Reminding her. The only time it had left was when she was out in Australia. With her sister, her family. The man she loved. She should have stayed. She knew that now. Talked it out. But she hadn't, and she couldn't change the past. All she could do was hope to change the future.

Turning away, she took in the furniture and the décor. It was classy, exuding style and luxury, but it wasn't homely. It was more like a hotel room, which in a way it was. So Hero did what she always did in hotels and went to check out the bathroom. Which was when she saw that the towels had been used and there was a wash bag next to the sink.

'Oh my God!' Her hand flew to her mouth in case whoever was here heard her. Should she find them and apologise for the mix up? The thought filled her with horror. No, best just to sneak out quietly. How could Rupert have forgotten that someone was already using the facilities? She felt her face flush with embarrassment as she backed out of the bathroom. Glancing around as she hurried back to the door, she caught sight of the open door to the bedroom. And Nick lying on the bed.

Hero gripped the doorframe to steady herself. Maybe it just looked like Nick. But she knew before she had even finished the thought that it was him. She didn't know why, or how long he'd been here, but what she did know was that Rupert knew the answer to both those questions. Hero took a step closer. Nick's breathing was deep and even. She took another step, so close now that she could touch him. He was dressed in a white T-shirt and the stone cargo pants she had bought him on a trip into Adelaide last year with Juliet and Gill.

She sat lightly next to him on the bed, and then bent and kissed him just as lightly on the lips as tears flowed silently down her face. His face was clean-shaven and he smelled of soap and warmth and Nick. She sat back, watching him sleep, not wanting to take her eyes off him, drinking in the sight of him and overwhelmed at the shock and absolute relief of being near him again. In his dream, Nick frowned and then slowly opened his eyes to see the woman from his dreams sitting next to him on the bed.

He lay there looking at her, afraid to move in case he was still dreaming, in case he woke and she wasn't there anymore. It wouldn't be the first time. And then Hero leant forward and kissed him again and Nick knew he wasn't dreaming anymore and he wrapped his arms around her so tightly that Hero had trouble breathing and it felt wonderful.

'How long have you been here?' Nick asked when he finally released her enough to look into the beautiful face he had missed so much.

'Not long,' Hero replied, running her hand through his hair. She opened her mouth to say something and closed it again. Then she smiled that smile that always sent Nick into a spin. 'I don't even know where to start.'

Nick looked back at her, his eyes shining with emotion. 'I've missed you so much.' His voice was hoarse and raw and soft, and the sound of it sent a shiver of pleasure through her body.

'I've been miserable ever since I left. I thought I could forget. That I would get over you, but every day it just got worse. And the longer I was away, the more I thought that it was too late, that you would find someone else—'

'There hasn't been anyone else,' he interrupted, taking her hands in his. 'I don't want anyone else, Hero. I want you.'

Hero looked at him, saw the taught muscles in his arms, and his hair that needed cutting, and his light brown eyes fringed with thick lashes, and her heart felt so full with the strength of her love for this man.

'I want you too.'

It was all the prompt he needed. Nick pulled her down onto the bed, kissing her hard and hungrily until the only thing she knew was him.

Chapter 22

'Can I ask you something?'

They were snuggled together on the sofa that looked out onto the city, wrapped in matching white towelling bathrobes, fresh from the shower. Nick was stretched along the length of the couch and Hero sat between his legs, resting against him. Empty Chinese food cartons were scattered on the table.

'What's that?' Hero said.

'How did you know there were condoms in the bedside cabinet?'

Hero adjusted her position so that she could meet his eyes.

'Forget it. I shouldn't have asked. I—'

'Rupert made a point of telling me, saying that I should order some food in, and that there were condoms in the bedside drawer if I felt the urge to jump the delivery guy. Sneaky sod.'

Nick laughed, snuggling into the curve of her neck. 'He's a pretty decent bloke, isn't he?' he said, in between placing tender butterfly kisses on the soft skin, 'Rupert, I mean.'

Hero took a deep, contented breath. 'Yes. He is. I owe him a lot.' She leaned into Nick and he cuddled her closer. 'Even more so now.'

'I owe him a lot too. I wasn't sure he would help me.'

'Rupert knows you make me happy. Happier than I've ever been.'

'But I stuffed up.'

'Yep,' she teased. 'You did. Big time.' He looked pained and she kissed him to soften the blow. 'But I should have stayed. Talked it through, worked it out. Forgiven you for being such an idiot.' Hero looked up through her lashes at him.

Her smile softened the words.

They sat for a moment in the silence, just enjoying the nearness of each other again, until Nick broke the silence.

'Hero?'

'Mm-hmm?'

'Can we start again?'

Hero took a deep breath, rolled her hip across Nick's leg and stood up. She walked to the window, gazing down on the night skyline. Behind her, Nick sat up and waited.

'I don't want to start again, Nick.'

Nick felt something in his throat contract. So that was it. It was over. Forever. He'd found her only to discover he really had lost her. When he didn't say anything, Hero turned. Seeing the look on Nick's face, she returned to him, taking his hands in hers.

'So, I really did stuff up then?'

Hero leant her head so that his fingers touched her cheek. Nick wanted to pull them away, to grab his clothes and just leave. Why do all this? Why hold him and make love with him if she was just going to tell him to rack off anyway? A brief thought that this was Hero's payback entered his mind, but he shoved it away. He knew her. No matter how much he had hurt her, she didn't have it in her soul to be callous.

'I don't want to start again,' she repeated. 'I'd really like to just pick up from where we left off.' His smile broke as he pulled her towards him once more.

'When do you have to be back?' Hero asked Nick, as she lay sated in his arms watching dawn break across London.

'When I get there,' he replied, sleepily.

Hero shuffled round, lying on her stomach looking up at him. 'Do Pete and Juliet know where you are?'

Nick rolled his head from side to side a couple of times. 'Nope. I left a note saying that I was going to stay with a friend.'

'So, nobody knows you're here.'

'Paul knows. I didn't want to get anyone's hopes up if I couldn't see you or if you told me just to rack off.'

'That makes sense.'

Hero pushed against Nick's chest and sat back, one leg tucked under her, the other, less flexible, resting against the side of the couch.

'So.'

'So?'

'So, what happens now?'

'What do you mean?'

'With us.' Hero watched Nick's expression and then made to push away from the couch, but he caught her wrist.

'Oh no! You're not running away from me again.' He smiled but Hero saw the uncertainty in his eyes. She leant forward and kissed his lips.

'I don't want to …'

'But?' Nick took a deep breath to keep the panic at bay. He was not going to lose her again. He couldn't.

'But,' Hero repeated, 'I need to know that you trust me. I'm not asking you to change. I know you have a jealous streak – I think we all do. When Rupert said about the possibility of you being with someone else, I couldn't bear to think of it. But I love you, Nick. Nobody else. I won't go through all this again and have you look at me again like you did that day – so coldly. I can't do that. I won't.'

Nick sat up on the couch, moving Hero with him. He caught

her chin with his hand and looked steadily into the bright, green eyes.

'I trust you.'

***

'Do you have a coat?' Hero asked as they left the apartment building. Return flights had been booked, Rupert had been thanked and also told what a devious mind he had, and there was still a day left for sightseeing. Hero had a whistle-stop tour planned. Nick shrugged into the summer-weight jacket he had brought in his rush.

'Is that the only one you brought?'

He nodded.

'Aren't you cold?'

'Bloody freezing,' he said as he hugged Hero to him for warmth.

She was wrapped in an ankle-length woollen coat with a scarf tucked across her face, a hat pulled down to her eyes and mittens warming her hands. Her outfit had the dual benefit of keeping her warm and preventing recognition.

'But considering I haven't really been out of bed for the past three days,' Nick continued, 'it hasn't exactly been a problem until now.'

Hero's eyes smiled up at him as she wrapped her arms around his body, trying to transfer some of her own heat to him. Without even seeing the rest of her face, Nick knew she was blushing, and he hugged her closer. The taxi ordered by the concierge pulled up and Hero leant forward.

'Oxford Street, please.'

Having first equipped Nick with more suitable attire, and filled up on a breakfast of soft croissants, Hero then led him down into the depths of the Tube. Purchasing two Oyster cards and credit, they tapped through the barriers and headed for the escalator that stretched away in front of them, taking them deeper under the city.

'What do you think?' Hero asked as they sat in the slowly moving bubble of the London Eye.

The weather couldn't have been better for Hero to show Nick the city that had been her home for so long. Crisp, cold, and bright, the views were spectacular. As they moved slowly in their circular route, Hero sat within his embrace, pointing out some of the more well-known landmarks of London, as well as a few of her own. Nick listened as she told him about a show she'd done for one of the big fashion names at Tate Modern, and some of the clothes she'd modelled for it.

'Does anyone really buy that stuff?' Nick asked, half laughing as she described a dress that had a huge funnel neck collar so tall she could barely see over it.

'Some. It really depends on how wearable things are. But you'd be surprised at what does sell.'

Nick shook his head, studying Hero for a moment, rather than the stunning views. 'Do you miss it? Any of it?'

'No. It was a different part of my life. I'll always be thankful to it for bringing Anya and Rupert into my life which was so much richer for having them in it. But I've moved on now to a different place, and that's where I want to be now.'

He gave a little nod, before she turned back to the scenery and snuggled closer, her back to his chest. Dropping a kiss onto the top of her beanie hat covered head, he sat content looking out at the city, the woman he loved within his embrace.

They'd decided to stretch their legs and take advantage of the weather to stroll along the riverside near Tower Bridge, watching as the Victorian engineering went into action, lifting the road in order for a huge cruise liner to pass under. They waited as it docked next to HMS Belfast.

'That's as far as they can go because of their size,' Hero said, stuffing another square of the salted caramel fudge they'd bought in Borough Market into Nick's mouth before taking one for herself. 'We might have to go back for some more of this. I don't think the one we got for Jules is going to last the journey.'

Having watched the ship dock, they wandered on, arm in arm, turning into Shad Thames.

'So all these' – she pointed up at the metal walkways criss-crossing the narrow street above them – 'were once used to get between the storage spaces.'

'And they're all apartments now?'

'The warehouses, yes. The walkways are the balconies for them.'

'Not sure I'd fancy sitting out on my balcony with all these people peering up at me.'

Hero shrugged. 'There is that. How the world turns though. In Dickens' time, all this' – she waved her arm to encompass the area – 'was terrible slums.'

Nick looked around, trying to equate the descriptions of disease ridden slums with the smart, expensive apartments either side of them. It was impossible.

***

'To us.'

Hero lifted her glass, tapping it gently against Nick's. 'To us,' she repeated softly, her eyes on his.

She took a sip of the champagne, turning to gaze out at yet another spectacular vista.

'Well, it's certainly different from cracking open a beer on the verandah with only sheep as far as the eyes can see.'

They'd made a late booking at 'Vertigo', London's highest champagne bar, for an afternoon refresher before heading over towards Piccadilly where Hero wanted to have a look around the huge bookshop, savouring her chance to stock up on some reading material for the flight home, as well as pick up some books she thought Joe might like.

Home.

She smiled and held her glass up once more. Nick tilted his head, enquiring with his eyes.

'To home.'

'To home.'

Nick plopped down heavily on the sofa and let out a huge sigh of satisfaction and relief. 'Crikey. I never thought being a tourist could be so exhausting.'

Hero smiled across at him as she hung up her coat. His head was lolled back, eyes closed, long legs stretched out, still fully muffled up against the biting cold outside.

'Do you want a cup of tea?'

He lifted a hand wearily and gave her a thumbs up sign. Hero flicked the kettle on, pulled off her boots and crossed the room. Nick opened his eyes and let out an 'Oof' as she sat down on his lap unexpectedly.

'No stamina,' she stated as she pulled his hat off and dropped it to the side of them. His hair, still in need of cutting, stuck up at odd angles. Hero ran her fingers through it, in an attempt to tame it.

'As you pointed out this morning' – off came the gloves – 'you've spent the best part of three days in bed' – then the scarf – 'and now' – she leant him forward to free his body from the coat – 'you're tired?'

Nick let her take the clothing, enjoying the feel of her body against him. He moved his hands to her hips, pulling her closer, enjoying the flush of colour it brought to her cheeks.

'Just because I spent the last three days in bed, doesn't mean I haven't been working hard.' He moved under her, his mouth smiling, his eyes darkening with desire.

'Really?' Hero replied lightly. 'I hadn't noticed.'

'Right!' Nick stood, tipping her off him. 'We'll see about that.'

Hero laughed and scooted into the kitchen, placing the breakfast bar between them. Nick strolled in and up to where Hero was standing, blocking her view of everything but him. He looked down into the beautiful face, shining now with laughter and mischief.

'I thought you wanted a cup of tea.' She pretended to stall him, recognising the look in his eyes, one corner of his mouth tilting up in a sexy half smile.

'Didn't notice, huh?' he said, still not touching her.

'Well, I …' she trailed off. Nick had a way of making her forget everything but him.

He moved closer, touching her now with his body, pressing her back into the counter top. Slowly he bent and kissed her, teasing her with his tongue and the promise of more. Hero's hands were trapped behind her back, her head was dizzy, her knees weakening as Nick leaned into her again, whispering into her ear, his voice thick and hoarse with love and wanting.

'I promise you you're going to notice this time,' he said, one hand sliding under the clothing layers until it found her breast.

Hero moaned as Nick's thumb teased the skin already swollen and tight with desire.

'You're going to notice everywhere. Every part of you. You're going to be noticing for a week.'

Hero pushed her hips towards him, wanting him but he held her back with the other hand.

'Nick …' Her voice broke, one word encompassing all the frustration and pleasure and wanting he was creating.

She felt him smile against her cheek.

'Are you beginning to notice?'

The moan she gave was enough of an answer.

'Good,' he said, straightening as his eye caught sight of something on the counter. He snagged the purple Liberty bag towards him, drawing out the long silk scarf Hero had bought. She watched as Nick pulled it from the bag, drawing it back momentarily before reaching around for Hero's wrists, draping the soft, slippery fabric across them, twisting it loosely underneath to draw them together.

'You know, I think this might help you notice.'

Hero pushed into him, claiming his mouth as Nick pulled her as close as he could. Without breaking the kiss, he lifted her against him, her legs automatically wrapping around his body as he took them into the bedroom in order to make good on his promise.

Chapter 23

Nick peeked over the top of his first-class duvet to where Hero lay next to him, sound asleep, her books so far untouched. Nick had been true to his word, making her notice him in all sorts of ways, the result of which meant they were both exhausted.

'Can I get you anything, sir?' a passing cabin crew member whispered in deference to the others sleeping around them.

Nick smiled, and shook his head before snuggling back under the duvet, content in the knowledge that everything he wanted was right next to him.

Acknowledgements

Thank you, as always, to James for his unfailing belief in me, especially in this past year when my own belief has definitely been in choppy waters. Thank you so much for all the support you give me both mental and physical. None of these books would exist without you.

Thanks to Clio, Nia, and all the team at HQ for believing in Hero and Nick's story and giving me the chance to share it with the world. Thanks also to my copy editor Dushi Horti.

A massive hug (I'm super big on hugs!) to all those fantastic book bloggers who, since I jumped into the deep end of this incredible – and sometimes scary – adventure, have given their time to read and review my books, helping spread the word. I really can't thank these fabulous people enough. They do a brilliant job – all unpaid – and their beautiful, thoughtful reviews have made me cry (in a good way!) more than once. You are all superstars!

Mahoosive hugs go to the fabulous Rachel Burton, and Annie Lyons for their unfailing support, advice, and ability to bring many giggles. Big thanks to Rebecca Raisin for her help with a couple of locality queries and also to Sarah Bennett, who is just a general fount of knowledge.

I'd also like to give a quick shout-out, and a huge thank-you, to the brilliant Mr Teo – plastic surgeon extraordinaire who inspired the surgeon mentioned in the book. Last year brought an unexpected and upsetting diagnosis which meant that I suddenly required surgery on my face. As I'm shy and also tend to scar badly, I was having a bit of a panic. However, I need not have worried as, in view of the location, I was referred on to Mr Teo. He and his team not only did a fantastic job, but actually kept me laughing (as much as one can in such a situation!) during the procedure.

See? I told you I wouldn't make you a baddie.

Ps – I'm still saving for the facelift.

And most of all, thank you to all the lovely readers. There is such a huge and wonderful choice of books out there and I am eternally grateful that you choose to spend precious time and money on one of mine. Hearing that I've brought a smile (and sometimes a tear) to someone is an amazing feeling, and also incredibly humbling. Thank you so much. Your support and enthusiasm mean more than you could ever know.

xx

Dear Reader

Thank you so much for reading *Second Chance at the Ranch*, and I very much hope you enjoyed Hero and Nick's story.

If you did, I'd be so grateful if you could leave me a review – just a short one is absolutely fine! They really can make such a difference in helping spread the word. I know Amazon isn't everyone's favourite, but as the market leader for digital sales, it really does help. But honestly, a review anywhere would be just lovely!

For those of you who've enjoyed my previous romcoms, don't worry – I'm still writing those too, and hopefully there will be more out in the world before too long.

Thank you again for all your support. I always love to hear from my readers, so please feel free to contact me on any of my social media channels or by email. I look forward to hearing from you!

Happy reading!

Love Maxi xx

Dear Reader,

Thank you so much for taking the time to read this book – we hope you enjoyed it! If you did, we'd be so appreciative if you left a review.

Here at HQ Digital we are dedicated to publishing fiction that will keep you turning the pages into the early hours. We publish a variety of genres, from heartwarming romance, to thrilling crime and sweeping historical fiction.

To find out more about our books, enter competitions and discover exclusive content, please join our community of readers by following us at:

@HQDigitalUK

facebook.com/HQDigitalUK

Are you a budding writer? We're also looking for authors to join the HQ Digital family! Please submit your manuscript to:

HQDigital@harpercollins.co.uk.

Hope to hear from you soon!

ONE PLACE. MANY STORIES

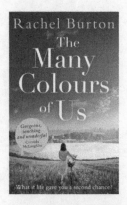

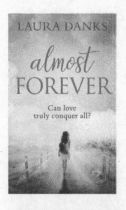

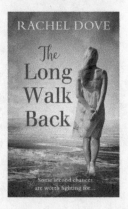

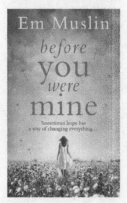